Endorsement Quotes

The Whispering of the Willows is an inspiring story full of twists and turns, freedom and redemption, the expected and unexpected. This book brings to light the struggles of young women past and present. God's goodness and provision flow from each page.

> – Linda Bottoms, Rocky Mountain Ministry Network
> Women's Ministries Director

Tonya Blessing's sweet, unassuming voice deals artfully with racism, sexism, and religious bigotry. Superb storytelling interspersed with practical faith portrays the difficulty and beauty of Appalachian life. An absolutely delightful read!

> – Marilyn Bay Wentz, author of *Prairie Grace* and
> *All We Like Sheep*

God's redemption rings true in the heartfelt story *The Whispering of the Willows.* The book's heroine, Emerald Ashby, is rescued from tragedy by the loving hand of Jesus. Christ is revealed time and time again by the care and kindness of others, poetry, song, and the beauty of the Appalachian Mountains. This story reads like a prayer and will most certainly capture your heart.

> – Diane Andrews, founder and director of R&R Retreats,
> national and international speaker

Publisher's
Note:

We offer this book to mothers and young daughters as a mutual reading opportunity for discussion. The Whispering of the Willows joins women's issues with the properties of a young adult novel creating a special genre of women's coming-of-age literature. Given a discussion on the events surrounding Emie's natural physiological changes, and the actions of the community surrounding her, young women may acknowledge how, *specifically,* girls are set apart from boys. The Whispering considers *how* the same transition can set a woman's future immediately. The abuse of young women among family members, community members, and strangers is a universal problem, not only an Appalachian Folk problem.

A trans-formative power resides in the clever choices of quiet individuals modeled in the Whispering of the Willows. This power inspires effort, protection, and provision in the face of social indecencies. What happens then, turns a community into the protagonist. We promote the George McDonald, Brothers Grimm, Charlotte Bronte, and Charles Dickens' style of story-telling here, because it provides another model of fictional realism. Imagination fostered can cure the inadequate responses of mere individuals who dare to care for another human being. If you have ever been the recipient of graciousness, you will know the heroic effect is never lost.

the *Whispering*

of the

Willows

Tonya Jewel Blessing

Names: Blessing, Tonya Jewel.
Title: The whispering of the willows / Tonya Jewel Blessing.
Description: Littleton, Colorado : Capture Books, [2016] | Includes
bibliographical references.
Identifiers: LCCN 2016931550 | ISBN 978-0-9971625-4-7 (print) |
ISBN 0-9971625-4-6 (print) | ISBN 9780997162554 (ebook)
Subjects: LCSH: Teenage girls–Abuse of–Fiction. | Rape victims–Fiction. |
Abusive men–Fiction. | Poverty–Appalachian Region–Fiction. |
Appalachian Region–History–20th century–Fiction. | Historical fiction. |
Bildungsromans.
Classification: LCC PS3602.L47 W45 2016 (print) | LCC PS3602.L47 (ebook) |
DDC 813/.6–dc23

Library of Congress Control Number: 2016931550
The Whispering of the Willows/Historical Fiction /Appalachia / Women
By Tonya Jewel Blessing
Cover Design: Laura Bartnick/Kathryn K. Swezy
Cover Photograph: Kara E. Hokes
Copyright © 2016 Capture Books
5658 S. Lowell Blvd. Suite 32-202
Littleton Colorado 80123
ISBN-10: 0-9971625-4-6
ISBN-13: 978-0-9971625-4-7

Dedication

This book is dedicated
to the original Ashby
siblings: my uncles, my
aunts and my mother.

A Note from the Author

In 1937, my mother, Virginia Ashby, was born in the rural hills of West Virginia. She spent several of her formative years in an area known as Big Creek.

I have borrowed my mother's maiden name, several names from her past, and the name Big Creek. *The Whispering of the Willows* is a fictional work. The characters and incidents are solely the concepts and products of my imagination and should not be construed as real.

Chapter One

"Beauty is skin deep, but ugly goes clear to the bone."
(Appalachian Folk Belief)

Emie was hiding in the barn loft. Well, not really hiding, since her two brothers and six sisters knew exactly where she would be.

She could hear the piglets below. The pregnant sows and those who had experienced the recent pangs of birth were sheltered in the barn. The males were relentless in their pursuits. Emie wondered why nature at times seemed to be so cruel, especially to mamas and babies. She could hear the piglets suckling. Their soft snorts coupled with the gentle sighs of the sows brought a fading smile to her face. She couldn't see the tenderness, her hiding place was in the dark corner of the loft, but her imagination allowed her to ponder the bond between the givers of life and nourishment and the always hungry young recipients.

The hay she generally used for a pillow was sparse. Winter had depleted the supply and harvest was still a few weeks in coming. From the shadows she could see out the barn window. The willows by Big Creek were still leafing. Big Creek was swollen like the sow bellies below waiting to deliver. The snow melt from the hills caused the creek to expand in width and depth. She loved this time of year in the holler. The stench from the hogs and the outhouse was diminished by the lilac bushes, blue bells, and yellow daffodils, mama's favorite. Her two brothers were responsible for enlarging the toilet holes, but spring births kept them busy. Even now she had to pee. Her full bladder called for attention, but the voice of fear inside her head called even louder.

"Emie, Emie!" She could hear Ernest in the distance. She shuddered knowing the inevitable was to come. A switch from one of the willows would be laying on her father's dresser. Daddy would be sitting in his wheelchair yelling for the girlie to come; his paralyzed legs covered in a quilt hand stitched with scraps from threadbare cast off family clothes, his bald head reflecting light from the bedroom window, and his prickly beard ready to be shaved. Mama razored the sparse and soft, yellowish-gray hair from his head each week, but it was the job of Emie and her sisters to bathe and shave Daddy daily. Seven sisters - one for each day of the week, at least that's what it would be like when the young ones grew a little.

If she cut Daddy with the straight edge razor, the switch was used on her legs and bottom; Daddy said it was a reminder to respect your elders. Emie thought the punishment had more to do with Daddy's anger at the world.

The willows brought both comfort and pain to Emie. Through the loft window they danced in the breeze. Branches raised in worship of the sun. Small green leaves and buds adding color to the dance. Delicate purple flags grew wild at their feet.

She thought only about the sting of the willow switch on her legs and shuttered. If today was an especially angry day, Emie knew the stripes would draw red welts and even blood.

"Emie, girlie − get down from the loft. Daddy's waitin'. He's been waiting too long. You'll only make it worse."

She could see Ernest on the floor of the barn. At least it was Ernest, not Lester, who'd come to fetch her. Lester with his gruff voice and even gruffer hand would have already drug her from the loft into Daddy's room. He would have proudly presented her, waiting for Daddy's approval for doing his bidding. Neither Lester nor Daddy would care about the bruises left on her arm.

"You're not making this easy for any of us," Ernest pleaded.

Both the softness of his voice and the gentle reminder that her foot dragging held not only consequences for her, but for Mama as well, brought her down from the loft.

"I'll walk you to the house, Emie." She loved Ernest. In fact, she loved him earnestly. The play on words was something shared between her mind and heart. Never out loud. Ernest would blush, and if Daddy or Lester ever heard − poor Ernest would again be the butt of their cruel jokes.

Ernest draped his arm around her shoulders. Emie found the weight comforting. Not a word passed between them as they made their trek from the barn, past the hog pens, past the outhouse, down the narrow dirt path toward the small wornout house that sat in a tiny gully.

At the back door of the kitchen, Ernest gently squeezed her shoulder and left her to face the consequences of her hesitations. Emie knew that Ernest wished there was something he could do, but Daddy was like a big black bear − no one crossed him.

The twins, Ruby and Garnett, were still cleaning the breakfast dishes, and said nothing as she entered through the door. Having experienced the switch themselves, they knew what waited. From the other room, she could hear Mama trying to soothe Daddy; Mama's voice soft and Daddy's loud. "It won't be just the switch today, but my belt, Alma. I'm tired of waitin'." Next came the loud slap.

Mama should know better than to get too close to Daddy when he's like this, Emie thought. Fate waited. She walked from the kitchen to the small narrow bedroom quickly. The red handprint on Mama's face was already raised. Ashamed, Mama lifted her hand to hide the mark. Adding insult to injury, Daddy hollered, "Dump the shitter, woman, and get the girlie here warm water! I won't be bathed in cold water!"

Mama carefully grabbed the white porcelain bucket of human waste. Her eyes full of pity, she glanced briefly at her daughter before she exited the room. Mama knew, as well as Emie, that Daddy always got his way. His meanness overshadowed their family and daily lives, like the West Virginia thunderstorms that caused Big Creek to suddenly rise and flood the holler, destroying everything in its path.

"Get the switch, girlie."

Emie obeyed. He struck her legs, beginning at the knees and rising to the thighs. Her bottom was next. The thin cotton dress passed down from sister to sister, and the worn, holey panties offered no protection. Emie thought of Big Creek. She pictured the tadpoles, trout, and nesting birds in the willows. She wasn't sure if her thoughts diminished the pain, or if pain upon pain numbed her skin until the feeling in her legs ceased. Her bladder released, and pee flooded her feet and the floor.

Mama entered the room carrying the cleaned bucket, placing it back in its resting place. Next, came the pitcher of warm bathing water. Emie was faintly aware of Mama taking her shoulders and pulling her from Daddy's reach. "Enough," was all Mama said, taking the willow switch from her husband's hand.

Anger spent, Daddy wilted. His lips were white from exertion and his face flushed. The rage was over. His victim was pale-faced, a faint line of blood dripping down her legs to her bare feet, seeping into the cracked linoleum. Mama moved the wheelchair to the corner of the room and wiped the urine and blood from the floor.

Emie took the worn washrag, dipped it into the water and lathered it with the bacon grease soap her mama made each season. She washed her daddy's feet and legs. She instinctively turned her back as Daddy washed his sensitive areas. As was his routine, he lifted the night shirt, to wash his private parts, and then slipped the shirt from his arms and chest, managing to cover what was foreign to a young girl. Emie re-wet and soaped her cloth, moving to his chest and arms.

Emie handed him the shaving cloth and lathered bar of soap. He washed his own face and neck, and then applied a thick layer of soap to his face for shaving. She took the straight edge in her right hand and shaving cloth in the left, and began her ministrations. Her hands were shaking from fear and pain. She nicked his chin twice, drawing a thin line of blood each time. He winced with each cut. Emie prepared herself for the worse, but when she finished, her daddy simply said, "Leave me, girlie."

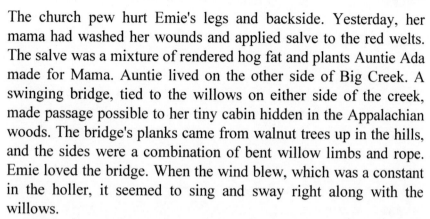

The church pew hurt Emie's legs and backside. Yesterday, her mama had washed her wounds and applied salve to the red welts. The salve was a mixture of rendered hog fat and plants Auntie Ada made for Mama. Auntie lived on the other side of Big Creek. A swinging bridge, tied to the willows on either side of the creek, made passage possible to her tiny cabin hidden in the Appalachian woods. The bridge's planks came from walnut trees up in the hills, and the sides were a combination of bent willow limbs and rope. Emie loved the bridge. When the wind blew, which was a constant in the holler, it seemed to sing and sway right along with the willows.

The salve stank worse than the hog pens, but Mama had insisted. Like the seasons of summer and winter, her mama's touch was gentle — so opposite of Daddy. Emie had lain over the feathered bed she shared with her four sisters, while Mama applied the medicine. It numbed the stinging stripes, opened her sinuses, and drew the flies. She hoped her smell wasn't offensive to Ernest, who sat on her right and Garnet, who sat on her left. Of course, the Ashby family wasn't overly sensitive to smells. They ran a hog farm after all, and while Mama and Daddy washed daily, the children bathed once a week, sometimes even in the creek.

The Ashby family lined an entire pew; Lester on the far end, then Mama, Ernest, Emie, and her sisters. Church was a requirement, not an option — except for Daddy. Only on rare occasions would he allow his chair to be pushed up the hillside by the house, onto the rutted dirt road that led to the country church. It would take both Ernest and Lester switching turns and pushing with all their might to get Daddy to the house of worship. Daddy would, of course, take the lead, boys behind, then Mama and the girls.

On those occasions, Emma thought they must look like a circus train. Not that she'd ever seen a circus train; she'd only read about them in her school primer. But she vividly remembered the picture of elephants stirring up clouds of dust as they walked.

The walk to church took some time. When it rained or snowed, the red clay was slippery. But in the summer, when it was dry, the red cloud rested on them like Mama sprinkling paprika on her deviled eggs.

As far as Emie was concerned, Pastor Eugene, her daddy's second cousin, had basically three messages:

1. hell with all its fire and brimstone,
2. women listening to the pastor and their husbands, and
3. the need for children to be disciplined with the rod.

When Pastor Eugene got on a roll, there was no stopping him – sometimes he preached all three sermons at once.

When the Ashby family returned home, Daddy would insist one of the boys share the entire message. It had to be the boys because women weren't to instruct men in spiritual matters. Emie thought Ernest did the best. His voice was soft and tender. He would quote the verses from memory. He even closed his eyes when reciting the Scriptures. It was obvious, however, Daddy preferred Lester's booming voice. Mama said, "Like father, like son."

Church was ready to begin when Pastor Eugene stretched over Lester to talk to Mama, "Alma, how's Ahab this mornin'?"

"Why he's fine, pastor, wishin' he could be with us this Sunday."

"Good, good, good to hear. Please let him know I'll be over this week to discuss our unfinished business."

Then Daddy's cousin did the oddest thing. He looked at Emie, spoke her given name, "Emerald," and with a slight nod, just walked away.

Something was wrong. Emie just knew it. Even Ernest sensed that something was out of place. His breathing changed and Mama was folding and unfolding her hands in her lap. Emie leaned toward her brother and began to whisper. Ernest shushed her just as the music began.

Tell me the story of Jesus. Write on my heart every word. Tell me the story most precious, sweetest that was ever heard. Tell how the angels in chorus, sang as they welcomed his birth. Glory to God in the highest! Peace and good tidings to earth...

Emie felt peace wash over her. Somehow being in church

brought her a sense of well-being. Ernest said it was Jesus showing her His love. Mama told her that Jesus loved her, but life in the holler was hard. Life in the Ashby family seemed especially hard. Where was God's love? Auntie Ada told her once to look at the willows – cuz they even praised God.

Tell of the cross where they nailed Him, writhing in anguish and pain. Tell of the grace where they laid Him. Tell how He liveth again. Love in that story so tender, clearer than ever I see. Stay, let me weep while you whisper. Love paid the ransom for me.

Auntie Ada was right – the willows did weep with us and whisper about the love of God. Even in the holler, the story of Jesus was tender. Moved by the music and her thoughts of the willows, Emie sighed and prayed in her heart, *Lord, help me.*

Chapter Two

"If your lips itch, it means you want to be kissed."
(Appalachian Folk Belief)

"Mama, where are Ruby and Garnett?" Emie asked as she poked a hole with her right index finger in the red soil. She then dropped in a corn seed. Emie enjoyed outdoor work far more than the tedious tasks of cooking, cleaning, and then cooking again, but gardening was generally reserved for the older girls.

Mama prided herself in the vegetables she raised for her large family. Last summer when Emie had pleaded to help, Mama had hushed her and said, "Your turn will come."

The vegetables they grew sustained the family throughout the year. The potatoes and onions were placed in the root cellar. Other vegetables were eaten fresh, and then later in the summer, they were canned and stored in the pantry. In late fall, any wilted greens left in the garden went to the pigs.

Apple, peach, and plum trees dotted the green meadow between the Ashby barn and Big Creek. Blackberries and raspberries grew in the wooded areas this side of Auntie Ada's home, but vegetables had to be planted and tended. Emie enjoyed the cool morning breeze. The sun was shining, but not directly overhead.

Mama avoiding Emie's question, chuckled as she worked alongside her daughter. "Them boys of mine sure eat like mules. I'm glad Lester took the time to plow the garden. Today's a fine day for plantin' seeds."

Lester had mixed the red clay with manure a few weeks earlier. The manure, baked in the sun, would break down and add nutrients to the West Virginia clay.

Mama often compared the boys to mules: they ate like mules, they stomped their feet like mules, and even fluffed like mules. "Fluffed" was Mama's word for passing gas. Emie didn't see the mule comparisons as compliments, but Ernest and Lester didn't find offense. They both laughed easily with Mama, especially when Daddy wasn't around.

Mama wasn't answering her question. Emie knew she'd heard her. It seemed Mama could hear her children fussing a mile away. With Emie standing right next to her, Mama had heard loud and clear.

"Why aren't Ruby and Garnett helpin'?" Emie tried again.

"Baby girl, some things are best left unsaid. But bein' your mama and all, I know you won't let up till I explain. Ruby and Garnett are off courtin'. Your daddy's done made arrangements for them to marry the Houston boys up the holler," Mama answered.

"The twins aren't even sixteen yet. They ain't old enough to marry," Emie interjected, not trying to hide the exasperation in her voice.

"Girlie, you know how things are done in these hills. Once a girl is through eighth grade, and has started her menses, it's time to marry. The daddies talk among themselves and make the matches. We've been tradin' our pork for beef with the Houstons for years. It's a good match," Mama explained.

"Don't Ruby and Garnett get a say?" Emie asked indignantly. "I've seen them Houston boys. They're none too handsome! I think Eugene might even be cross-eyed."

"Emie, mind what you say," Mama said, shaking her head. "The twins know how things is done. They'll farm and raise babies with their husbands. Now hush and get to work. The sun will be hot before you know it."

Emie and Mama continued their work in silence – both enjoying the spring morning in the holler. Emie worked as hard as a grown woman. There was no complaining or making excuses.

Even when the outhouse called, she continued her planting. She didn't want to disappoint Mama. Hard work was a given in the hills - just like marrying young and raising a family.

Emie was fourteen. She'd finish eighth grade in just a few weeks. She wasn't sure what "menses" was, but now didn't seem the time to ask. Mama was preoccupied with her thoughts. Emie enjoyed seeing the smile on her mother's face. Mama had told her once that working in the garden was better than church any day. "I can pray clearer and worship sweeter with my hands in the red clay," were her mother's words.

When the rows of corn, peas, and beans were planted, Mama said they could call it a day. The root vegetables and greens could wait.

Emie's back and knees hurt. Mama believed in using your hands for planting. The rows were made straight by pounding stakes in the ground and tying twine between the stakes for guidance. The burrows were done with a hoe, but each seed was planted and covered by hand. Mama said it made the vegetables sweeter, and Emie didn't argue.

Emie and her mother headed to the water pump by the house to wash their faces, necks, hands, arms, feet, and legs. Mama called it, "Takin' a bird bath."

"Oh, doesn't that feel good, Emie?" Mama splashed her face with cool water from the pump. "Nothin' like feelin' the sun on your back and dirt in your hands. You did a good job today, baby girl."

Emie could hear Ruby and Garnett inside the kitchen, giggling and whispering. She wondered if once they married if cooking would become her chore. She hoped not. She'd rather work with Ernest feeding the hogs. Heck, she'd rather clean the outhouse than stand by the hot wood-burning stove. Stink was better than heat any day. She'd put some of her mama's lavender oil under her nostrils, and cover her mouth and nose with a rag. The smell wouldn't be too bad. She could manage.

Her mama said electricity and running water in a house worked well in the city, but would never make it to the holler. "The hills are too selfish and stubborn to ever help a poor woman," Mama had muttered more than once.

Courtin' must be over, Emie thought. Maybe it's none too bad if they're laughing. I wonder if they kissed, or did other things. She wasn't sure what the other things were exactly, but she'd seen animals mate, and she'd heard her mama and daddy in their curtained off bedroom. Daddy, who was always gruff, spoke softly at night to Mama, and Emie figured with eight children something was going on. She knew that mamas didn't get pregnant on their own - except for some reptiles and amphibians. She'd learned about that in her reader at school.

Daddy said boys were needed to run the farm. Lester was the oldest and then Ernest. Next came the twins, Ruby and Garnett, then Emie. Her four younger sisters followed suit.

Emie saw Daddy pinch Mama's bottom once through her cotton nightgown. Mama slapped his hand, but was smiling - like she wasn't really mad. Daddy laughed and told Mama that he needed more sons. Mama had said she wasn't ready for another big belly. Emie knew Mama and Daddy had been married for twenty years. Sapphire, her youngest sister, was almost four, and Lester was nineteen. Emie had done the math in her head. She was proud of knowing all her tables. She was the only girl in eighth grade who could multiply and divide her twelves. Mama had a big belly every two or so years, and was past due for the next baby.

Mama smiled lovingly at Emie. "I know you must be worn out, but would you mind taking some things to Ada?"

Emie could hardly believe her good fortune. Usually Ernest made the trek to Auntie's. A visit to Aunt Ada was like walking on sunshine. A visit by herself meant shared secrets, tasty treats, and lavish love.

The walk to Auntie Ada's was wonderful. The meadow was lush from the spring rains. Walking under the blossoming fruit trees made Emie feel like a princess. She'd read about real princesses in her school reader. She imagined herself as royalty, sitting on a throne, summoning servants to do her every whim. The servants would be dressed like jesters, doing her bidding and entertaining her with stories from afar. The swinging bridge over Big Creek was her moat, and the wooded area leading to Auntie Ada's was her secret forest.

Auntie's tiny cabin was Emie's hideaway in the pretending and in real life. The arched wooden door seemed too large for the tiny home. The willow branch wreath was welcoming. Ada was known for her willow wreaths and baskets. She picked young willow shoots and wove them with her hands. What lay behind the door were treasures − not treasures of gold and wealth, but of love, assurance, and comfort.

Auntie Ada was a "love & pick aunt." She wasn't related by blood, but by heart. Since Emie was little, Auntie had been her confidant. She had no fear of willow switches, growling tummies, or shushing. As a little girl, Emie had worried that she'd suffocate in Auntie's amble bosom. Ernest said Auntie hugged like a bear. Emie asked Ernest when he'd ever been hugged by a bear.

Emie was barely through the front door, when her pent-up words of frustration began to flow. "Auntie, why is Daddy so mean? He took a switch to me on Saturday. It hurt like fire, but I tried not to cry. I figured Mama would cry enough for both of us. Sometimes he's sweet to Mama, but never to us girls. He almost slapped Sapphire yesterday, but Mama stepped between. She's only four, and she don't know better than to pull at his leg quilt. He and Lester seem to get on, but not so much Ernest." Emie spoke the words softly, knowing she could trust Auntie Ada with her rambling thoughts.

"Darlin', your daddy ain't always been so mean. He and your mama married right under them willows by Big Creek the spring of 1910." Auntie rose from the wooden rocker and gazed out the window toward the creek. "I remember how he looked at your mama that day. When they kissed, even the willows clapped their hands. Your granddaddy ran the pig farm then. Ahab had worked with his daddy since he was a wee thing. He had loved your mama for years, but was waitin' for her to grow up. They was happy. Married less than a year when your mama gave birth to Lester, and then Ernest came not too far after." Emie waited for Auntie to finish the story. Minutes crept by, but Emie remained quiet. Even at fourteen she understood Auntie Ada could get lost in her thoughts.

"Your daddy loved them boys. I saw him tuck baby Lester in his front overall pouch once. I laughed till I cried." Auntie smiled at the memory and paused once again.

Ernest had told Emie that when Auntie got lost, she was simply wandering from this world to heaven where she was talking with Jesus. Emie guessed that Ernest was right. Aunt Ada had even told her once that sometimes an old woman's thoughts got stuck between earth and the ever after. The idea of getting stuck didn't make sense to Emie. When Auntie went wandering, did her thoughts get trapped somewhere?

Emie thought of Lester's raccoon trap. The cage had kept the animal penned. Emie remembered how the raccoon had fought to break free. Its struggle had grieved her. Lester had laughed and called her a "baby." Ernest had wiped the tears from her cheeks and reminded her that farm life could be cruel. She was older now and understood the mischievous nature of a raccoon, but at the time not even Ernest could bring her comfort. A few days later, when the trap caught a skunk, and Lester was sprayed, Emie had giggled, not where Lester could see or hear, but behind the outhouse. When Ernest saw her, he smiled and winked. The memory warmed Emie. How she loved her brother!

When Auntie started talking again, Emie was drawn back into the present. "Every man in these hills wants sons. Boys are needed to feed the family and carry on the farmin'. When the twins was born, your daddy was disappointed, but he said they was so pretty he couldn't help but love them. He's the one who named them Garnett and Ruby, his gems he said. Emie, you were less than a year old when your daddy left for the Great War. Most of the men left the holler to fight. With the men gone, we women helped each other best we could. Most days I watched you and your brothers and sisters, so your mama could work the pigs. Times was rough. Food and milk was scarce. Your mama worried that you babies would starve."

Auntie Ada returned to the worn rocker and continued her soliloquy. "The war changed the proud hill men. Most had never left the holler before. They came back to us different. Your daddy came home changed in body and mind. The day he came home was a sad day for us all, especially your mama. She met him at the train station in Charleston. She wasn't sure what to expect. The wire said he'd been wounded in battle, but nothin' about the wheelchair. Your daddy rode home part way in a borrowed car with a war buddy at the wheel, and then he and your mama came up through the holler in a mule drawn cart; your daddy lay in the back with your Uncle Eugene drivin'. Your mama told me that she tried to talk with your daddy first about you children, and then about the weather and the hogs. Your daddy said nothin' the entire way home. He wouldn't even let Eugene give thanks to the Lord."

Auntie took a deep breath and then looked closely at Emie. "Girlie, ain't your mama or daddy done told you that story?"

"No, Auntie. Daddy doesn't talk much and Mama gets tears in her eyes whenever someone says somethin' about Daddy's legs."

"Honey, it's not his legs that make her cry. She misses who he used to be. His joy of livin'." Auntie paused, like she was remembering Emie's daddy of old.

Emie couldn't imagine him any different. He was hard, like the Appalachians. She'd read in her *McGuffey Reader* that the mountains were formed by the earth plates colliding together. Her teacher said that the continents were different back then. Emie didn't quite understand about the plates or the continents. She just knew that her daddy had collided with the war and come home different. She prayed that someday she could love him like she loved the mountain plateaus, ridges, and valleys.

"Emie, let's eat us some cornbread. Do you want buttermilk or honey? I thought Ernest might be comin', so the bread ain't quite as sweet as I know you like."

Emie smiled slightly. She enjoyed cornbread, but thoughts of her daddy's story had sobered her mood. She prayed in her head that when daddy had angry days she could remember what Auntie shared.

"I think my girl would like honey." Auntie Ada rose from the rocker and took the few steps to the tiny kitchen. The cornbread baked that morning in an old iron skillet had already cooled.

Auntie served generous pieces, placing hers in a bowl with buttermilk, and Emie's on a faded white chipped plate with sugared honey dripping from the bread's sides. A small piece of the honeycomb rested on the side of the plate. How well Auntie understood Emie, who loved to swirl and nibble the wax-like honeycomb in her mouth.

Emie knew that Ernest had brought Auntie Ada the honey last fall. It was still too early in the spring for fresh honey. Last summer Ernest had found a large beehive in a walnut tree in the woods. He'd been squirrel hunting when he heard the humming. He told Emie that the ground had vibrated from the buzzing of the bees. Daddy had criticized Ernest for not collecting the honey right away. Even when Ernest explained that he didn't know how, Daddy had ridiculed him. Mama had taken Ernest aside, and explained how to smoke the bees into leaving their hive. The Ashby family had enjoyed honey all summer and fall. The honey was now sugared. It still tasted good, but had lost its clarity. Emie enjoyed the sweetness even if the texture was slightly different.

Chapter Three

"If you dream about crossing water, there will be trouble in your family."
(Appalachian Folk Belief)

The water was rising a little bit each day in the creek. The snow from the high country was just about melted, the runoff trickling into Big Creek. The water was muddied, but the frogs, salamanders, and turtles didn't seem to mind. It wasn't warm enough yet for rattlesnakes and copperheads. She loved the swinging bridge, but somehow the water called to her. Like the willows, the creek seemed to have a voice.

The rocks were sharp at the creek bottom. Emie wished that she'd left her shoes on, but fear of muddying and ruining her only pair had caused her to reason at the bank. The water was cold – so cold that the first step had taken her breath away. She usually liked to dawdle in the water, but today she hurried.

Just as she reached the opposite shore, Ernest appeared from the orchard, his head and shoulders covered with blossoms. Earlier, Emie had dreamed of being a princess. With her dream now faded, she saw Ernest as royalty, not herself. He looked like a prince, or better yet, a groom waiting for his bride. She often asked Ernest why he hadn't found a girl yet. He only smiled. "No one would have me with a sister like you."

"Girlie, I was just comin' to fetch you. How's Auntie?"

"Fine. She was expectin' you. Made you cornbread, but don't

worry none, I ate your share," Emie said in a sassy tone.

"I bet you did. Honey or buttermilk?" Before Emie could answer, Ernest shushed her, "No wait, let me guess." Ernest then moistened his index finger with the tip of his tongue and wiped sticky honey from the corner of her mouth.

"I'm gettin' too old for this," Emie said while waiting impatiently for her brother to finish. Ernest had been giving her spit baths since she was a baby.

Emie sat down on a log next to the creek and put her shoes on. She hoped her brother wasn't in a hurry. She had some questions that needed answering, and Ernest wasn't shy about telling her the truth.

"Ernest, what does it mean when a girl has her menses?"

At first Ernest looked surprised, then he started to chuckle, next came the belly laughs. He barely got the words out, "Emie, the things you ask."

"Brother, I'm serious. Mama said that girls get married after they start their menses. I'm a girl, and I don't even know what that is." Emie took a deep breath. She wanted Ernest to see that she wasn't fooling.

Ernest pulled Emie up from the log, and started walking toward the meadow. "Menses means that a girl can have a baby. Garnett and Ruby are old enough to have babies, so they're ready to be gettin' married."

"Mama also said that girls have to be through eighth grade to get married."

Ernest started to laugh again, "They also have to be too old for spit baths, and not have the bossy toe."

Tradition in the hills said if a girl had a second toe longer than the big toe that she was bound to be bossy. Emie was the only girl in her family with the bossy toe. Daddy had bossy toes, but like so many other things in the holler, it was okay for a man, but not a woman.

Emie rolled her eyes at Ernest and shook her pretty blonde head.

"Emie, did I ever tell you about the piglet who rolled her eyes? She had big blue eyes just like you. I think she even had a few blonde hairs comin' out her snout."

Emie tried hard not to laugh. Ernest always had crazy stories about the hogs.

"She rolled them eyes back in her head and they never came down. It was a sight, alright. Sight for me to see, and that poor pig could barely see a thing. She tried to suck her mama's tail — thought it was a teat to latch onto."

As they traveled the meadow together, Ernest continued to make Emie laugh. Being with Ernest was like being at home. Not home where Daddy was yelling, Mama crying, and the little ones fussing — but home without fear, and where love and joy were plentiful.

"Ernest, the outhouse stinks," Emie declared loudly. "I need to do a big job and can't stand the thought of sittin' in there."

"Emie, I've been too busy birthin' pigs, milkin' cows, and feedin' chickens to worry about the shitter. Now, if you've a mind to help me tomorrow, I'll work on the outhouse. 'Til then I reckon you'll have to wait or sit in the stink."

Emie with her voice raised, headed toward the house. "Mama, Ernest is needin' my help tomorrow. Can you spare me to work outside?"

Mama met her at the back door leading to the kitchen. "Girlie, since when do you enter my house yellin' like something's on fire? We have company, and I need you to mind your manners. Garnett and Ruby went back up the holler. Put coffee on and slice and butter some of that sweet bread. Pastor Eugene is here visitin' with your daddy."

Emie wondered why her mama hadn't already put the coffee on and gotten the bread sliced and buttered, but the stern look on Mama's face told her now was not the time for questions. Emie got busy, but not so busy that she didn't notice Mama sitting outside the curtained-off room, listening to Daddy and Pastor Eugene talk. Mama was wringing her hands again — a sure sign that trouble was brewing, brewing like the coffee Emma had placed in the worn, porcelain, speckled pot on the back of the wood stove.

The girls' room was a small curtained-off area toward the back of the run-down mountain home. Through the curtain and to the immediate right was Daddy and Mama's room. The tiny central room was where Ernest and Lester slept. It was still cool enough at night that Ernest had built a small fire in the wood burner. The curtain that separated the rooms was thin and worn, so Emie could see the glowing embers. Sleep wouldn't come to Emerald.

The bed was crowded with her and four of her sisters. The girls slept sideways on the bed. Mama said that it didn't matter if their legs hung over the side. "It's the way of the mountains. You use what you have and are thankful for it."

The twins, Garnett and Ruby, had fallen asleep giggling about the Houston boys. Between Emie and the twins lay Coral and Opal.

Emie had tried to explain once to Mama that coral wasn't really a gemstone. "It's formed at the bottom of the ocean by tiny sea animals," Emie clarified. "Coral's name doesn't fit with the rest of the sisters."

Mama had shook her head and hushed Emie. "I saw coral once in a store window in Charleston. It was lovely. All my girls is beautiful, Emie. Don't be tellin' your sister she don't fit. She has enough trouble being sandwiched in the middle of all of you."

Mama was right. Coral was smashed right in the middle - the middle of the bed and the middle of the Ashby family life. Emie sometimes forgot she was even there. Coral was so quiet. Often on the walk to school, she wouldn't utter a word. She seemed to blend with her surroundings and become invisible. She hid in the shadows like a mouse who only came out at night and scurried close to the walls.

The two youngest girls, Sapphire and Pearl, were sleeping on a pallet on the floor, both clutching rag dolls that had been passed down from sister to sister. Emie could hear the boys sawing logs – that's what Mama called their snoring.

Just like Daddy, Lester was loud even in his sleep, and Ernest was, well, just Ernest. Even in sleep, he seemed serene. Emie somehow found reassurance in Ernest's heavy breathing.

The west wall of the girls' room separated their sleeping

quarters from the kitchen and eating area. Emie could still smell the residual odor from the fried trout her family had for dinner. At dusk, Lester had come home with freshly caught rainbows. His surprise had distracted Mama from questioning his whereabouts. Emie had wondered if that was Lester's plan all along. He disappeared a lot these days. Not that Emie minded. Her brother was difficult at best, and the sisters had all grown tired of his bossiness. He reminded Emie of a volcano she'd read about in school. It had erupted without warning, killing the living and destroying nature. The red molten lava hadn't discriminated between young and old, wicked and wise, or beautiful and ugly. Like Daddy, Lester's temper would be his destruction, and the destruction of those around him.

Emie heard her parents whispering in the dark. Their voices were hushed, yet their words were intense. She then heard her mama's quiet crying, and her daddy's slightly raised voice, "Alma, it's our way. Eugene and I agreed. There are too many mouths wantin' food. She ain't a boy that can carry his weight."

Her mama answered, "She ain't ready yet."

"Alma, you didn't act like this about the twins. Daddy's voice was raising slightly more in volume.

"They're goin' together, Ahab. They're older. It's not the same."

"Now, Alma..."

Mama interrupted, "Leave me be. I need to grieve."

All grew quiet. Emie tried to focus on Ernest's breathing, but comfort wouldn't come. She hadn't heard her name, but sensed the conversation had been about her. Sleep eluded her until the wee hours of the morning when exhaustion and worry laid their claim.

Chapter Four

"Putting a handful of salt on your head will cure a headache."
(Appalachian Folk Belief)

"Girlie, what's wrong with you today? Yesterday you begged Mama to help me and now you're lollygaggin'." Ernest was exasperated, yet Emie couldn't find the gumption to move any faster.

While her mind raced with worry, her body moved in slow motion. Her stomach hurt and her head ached. She felt mean as a polecat and was doing her best to not make Ernest the victim of her verbal swipes. So far he'd been fairly patient, but Emie knew she was trying him. She couldn't seem to help it.

Finally, Ernest relegated her to the barn. Her chore was to check on the piglets and mamas. Fresh water and food were needed. She also needed to investigate their overall health. Were the sows bearing up under the constant demands of the young ones, and were the piglets pink and chubby? The stalls needed mucked and most of the pigs needed washing. They were covered in manure and mud. Emie knew they rolled in mud to keep cool, but her ministrations required her to actually examine their bodies from snout to tail. She didn't want to disappoint Ernest.

She could hear Ernest in the outhouse. He was singing, "When the Roll is Called Up Yonder." Cleaning the potty was a disgusting job. When Ernest was disgusted, he sang hymns. He'd once told Emie that singing to God kept him from swearing. His voice grew louder with each verse.

In spite of feeling melancholy, Emie couldn't help but smile. "He must really feel like cussin' up a storm," she whispered to the squirming piglet she was bathing. Daddy cussed and so did Lester, but never Ernest. Emie felt that God should make allowances for cussing when a person lived in a West Virginia holler, but Ernest disagreed.

When Mama called for lunch, Emie replied that she wasn't hungry. She felt funny. She wasn't sure if it was lack of sleep, aching arms from wrestling pigs, or exhaustion from hauling water and cleaning stalls. Maybe it was Ernest's singing.

Emie thought something a little more upbeat would be nice. Out in the barn, where no one could see, she could even dance the Charleston. Mama said that dancing led to other sins − like carousing. Mama also believed that dancing paved the way to hell, where you'd dance with the devil throughout eternity.

Ernest had told Emie privately, "Dancin' won't send you to hell. Now if you go places that have dancin', smokin', and moonshine, you might smell like hell. Heck, Emie, in the Bible, King David danced almost naked in the streets."

Mimi, her friend at school, had taught Emie the Charleston at recess a few weeks ago. Emie didn't want to forget the steps. With spring planting break and school starting in just a couple days, she wished she'd taken time to practice. Emie thought Mimi was so sophisticated, and she had already embarrassed herself by innocently asking, "Can I still learn the Charleston if I keep all my clothes on?" Mimi had giggled and smiled, but Emie's face still flushed thinking about the exchange of words.

Emie's thoughts were interrupted by Ernest's approaching steps.

Emie smiled at her brother as he entered the barn.

"Nice job, girlie." Ernest jokingly grabbed his heart and stumbled through the barn, like he was in shock.

Emie's smile broke into laughter. Amid her giggles she told Ernest, "I separated two little ones that don't look good. I just need to gather some fresh bedding straw for the stalls."

"I'll be happy to help. You done good today, little sister."

Ernest lovingly placed his arm around Emie's shoulders. They stood for just a moment in silence, admiring the cleanliness of the barn, and listening to the squeals of the piglets searching for their mothers.

Emie agilely climbed up into the barn loft. She tossed one of the few remaining straw bales to Ernest, who in turn removed the twine and separated the bale into sections for the stalls.

Emie's gaze traveled to the willows. Their leaves were continuing to bud. It was a beautiful sight. The creek, and the trees along its bank, seemed to change daily. Spring had a way of bringing life to the holler.

Emie placed her long slender legs on the first rung of the worn wooden ladder, and then jumped to the barn floor. She felt wetness between her legs. Her first thought was that she'd peed herself like a baby. Then she saw the blood − enough blood that it was trickling down her legs onto the dirt floor of the barn. She started to panic, and began twisting and turning in self-examination. She whimpered, not because she felt pain, but because she was afraid.

Ernest heard her soft cry and hurriedly took the needed strides to reach her. He first saw the fear in Emerald's eyes and then noticed the blood.

Emie started to cry. "Ernest, I'm dyin'. Pray for my forgiveness. I've been dancin' the Charleston with the devil."

Lovingly and patiently Ernest began his own examination. "Emie, where does it hurt?"

He paused waiting for her to answer. Emie was too busy praying, "Jesus, forgive me. I don't want to dance for eternity in hell..."

Ernest waited a moment and then gently placed his hand over Emie's mouth, silencing her prayer. "Emie, you're not going to hell. You started your monthly."

She swooned into the loving arms of her brother.

Alma tapped softly on Ada's front door. She knew that Auntie often gave her eyes a rest during the late afternoon. She waited. Not wanting to wake her aged friend, but at the same time, burning with need to unburden her soul, she knocked a little louder, feeling selfish for interrupting Auntie's nap. Alma listened closely and finally heard the shuffling of the older woman's feet.

As the door opened, Ada's sleepy eyes widened in surprise. "Well, Alma, it's been awhile since you came callin'. Usually Ernest brings your biddin'." Auntie's arms drew Alma into a firm and loving embrace. "Come in. Come in. I'm so glad to be seein' you."

"Sit, sit. I'll get us some milk tea." Ada gathered wild plants and herbs each summer. She crushed them with a wooden mortar and pestle passed down from her own mama. She seeped the crushed leaves in boiling water, and then added milk and sugar. Each cup tasted slightly different, but delicious, nonetheless.

The longtime friends sat quietly sipping their warm tea. Auntie waited for her caller to speak. Alma waited, not knowing how to begin. The ache of her heart kept her from making small talk.

Alma's tears started the wordless conversation. They flowed in trickles at first, and then gave way to sobs that stained her cheeks. Auntie didn't ask questions, but took Alma's hand, like a mother would a child, and comforted her through gentle squeezes and taps. She patted her in series of threes, allowing her touch to speak the words, "I love you."

When the tears subsided and silence reigned again, Alma began her story. "He's done it. Ahab told Eugene that Emie would marry his boy."

Alma began wringing her hands in her lap. "I was holdin' out that she'd be a late bloomer, but yesterday she started her monthly. Ahab's lettin' her finish the school year, and the weddin' will take place late summer. A few weeks after the twins'."

Alma stopped speaking. Her glistening eyes roamed Ada's cabin. She was looking, but not really looking. When Alma's words didn't come, Auntie rose from her worn rocker, and kissed Alma's forehead, her lips lingering. Ada then took the tea cups from the small wooden table separating the chairs, and headed to the kitchen to warm the brew.

Alma understood that Ada knew all about Eugene and his son, but nonetheless, her own needs required that she tell the story. "I know Eugene's the church pastor, but he's not my pastor. I'm polite enough, but I'm not fooled. He's like a rooster, strutting in the hen house causin' all the chickens to cluck and run. He sees God as a tool to get what he wants. Sayin' one thing on Sunday and livin' different the rest of the week. And Charlie, his son, is just the same.

Alma paused, rubbing her hands and lower arms like she was washing away dirt and grime. "Eugene killed his wife. He didn't shoot her with a gun, but worked her too hard and preached her to death. Tellin' her that hell was waitin' if she didn't do his biddin'. In the end, she was thankful to leave this earth and go to Jesus' arms."

Auntie returned to the rocker, but had yet to speak.

Alma continued. "Emie will be nothin' but a workhorse for Eugene. Charlie and him both will break her will. She'll lose herself in Eugene's preachin'." Alma paused momentarily. "Ahab can't be reasoned with. He thinks the match is a good one."

Ada instinctively knew when Alma had finished. Her long sigh and faraway look told Ada that her friend had resigned herself again to Ahab's distorted wishes. Inside Ada felt like sizzling lard. The chicken she'd fried last night in grease had popped and smoked. Her emotions were doing the same. She worried that if she spoke, her words would injure, like the grease splatter that had stung her right wrist. She whispered a prayer for wisdom.

"Alma, all you're sayin' is right, but as the mama, it's your job to protect Emie."

"Ada, I can't go against Ahab. You know how he is. There's no reasonin'."

"I know he hits and slaps and punches with body and words. You even more than the children. You've tolerated his meanness far too long. Leave Lester and Ernest with their daddy, they can protect themselves and work the hogs, and bring yourself and the young ones here with me," Ada's voice pleaded with her friend.

Alma responded emphatically, "I can't!"

Ada answered passionately, her voice sounding like a mother

charging her child to make the right decision. "Alma, it's not that you can't, but you won't. Don't be thinkin' that your children don't know that it's your job to keep them safe. In time, they'll resent you even more than their daddy."

By the look in Alma's eyes, Ada knew that the walls were starting to cave in on her friend. Alma's breathing grew labored, like she was suffocating. She rose from her chair, kissed Auntie Ada on the cheek, and simply left without another word.

Chapter Five

"If you sweep after the sun goes down, you will never be rich."
(Appalachian Folk Belief)

Ernest knew that Lester was up to something. He was also tired of carrying the workload. All the chores were swirling around his neck, like the laundry hung out to dry on a windy day. Lester wasn't lazy; he was a hard worker. He was just off working somewhere else, but where?

For all Ernest's efforts, things weren't getting done. He needed Lester's help. The fences needed mending, the hen house needed cleaning, and the male piglets needed castrating. Ernest had planned on doing the snipping yesterday, but with Emie sharing the outdoor chores, and her propensity to cry at injustices to animals, he had wisely made the decision to wait.

Lester disappeared for hours at a time, the breeze blowing him in and out of the farm. Mama appeared to notice that something was amiss, but Daddy was Daddy after all, and Lester was the favored. When Lester, as the oldest son, made the evening hog report, Daddy only nodded. Lester acted like all was well, and that he knew the ins and outs of each day's activities, but Ernest knew better.

The wind had kicked up that morning, dropping needed rain from the dark clouds above the holler. Lester, pretending concern over repairs to the pigpen this side of the orchard, had set out early.

Ernest wasn't fooled by Lester's deception. Why, his brother hadn't even bothered to take the needed tools, especially the hickory hog stick.

Yesterday, Emie had helped with the mamas and piglets, but Ernest would never let her, or any of the sisters, close to the boars used for breeding. They had too much passion, passion for the sows, but also passion, albeit a different kind, for anyone or anything that got in their way. His daddy had warned him and Lester, from the time they were old enough to work the hogs, to always carry the stick. Lester had beaten a number of the beasts to within an inch of their lives, only to have them dangerously charge again and again. Hog tusks could easily tear a man's flesh. Many a hog had killed the hand that fed him.

Lester and Ernest never tended to the boars without the hog stick. Ernest found it best not to rile the animals with threatening shouts and waving of the hickory. Lester, on the other hand, seemed to stir up trouble wherever he went, including working the hogs. Ernest thought at times that Lester, in some sort of off-kilter way, enjoyed the altercations.

Daddy had scared his boys early on with a horrific story about a fellow farmer. "A farmer, just like you boys, was out in the pens workin' the hogs, when a big boar came up from behind and laid hold of his Achilles tendon. The hog cut the tendon right in two, and the man fell to the ground. The hogs gathered 'round the farmer, tearin' at his body. Bless his wife, she found him later in the day. She was a good woman, but a better woman would have found him before he died."

Ernest knew that raising hogs wasn't for the faint of heart. He enjoyed farming, but he also longed for further education. He wanted to be a teacher, and needed to leave the holler, for a season, to attend college. Most of the mountain children quit school after eighth grade, but Ernest, with Mrs. Randolph's help and patience, had studied through the twelfth grade. She had encouraged Ernest to register at the Charleston Teaching School, her alma mater. The faithful teacher, despite her advancement in years and certainly being tired at the end of each school day, met with Ernest some evenings to help prepare him for college. It was their secret, although Ernest suspected that Auntie Ada knew all about his tutoring from Mrs. Randolph.

Ernest's dream often held his mind and emotions captive. The thought of teaching children one day brought him hope for the future, but his heart was torn knowing that the price for his dream would be costly, not just monetarily, but with relationships as well. He would have to defy Mama and Daddy in order to leave. They wouldn't understand − it was their heritage; the hill people stayed close to home. He would also have to leave Emie. Ernest loved all of his sisters, but with Emie it was as if God had given him an extra portion of love. Sometimes he felt there was a tether connected to his heart and hers. With a just a look, she could pull the chord to the place where his heart bubbled with joy, or sank in the murky creek mud with sadness.

Lately, Ernest's concerns over Lester's frivolity only added to his internal struggle. How could he leave his family, if Lester couldn't be trusted to carry on the farm? As much as Ernest was a dreamer, Lester was a schemer.

As the day warmed, Ernest, not generally prone to anger or frustration, began singing, *"What a fellowship, what a joy divine, leaning on the everlastin' arms. What a blessedness, what a peace is mine, leanin' on the everlastin' arms. Leanin', leanin', safe and secure from all alarms. Leanin', leanin', leanin' on the everlastin' arms."*

As Ernest walked toward the orchard, he continued with raised voice the second verse, *"Oh, how sweet to walk in this pilgrim way, leaning on the everlastin' arms. Oh, how bright the path grows from day to day, leaning on the everlastin' arms."*

When his steps grew in distance and force, and singing became impossible, the chorus still continued to ring through his mind and heart, *"Leaning, leaning, safe and secure from all alarms. Leaning, leaning, leaning on the everlastin' arms."*

As he approached the orchard, he saw Lester's large footprints leading toward Big Creek. Ernest needed to know what Lester was scheming, yet he didn't want to know. He understood that sometimes in knowing, action was required. He liked to believe that he wasn't afraid of Daddy and Lester. He knew he was afraid for Mama. Heartache upon heartache could push a person to places where only God Himself could bring one home. The journey from those places was long and difficult, and Ernest knew that people didn't come home the same way they left. Mama appeared to be strong, but she was fragile, like a bruised reed or a smoking candle.

The rain earlier in the day made Lester's steps easy to follow. The mud trail led Ernest across the swinging bridge. He followed the impressions on the ground through the meadow; they then veered off, going the opposite direction of Auntie's. Ernest had tracked deer through these same woods. The terrain was familiar, and self-assured Lester, not knowing that he would be followed, had made no attempt to hide his wanderings.

Ernest slowed his pace, and began praying as he walked. His conversation flowed easily toward heaven. He had no trouble talking to God; the trouble lay in hearing back. Ernest longed to hear the Lord speak his name and call him friend. His meditations brought peace to his troubled heart. He sensed the presence of God leading him forward in his quest to find Lester.

The lyrics of his earlier song were a wonderful reminder of God's omnipresence. Whether in Charleston at the teacher's college, or in the holler of his ancestors, Ernest would lean on the Lord's everlastin' arms, safe and secure from all alarms.

He heard Lester's booming voice before he saw him. He also heard the voice of another man. Ernest stopped in his tracks and listened, wanting to identify who was present with his brother. He was too far away to hear with clarity the words being spoken, but the rise and fall of the man's voice was familiar.

It took a moment for Ernest to pinpoint the speech pattern, but it came to him like a hidden marble being swept from under a bed. The voice belonged to Charlie, Pastor Eugene's son. The hair rose on Ernest's neck. Whatever Lester was up to wasn't good. Mama had compared Charlie and Lester's friendship to lantern oil and a lit match, and Ernest knew that Mama's words rang true.

Although he moved closer, Ernest didn't approach the clearing, but stayed hidden among the trees. He wanted to observe Lester and Charlie without detection.

He could see that the cleared land had been planted in corn.

The seedlings were barely through the soil, but still identifiable. Ernest estimated that close to three acres had been planted. The process would have been time consuming, explaining Lester's absence of late. The corn had also been planted very early. Lester and Charlie's secret had even defied nature, which hadn't brought a spring freeze.

Off to the side, Charlie and Lester were working on some type of equipment. At first, their backs obscured Ernest's view, but he waited quietly and patiently for his brother and friend to move. Waiting in the woods wasn't a new experience for Ernest. He was a skilled hunter; the health of his family depended not only on hog farming, but on the deer, quail, turkeys, and squirrels that he and Lester harvested.

He smelled the muskiness of the coming rain, and felt the air grow heavy with moisture. He heard the rain before he felt the drops on his head. The trees acted as a canopy. On any other day, Ernest would have enjoyed the fresh feel of rain on his being, but today his body was wound tight. He was focused and would not allow himself the luxury of enjoying nature's watering.

Some time passed before Charlie and Lester moved, the rain driving them under their own canopy of trees. The equipment wasn't yet assembled, but Ernest recognized the makings of a still. A remote speakeasy had opened further up the holler. Ernest had wondered where the bootleg liquor would come from, and now he knew.

The argument over prohibition was a heated one. Mama said that it wasn't good for families and that drunkenness would send men to hell. Daddy said that men would drink whether it was legal or not. Ernest wasn't sure. He wasn't a drinker himself, but he knew that Lester enjoyed partaking.

Ernest headed back to the Ashby farm. Today wasn't the day to confront his brother. He needed to think. He needed to pray, and he needed to talk with Auntie Ada.

Chapter Six

*"If you look in a mirror held over a spring, you will see
the face of the person you will marry."
(Appalachian Folk Belief)*

Emie loved school, and all it's special gatherings. She could hardly believe her graduation was less than a month away. She had raced through her morning chores and was waiting impatiently for Coral and Opal to put on their shoes. Mama had already cautioned her, "Emie, be patient. Speak kindly to your sisters. Don't be rushin' them. They'll be ready soon enough."

Emie knew that Coral's shoes were tight, so it would take extra time to push her growing feet into the weathered leather. She smiled at her sisters, but inside her heart raced with anticipation. She wanted a chance to talk with Mimi before Mrs. Randolph rang the morning bell. Emie could almost run the distance, but the shorter legs of her younger sisters made the journey awfully slow.

The one-room schoolhouse was over two miles away. The school was located right next to the privy and the church. Pastor Eugene acted like it was his responsibility to oversee the proper education of the young ones.

Just as the girls reached the dirt road, Coral spotted a box turtle. "Emie! Opal! Look!" Coral exclaimed. The turtle's head popped back into its shell just as Coral knelt to take a closer view.

Emie wanted to yell at Coral to forget the turtle and hurry up, but thankfully caught herself before the words passed her lips.

Coral rarely spoke, and when she did the words were said so softly that Emie had to pay her close attention. Emie remembered her conversation with Mama about Coral being squished in the middle of the Ashby family. It was important that her next-in-line sister felt that she was heard and valued this cool morning.

Coral tried to coax the turtle into reappearing by softly tapping its shell with a stick. Emie finally took Coral gently by the hand leading her down the rutted road. Opal nonchalantly took Emie's other hand, and the three sisters continued on their path. Their innocence was sweet as the morning dew that was already evaporating from the early sunshine.

For a brief moment, Emie wished that she could hide like the turtle from the struggles of the holler, but then she thought about Big Creek, the willows and the morning glories along the road where she was walking. *It would be a shame to hide my head and miss seeing the beauty of the mountain land*, she thought.

Emie talked with Coral about the turtle's ornate shell and how easily turtles become frightened. "Did you know that turtles can hide in their shells for hours? On our way home, we'll check and see if the turtle is still by the road. Maybe Mama will let you keep him − or her. I'm not sure which it is."

Coral smiled in response, but didn't utter a word.

Emie continued her prattle, "Coral, we'll need to look closer at the shell to see if it's a boy or girl. We can also look at the tail and claws. Girls have shorter tails and claws. I read all about it in my school reader."

Opal interrupted by squeezing Emie's hand. "I have to pee," she squeaked.

"Opal, we've talked about this before," Emie reprimanded her little sister. "Mama said for you to go before we leave home."

Coral rose to Opal's defense, "She couldn't use the potty. Lester was in there, and he yelled real loud when Opal asked him to hurry. She even asked real nice."

Emie was about to ask Opal if she could wait, when her sister started doing the potty dance. The crossing and uncrossing of Opal's legs and her frantic jumping up and down was a clear indication that she needed to go and now. She slipped down her faded hand-me-down panties, squatted in the road, facing the ditch where the morning glories were blossoming, while Emie and Coral made a circle around her backside, using their slightly flared dresses to shield their sister.

"Emie, I dribbled." Opal sounded like she was ready to cry.

"Let me see," Emie replied. "It's just a couple spots. It'll be dry before we get to school."

"Mama says if big girls wet their pants that they'll stink. I don't want to stink," Opal said through her tears.

Emie began to sniff loudly. "I don't smell nothin' but the sweetness of the mornin'. What do you smell, Coral?"

Coral, quickly catching on, put her nose in the air like a hound dog, and began sniffing as well. "I smell wild flowers, nothin' else."

The girls then broke out in giggles and continued their walk toward the country school. They arrived just as Mrs. Randolph was ringing the bell.

At lunch recess, Emie finally had the opportunity to visit with Mimi. They laughed and shared secrets, almost forgetting to eat their lunch. Emie would miss coming to school. She'd miss Mrs. Randolph; she'd miss reading and learning. Mostly she would miss her best friend, Mimi.

"Mimi, what will we do when school's out? I don't think there will ever be a time when I don't have secrets to tell you," Emie spoke softly.

Emie was ready to share about her bleeding, when Mimi suggested they dance the Charleston. Even without practice, the steps came back to Emie quickly. Mimi was dancing and singing at the same time. The song was unfamiliar to Emie. Of course, she only knew hymns, while Mimi − so much wiser and worldly in the eyes of her friend − knew all kinds of songs.

Mimi's sweet singing, and Emie's soft giggles drowned out the approaching footsteps. "Emie, dancin' will send you to hell. My daddy says that it's a man's responsibility to tell women folk about sin," Charlie declared loudly, interrupting the girls' fun.

He then grabbed Emie by the arm and tried to pull her away from Mimi. Emie resisted, finally kicking Charlie in the shin.

"Stop it, Emerald, or I'll have to get rough," Charlie said angrily, applying more pressure to Emie's arm.

Charlie was hurting her, but Emie continued to struggle. "This ain't none of your business, Charlie. Let me go! Were you spying on us from the church window? You were, weren't you? Let go of my arm," Emie yelled loudly.

The ruckus was loud enough that Mrs. Randolph heard from the front of the school building and came running. "Charlie, you let go of Emie this instant. You've already graduated. You don't belong on school property." When Charlie hesitated, the teacher continued more firmly, "I'll be forced to send for your daddy and then the sheriff, if you don't release Emerald."

Charlie gave his captive's already sore arm another harsh squeeze before letting her go. He then spoke under his breath for her ears only, "Emie, I won't tolerate this type of behavior. Get yourself in line, girlie, or there'll be trouble."

Emie responded by once more kicking her aggressor. "Why were you spyin'? Were you hopin' to see us dance naked like King David? If I were you, I'd be worried about my own soul goin' to the devil. Now, run back home to your daddy like a good little boy!"

Charlie glared at Emie and then stomped back toward the church building. Mrs. Randolph led the girls to the front of the schoolhouse, and then rang the bell indicating that school was back in session. Other than Rudy, who was the same age as Mimi and Emie, the other children immediately took their seats. Rudy hung back. His concerned look brought a smile to Emie's face. She had known Rudy since first grade. His red hair with the cowlick and his freckled face brought to her remembrance a picture she had seen in her school reader. In the story, a young lad had been fishing with his grandfather along a river bank. The character had reminded Emie of Rudy, and the setting had reminded her of Big Creek. The story was about the big fish that got away. At times Emie adored Rudy. At other times she wanted to throttle him. Ernest had told her, "Emie, that's the way of boys and girls."

While the other children took their seats, the teacher spoke with Emie privately. "Emerald, what was that all about? Do I need to speak with Pastor Eugene about Charlie's behavior?"

"Mimi and I were just havin' fun. Mimi was singin', and we were dancin'. I don't know why Charlie was even lookin' at us," Emie was still confused about Charlie's actions.

"Thank you, Emerald. You may take your seat," Mrs. Randolph instructed.

As the afternoon wore on, Emie had a hard time concentrating on her work. Her arm ached. When she lifted her cap sleeve, her upper arm had red welts from Charlie's hand, and bruises were forming.

At the end of the school day, Opal and Coral played on the swings, while Emie said goodbye to Mimi. Emie enjoyed hearing the joyful sounds of play from her sisters. Her arm ached, but she was determined not to complain. Mama had told her more than once, "Complainin' is for city girls, Emie. In the holler, there's no time for whinin'. There's work to be done, and you best get to it."

Emie noticed Rudy standing on the front steps of the school building. When she glanced his way, he nodded his head and walked away. *How odd*, Emie thought. *Ernest is right. Boys and girls are sure different. Why didn't Rudy just come over and visit with Mimi and me?*

As Emie hugged her friend goodbye, promising to see her tomorrow, Mrs. Randolph caught a brief glimpse of her injury. "Emerald, please lift your sleeve and let me look closely at your arm," the teacher kindly requested.

Emie's upper arm was dark purple, almost black, and the skin was raised, outlining Charlie's large fingers. The teacher spoke gently to Emie, her voice filled with compassion and concern, "Why didn't you tell me? Emerald, this must have pained you all afternoon. Let me quickly write a note to your parents explaining what happened. It's my job to protect my students. In the future, I want you girls to stay in front of the building so I can see you. Rest assured that I'll be visiting with Pastor Eugene this afternoon. Charlie will be reprimanded for his actions."

Mrs. Randolph quickly wrote her note and returned to the front steps of the schoolhouse. The generally passive teacher watched

Mimi head for home in one direction, and the Ashby girls in the other direction, before she stormed across the schoolyard to the neighboring church.

Emie, Coral, and Opal were all disappointed that the turtle had disappeared, but were delighted to meet Ernest on the dirt road just outside the Ashby homestead. The sun had begun to dip slightly in the sky. The warm spring weather put the Ashby siblings in a playful mood. "I've been waitin' for my naughty sisters to get home," Ernest teased.

The towheaded girls smiled lovingly at their older brother. Coral's and Opal's blue eyes danced with delight. Ernest smiled in return and affectionately drew the three sisters into a group embrace. Ernest was disappointed when Emie pulled back from his brotherly display of love. The hurt look on his face made Emie break Mama's rule about complaining and whining.

"I hurt my arm at school today, Ernest."

"Let me see, Emie."

In response to Ernest's request, she lifted her sleeve.

"You didn't hurt your arm. Someone hurt you. And by the looks of the bruisin', it was someone bigger and stronger. What happened?"

Before Emie could get the entire story told, Ernest started humming, "Savior Like a Shepherd Lead Us." Ernest had previously told Emie about the song's history. During the Civil War, a Confederate soldier stood ready to shoot a Union officer, when the officer began to sing, *"Savior like a shepherd lead us. Much we need Thy tender care..."* The Confederate soldier turned away; he couldn't take the life of someone calling out to the Lord for love and care.

"Tell Mama that I'll be payin' a visit to Pastor and Charlie." Ernest left the girls on the road, and walked purposefully toward the school and church. When he was out of sight from his sisters, he lit out like an arrow shooting from a bow. He didn't condone violence, but recognized that at times aggression was the only way to defeat an enemy. From the time he was little, Mama had taught him that it was best to get along with your neighbors. Ernest knew Scripture said that a man was to be at peace with others as much as possible. He reasoned that God must have included the "as much as possible" part because of people like Charlie.

When he arrived at the church, he didn't bother to knock or give warning. He found Pastor Eugene, Charlie, and Mrs. Randolph talking in the small foyer. He boldly turned to Mrs. Randolph and asked her to remove herself, "We've some man business that needs attendin."

Ernest pushed Pastor Eugene aside and laid into Charlie. It didn't bother Ernest, in the least, to be a little rough with Eugene. In the back of his mind, he knew that his daddy's second cousin was somehow involved − directly or indirectly − in the offense against his baby sister.

For a few seconds, Charlie was stunned like a cockroach when the kitchen cabinet doors swing open. Instinctively he began his own fist throwing. Charlie was bigger and stronger than Ernest, but Ernest had the love of family on his side. He knew that Charlie's stature and mass overshadowed his own flesh. He also knew the love in his heart outweighed anything that Charlie could muster.

The altercation waged for a few minutes, both parties stepping away from the fight winded and bloodied. Pastor Eugene was beside himself, and Mrs. Randolph, hearing the commotion, had come back inside the church. She placed herself between the boys and insisted that the fighting cease.

Ernest remembered her doing the same thing when he'd gotten into a pushing match with another student in elementary school. He also thought it interesting that Pastor Eugene stood by, not interfering. Ernest had always known that Eugene was coward.

"Don't you ever lay a hand on Emie again," Ernest declared, still breathing heavy from the fight.

"So, that's what this is all about?" Charlie stammered through his own labored breaths.

"You've no right to get involved in my family," Ernest said, raising his right fist ready to swing at Charlie again.

Charlie, not the least bit intimidated, continued the argument, "I have every right. Your daddy has done promised Emie to me. We'll be married before the summer's through."

Ernest stepped back, stunned. No one said anything for a minute. Then when Eugene deemed to speak, Ernest held up his hand signaling the pastor to keep silent.

"Does she know?" Ernest said softly.

Mrs. Randolph stepped away from the boys and began to quietly weep. The thought of Emie's future brought sorrow to the teacher. Charlie said nothing. It was as if time stood still. Then Pastor Eugene began his own tirade directed at Ernest. "How dare you enter the House of God with your filthy ways?"

Ernest didn't stop to listen. He exited the church building before any more words were spoken. Charlie followed him outside.

"She's mine, Ernest."

"You don't know Emie. She can't be bought or sold. She's like a lit match in the darkness. She'll expose who you are, and who your daddy is." Ernest knew that his words were true, yet he felt as if his very life had been drawn from his being, like a bucket drawing water from a well.

Charlie shrugged. "She'll listen, or else."

"Or else, what? What's in this for you? Or better yet, what's in this for your daddy and my daddy?" Ernest questioned.

"Well, seein' you're gonna be my brother an all," Charlie said sarcastically, "I don't see the harm in lettin' you know that the match will benefit both our families. Lester and me have done started a business. My daddy helped us with some money to get started. And your daddy agreed to let me marry Emie in exchange for sharin' the profits."

"Your bootleg business! My daddy agreed to let you marry Emie for profits from moonshine?" Ernest shook his head in disgust and started to walk away.

Just as Charlie reached the front door of the church, Ernest turned around, "Charlie, you didn't answer my question. Does Emie know?"

Without even turning to face Ernest, Charlie answered, "Not yet."

Chapter Seven

"A pinching crawdad will hold on until it hears thunder."
(Appalachian Folk Belief)

Ernest's footsteps blindly took him home − if home was a place of bribery, manipulation, and illegal activity. His thoughts and feelings were elsewhere. His mind raced. He and Lester had once raced Auntie's two horses across the meadow. Lester had won, not by much, but he'd won nonetheless. Now, he had won again. Emie had cheered for Ernest, but who would cheer for Emie?

Ernest's mind traveled to politics. He and Mrs. Randolph had recently discussed Andrew Jackson's 1828 campaign. *To the victors belong the spoils.* President Jackson had given government jobs to his voters. Their employment had nothing to do with merit, only loyalty to a political party. Now it seemed like Pastor Eugene headed the "Moonshine Party." Charlie, Lester, and Daddy were the party's loyal followers, and Emie was the spoils.

"God help us all," Ernest prayed. On the journey home, he continued to pray and sing. Just as he approached the worn house in the small gully, he felt the presence of God wash over him. It was almost as if a mist surrounded him. The Lord began to massage his heart. The core of his being, the center of his body, was being touched by a hand from above. The anger faded. The feelings of defeat diminished, and in their place was a peace unknown and never experienced before by Ernest.

When he arrived at the homestead and entered through the back door, he found his mother working in the kitchen. "Mama," Ernest questioned, "where are the girls?" The calmness in his voice surprised him. His voice seemed almost melodious.

Not looking up, Alma answered, her hands in biscuit dough for the evening meal. "Sapphire and Ruby are up the holler makin' wedding plans, and I sent Emie out to play with the little ones."

"I need to talk with you and Daddy," Ernest said.

"Your daddy's sleepin'. We best not wake him," Mama responded, looking up from the floured dough board.

Before she could question her son about the bruises and blood on his face, Ernest left the kitchen and headed toward the back bedroom his parents shared. The room was simple and uncluttered. It had a worn-out look, like his mama. Ahab lay on top of the tattered covers, his leg blanket hiding his injuries. His mouth was slightly open and his breathing was heavy. He looked almost placid, yet Ernest knew that his daddy had been a stranger to peace for years. There was a battle that raged inside of his daddy, and when the war grew too big for his insides, it spilled out onto the entire Ashby family.

"Daddy, wake up," Ernest spoke in a composed voice.

Ahab growled like a bear and then opened his eyes. "Leave me be!"

Ernest moved the wheelchair from his daddy's bedside. "Daddy, you need to listen and listen now. They'll be no escapin' what I got to say." Ernest felt resolute, yet tranquil.

Struggling to sit up in bed, Ahab yelled, "Get my switch! I'll teach you to disrespect me! Looks like somebody done bloodied your face, a few more swipes across the mouth might teach you a lesson!"

"Daddy, I'm eighteen years old – too old for a switch. I'm grown and need to talk like a grown man."

Alma entered the room, wiping her hands on a faded dish towel. "Ernest, I told you your daddy was sleepin'!"

"This can't wait," Ernest began. "Charlie hurt Emie today. I went to the church to have it out with him. Daddy, he told me what you did."

"I ain't done nothin' that hasn't been done by my daddy and his daddy before. I made a good match for my daughter!" Ahab defended himself.

"A match based on money from moonshine."

His mama at first looked shocked, then her brown eyes fell to the floor in shame. Ernest knew that his daddy felt no shame. He also knew that his mama experienced enough for herself and her husband. His mama's shame shifted to another emotion, and she looked at Ahab with disgust. "You lied to me," she said through clenched teeth.

"I did no such thing, Alma. There's some business that's only for men folk. Eugene and me came to terms, that's all," Ahab said in an unusually calm voice.

Ernest knew that his daddy was already trying to win his mama over. His mean ways always softened when Mama's heart started to divide.

"Ernest, leave your mama and me be. We got things to discuss," Ahab, now sitting upright in bed, gestured with his hands for his son to leave the room.

"When all the truth is told, I'll be leavin'," Ernest paused as if to catch his breath. "Eugene gave Lester and Charlie money to plant a corn crop and build a still. They've done made arrangements to sell the liquor to the speakeasy up the road. In exchange for Charlie marryin' Emie, Daddy's been promised a portion of the profits."

"Ahab, how could you?" Alma said, using the dishcloth to wipe her already tear-filled eyes.

"There's more I've got to say," Ernest uttered. "After Emie's graduation, I'm leavin' the holler and takin' her with me."

Ernest quietly left the room. When Alma started to follow her son, Ahab spoke up, "Darlin', don't be leavin' me. I need to explain."

Ernest stood outside the tattered room watching and listening. Even though his parents were speaking softly, the curtain that separated the room was partially open and did little to hide the voices. When his daddy reached his hand toward his mama, the draw was too strong, and she came and sat next to her husband on the bed. When Alma shifted her weight, the bed squeaked like a bawling cat, the way a mother cat cries when she has lost one of her kittens.

Ahab began to rub her back and speak to her in a soothing voice. "Don't cry. Alma, I did this for you, for our girls. Our boys is grown. You heard Ernest; he's leavin'. Who'll care for the hogs? We'll be needin' the money to hire a hand. If not, our babies could starve."

It was all Ernest could do to stay put and stay silent. Yet, he knew this was between his mama and daddy. He'd said his piece, now he had to wait and let the chips fall where they may. He thought of Lester chopping wood and the chips scattering in a haphazard pattern.

His daddy paused. Ernest knew he was trying to gauge his mama's emotions, and scheming on how to convince her that his plan would work.

He gently continued his persuasion. "Alma, don't be cryin' or worryin'. I'll talk with the sheriff. He's a friend of Eugene's. Ernest won't be takin' Emie from the holler. You'll see − everything will be fine."

Ernest heard the bed squeak as his mama stood. His daddy, of course, had to have the final say, "Let's not tell Emie about any of this. We should be lettin' her enjoy her graduation."

Ernest wondered if his mama recognized his daddy's words of deception. If she did, she didn't say anything. He wished for once that his mama would confront his daddy's lies. He guessed that it was too ingrained in her to ignore her man's meanness. Ernest knew that his mama thought of herself as a poor mountain woman without means. Her actions always showed that her first responsibility was to her husband. Didn't she realize that her children needed her to defend them? Right now, Emie especially needed her.

Ahab lay in bed. He thought to call Alma back to get his wheelchair, but then thought better. Now wasn't the time to remind her of his needs. It was best that she focus on the girls and how the extra money would benefit them. Besides, he wanted to ponder on the situation a bit. He knew if somehow Emie escaped the holler with Ernest that another plan needed to be put in place. Alma wouldn't like it, but he'd convince her it was the right thing to do. She'd cry a little. He'd comfort her best he could, hold her, and speak sweet nothings. She'd come around to his way of thinking; she always did. What choice did she have? Eugene wouldn't like it either. He would say that Coral was too young. She was only twelve, a might young, but it had been done before.

Chapter Eight

*"Bury a hickory stick in a moist place, and
it will turn to stone in seven years."
(Appalachian Folk Belief)*

Ernest headed out the kitchen back door. He spotted his sisters playing in the meadow. Emie had corralled them like a mother hen. The five of them with their heads together looked like a giant sunflower. He and Lester had darker hair, favoring their mother. Even their skin was a darker shade, tanning easily in the mountain sunshine. The younger sisters were all blonde and blue-eyed like daddy, and the twins were somewhere in between. The siblings ranged in temperament from hot to cold, like the heat of August and the cold in January.

The sun was setting, yet still shining at an unusual angle down upon his sisters. He often thought that sunshine was God's way of kissing His children. *Lord, shine your love and mercy upon us*, Ernest silently prayed. His spiritual experience on the road home lingered in his mind and soul. God was at work. Ernest knew that God worked in His own way and in His own time. The plan to rescue Emie was divinely inspired, but Ernest wondered how the plan would specifically play out. In stories and in real life, the plots were often more complex than first imagined. He knew characters in novels and in real life could change and grow, while at the same time remain the same.

He reflected on his daddy's words about summoning Sheriff Robbins. For just a moment or two he felt panic, and then he strengthened himself in the Lord, refusing to let fear and worry overtake him. He reminded himself that the mysterious ways of heaven were about to be revealed in the holler at Big Creek. If there was fear to be had, it need only be the fear and reverence of God.

He headed toward the meadow, wanting to enjoy his sisters' play, before heading to visit Auntie Ada. The young ones were now laughing and running; all but Emie were preoccupied with foolery.

"Ernest, are you hurt?" Emie asked with concern.

"No, girlie. I need you to stay away from Charlie. You hear me?" Ernest said firmly.

"I'll listen. I promise," she spoke reassuringly.

"You're a good girl, and I love you," Ernest replied.

"I know you do, but you rarely say it. Is somethin' wrong?" Emie asked intuitively.

"Emie, if you think something's wrong when I tell you, 'I love you,' then I haven't been a very good brother." Her words had revealed truth to Ernest, but now wasn't the time to make amends.

Emie smiled. She took her brother's hand and squeezed his fingers affectionately. No words were needed.

"Take the little ones and head home. Mama's workin' on supper. I'll see you in a little bit," Ernest instructed.

Emie, normally more curious than a kitten, didn't question her brother about where he was headed. She called to her sisters, gathered them close and headed toward home. Ernest stood watching. He wanted to protect those he loved, but he knew as a mortal man that his powers were limited.

"Auntie!" Ernest announced his arrival, not bothering to knock at the door. He was eager to know what the wise woman would think of his plans.

"Ernest, what a pleasant surprise!" She embraced him firmly, holding him tighter and longer than usual. It was just like Ada to know what was exactly needed in the moment.

"Your mama came callin' a couple days ago, and Mrs. Randolph just left." Ada spoke as she stepped away from Ernest. With one hand still on his arm, she used her other hand to signal him to sit. They took their usual places: Auntie in the willow rocker by the window and Ernest in the upright chair.

"I won't repeat what you already know," Ernest spoke. "It's too hard to speak of anyway. I'm relieved to not be the bearer of bad news."

Auntie rocked and sighed in response.

"I've a plan, Auntie. And I need you to tell me your honest thoughts," Ernest continued.

"Have I ever been anything but honest with you?"

"No. That's why I'm here." Ernest reached across the small round table and patted her hand.

"I'm leavin' the holler and takin' Emie with me." He paused, looking at Auntie and wondering if she had something to say; instead of words she only nodded her head.

"As soon as her graduation's over, we're goin'."

Ada still said nothing.

"I'm nervous, Auntie. I don't know where to go, or how I'll get there. And do I tell Emie now or wait? What happens if she won't go with me?" Ernest confessed.

Ada's mouth opened and words of wisdom began to flow like the waters of Big Creek. Ernest found solace in her words.

"Son, I knew you wouldn't stand for your daddy and Eugene's nonsense. Me and Mrs. Randolph are gonna help. I done gave her money for you to attend teachin' school in Charleston. I'll talk with her about arrangin' your travels. She'll know where you and Emie could stay."

Auntie rose from her rocker and stood behind Ernest. She placed her weathered hands on his shoulders. He felt the love of God transfer from Auntie's hands into his body. "When Jesus was baptized in the Jordan, God spoke to Him from heaven, 'This is my son and I am pleased.' Ernest, God is sayin' the same to you today. You're His child, and He is pleased."

"Thank you," he responded. Ernest then pondered a moment on

Auntie's words before continuing, "Do you think I should tell Emie now, or do I wait?"

Auntie confirmed what was already in his mind, "Wait. Pack what few things she has and be ready to leave right after graduation. She'll be surprised, but she'll go."

"Who'll take care of Mama and the little ones, Auntie Ada?"

"It's enough to take care of Emie. Eugene, Charlie, and your daddy done built a web around her. If she don't leave now, she'll be caught, and there won't be no escapin'."

Ada walked over to the window. Ernest knew that she wanted to witness the final moments of the sun's setting. She pulled matches from her apron pocket and lit the two oil lamps in her living room. They smoked at first and then illuminated the room. Even in darkness there was always a measure of light.

"Ernest, don't be worryin' none. I may be an old woman, but I done planned a couple escapes from this holler in my time."

Ernest looked curiously at Ada.

"I'll be savin' my stories for another day. Son, you best get home now."

"Let me light your evenin' fire first. It'll take the chill off, and then I'll be goin' home."

Ernest's love for Auntie Ada was often expressed in the way he helped. He remembered, however, Emie's earlier surprise at his verbal expression of love. He looked toward his dear aunt and softly said, "I love you."

Chapter Nine

"To stop bleeding from a wound, apply chimney soot."
(Appalachian Folk Belief)

Emie woke up early; in fact it was still dark outside. She couldn't believe that graduation day had finally arrived. Last night after dinner, Ernest had mentioned that he had a special graduation surprise for her. The graduate was to meet him right after the ceremony.

"Emie, they'll be quite a few people celebratin' tomorrow. I'll be waitin' for you by the maple tree in the school yard," her brother had told her.

When she started to squeal in delight, Ernest had hushed her and whispered, "This is a secret, girlie. Just between the two of us."

She had hardly slept. First, Mrs. Randolph had asked her to make a speech at graduation, then Auntie Ada had insisted on making her a new dress and buying her satin slippers, and now Ernest had a gift for her.

Emie rose from the bed quietly, trying not to disturb her sisters. The small home felt eerie. The darkness seemed to cast shadows on the walls. She left the bedroom clothed in her nightgown. Lester was still sleeping. She thought Ernest might be awake. His body had shifted when she entered the tiny central room. She fought hard not to whisper his name. Emerald enjoyed sharing special moments with Ernest, yet she wanted her own private celebration this morning.

She stood outside her parents' bedroom, listening for any morning movement, and then made her way into the kitchen. Emie walked slowly, not wanting to stumble in the darkness. Her shoes were by the back door. She slipped them on and headed toward the meadow, her final destination being the willows and Big Creek.

She took her time taking in the morning. At first, silence surrounded her, and the darkness seemed overwhelming. The girl could barely see her feet moving across the meadow. During the day, the meadow was green and lush from the spring rains, but in the darkness, the grass and spring flowers made a damp, gray blanket. As she walked, the taller plants tickled her legs. The sun was just starting to make an appearance. Emie needed to hurry. Mama would be worried if all her children weren't accounted for at breakfast.

She heard the creek before she reached its banks. She stood among the willows waiting for the sun. Emerald took pleasure in its faint glow on the horizon, the yellows and oranges overtaking the darkness by small measures. She felt her body wake, along with the willows and the creek, as the celestial ball of color lifted bit by bit.

As the sun rose in the sky, her spirit rose. Today was an ending and a beginning. She breathed in the mountain air, her lungs expanding with excitement. In a rash moment, she slipped off her gown and shoes and waded into the creek.

The water was frigid, but the sun above was starting to warm the day and her body. Emie waded to her waist, and then splashed the cold water over her torso, breasts, arms, and face. She shivered from cold and from delight. How she loved this place! It was as if God designed the waters of Big Creek and the whispering of the willows just for her. She hesitated a moment longer. She left the stream, slipping her gown over her wet body and her shoes over her muddied feet. Emie was surprised that Daddy had made the decision to attend her graduation. Unless it was his own birthday, or somehow he was the center of attention, he wasn't the celebrating type. Yet, there he was, leading his family down the dirt road toward the schoolhouse. Lester was pushing Daddy's wheelchair with Mama behind; next all the girls, but her, were walking two by two; then she and Ernest were following. Ernest was, in fact, holding her hand. It all felt strange to Emie. The Ashby parade was out of sync; usually Ernest walked by Lester and Daddy, and she couldn't remember a time when her brother had ever held her hand.

Exasperated she said, "Ernest, my hand is gettin' sweaty."

"Sorry, Emie," he replied, releasing her palm.

She shifted the slippers she was carrying to the hand Ernest had been holding. She also noticed that Ernest shifted the large satchel that he was carrying. Emie wondered if her present was inside.

She was wearing her school shoes with the toe worn through, so she didn't soil her special graduation slippers on the dirt road. Auntie Ada had made her dress from a used white sheet. The material had been bleached, scrubbed, and then patterned especially for Emie's frame; the bodice fit her slim torso just right, the waist was fitted and then the dress flared, stopping just below her knees. Auntie had added pearl buttons to the back, and a dainty pink crocheted flower to the front, along with a matching pink ribbon belt.

All three graduates sat in roped-off special chairs in the first row on the left side. On the right side, Mrs. Randolph was sitting with her daughter and family. Her daughter had come all the way from Charleston to celebrate. Emie noticed Mrs. Randolph introducing Ernest to her daughter and son-in-law. Pastor Eugene opened the ceremony with prayer, thanking the good Lord that there were at least three children in the holler smart enough to graduate eighth grade.

Next came Mrs. Randolph. She politely thanked Pastor Eugene and then talked about how smart all the children in the holler were. She added special praise for Emie, Mimi, and Rudy. "I am so proud today of our three graduates. They have all worked hard to complete their eighth grade exams, and I am pleased to say that each has graduated with good marks." Mrs. Randolph then paused, asking the families and friends present to join her in applause for the honored students.

Emie applauded loudly for Mimi and Rudy, whose name was really Randal. He was one of the few holler boys, other than Ernest, who wanted to continue school through twelfth grade. Emie then looked back to see her family. They were all clapping, except for Daddy. He was busy whispering to the sheriff, which Emie thought was very strange.

Next, Mrs. Randolph introduced Rudy by his given name. He proceeded to read a poem that he had written about his cowlick.

Then, Mrs. Randolph introduced Minerva, who was really Mimi. Emie's best friend sang "Slumber My Darling." Mimi and Emie had been hoping for something a little more modern and upbeat. In fact, Mimi had wanted to dance the Charleston while she sang. Mrs. Randolph felt that the Appalachian folk song, which dated back to the Civil War, was more appropriate. She, however, suggested that Mimi incorporate a few waltz steps.

"Slumber, my darling, thy mother is near, guarding thy dreams from all terror and fear. Sunlight has pass'd and the twilight has gone. Slumber, my darling, the night's coming on. Sweet visions attend thy sleep, fondest dearest to me. While others their revels keep, I will watch over thee..."

Then the kind school teacher introduced Emie. "Family, friends, and Big Creek community, please welcome Emerald Ashby, who will be giving our graduation address."

Emie's heart began to race. She willed her body to move from her seat. As she rose from her chair, Mimi, who was sitting next to her, gently squeezed her hand. Emie looked at Rudy. He smiled at her, encouraging her, not with words, but with the familiar facial expressions of a long-time school companion. Emie found her composure and approached the wooden podium. The graduates had practiced their ceremony a number of times, but standing behind the lectern and looking at the crowd made everything real.

Emie began her address by thanking Mrs. Randolph, Mimi, and Rudy. She then thanked her family, including Auntie Ada. Mrs. Randolph had worked with Emie on her speech. She had instructed her to speak slowly and loudly. "Emie, please use proper grammar, and represent your teacher and school in a manner fitting a delightful young woman."

"The Good Book tells us that when God's people wanted to return home from their slavery that they sat and cried under the willows. The willows of Big Creek call to the people of the holler. Under the trees we can share our hopes, joys, and concerns. The holler can be a difficult place. Life can be harsh for the Appalachian people here, yet there is wonder in the nature that surrounds us. Mimi, Rudy, and I have had the privilege of attending Big Creek School since first grade. It is with great pride that we celebrate our graduation this afternoon. The three of us have enjoyed our community, the people who live here, and the beauty of the mountains. Thank you for celebrating this special occasion with us."

Emerald returned to her seat as the audience stood and applauded.

Mrs. Randolph motioned for all three of the graduates to stand and face their guests. After a moment, she asked those present to take their seats and called Emie, Mimi, and Rudy back up to the podium. Each student was presented with a graduation certificate, pen, and a journal covered in willow tree bark. Mrs. Randolph then spoke briefly about the importance of the three graduates continuing their education. Her eyes seemed to glance back and forth between the families of her three accomplished students.

Pastor Eugene came forward and prayed a blessing over the graduates, "Lord, we thank You for our three young ones. They have studied hard and done good. May they faithfully serve You and the mountain people." Then Pastor Eugene blessed the food and dismissed the attendees to eat and celebrate in the schoolyard.

The graduates took a few minutes to congratulate each other. Rudy seemed uncomfortable with the hugs he received from Emie and Mimi, especially from Emie who also kissed him gently on the cheek. Rudy's weathered cheeks felt rough, just like Ernest's, beneath Emie's soft lips. Like most of the boys in the holler, Rudy helped his family in the fields. He also helped his daddy run the local grocery store. Rudy shook his red head in confusion when the two best friends squealed in delight and hugged each other lovingly. Mimi then began to sing loudly and the girls started to dance. Rudy stood back chuckling at the two girls. It had been this way all through their school years, Mimi and Emie giggling and sharing secrets, while Rudy watched, sometimes in boyhood confusion, and other times with admiration toward the two young women, especially toward Emie. The three enjoyed the special time together with the familiarity of long-time friends, each treasuring the moments of closeness before life carried them to different places.

As the three companions headed outside, Emie looked toward the maple tree to see if Ernest was waiting for her. When she didn't see him, she filled her plate with food and sat with Mimi on the swings. It was only then that Emie noticed Ernest talking with the sheriff. Her brother's lips appeared glued together. Emie knew that he was humming and that something was wrong. She sat her food on the merry-go-round next to the swings and excused herself. As she headed toward Ernest and the sheriff, Mama and Daddy came forward blocking her path.

"Congratulations, girlie," Daddy spoke.

It was the first time that Emie remembered receiving a compliment, or an acknowledgment of a job well done, from her daddy. She felt the sun shine brighter and the breeze blow sweeter.

Mama added her own thoughts, "Emie, we're proud. You done good with your speech and all." Then she gave her daughter a gentle squeeze.

Daddy spoke up, "Charlie's wantin' to take you for a walk, Emie. Go get your plate and finish eatin'."

"Daddy, I ain't wantin' to go for a walk with Charlie. I don't like him none," Emie responded to her father.

"Don't sass me, girl. Charlie's done sorry for what happened. He's wantin' to apologize. Emie, now do as I say, or they'll be trouble when we get back up the holler."

Emie realized that her daddy's praise was not because he valued her, but because he wanted something from her. The sun moved behind a white cotton ball cloud and the breeze stilled. Emie hung her head in submission and walked slowly back to the swings to gather her plate. She was relieved that Mimi had already left the play area and was visiting with her family. The two girls had agreed to never talk to or even look at Charlie again. Emie didn't want Mimi to witness her broken promise. She looked around for Ernest, but didn't see him or the sheriff. She didn't want her brother to worry when she wasn't able to meet him.

When Emie glanced back at her parents, Charlie was standing beside them and her daddy was motioning for her to hurry.

She finished eating the fried chicken leg, seasoned potatoes, greens, and homemade applesauce while Daddy and Charlie visited about corn crops. She hoped that some of the greens were stuck in her teeth. She wanted to be sure and smile real pretty for Charlie. None of it made sense to Emie, including the way Mama was standing with her hand on Emie's shoulder, occasionally patting her in a reassuring fashion.

Charlie left momentarily to get Emie some dessert. She thought it arrogant that he didn't even bother to ask what she liked. "What a nice young man," Mama voiced. Before Emie could disagree, Daddy gave her the skunk eye, at least that's what Ernest called Daddy's mean look. Emie felt frustrated – this was supposed to be her special day, and now Daddy was forcing her to take a stroll with Charlie – and where was Ernest? She was worried about her brother.

"Mama, do you know where Ernest is? I saw him talkin' to Sheriff Robbins."

Before her mama could answer, her daddy interrupted. "Don't be worryin' none about Ernest. He and the sheriff had a little business to attend. You go off with Charlie and enjoy yourself."

Emie ate only a couple bites of her dessert. Charlie had brought her mincemeat pie, which wasn't one of her favorites. She preferred moist white cake with sweet cream icing. Mama took the plate, fork, and napkin from her daughter, while Daddy stared at Charlie looking very pleased.

Charlie, behaving like a perfect gentleman, took Emie by the elbow and led her away from her parents and the crowd at school. "Emie, thank you for agreeing to take a walk."

As soon as they rounded the bend and were out of sight, Charlie let go of Emie's elbow and gripped her hand firmly.

"Hey, you're hurtin' me, Charlie."

"I'm just takin' what's mine, Emerald."

"What are you talkin' about?"

"You done been promised to me. Your daddy and my daddy made the arrangements. We're gonna marry in a few weeks and we got some talkin' to do. Emie, I got worries about your soul. It's my job to make sure you're heaven bound. I can't be toleratin' the way you act − dancin' and laughin' with that girl. You better straighten up or the devil's comin' for ya. My daddy said it was the same with my mama, and that I need to take a firm hand and show you what's right."

Emie shook free of Charlie and yelled in response, "You're a liar. And you know where liars go. They go to hell. I ain't never gonna marry you, Charlie."

Emie stormed off, taking hurried steps back toward the safety of the schoolyard. She needed to find Ernest. He would know if Charlie was lying or telling the truth, and if he was telling the truth, Ernest would know what to do next.

Charlie quickly grabbed her, practically dragging her down the dirt road further away from the school. Emie yelled as loud as possible, "Let go! Leave me be!"

"Shut up, Emie, or I'll make you sorry."

At first, Charlie said nothing more. He continued his pull on her arm, and, after a few minutes, he drug her off the road, through the ditch and toward the woods.

When he grew tired of Emie's yelling, he slapped her hard across the face. She knew if she didn't escape that Charlie would hurt her and hurt her bad. She made her body limp thinking that would slow down her captor. Instead, Charlie picked her up and roughly threw her body over his right shoulder, using his arm to hold her securely in place. Her dress hiked up and caught about her waist. When she struggled to hide her step ins, Charlie simply laughed. "Emie, your worn-out, raggedy underwear don't interest me. It's what's beneath those rags I'm wantin' to see."

Emie kicked his stomach and clawed his back. She even bit his shoulder till it drew blood, but Charlie never slowed. When he had carried her well into the woods, he threw her down on the mossy floor. Her head struck the trunk of a tree and started to bleed. She was frightened and hurt. She struggled to get up only to have Charlie kick her back to the ground. He held his foot on her breasts. He then bent down, replacing his foot with his hands. He ripped the white dress from her chest and started to laugh, "Girl, you got a little pair. I was hopin' for more. You sure ain't no woman." He began to roughly fondle her chest. With each touch, his hands grew rougher, scratching and tearing at her flesh.

She continued to fight, clawing at his face and kicking wildly. When she cried out loudly, he told her, "No one can hear you. I told you that I was takin' what's mine."

Hoping to escape, she continued to writhe and twist. When Charlie grew tired of her breasts, he began to roughly kiss her lips and neck. When she bit his lip and spat on him, his anger was roused further. He clasped her arms together above her head with one hand, and then tore at his britches with the other hand, exposing himself. When he laid on top of her, the weight of his body kept her from moving. She looked away, and then closed her eyes, willing her mind to travel to the willows. She pretended to sit among the top branches of her favorite tree, hidden from the evils of the world. She felt a sharp pain, and in shock she grew silent. She said nothing, as the tears flowed silently down her checks.

When Charlie climbed off of her, his voice was filled with hate, "What? No more yellin'? No more cryin'? I told you I'd shut you up. I said I'd take what was mine. You ain't got nothin' to say. Well, just lay here girl, till someone finds you. They'll laugh just like me at your no account who who's."

Emie rolled onto her side, trying to hide herself.

Charlie paid her no mind as he attempted to straighten his clothes. His face was scratched; his stomach was bruised; and his back was clawed to pieces. She was a fighter; he would give her that much.

"Emie, I'm given you fair warnin', don't be tellin' this to no one."

She drew her legs closer to her chest, attempting to draw her body into a tight ball. She still said nothing.

"Funny thing, girl, now that you're mine, I ain't wantin' you."

Charlie kicked her one more time, square in the back. "I best get home and tell my daddy to be changin' the arrangements. Emie, you best learn that men rule the holler, not no account little girls."

He walked off leaving her laying among the trees. There was blood between her legs. The gash on her head hurt like fire, and her limbs were bruised and sore. She tried to stand, but couldn't get her body to rise. She was able, however, to prop herself against a tree. It was ironic, the same tree that had wounded her head was now her support. She looked down at her bare breasts; they were scratched and raw. She tried to cover herself with her torn dress, but it offered little protection. Charlie had ripped the material to shreds. She was both frightened and exhausted. She tried to stand again, and this time made it to her knees, but no further.

The young woman closed her eyes and allowed her thoughts to drift to Big Creek. She was wading in the creek. At first, the water soothed her, then it became a raging torrent that drew her to the depths of its center. She couldn't breathe; she was drowning. A limb from one of the willows was her savior. It stretched toward her and lifted her from the water, but once she reached the banks, the limb started to choke her.

Gasping for breath, Emie's eyes popped open. The sensation of being awake, yet asleep felt very strange to her. She shivered from shock and fear, and felt cold. From what she could tell from the sun, it was late afternoon. She heard footsteps approaching and wondered if Charlie was coming back. To hide his sin, he would kill her for certain. He'd bury her body in the woods and take the secret with him to the grave. Emie willed her body to move. Still on her knees, she stretched out her hands and began to crawl.

She made it only a few feet from the tree, when she heard a gasp. The sound had come from a man. She turned her head toward the voice and recognized Rudy. Sobs of relief wracked her body. Her arms and legs gave way, and she was once again lying on the forest floor – this time face down.

"Emie, is that you?" was all Rudy said before kneeling beside her. "Lord, help us," he prayed, taking off his shirt and placing it over her back. He then helped her sit. Her breasts were exposed, and she fumbled to place her arms through the sleeves of his shirt.

"I won't look, Emie," Rudy spoke softly. While she struggled to cover herself, he looked away and then with amazing dexterity buttoned the large shirt without touching her flesh. He sat down next to her on the mossy floor. When he placed his arm around her shoulders, she shuddered and recoiled. "Emie, it's me. I won't hurt you. I just want to warm you a minute before we decide what to do."

"Thank you, Rudy." Emie said leaning her head against his shoulder.

"Do you want to tell me what happened?"

"Not now. Probably not ever," she whispered.

Emie knew that questions must be racing through Rudy's mind, but she couldn't bring herself to tell what Charlie had done.

"Just tell me who, Emie."

"It was Charlie." She buried her head in his undershirt and cried.

Rudy didn't ask any more questions. He kept his arm around Emie and let her cry. With her head buried against him, he looked at her injuries. Nothing appeared to be broken, but there was blood and bruising. The knot on her head looked bad. Her legs and arms were scratched, and the blood on her thighs left no doubt about what Charlie had done.

Rudy shifted his weight. He knelt and lifted her into his arms, and then rocked her like a baby. Emie knew that Rudy was praying and that he was crying right along with her.

"Emie, would you like me to take you to the doctor? Or the sheriff?"

"I want to go home," she mumbled into his chest.

After several moments, he stood. Still holding Emie, he began to walk through the woods. It was slow going. He was concerned that the hanging branches would injure her further, and though Emie was light, he struggled some with the weight of her.

"Rudy, I think I can walk if you help me."

He slowly put Emie down. At first her legs were wobbly, but the team soon developed a slow rhythm to their walk. Rudy held her by the arm gently, yet firmly enough that if she stumbled he could keep her from falling.

"Don't worry. I know where I'm goin'. Instead of takin' the road by the schoolhouse toward your home, we're takin' the woods. I don't want to run into Charlie on the road, and I'm thinkin' you don't want to be seen just now." Rudy spoke in a protective manner.

"Thank you," Emie replied softly.

The way home was slow going. The pair stopped frequently to rest. Emie never complained of her injuries, in fact, she was extremely quiet. Too quiet, as far as Rudy was concerned. Emerald had been a part of his life for as long as he could remember. She was always talkative, and always, as far as he was concerned, very lovely; even in third grade when she was missing her front teeth and had tried to cut her own hair − she was still pretty. He'd spent more time in the corner of the schoolhouse than he wished to remember, all because of his dreaming (at least that's what Mrs. Randolph called his mental walk-abouts), and most of his dreaming had involved Emie.

Rudy was angry. Angry mostly at Charlie, but also angry at the circumstances that had put Charlie and Emie together. There had been whispers in his dad's store that Ahab and Pastor Eugene had made arrangements for the two to be married. In his youthfulness, he had ignored the rumors; he should have known better. He treasured Emie, but it was foolish to think that Ahab saw her as anything more than a commodity.

Twilight was upon them, as they approached the swinging bridge at Big Creek. He knew that Emie was emotionally and physically spent.

She whispered, "I need to wait here on the bridge. Please go get Ernest, and don't tell anyone what's happened."

Using a willow post as a backrest, he helped her sit down at the end of the bridge closest to the meadow. He looked at her bruised faced and holding back his own tears told her, "Emie, soon the moon will rise and the stars will appear. Today was a horrible day, but God has not forgotten you."

Rudy headed toward the meadow. The apple trees still had a few blossoms, reminding him that fall would be bring sweet, delicious fruit. His poetry about the moon and the stars were reminders to Emie that there were better days ahead. His notice of the meadow was a reminder for himself that this season would pass, and that the future would be bountiful. He spoke aloud for his own ears and for the ears of heaven, "There is always hope. Hope in God."

Rudy found Ernest, just as he suspected, in the barn giving the sows and piglets their evening feed. Ernest's back was turned, and not wanting to startle him, Rudy cleared his throat announcing his arrival. "Ernest, it's Emie. She needs you."

Ernest instantly turned to face Rudy, "What's happened? Where is she?"

"She's waitin' for you on the bridge. I'll let her tell you what's happened, but it ain't good."

The brother took off running with an oil lantern in hand. Rudy followed close behind.

Emie sat on the bridge waiting for Ernest. She needed her brother. She prayed that Ernest would know what to do. She felt the wind rising and the bridge swinging. She closed her eyes and for a moment felt lulled by God.

When Ernest got to the bridge, he knelt down and looked closely at her. There was only a glimmer of daylight remaining, but the lantern illuminated enough for Ernest to realize that she had been raped.

He sat the lantern down, wrapped his arms around his sister and openly wept. Emie lacked the energy to embrace her brother, but instead buried her head against his chest. Ernest began to sing "A Mighty Fortress is Our God." *"And though this world, with devils filled, should threaten to undo us, we will not fear for God hath willed, His truth to triumph through us..."*

Before Ernest could finish, Emie whispered, "It was Charlie."

Taking a seat next to his sister, Ernest clenched his fists tightly. Emie shifted her body in order to gently place her hands over her brother's. "Is it true that Daddy promised me to Charlie?"

"Yes, Emie."

"And you didn't tell me?" She shuddered in the darkness.

"Auntie Ada and I had a plan. We were gonna leave today – you and me, Emie. That was my surprise. We were supposed to ride with Mrs. Randolph's daughter back to Charleston." Overcome with emotion, Ernest paused. "I'm so sorry. Forgive me."

"Ernest, this isn't your fault. It's Daddy. It's Mama. It's the holler and its backwoods ways. What are we goin' to do now?" Emie asked. She paused, hoping that Ernest had a plan. When he didn't immediately answer, she called to her friend, "Rudy, are you still here?"

"I'm here, Emie. I'm waitin' in the willows. Just givin' you a little time with your brother."

"Girlie, do you think you can tell me what happened? Not everything if you don't want, but enough so we can decide what to do," Ernest asked.

"I'll tell, but only bits and pieces," Emie responded beginning to shake uncontrollably. "Daddy m-made me go for a walk with Charlie. Ernest, Charlie said that I belonged to h-him. Like he owned me. Nobody o-owns me, do they?"

"You belong to God and only God, Emie."

"Charlie got mad. He drug me into the woods and pushed me down. I, I f-fought h-hard," she stuttered. "I really d-did."

"I know you're a fighter," Ernest spoke reassuringly.

"He tore my c-clothes, and then h-held my hands o-over my h-head. I saw his t-thing, Ernest. I looked away, but h-h-I still s-saw it."

"I'm so sorry, girlie. That should *never* have happened," Ernest spoke hoarsely trying to decide how best to comfort her.

"He laid on top of-f m-me. I felt like I couldn't br-breathe and oh, it h-hurt, brother." Overtaken with emotion, Emerald's shivers turned to shudders. Next, came the heart-wrenching sobs.

Ernest placed his arm around his sister. "That's enough, Emie. You don't have to tell me any more."

Ernest then called to their friend, "Come on over, Rudy."

When Ernest heard Rudy's steps on the bridge, he asked, "Where did you find her?"

Rudy described the location, as well as Emie's condition, and the wooded path that had brought them to the Ashby home.

"Emie, I need you to listen close. Can you do that?" Ernest asked.

"I'll try," she answered.

"Charlie robbed you today of somethin' precious. He took away somethin' that was only yours to give. I don't want to be makin' decisions about you without your say. I got some thoughts about what's needin' to be done, but if you say, 'no,' then no it will be."

"Okay, brother."

"Sit down, Rudy. We'll be needin' your ideas as well." Ernest motioned for Rudy to sit on the other side of Emie.

The three sat in a half circle with the lantern in-between them. Their faces were shadowed from each other. Ernest on one side held Emie's hand and Rudy on the other side placed his hand on her shoulder. She felt safe, protected from evils of the world.

Ernest expressed his ideas slowly, pausing and giving thought periodically, "I think Rudy should go get the sheriff and the doctor. I don't think we should be keepin' this a secret. Charlie needs to be punished for what he's done. Emie, Daddy and Lester will lay fault with you, and Mama, like always, will come round to their side. She'll be wantin' to keep peace. I'm sorry, girlie, but it's the truth, no use sayin' different. I'll protect you much as I can, but I won't be lyin' to you, this will be hard."

Rudy gently patted Emie's shoulder. "I think Ernest is right. No good comes from keepin' dark secrets."

Emie, at a loss for words, squeezed Ernest's hand.

As Rudy left to find Sheriff Robbins and Dr. Bright, Ernest helped Emie make her way to the house.

A few steps from the back door, Emie looked lovingly at her brother, "Ernest, thank you for wantin' to save me from marryin' Charlie." She glanced down at her feet. "He don't want me no more. Probably no one will be wantin' me now."

Ernest drew Emie into his arms, and held her tightly, his words tickling her ear, "You crazy girl. Who wouldn't be wantin' you?"

Chapter Ten

"To keep evil away, put salt on the fire or carry
the left hind foot of a graveyard rabbit."
(Appalachian Folk Belief)

Mama and the twins were cleaning the kitchen when Ernest and Emie entered the back door. The dishwater was warming on the back of the wood stove. The house smelled of fried pork and seasoned potatoes. A clay bowl sat on the table holding the leftover green beans that Mama had cooked with onion and bacon. There was even a sole buttered biscuit left sitting by the sticky honey jar.

Alma turned from the dishes when she heard the door open. When she saw Emie, the dinner plate in her hands dropped to floor and a scream escaped her lips.

"Alma, what the hell's goin' on? I'm waitin' for my coffee and pie," Ahab yelled from the back room.

Alma answered her husband before inquiring about her daughter's condition. "I'll be right there."

Emie knew that Mama favored Daddy over her children, and she supposed that was right in most circumstances, but in this moment with what had happened, she wanted her mama's undivided attention. She wanted to be the most important person in her mama's world for just a little bit of time.

"Mama, I'm gonna help Emie to bed. The doctor and sheriff are on the way," Ernest said.

Mama told the twins to get a warm bath ready for Emie, and then busied herself getting dessert and coffee for her husband.

"Alma, what's takin' so long? Send one of those girlies with my pie," Ahab yelled once again.

As Mama served Daddy, Emie could hear her, "Ahab, Emie's been hurt real bad. Ernest has done called for the sheriff and doctor."

"That girl's nothin' but trouble," Ahab responded angrily.

Emie closed her eyes willing her mind to travel to the willows. She remembered the feel of the evening breeze and how it had soothed her, while she had waited for Ernest on the bridge.

Mama entered the girls' bedroom, wringing her hands. "Emie, what's done happened?"

Ernest answered on her behalf, "Charlie drug Emie into the woods and raped her. Rudy found her and brought her home."

"Oh, Emie, girl," Mama said through her tears, as she kissed her daughter's soiled forehead. She then took a moment to examine the cut on Emie's scalp. The dried blood mixed with dirt and grass made it difficult to assess the wound.

Emie could hear her daddy's wheelchair leaving her parents' room and traveling across the center of the house toward where she lay. "What's the girlie done now?" Ahab asked, struggling to enter the room.

Again Ernest answered, "Daddy, Emie's hurt. She ain't done nothin'. Charlie attacked her and stole her innocence."

"Alma, ain't you taught your daughter not to be sexin' with men? Look at what she done. Charlie wantin' to marry her and all..."

Ernest interrupted his daddy's words by grabbing the front of the wheelchair and pushing him with all his might out of the bedroom. Emie could hear the chair hit the wall, and her daddy cussing. "Clean that girl up and fetch Eugene. Tell the sheriff and doctor they ain't needed," Ahab barked.

"Ernest, get the tub. The twins are warmin' water," Mama requested.

"We need to leave her as is till the sheriff and doctor have a look." Ernest spoke with defiance.

"Son, you heard your daddy. Go get Eugene. We won't be needin' the sheriff or the doctor. This is family business. Your daddy and Eugene will settle the matter."

"Mama, you don't understand. Rudy has done gone for the law. The sheriff and doctor are both comin', and I'm not leavin' Emie to fetch anyone."

Alma's hands went to her face to wipe her tear-stained cheeks. Emie knew that some of her mama's tears were born of compassion for her daughter, but most of the tears came from fear of her husband. Alma's eyes looked red and swollen. Her face was pale and her hands were shaking slightly.

Emie closed her eyes. She could hear her daddy struggling to move his chair, the footsteps of her mama leaving, and the rolling of the wheelchair into the back room. When Daddy's yelling grew louder, she felt Ernest take her hand. The noise from the other room seemed to magnify and echo, and she felt once again that she was drowning.

Ernest patted her hand. "Emie, I need to talk to Daddy and Mama. I'll be back in a few minutes, try and rest."

Ernest felt overwhelmed. His relationship with his parents was complex. How did he love and honor them according to Scripture, and defy them over Emie's care? And did he really love his daddy? He feared him, yet knew his daddy lacked the strength to cause him physical harm. He also felt conflicted with emotion over his mama. As much as he wanted to protect her, he couldn't shield her from the consequences of her own choices. He was a man, yet he trembled like a boy. His heart was pounding and his palms were sweating. His prayer was simple as he entered his parents' room, "God, I need you here."

"Daddy, Mama, please let me speak." Ernest was surprised that his parents both quieted.

"You've done the best you could in raisin' us, but the traditions of the holler have clouded your thinkin'. Charlie hurt Emie. He stole from her and then left her layin' in the woods. He's not wantin' her anymore. Daddy, you and Pastor Eugene can't fix this.

Like it or not, Rudy's done gone for the sheriff and doctor."

"She was spoken for. It was Charlie's right to take her if he wanted," Ahab spoke, his voice quaking like an earthquake ready to divide the land and damage its occupants.

Ernest did all he could to remain calm, yet his voice quivered, "Daddy, you know that's not the law. When the sheriff questioned me today, I knew it was your doin'. I can understand not wantin' me to take Emie to Charleston, but tryin' to marry her to Charlie for money ain't helpin' no one."

Ahab answered back through clenched teeth, "I'm the father. I'll be doin' what I think's best for my family. If you don't want my wrath, send Sheriff Robbins and the doctor away."

"Daddy, I'm a man, not a boy. I'm bigger and stronger than you. I'm not afraid of you anymore." Ernest spoke the words convincingly, but in his heart they didn't ring true. "The sheriff won't be leavin', nor the doctor." Ernest turned and left the room.

He could hear his daddy turn on his mama, "Alma, this is your fault. You're always takin' up for those children. Your son's done disrespected me and your girl's done messed with a boy. What's next, woman?"

When Ernest heard his daddy's slap and his mama's cry of pain, he returned to his parents' room. Like a deranged man, Ahab's arms were flailing wildly. Ernest stood between his parents, taking strikes on his back, and then leading his mama by the hand to the worn wooden chair by the wood stove.

He was mad at his mama, but he also pitied her. He felt hostility because Emie lay in bed needing the comfort of a mother, and felt pity because he knew his mama lacked the strength to change her life and the lives of her children. Ernest addressed his mama, but the words rang true for him as well, "Mama, he only has the power that you give him. He can hardly move his chair. He can't come after you. Next time, just walk away."

"You don't understand. He's my husband," Alma answered.

That was Mama's answer for all of Daddy's injustices. Ernest longed to see courage and strength written on her face. He wanted to draw from those virtues, but all he saw was shame and defeat, neither of which he wanted to embrace.

Chapter Eleven

"Grass won't grow where human blood has been spilled."
(Appalachian Folk Belief)

The knock on the front door roused Ernest from his thoughts. When he opened the door, he felt the cool evening breeze. He ushered Rudy, Sheriff Robbins, and Doc into the Ashby residence. Ernest noticed the sheriff looking around. The shabby furniture, worn linoleum, and smoke-stained walls were evidence of the poverty that existed in most homes in the holler, but in the Ashby household, they reflected not only material poverty, but relational and spiritual poverty as well. The family was separated by a chasm so large that only God Himself could build a bridge over the divide, and Ernest knew that even the hand of God required cooperation from the people He created.

Ernest heard his daddy struggling to move the wheelchair. His mama rose immediately, assisting Daddy to where the group was gathered by the front door. She had yet to greet those who had come on Emie's behalf.

The sheriff spoke first, "Ahab, Alma, sorry to hear about Emie. Rudy told me some of the story, but I'll be needin' to hear it from Emie firsthand."

Ahab interrupted, "Sheriff, we ain't needin' ya here. This is family business. Eugene and me will be gettin' the truth from our children and making decisions from there."

"Ahab, that's not how it works. I'm duly sworn to follow government law, not the laws of the holler. With or without your cooperation, this is needin' to be investigated."

"Sheriff," Ahab's fury was once again evident. "You ain't talkin' to Emie. I'm her daddy, and I forbid it."

"Ahab, don't make this difficult. I stretched the law for you earlier today by takin' Ernest to the jailhouse for questionin', and I won't be doin' that again. I'll put handcuffs on you for interferin' before I'll let Emie suffer further." The sheriff then turned to Alma, "Where's the girl?"

When Alma hung her head, refusing to even make eye contact with the sheriff, let alone answer his question, Ernest directed the sheriff to the back bedroom where Emie lay.

The sheriff nodded thanks to Ernest, "You and Rudy did a great job helpin' your sister today, but I'll be needin' to talk with her alone."

Ahab shouted at the sheriff, "You won't be lookin' or talkin' to the girlie without her mama present."

Alma followed the sheriff into the bedroom. She stood in the corner with her hands folded across her chest.

Emie had been fitfully resting. Her parents arguing, and her concern about the arrival of the sheriff and doctor, prevented any real sleep. When she would give into exhaustion, Charlie's wicked presence would fill the room, like a monster that came haunting at night. She was doing her best to be brave and had purposed not to cry out.

This time when she opened her eyes, Sheriff Robbins was standing over her. He then skirted around her mama and moved the cane chair from the corner of the room next to her bedside. She thought to warn him about the broken seat, but somehow the words wouldn't travel from her befuddled brain to her pretty mouth. The sheriff's presence only added to her anxiety. He had always seemed nice enough, yet she knew he was an acquaintance of Daddy's and a friend of Pastor Eugene's.

The sheriff reassuringly laid his hand on her shoulder. It was all she could do not to recoil. Emie thought that he must have sensed her internal reaction, because he removed his hand quickly and then spoke softly. "Emerald, I'm here to help. Rudy did the right thing comin' to get me. When we're finished talkin', the doc will take a look at you. He's a good man. Why, he probably helped your mama birth you. Now, I'll be needin' you to tell me the truth, Emie, all of it."

Emie sat up in bed and adjusted the pillow behind her. If you could still call it a pillow. Long ago it has been filled with goose feathers, but the feathers were now compressed, offering little comfort. It was the only pillow in the room. The little girls who slept on the floor shared the pillow. Emie and the other sisters cushioned their heads with the mattress alone.

"Are you ready to tell me what happened?" the sheriff asked.

Emie looked to where her mama was standing; her pleading eyes asking for her mother's approval. Alma didn't speak a word or move a muscle. She stood with a frown on her face and her arms folded across her chest. Even in the pale light, Emie could see the dark circles under her mother's eyes. Emie knew it was useless to seek her mother's help. She would never go against Daddy. Emie felt belittled once again by the one who gave birth to her. Her mama had suckled her, yet when Emie now needed to feel the security of being warmed and fed, her mother refused. She knew her mother loved her the best way she knew how, and that somehow that love was squashed by Daddy.

Emie shifted her focus and looked at Sheriff Robbins. "I have a question." She wanted him to understand that she expected the truth from him just as he expected the truth from her.

"Why were you talkin' to Ernest today?" she questioned. "He was supposed to help me leave the holler. We were goin' to Charleston."

The sheriff paused. Emie was certain that he was weighing his answer. She hoped that the scales were balanced. If they weren't, she would refuse to tell her story. With all the wounds of the day, only a trustworthy soul would hear about her sorrow. Anything less would diminish what she had lost. Emie had learned from a young age that it was better to bare her own heartache than to share her disappointments with someone who would ignore, mock, or make light of her pain.

The sheriff maintained eye contact, "Your daddy and Pastor Eugene asked me to visit with Ernest. They were concerned that he would take you away. I needed to explain to your brother that without your parents' permission, he didn't have the legal right to leave with you."

"You best watch the chair you're sittin' on, sheriff. It'll give out on ya," Emie instructed.

"Thanks for the word of caution. I got a few wobbly chairs of my own."

Emie then lowered her eyes to the mattress beneath her injured body, "I'll tell my story now."

"Take your time. I'll be needin' to take notes while you talk."

Emie began by sharing what happened in the schoolyard with Charlie while she and Mimi were dancing. She talked about her confusion and Mrs. Randolph's concerns over Charlie's actions. She even mentioned the school teacher's intention of talking with Pastor Eugene. She told the sheriff, "You'll have to ask Ernest what happened with him and Charlie. My brother didn't tell me. I just saw the bruises on his face."

Emie then moved the conversation to graduation day. She talked about the ceremony and eating lunch on the swings. She shared about her worry over Ernest. When she talked about her brother, she lifted her head and looked at the sheriff. She noticed that his eyes were deep brown like Ernest's.

Mama said that Ernest's eyes were the color of the West Virginia soil. Emie wasn't sure if Mama's words were a compliment or not, but Ernest took pride in working the land, and felt it only right that his eyes reflect what he loved. "Emie, my eyes are like the dirt, and your eyes are like the deep blue pools of Big Creek," Ernest had thoughtfully told her. Maybe Mama's words were an adulation after all. Emie had certainly treasured the thought of her eyes being compared to the creek.

She continued to tell her story, but felt stuck in the details of the graduation party. She talked about the food she ate, and Daddy's praise that wasn't really praise. She even mentioned the clouds hiding the sun, and her love for white cake. She knew she was rambling but couldn't get her thoughts past the schoolyard. What had happened next was too difficult to talk about.

The sheriff held her gaze, "Emerald, it's time to tell me what happened with Charlie."

Her eyes fell again. She couldn't look at Sheriff Robbins and talk about what Charlie had done. Emie looked once again to her mama. The tell was there; the wringing of her mother's hands. The oil lamp was casting a shadow, yet Emie could see the glistening of tears on her mother's face. Quietly her mama took two steps forward and softly patted Emie's leg in Auntie Ada's fashion, three distinct touches. Her mama's gesture gave Emie the strength to continue her story.

"We left the schoolyard. Both Mama and Daddy were smiling. At first, Charlie was nice. Then when we were out of sight, he grabbed my hand hard and talked about how we were gettin' married. I called him a liar and tried to run back to the school. He grabbed me and drug me a little ways. Then he threw me over his shoulder. He took me into the woods and hurt me."

"Emie, I need you to tell me exactly how he hurt you," the sheriff said in a soothing voice.

She recounted what happened the best she could. With each word, she felt like she was reliving what Charlie had done. The sheriff was patient in drawing out the needed information. He was kind when he asked questions. He even told Emie about his own two daughters, and how it would destroy him if something happened to one of them.

When Emie had finished, the sheriff asked, "In your struggle with Charlie, did you injure him in any way?"

"When he threw me over his shoulder, I bit him hard." Emie answered.

"Is there anything else?"

She thought for a moment, "I also scratched his back." Emie showed the officer her broken, dirtied fingernails. "When he was kissing me, I also bit his lip." Subconsciously, she took her right index finger and touched first her upper lip, then her lower lip.

The sheriff watched her movements. With tears pooled in his eyes, threatening to drip onto his face, he quietly spoke, "Emie, Charlie didn't kiss you. A kiss is something more than two mouths touching. A true kiss is intimate, almost sacred. It represents shared loved, not Charlie takin' what wasn't his."

Sheriff Robbins took her hand. "Emerald, we're done for now. I'm going to ask Doctor Bright to examine you. You're a very brave young woman."

"Sheriff, what happens to Charlie? I'm scared." Emie confided.

"I need to do a thorough investigation. I believe he hurt you, but I need to be sure there's enough evidence to put him in jail. In the meantime, I will ask Ernest and Rudy to watch over you. Charlie won't be hurtin' you any more, Emie."

She hoped Sheriff Robbins was right.

The Sheriff glanced back at Alma, "You should be proud. Your girl was courageous and fought hard."

Her mother wiped the wetness from her checks, nodded at Emie, and then escorted the Sheriff to the central room.

Doctor Bright was a kindly older gentleman. His gray hair, wrinkled forehead, and portly middle gave him the appearance of Santa Claus without a beard. He had grown up in the holler, and after his schooling had returned to doctor the mountain people. As far as Emie knew, he had never married nor had children of his own. She had met the doctor only a couple times. Mama believed in hill remedies, and rarely took her children into town to see Doc Bright.

Before he began his ministrations, he spoke reassuringly, "I consider all the children of the holler my own. In fact, Emerald, I remember the day you were born. I'll be gentle and take good care of you, just like you were my own flesh and blood."

He was true to his word. She was embarrassed for him to see her girl parts, but he distracted her by talking about her siblings. He hadn't delivered the boys, but when the twins were ready to be born, he told her about Daddy running into town to fetch him. "Your mama was having a tough time. I'll never forget the fear on your daddy's face when he arrived at my office. He was out of breath, and so worried about your mama and the babies. I grabbed my horse and your daddy, and I rode up the holler. Your Aunt Ada was with your mama. It took a while, but your sisters came into the world safe and sound."

The doctor continued his stories until the examination was finished. He then took her face lovingly in his wrinkled hands, "Emerald, you're a strong young woman. Physically you'll be just fine. How you heal in your soul is up to you. Nothing can change what happened. Grieve what you've lost and then continue living."

A few minutes later, Mama arrived with a basin of warmed water scented with lavender. Her mama washed her like she was a small child. Doc had already cleaned some of her wounds, but Mama rewashed and examined, it seemed to Emie, every inch of her being. She knew that Daddy must already be asleep, or Mama would not be taking so much time.

The gentle hands of her mother soothed her. The washing seemed to cleanse away the bad of the day. Her mama spoke very little, but in those few moments, Emie felt loved and sheltered. She thought about the hens who gathered their chicks under their wings. She also thought about Mimi's graduation song, *Slumber, my darling, thy mother is near. Guarding, thy dreams from all terror and fear. Sunlight has pass'd and the twilight has gone. Slumber, my darling, the night's coming on. Sweet visions attend thy sleep. Fondest, dearest to me, while others their revels keep, I will watch over thee.*

"Emie, your sisters are sleepin' out by the wood stove tonight. You rest, girlie. Tomorrow is soon enough to be thinkin' about what's next." Mama smiled, but Emie could still see the worry in her furrowed eyebrows. She helped Emie place a fresh nightgown over her head, through her bruised arms, and across her marred chest. The gown was made of pale blue muslin and slightly worn. It was a hand-me-down from one of the twins, but Emie relished the feel of something clean and familiar. She was relieved to be rid of the dirt and blood from her ordeal.

Doctor Bright had left medicine to help her sleep. Mama mixed the fine, white powder with water and instructed Emie to drink it down quickly.

Ernest bid her goodnight and then the oil lamps were put out. At her request, Ernest had left the curtain to the girls' room partially open. Emie found comfort in seeing her brothers and sisters strewn about the center room. She watched the shadows from the fire dancing on the walls until her eyes grew heavy and sleep came upon her.

In the wee hours of the morning, while the stars were still shining over the dogwood flowers, making each tree glow like earth-bound galaxies, she woke to find Coral asleep beside her. Coral's small, innocent, pale hand lay, fingers slightly bent, next to Emie's marred one. The older sibling sensed that Coral had held her hand in the night. Tears rolled down Emie's checks, not tears of sorrow, but tears of thankfulness as she thought about the special bond shared between siblings. Enveloped in love, Emie closed her tired eyes and slept soundly until late morning.

Chapter Twelve

"The leaves and bark of a willow are a remedy for heartache."
(Appalachian Folk Belief)

Emie woke to the sound of whispering voices. The faded bedroom curtain, now tightly closed, offered little in the way of a sound barrier. Coral was no longer by her side, but if Emie listened closely, she could hear her quietly chastising the younger sisters, "Baby girls, Emie was hurt yesterday. Hush now and let her sleep."

Emie couldn't help but smile; the little girls hated being called babies. The one window in the bedroom allowed the mid-morning sun to dance across her face. She yawned and stretched; the stretch instantly reminding her of yesterday's injuries. As slumber gave way to the morning light, she became more in tune with the aches in her body. The pain radiated from bow to stern. Her body willed her to lie as still as possible, yet her mind raced, calling her to face a new day.

When Ernest peeked around the curtain offering her breakfast in bed, she kindly declined. "Emie, I'll get Mama to help you dress."

A few minutes later, her mother entered the room, water basin and cloth in hand. Mama stood silently while Emie wiped the sleep from her eyes and cleaned her teeth. Emie knew that her mama was trying to forget the wrongs of yesterday. The holler people believed that talking about the bad brought even worse to someone's life.

"Let me help you dress and get to the stinky," Mama said, helping her daughter rise from the bed.

"I think I'll be fine. You have enough to do without babyin' me," Emie replied.

"When you're finished, come eat breakfast at the table, girlie. You shoulda ate the food Ernest offered. I ain't never had breakfast in bed, and you probably won't neither."

Emie walked slowly from the bedroom. She knew that her mother was troubled; she could tell from her curt tone. Emie already felt undone. Exposed and vulnerable from the cruelty of yesterday, she wondered where the strength would come to face the trials of today. The words, *"I will strengthen you,"* came to mind. She knew it was God reassuring her of His presence. She wondered where God was when Charlie was raping her. Her heart then radiated with the words, *"I was with you. I didn't leave you."*

The kitchen was empty except for Mama and Ernest. Mama was red in the face, and Ernest was humming a hymn. She slowly walked outside to the privy, and then returned even more slowly to the kitchen. Her body was aching. As she sat down to eat, Mama pulled a chair close by; Ernest did likewise, placing himself on her other side.

Mama put her hands on top of the table and then folded them together. Emie knew that her mother often played with her hands when she was nervous or upset. Mama looked toward the back bedroom, and when she spoke softly, Emie figured that Daddy must be having his late morning rest. "Ernest has news from the sheriff."

Her brother smiled. "Emie, it's good news. I walked to town this mornin'. Charlie's in jail. Sheriff Robbins arrested him late last night. The sheriff said that Charlie's injuries were just as you told."

"Whether it's good news or not remains to be seen," Mama interjected. Her sarcasm wasn't lost on either one of her children.

Ernest ran his hand through his brown hair, "Mama, this is out of Daddy's hands. It's out of your hands. The law's done taken up Emie's cause."

"Girlie, how could you let this happen? It'll be the end of us,"

Mama spoke accusingly.

Her brother pounded his fist on the table, "Enough. She's done nothin' wrong."

Again, her mother looked toward the back room, anxious that her husband might be awakened. "Take back what you've said, Emie. Tell the sheriff you made it up. You can't send Charlie to jail. Pastor Eugene and your daddy won't have it."

Emie had no appetite. She pushed her plate away and slowly rose from the chair. "Ernest was right. He told me that you'd take up for Daddy no matter what. I can't take back what's true. I'm not sendin' Charlie to jail. He's sendin' himself there. His own actions broke the law, and broke a piece of me, too. That should matter. He hurt me, Mama."

Ernest took his sister's elbow, "Let's enjoy a few minutes of mornin' air."

They walked out the back door to the closest patch of grass next to the house, by Mama's spring flower bed, and sat down. "Emie, I know you're hurtin' some, go ahead and lean on me."

Emie shifted her body slowly, until her back was against Ernest's back. "Let's sit like we did when we was little."

The two sat quietly. In the midst of disappointment, the brother and sister, without words, comforted one another. The sunshine felt wonderful on Emie's face; she closed her eyes and pressed her weight against her brother. Ernest sighed and began to hum. Among the tulips and daffodils, Emie wondered what Ernest's sigh meant; was it born of worry or contentment, or maybe both? She was worried, yet she felt content in the moment, and maybe for Ernest it was the same.

Taking shade under a gloriously blossomed red bud tree, Ernest cupped his hand over his brow and noticed Auntie coming across the meadow. Even from a distance, her familiar stride and gray hair made her recognizable. It wasn't often that Ada came to the Ashby residence. Visits with Auntie mostly took place at her cabin in the woods. Ernest got Emie's attention by pressing his back firmly against her back, and then motioning with a nod of his head for Emie to look.

"Well, if it ain't two of my favorites sittin' here in the sun! Scoot on over and let me sit beside." Like a cold glass of lemonade on a hot August afternoon, Auntie quenched the parched spirits of those she loved. She was like the prophet of old who commanded to the dry bones to live. Ernest helped Ada carefully situate herself on the sedge grass.

She took Emie's hand and patted her usual series of three. "Girlie, I done heard the news. I'm sorry. There ain't words I can be sayin' to make this better. Just know I love you and I'll be prayin'."

"Thank you, Auntie," Emie managed in response.

Ernest headed toward the barn, "I'll be back, ladies. I'm needin' to check on the mamas and babies. I'm wantin' to be sure those sows are takin' good care of their young ones."

Auntie looked at Emie and then took her aged, rough hands and placed them on either side of Emie's young smooth face, "So, your mama ain't takin' good care of you?"

"Subtle, ain't he?" Emie smiled.

"Well, at least he got your mouth curved up. You got a big hurt right now. Your mama's hurtin' too, and she just plain don't know what to do."

"I know, Auntie, but I'm disappointed. I want things from her that she won't give me."

"I know it doesn't make it better, but she don't know how to give those things, darlin'."

Emerald hung her head. "She wants me to make things right, when I did nothin' wrong. I guess I can't give her what she wants neither."

"When I was a little girl, almost every Christmas my folks gave me an orange. It was a real nice treat," Auntie began. "One year, I wanted an apple instead of an orange. I was a might disappointed when I didn't get what I asked for. Emie, sometimes in life, we ask for apples, and we get oranges. I don't know why, but folks don't always give us what we want or need."

Although she didn't understand the entire meaning behind her aunt's words, Emie nodded. "How will I get through this?"

Ada lifted Emie's chin. "You can live a thousand lives in the past, or one life with purpose, girlie. I'm needin' to tell you a story."

In sync, Ada and Emerald shifted their bodies to face one another. To an onlooker their profiles would seem stoic, but in truth, Ada was thinking of how to start her story, and Emie was waiting with anticipation for what was to come.

Auntie's eyes grew misty. "I grew up in these hills. My folks was good people. Protective-like, but somethin' bad happened just the same. I experienced somethin' that cut me to the core. I was a little older than you. The wrong changed me."

Now it was Emie's turn to extend comfort. She placed her hand on Auntie Ada's shoulder and gently squeezed. The look of thanks from her aunt warmed Emie.

"Emie, you know I ain't never married. Your mama's like the daughter I never birthed, and you and your brothers and sisters are my hope for the future in this holler. I didn't marry because of what happened to me," Ada confided.

Emie thoughtfully spoke, "Auntie, you're beautiful. You must have had a beau?"

Ada smiled at Emie's compliment. "Doc Bright was my beau. I never told him why I wouldn't marry. He left the holler because of me, and when he came back and started doctorin' in these hills, I ignored him best I could. The years passed and... well, here I am."

Emie could see the waves of sadness wash over Ada. "Darlin', if I had to do it all over again, I would have lived past the hurt. It was my choice to allow the pain to cloud over my future."

Emie glanced toward the barn, wishing Ernest had been present for Auntie's confession. She smiled. Doc Bright was standing outside the barn with her brother. Her gaze remained on the older gentleman, "It's never too late, Auntie."

When Ada turned to see who or what had captured the girl's attention, she gasped. Her face flushed and her heart raced. This was her moment to make things right. She was scared. She had hurt Doc Bright badly. She had also hurt herself. She didn't know if her heart could take his rejection, or worse yet, indifference from the man she once loved. Ada knew it was time to make things right. In fact, it was way past time. It was also Emie's moment to see how a wounded soul could continue living.

Ada stood nervously. Emie rose and stood beside her; hand-in-hand they walked to the barn. A florescent hummingbird buzzed by, and returned in curious flitting circles around them.

Ada's voice trembled. "Doctor Bright, I have somethin' to tell you, and I'm wantin' Emie to hear what needs said."

The good man nodded in response.

"May I call you by your given name?"

For a brief moment, the doctor hesitated. "Although it's been some years, Ada, you may do as you've asked."

Auntie let go of Emie's hand and placed the same hand on the doctor's arm. "Christian, I'm sorry. When we were young, I loved you, but I dishonored you by not tellin' the truth."

"I knew some of what happened, Ada, but I didn't know how to help. I went to school hoping that when I returned you would love me again."

"I did love you, but I felt such shame." Ada lifted Christian's hand to her lips. "Please forgive me."

Chapter Thirteen

"To keep away crows, kill one and hang it from a garden post."
(Appalachian Folk Belief)

Ernest could tell that his mother was worried about Lester. He hadn't come home since Emie's graduation. In a way, he envied his brother. Lester had missed all the craziness: Daddy blaming Emie, Mama wanting to keep peace, and Emie doing her best to pull herself up by her boot straps. Like dirt when the fields were being turned, tension hung in the air at the Ashby home. Ernest would never leave Emie or the little girls, but right now the weight of being the older brother seemed far too much to bear. He couldn't fix the trouble in his family; why, even his attempt at protecting Emie had gone all wrong.

Lester Gillis was the real name of the well-known gangster, Baby Face Nelson. Ernest wondered if the name "Lester" was cursed. His brother had been nothing but trouble lately. He was tired of Mama saying, "Like father, like son." At some point, Lester needed to be accountable for his actions.

He had promised Mama that if Lester wasn't home by morning that he would go looking. She had pressed him to go tonight, "Son, don't you care none for your brother? He's been gone more 'n two days. Something bad coulda' happened. That's all we need is more trouble."

Ernest had simply shook his head. "Mama, if there's trouble,

Lester's causin' it. I wouldn't worry none. He'll come home when he's good and ready."

So much had happened in the last two days: Emie's rape, Charlie being jailed, Auntie's revelation. "My head is spinnin', Lord," Ernest prayed. He could hear the girls getting ready for bed in the next room. His parents were whispering. *"More secrets,"* Ernest thought. He started to imagine what trickery his father was scheming and his mother believing, but stopped himself. He needed to take control of his mind and set his heart on seeking God.

"Jesus, I've known you since I was little. I've given my life to doin' your will. I'm strugglin'. I don't know what to do here. Help me. Help Emie. Help Mama and Daddy, and even help Lester, wherever he is. Protect him from whatever mischief he's up to." Ernest stopped and reconsidered what he had just prayed. "Lord, I'm not sure I should be prayin' for Lester to be protected from his sin, but yet I care for him and it's hard to pray otherwise. I think I should be askin' that he repent from wrong and turn to you. Amen."

Emie lay quietly in bed trying not to disturb her sisters. Generally the girls pinched, whispered, and tickled until Mama or one of the boys yelled for them to be still, but tonight the air was somber. The twins had said very little to her since the rape. She wondered what they were thinking but didn't ask.

Sharing a room with six sisters gave little privacy; the girls were accustomed to dressing and undressing in front of each other, but tonight Emie sensed her older sisters staring when she slipped off the day's worn dress and put on her gown. Having seen her almost naked, except for panties, she was certain the twins had seen her bruises.

Girls in the holler knew little to nothing about sex. Emie wondered herself what all sex entailed. She knew according to Sheriff Robbins that what Charlie did to her wasn't how things were supposed to be. Emie wished she knew more about the ways of a man and woman. She was worried for Ruby and Garnett. Their wedding day was fast approaching. The twins up the holler were nice boys, but would sex be painful for her sisters? Would the boys be tender and loving? She hoped her sisters' husbands wouldn't say and do cruel things.

The little ones were asleep; she heard their steady breathing, but she was almost certain that Ruby and Garnett were still awake. They kept tossing and turning. "Ruby, Garnett, are you excited about the weddin'? I'm sure it will be beautiful with all the plannin' you been doin'."

One of the sisters mumbled, "Yes." Emie wasn't sure which one. In the light of day, she could easily tell her sisters apart, but at night when she couldn't see their faces clearly and with their sleepy voices sounding so similar, it was difficult. She thought it might be Ruby.

"Was that you, Ruby?"

"No, Emie, it was me," corrected Garnett.

"It's funny ain't it, twins marryin' twins?" Emie tried to be light-hearted. Most of the time her older sisters ignored her, especially lately with the wedding approaching, but in her heart she knew they loved her and she loved them. They had put aside their own joy tonight and were grieving with her in their own way.

"We're sorry, Emie."

"Yeah, we're both sorry."

She didn't bother to ask who said what. "I learned some things from Doc Bright and the sheriff about man stuff."

"Really?" one of the girls asked, with piqued curiosity.

"Do you know that kissin' is supposed to be intimate? Sheriff Robbins told me that it's almost sacred, and that it should be nice and not hurt anyone."

Emie waited for Ruby or Garnett to say something. She wondered if they had engaged in kissing their beaus. She had even asked Ernest about it, "Brother, do you think the girls have been kissin' on the twins?"

He had only laughed, "Emie, I'm sure they've been kissin' up a storm − not that's it any of your concern."

"Do you think they get confused about who's kissin' who since they all look alike?"

Ernest had shaken his head and chuckled, "I'm sure those boys know exactly who they're kissin."

At the time, she wondered. Was Ernest a kissing expert? As far as she knew, he had never even had a *girlfriend*. Once at the county fair, there had been a kissing booth. All the holler boys lined up to smooch on a pretty girl she'd never seen before. Emie had tried to goad Ernest into taking a turn. She'd teased him until he turned red in the face. Then, she made kissing sounds and even pretended to faint with desire.

Sure, Ernest laughed at her antics, but he'd said, "Emie, when I kiss a girl, I want it to be special. I want it to mean somethin', and the price I'll be payin' won't be with money, but with my heart."

She hoped that someday she would kiss a boy and have it mean something. "Doc told me that I would be just fine. That in time I needed to move past what Charlie did to me. I'm thinkin' on it, but it'll take a while. Why, someday I may even want a husband who'll kiss me nice and treat me special. Maybe he'll even serve me breakfast in bed."

Emie quietly got out of bed. She didn't want to disturb the little girls. She slowly and softly walked the few steps around the bed to where the twins lay and stood by their feet, "I know the both of you will have nice husbands. They'll treat you good. I don't think your weddin' night will be anything like what Charlie done to me."

As far as Ernest was concerned, morning came far too early. Mama woke him before dawn. "I'm gettin' your breakfast. Your brother still ain't home. Get dressed, eat, and head to town. See what you can find out."

On his way out the door, Mama added to her instructions, "Your daddy's wantin' to see his cousin. Tell Eugene, if he can, to head up the holler today."

Ernest walked swiftly to town. Usually, he enjoyed the fresh morning air, but today he was in a hurry. He wanted to appease his mother, but at the same time, he didn't want to leave Emie for very long. Yesterday, Doc had come to make sure that she was feeling alright. He expected that the sheriff would come today, and he felt it best to run interference between the law and his daddy.

He made the decision to stop by the parsonage first. It was early, and more than likely Pastor Eugene would still be sleeping. He would call on his daddy's cousin, make a few inquiries in town and then, hopefully, walk back up the holler with Eugene. He wanted to get a sense of what the pastor was thinking. It wouldn't be good for Emie if Eugene and Daddy made plans. In fact, he was considering talking with Mama about sending Emie to Auntie's. He didn't know what his mother would say, but he was praying on the matter.

Ernest knocked on the front door of the pastor's home. The parsonage was small, but well maintained by mountain standards. The ladies from the church had planted spring flowers by the porch, and last year the men had painted the exterior – which was considered by some a luxury. Most of the holler homes were constructed of simple clapboard without any paint.

For a fleeting moment, he felt sorry for Eugene. It had to hurt to have your only son locked up in jail for rape. He also felt anger. Eugene had taught his son spiritual untruths. He had misrepresented the wonder of how God had created the female gender. He had also spoiled Charlie. "My boy, you're like the sun in the sky. If you play your cards right, the world and what's it in will revolve around you."

Ernest's thoughts drifted from Charlie to Lester. They were like two peas in a pod; willing to hurt others to get what they wanted, and feeling like the world owed them something.

When no one answered the door, Ernest knocked again. Finally, to his surprise, Charlie opened the door, dressed in nothing but his drawers. His dark hair was standing on end, and his face was unshaven. Obviously, Ernest had woken him up.

"Why, cousin, what brings you callin' this early morn? Are you here to defend the righteous Emerald again?"

Ernest was speechless; his mouth gaped open and his mind was whirling like a dirt devil. Why was Charlie out of jail? What happened that Sheriff Robbins released him?

"You might want to close your trap before the flies get in," Charlie smirked.

After gaining some composure, Ernest stammered, "What...what...what are you doin' here?"

Smugly, Charlie answered, "Why, I live here. Ernest, they only keep guilty men in jail. Your sweet little sister lied. I did nothin' to her, and I've an alibi to prove it."

Ernest was dumbfounded. He closed his eyes and began to shake his head in confusion. He needed to think. He needed to pray.

"Little brother, cat got your tongue?"

Ernest opened his eyes and saw Lester standing behind Charlie. He should have known that the two would be together making trouble like lightning and rain on a stormy day.

Charlie casually placed his arm around Lester's shoulder. "What Emie's doin' is wrong. I wasn't even with her; I was with Lester."

Ernest had experienced Lester's deceptive ways since they were small children. In fact, one of his earliest memories involved Lester lying to mama about a broken toy. Lester had played innocent, and Ernest had received a swift swat on his behind from his mother's hand. "Little boy, you know we ain't got money for toys. You done broke the one you had. There won't be any more comin', and don't be askin' your brother to share. He don't have to share with a brother who breaks things."

Ernest looked at Lester straight in the eye and tried to gauge his brother's emotions. At first, his brother boldly stared him down. Then when Ernest refused to look away, Lester turned his own eyes away. Both brothers had dark eyes, but today Lester's eyes looked sinister, like a villain in a dime store novel. Only this wasn't a made-up story where the bad men went to jail, and the damsel in distress lived happily ever after. This was his brother bold-faced lying about his sister's rape. Perhaps his downward glance indicated remorse, but given Lester's pattern of living, Ernest wasn't hopeful. He felt sick all over. His heart ached, so did his body; his head felt ready to explode and his stomach was churning bile. Ernest turned to walk away. "I'll be back. I'm goin' to see the sheriff."

Lester said nothing, but Charlie, with his hairy chest puffed out like a robin full of worms, called after him, "Won't do you no good. I'm a free man, and I'm stayin' that way. Lester done vouched for my whereabouts. Some Negro raped your sister. That black face is sittin' in jail. Go on over there and meet him."

He could hear Charlie's harsh laugh and booming voice as he walked past the church heading toward the sheriff's office. "Hey, Ernest, tell the sheriff that I'm a might thankful for his hospitality."

The door to the Sheriff Robbins' office and the local jail was locked. It was still early. Ernest took a seat outside the building on a weathered bench. On either side of the bench were potted plants – pansies, he thought. They were wilted and needed water. He closed his eyes, and felt the morning sun on his face. To a passerby, it looked like he was sleeping, but in reality he was humming a hymn, trying to calm himself before the sheriff arrived.

Ernest needed more strength. He needed the peace of God that he couldn't get by his own understanding now. He needed to experience the Lord's love without limit. "Lord, you have no boundaries. You give and give and give again," he prayed.

Ernest felt a tap on the shoulder. "I was expectin' to see you today, just not quite this early," Sheriff Robbins spoke. "Come on in, where we can talk in private."

The sheriff unlocked the door and called out to his only prisoner, "Justice, you doin' alright?"

"Yes, sir," the man replied.

"My misses will be bringin' you breakfast soon."

"Thank you, Sheriff," came the sober response.

"Have a seat, Ernest," the sheriff instructed, pointing to the wooden chair across from his desk. "If you're needin' to yell or pound your fist, go right ahead. I did some shoutin' myself last evening."

"Much as I'd like, I don't think yellin' or poundin' is gonna help. I just need to know what happened," Ernest said.

"After talkin' with Emie, I headed to the parsonage to question Charlie. He was nowhere to be found, but Eugene promised to bring him my way as soon as he came home. The Reverend was visibly upset and more than anxious to clear things up." The sheriff rose from his chair and started a pot of coffee.

"I waited past midnight before Charlie done showed his face. His injuries were just as Emie described. He admitted to leavin' the schoolhouse with Emie, but was close-mouthed beyond that."

The sheriff returned to his desk and started to rifle through papers. Ernest knew by the haphazard way the sheriff was stacking and unstacking the paperwork that he wasn't looking for anything in particular. He was upset and in an attempt to release his frustration, he kept his hands moving. Ernest was doing the same. He wasn't shuffling papers, but his legs were bouncing in slow rhythmic time to some unknown sorrowful song.

"By mornin' Eugene was back with Lester, who claimed that he was with Charlie when he got his injuries. When I refused to let Charlie go, Lester and Eugene paraded in a couple other witnesses, two moonshiners from far up the holler. They all claimed to have witnessed a fight between Charlie and some travelin' man, who, of course, can't be found."

Ernest heard the bell over the door ring and turned his head to see the sheriff's wife bringing breakfast. MayLou Robbins was known for her kind heart and excellent cooking skills. She was a good woman, who served the Lord not only with her words, but with her actions as well. She often baked bread for those in need. Her homemade jams and churned butter seemed to hold the mysteries of heaven. Normally, Ernest's mouth would be watering with anticipation, but this morning he had no appetite.

The sheriff took the willow basket from his wife, "Thank you, darlin'. I appreciate you making Justice somethin' to eat."

Mrs. Robbins smiled kindly in response, "I brought a couple extra cinnamon rolls. You and Ernest can enjoy those. I'll be back later to gather things up." She removed the red cotton cloth that covered the basket, laid a roll in front of Ernest, and then gently patted his shoulder.

He felt tears in his eyes and was embarrassed when they rolled down his checks. He wiped his face with the back of his hand.

"You're a good brother, Ernest. Emie couldn't ask for none better. I've been prayin' since Edward told me what happened, and

I'll keep prayin'. See that red cloth. I covered the basket with it on purpose. Red is the color of redemption. You remember that now. When you leave here today, you put that red cloth in your pocket. Wipe your tears on it and remember God's redemption is comin' for Emie."

MayLou placed a cinnamon roll on the desk in front of her husband's chair, and laid the red cloth in the center of the work space. She smiled sweetly at the sheriff and left the two men alone.

Sheriff Robbins walked toward the cell where Justice Smith was being held. When Ernest started to follow, the sheriff motioned for him to stay put. "I'll be right back."

Ernest could hear the rattle of keys and the words of gratitude from a man being held for a crime he didn't commit. He wondered how Justice could be thankful when he was being treated so unfairly.

"He ain't guilty, sheriff."

"I know it, Ernest. I'm not sure why he showed up yesterday and confessed. Swears up and down that he hurt your sister. I ain't abidin' to holding an innocent man, but if he doesn't take back his confession and with Charlie now havin' three witnesses, I ain't got a choice," the sheriff spoke.

"What do we do now?" Ernest asked.

"I've sent someone for the judge. I'm hopin' he can sort out this mess. Justice is a good man. He and his family live in a small shack several miles past your family's place. He works hard for a corn farmer. Gets paid hardly nothin' but has a place to live and food provided. He ain't never been in trouble before."

"Can I talk with him?"

The sheriff shook his head. "He says he won't talk to no one. Don't even want a lawyer."

The bell over the door rang again. It was Rudy. "I heard the news at Daddy's store, and I come to help. What can I do?"

Ernest first looked at Sheriff Robbins, then at Rudy. "I have an idea. Let's have Rudy fetch Emie and see if Justice will talk with her. She's hard to refuse at times."

Rudy started thinking about Emie's honey-blond hair and big blue eyes and couldn't help but nod in agreement with Ernest.

"Heck, I've had a hard time telling her 'no' since first grade. I think it's the way she peers into your soul, like she knows all your secrets."

A faint smile crossed Rudy's lips. He looked into the sky and noticed a broad-winged hawk circling over them. "I'll head back to the store and saddle a horse. I'm not sure if Emie's up to walkin' to town, and it'll be quicker on horseback anyway. What should I tell her? You know Emie, she'll be askin' more 'n a few questions."

Sheriff Robbins gave Rudy the rundown on Charlie, Eugene, Lester, and, of course, Justice Smith. Ernest hesitated and then asked Rudy, "Would you please be sure and let my mama know that Lester's just fine?" He was angry with Lester and struggled to even mention his name, but he knew it wasn't fair to keep his mama worrying about her prodigal son.

As Rudy readied to leave the sheriff's office, Ernest took the scarlet cloth from the center of the desk. Using his teeth, he tore a small hole along the outside seam and then ripped the cloth in half. "Rudy, this will help Emie remember that Jesus loves her. Tell her that Job in the midst of losin' everything knew that God was still workin' in his life."

Ernest decided to head back to the parsonage. He wanted to talk with Lester, hopefully alone. When he exited the sheriff's office, he noticed that someone had watered the pansies. He figured it was MayLou. She had watered both the plants and his soul this morning.

There was no need to knock on the front door; both Lester and Charlie were sitting on the front porch. Lester had dressed, but Charlie was still without the benefit of a shirt or trousers. Ernest couldn't help but laugh. It was just like Charlie to think his hairy chest meant something more than it did.

"Did you meet the Negro?" Charlie yelled.

Ernest took the two steps leading to the porch in one stride, "It ain't necessary to yell. I'm right here."

"Take your shirt off, Ernest. We'll see who's more a man."

"I'm not taking my shirt off, Charlie. I guess I should be

thankful that you're not askin' to compare anything else." Ernest smelled Charlie's coffee and then Lester's. "You boys are drinkin' early today."

Lester pulled back his stoneware mug that had been made from the red West Virginia clay. "We're celebratin' Charlie's release from jail."

"Lester, why don't you and I take a little walk?" Ernest asked.

"Why, brother, it is a lovely day for a stroll, but I do believe it would be wrong to leave our dear cousin sittin' on this porch by himself." Lester's sarcasm dripped like honey from the comb. "Say what you come to say and be done."

Ernest struggled with where to begin. "You both are lyin'. I know it and the sheriff knows it." He turned toward Charlie. "Have your daddy get you a good lawyer. Face the consequences of what you done."

"I ain't done nothin'. Now get."

"I'll get," said Ernest. "But first, I'm wantin' to arm wrestle my brother. If I win, Lester and I take a walk. If Lester wins, I won't say another word and I'll leave right 'way."

Lester slapped Charlie on the back. "Cousin, he ain't never beat me at arm wrestling. Watch and learn!"

Lester placed his elbow on the porch rail, and Ernest did likewise.

"Lord, give me the strength of Samson," Ernest prayed.

Both Charlie and Lester guawffed in unison at his prayer.

The brothers gripped hands and the match began. While the elbows stayed in place, as much as possible, the hands and forearms went back and forth. Charlie cheered for Lester, whose knuckles soon turned white from exertion. Ernest felt his strength wane. Lester was right, in all their years of boyhood play, he had never beaten his brother at much of anything, especially arm wrestling. Just as Ernest was ready to give into defeat, he felt a surge of power, and with strength unknown, he forcefully and deliberately pushed Lester's hand down to the rail.

Lester came away from the match first shaking his sore hand and then rubbing his shoulder. He shrugged at Charlie and then addressed Ernest, "Looks like you won, Samson. Let's stroll."

Before they were out of earshot from Charlie, Lester spoke up, "This ain't gonna change a thing. I saw what I saw. Emie lied."

Ernest waited until they rounded the church house. "Lester, why are you doin' this?"

"I ain't doin' nothin'."

"This'll bring shame on you and our family."

"Like our family ain't already full of shame. Daddy and his ways. I'm just like him, Ernest. I've tried not to be, but I am," Lester pronounced.

"You can't change Daddy. I can't change him neither. This is about Emie. This is about our sister."

"You're wrong, Ernest. This is about me escapin' the hell of livin' in this holler." Lester turned and headed back toward Charlie.

"Brother, please look at me."

Lester just kept walking. Ernest thought he heard in the wind the words, "I can't."

Ernest shuffled his feet trying to decide whether to follow his brother or not. He called after him, "Lester, none of us can change without God's help."

The prodigal son sauntered toward the parsonage. Ernest decided to head back up the holler. He knew he would probably meet Emie and Rudy along the way, but he wanted to be sure that Eugene, Charlie, or Lester didn't interfere with Emie talking to Justice.

Chapter Fourteen

"If you point your finger at a cucumber bloom, the bloom will fall off."
(Appalachian Folk Belief)

Rudy was puzzled. He wasn't quite sure how to address Emie about riding double on the horse. "Emerald, we got two choices here, and I'll be lettin' you choose. I can ride in the back, but it will mean me placin' my arms round you tightly. It won't bother me none, but with what you been through you may not like it, or you can ride in the back and hold onto me."

She thought for a moment. "I'll ride in the back."

Rudy gave her a boost onto the horse. "Emie, Ernest asked me to give you this cloth. Red is the color of Jesus' blood; it's the color of freedom. Your brother wanted me to remind you of Job, who remembered in his trouble that God loved him and would take care of him."

He looked into the pool of Emie's blue eyes, framed by her long blond lashes, "May I keep a piece of this?"

When she nodded "yes" in response, Rudy took a small knife from the pocket of his jeans and cut a slit in the cloth. He tore a piece from the whole and placed it and the knife back in his pocket. The knife had been a gift from his daddy and mama on the day he was baptized. His daddy had told him that a good knife and a good relationship with Jesus was all any man needed.

Rudy handed the cloth to Emerald, and mounted the horse in front of her. When she hesitated to grab hold of him, he turned around. "Emie, we've been friends a long time, and part of bein' friends is bein' familiar. Remember when you got mad and bit me in second grade, and in fourth grade when we tripped and fell on each other on the playground? I broke my arm and had to wear a sling all summer. There ain't no reason for you to be nervous with me. I'm the one who should be scared. I ain't never bit you and never caused you to break a bone. Now, grab hold of my waist tightly. We're ready to ride."

She did as she was told. Rudy felt guilty. He knew that Emie was miserable, yet he found their closeness extremely enjoyable. He could linger in her light all day. He only wished the ride to town was longer.

"Emie, I'm sorry the ride is so rough. Betsy ain't got the best gait, but in her defense the road ain't exactly smooth. You can lean against me if you want."

He was surprised when she leaned into him. "Have you ridden before?" he asked.

Emie sighed, "Not in a saddle, a time or two bareback. Auntie used to have a couple old mares, and everyone once in a while, Ernest and I would ride together."

"Did you enjoy it?"

"I did. Ernest always took me through the meadow toward the creek. The smell of the water and the wind on my face was nice."

Rudy patted her hand. "Emie, pretend that we're in the meadow headed toward the creek. Maybe someday we can ride there together."

Surprisingly, she giggled. Rudy didn't dare look back, but he could picture her smiling.

"Pretend, Emie. Do you smell the water and feel the breeze, girlie?"

She sighed again; Rudy knew it wasn't a sigh of despair, but a sigh of pleasure. He desperately wanted to hold her hand, but knew that now wasn't the time. He would be patient and wait. Hopefully, someday, Emie would want to hold his hand in return.

They were almost to town when they met Ernest. Emie loosened her grip and waved to her brother. When Rudy slowed the horse, Ernest held out his hands to help Emie down. Rudy parted from the horse as well, and grabbed Betsy's reins to lead her back to the store.

Emie had been surprisingly quiet with Rudy; usually she was full of questions. He wondered if their closeness on the mare had made her uncomfortable.

Now she prattled on to her brother, "Rudy told me about Lester. I ain't surprised none, but he's my brother, and his lyin' about me hurts."

"It hurts me too, Emie," Ernest replied.

"He also told me about Justice. I prayed on the way down from the holler that God would help me know what to say, Ernest."

"I've been prayin' as well. Did Rudy give you the red cloth?" Ernest asked.

Emie looked at her brother and then at Rudy. "He did and took a piece for himself. Like the three strands of rope that can't be broken."

She then tied the crimson threads, like a bracelet, around her wrist.

Sheriff Robbins led Emie through the office to the jail cell where Justice was being held. He introduced the two of them, and after mentioning that Justice had a daughter about Emie's age, he left them alone.

"Mr. Smith, it's nice to make your acquaintance."

"Miss Ashby, I ain't wantin' no visitors."

"Please call me Emie."

"Alright. You can call me Justice, but I still ain't wantin' to talk."

"How come your mama named you Justice?"

When he had confessed to the crime, he had never counted on meeting the infamous Emerald Ashby. She was cute as a button. The sheriff was right, she was about the same age as his own daughter. Emie's fair skin, blonde hair, and blue eyes were just the opposite of Mercy's coffee-colored skin, black hair, and dark eyes.

"She named me after her father, who was a slave."

"Is your mama still alive?" Emie asked.

"No. She been gone a few years."

Emie shook her head in disbelief, "Well, it's a good thing she's in heaven, cause if she was alive, she'd be wishin' she was dead, knowin' that her son was givin' himself to a life of slavery. Jail ain't nothin' but slavery, Justice. I read all about it in my reader at school. They'll be chainin' you like you was a slave. They'll be tellin' you when to eat, sleep, and even use the stinky. Shame, shame, shame."

"That's enough, Miss Emie."

"Remember, it's Emie - just plain Emie."

Justice knew the girl wasn't through with him yet. She was sassy and sweet at the same time, like the sweet pickles his wife canned each fall, but he had made his decision. He had to protect the ones he loved. The thought of his wife being hurt, or the threat of his daughter being molested sent shivers through his body. What kind of man was he, if he didn't take care of his own?

Sensing Justice's fight within, Emerald took his hand through the bars. The sheriff had told her not to go near the cell, but she couldn't help herself − Justice was hurting. She didn't understand the source of his pain, but she remembered how both Rudy's and Ernest's touch had brought her such comfort after her ordeal with Charlie.

"Do you believe in Jesus, Justice?"

"Yes, I do."

"Then why are you lyin'? You know and I know that you didn't hurt me. Why, we ain't never met until now."

"Emie, you're a young girl. There's things that you can't begin to understand."

"I understand plenty," she retorted. "I know that you have a wife and a daughter. I know that you're a God-fearin' man, and there must be a good reason for your lyin', but lyin' is lyin' nonetheless." She released Justice's hand and struggled to untie her red bracelet. When it was freed, she tore a strand from the cloth and handed it to the jailed man. "Jesus is the only one who can truly pay for another's freedom. Justice, do you think you're God, and that you hold the world in your hands?"

Justice moved away from the bars and took a seat on the bunk.

He hung his head, and placed his face in his hands. Emie strained to hear his muffled voice, "Leave me now and get the sheriff."

While the sheriff talked with Justice, Ernest waited with Emie in the outer office. His sister looked tired. It was only noon, but they lived a full day in the span of a few hours. He felt weary himself, bone-tired. "Emie, what did Justice say?"

"Not much of anything. I did most of the talkin'. You know he has a daughter 'bout my age?"

"Yeah, Sheriff Robbins told me."

"What's gonna happen, Ernest?"

He wanted to comfort his sister, but in truth, he didn't know what was going to happen. "Emie, I'm thinkin' of talkin' with Mama about sending you to Auntie's. With Charlie and Lester lyin' and knowin' Daddy and Pastor Eugene, I don't think home's the best place for you."

"I don't want to leave you, Ernest, but I'll go, if you say. Will you visit? Do you think Rudy will come see me?"

He knew his sister was frightened, "I'll come see you, every day if I can, and Rudy will come, as well. You know he's sweet on you."

"Ernest, now's not the time for foolin'. Rudy just feels sorry for me."

The conversation between the siblings was interrupted when the sheriff re-entered his office. "Ernest, is that old shack next to Ada's house still standing?"

"It's leaning', but still there."

"Justice and his family will be needin' a place to hide. Seems like Lester and Eugene threatened to harm his wife and daughter if he didn't confess to hurtin' Emie. I can't send him home. Besides the man Justice is workin' for ain't nothin' but a stingy moonshiner, and our friend ain't wantin' to run a still."

Ernest placed his arm around his sister. He gently squeezed her shoulder. He was proud of her. Rudy was right, Emie could look inside and see a person's secrets.

"Sheriff, is it okay if Emie and me head on up the holler? I'm gonna see if we can borrow Rudy's daddy's horse. It'll save some time. I'm thinkin' of takin' Emie to Auntie's anyway. While I'm there, I'll help get things ready for Justice and his family."

"Sounds good. I'll get his wife and daughter over there late afternoon, and bring Justice after nightfall." The sheriff then looked at Emie, "I don't know what you said, girlie, but Justice done bore his soul."

Chapter Fifteen

"Red-headed gardeners grow hotter peppers."
(Appalachian Folk Belief)

When Ernest arrived at Auntie Ada's, he found her sitting on the front porch enjoying the afternoon sun. Her eyes were closed, but he could tell that she wasn't actually sleeping. He had witnessed her naptimes before and knew they included soft rhythmic snoring. Her head was tilted back against the porch chair made of willow shoots, and she was gently smiling as if she had a secret that was hers alone. On the porch were several willow baskets filled with wild flowers and greens. Auntie took pride in weaving the baskets herself. The yellow daffodils with their darker yellow centers were in full bloom in front of the porch, and the lilac bushes were budded, promising the soon arrival of fragrant blossoms. Ernest thought it odd that Ada was holding an empty Mason jar in her hands.

With her eyes still closed, she quietly spoke, "Well, son, are you gonna say 'good afternoon' to an old woman or not?"

"You're hardly old, Auntie."

"Well, now you're lyin', and both me and the good Lord done know it. How's my girlie doin' today, Ernest?"

"She's on her way home from town. Rudy's with her. I'm a little worried. Wishin' I was with them. Emie convinced me that she would be fine. Auntie, she needs to come stay with you a spell. The peace here will do her good."

Like it was a treasure, Ada gently placed the Mason jar on the worn wooden planks next to her chair. "I figured she'd be comin'. I'm thinkin' your mama and daddy won't put up much of a fuss. Rudy gonna bring her and her things over in a bit?"

In response, Ernest nodded. He noticed there were several small holes in the lid of the jar Auntie had been holding, but before he could ask if she had taken up bug catching, she broke into song – one that Ernest had never heard before.

"Glorious, glorious morning the Lord has given to me. My heart swells with wonder when I consider His majesty..."

The lyrics were simple and heartfelt. When Ada lifted her hands in worship, Ernest joined her in giving thanks, his humming harmonizing with her song.

"The Lord has somethin' special for me today, Ernest. I can just feel it. I've been singin' Him songs all day; made up songs comin' from deep inside."

As he sat down on the porch steps, Ernest couldn't help but smile. The mysteries of God constantly amazed him. He shifted his lean body to face Auntie Ada. She was a wonder; a gift from heaven wrapped in untold beauty; fragile like a piece of china, yet strong like brewed coffee before it's cut with cream.

"Auntie, I got some news. If you're willin', some good folks are needin' a place to stay. The sheriff was hopin' they could live in your shack out back."

Ada rose from her comfortable porch chair and took a seat next to Ernest on the steps. She patted the young man's leg. "Why, Ernest, that old shed ain't hardly fit for mice."

"Auntie, for some a shack can seem like a palace."

Ada nodded and motioned for Ernest to tell her more.

"Eugene, Charlie, and Lester are lyin' about Emie. They threatened a Negro man, by the name of Justice. Told him if he didn't confess to hurtin' Emie that they would harm his family. Our girl got Justice to tell the sheriff the truth. He can't go home, Aunt Ada. It's not safe for him or his family. There's three of 'um: Justice, his wife, and daughter."

Before he could finish, Ada was on her feet heading toward the shed. Ernest quickly followed. It took a crowbar to pry the weathered door open. There were two small rooms; the back room contained old worn-out household furnishings, and the front room held rusted, used-up farm supplies. Together Ernest and Ada began the process of emptying the front room. It was slow going, but some progress had been made when Doc Bright, at the sheriff's request, arrived to help.

Ada welcomed the man, "Christian, what a pleasant surprise."

"Did you receive my thoughts, Ada?"

Blushing, she answered, "Now exactly what were those thoughts behind the jar of lightening bugs sittin' on my stoop this lovely morn?"

Doc reached for Ada's hand, "The same thoughts as they were all those years ago."

Ernest had heard about movies, where people went to a theatre and watched a big screen. He had never been to a movie himself, but imagined that it must be similar to what was transpiring between Doc Bright and Aunt Ada; a story was unfolding. He wasn't sure of the plot, but found himself cheering for a happily-ever-after ending.

In order to give the couple a moment of privacy, Ernest returned to the work at hand. Soon the good doctor was working alongside him. Ernest hoped that before the afternoon passed, Rudy would be joining their efforts. It would also do his heart a world of good to see Emie safely settled with Auntie.

Rudy was leading the brown mare named Betsy, as he and Emie walked across the swinging bridge toward Auntie Ada's home. "Emie, are you sure that you don't want to ride Betsy?"

"No. I'm enjoyin' the walk. I know it's slow goin', but it gives me time to think."

Rudy took hold of her hand. He was surprised at how smooth her skin felt. She was a farm girl accustomed to hard work, yet her hand felt soft to his touch. It made him conscious of his own rough skin and calloused palms. He almost drew his hand back, but the pleasure of his fingers entwined with Emie's overshadowed his embarrassment. "I'm both relieved and sorry that your mama and daddy didn't put up a fuss."

Rudy had been shocked that Alma and Ahab hadn't argued over Emie moving to Ada's cabin. Her daddy had basically said, "Good riddance," and her mama, though she shed a few tears, had said nothing to discourage Emie from packing.

Emie gently squeezed Rudy's hand. "It's okay. I wasn't expectin' it to be different. I know Ernest was worried, but I knew in my heart that they wouldn't want me to stay. It's the way of the holler. Girls are nothin'."

Rudy stopped walking; still holding her hand, he looked her in the face. The sun had shifted and was shining in his eyes; he had to squint in order to see her flushed cheeks. "Emie, it's not the way of everyone in the holler, just some."

She nodded in response and let go of his hand; she then took the lead rope from his other hand and walked Betsy the rest of the way across the bridge.

Deep in thought, Rudy slowed his pace. He wanted to comfort her, but he didn't know how. It seemed like he was walking in a foreign land, where an unknown language was spoken. Emie had been his friend for years, seeing her this way hurt him to the core. He cared for her, even loved her, and he knew that Ernest and Ada felt the same. Everyone who knew her enjoyed her kind nature and spunky spirit. How did he tell her about the affections of others, and even more complicated, how did he reveal his own heart?

When Emie turned and looked back at him, Rudy hurried to catch up with her. "Are you sure we got all you'll be needin'? Betsy's only carryin' a small parcel."

"That's all I got, Rudy."

He subconsciously frowned and shook his head in frustration. His family didn't have much, but they were better off than most. He knew from the condition of the Ashby residence that poverty was no stranger; in fact, he was certain that it had lived there for quite some time. He thought of the pile of empty feed sacks in the back of his daddy's store. His mama saved them for MayLou Robbins, who made clothes from the sacks for those in need. If he had a moment alone with Auntie Ada today, he would talk with her about making some things out of them for Emie. He knew his mama would help.

Misunderstanding the look on Rudy's face, Emie glanced downward and spoke quietly, practically whispering, "Don't pity me, Rudy."

He wanted to take her hand again, but he wasn't sure if he should or not. "Emie, why would I pity you? You're the sweetest, prettiest girl in the holler." He felt embarrassed by his words and looked down at the meadow grass, yet he was glad that he had spoken them.

For the most part, they continued their walk in silence. Occasionally, Rudy would inquire about Emie's well-being. Although they were taking it slow, he was concerned about her stamina. She always responded to his questions with a smile. "I'm just fine. Thanks for askin'."

They had walked some distance when Emie began sharing a story. "Last summer Daddy sent me outside to cut weeds in the ditch along the front of the house. I only had an ax to use. It was slow goin', but I stayed at it. I was tryin' to be real careful. Lester had just sharpened the head, and I didn't want to cut myself. The little girls were playin' in the road, and I got side tracked; I ended up cuttin' my big toe and bossy toe pretty bad."

Rudy cringed when he thought about how the accident must have pained her. He was also trying to figure out exactly what she was talking about. What the heck was a bossy toe?

As if reading his mind, Emie clarified, "Does anyone in your family have a bossy toe? You know, the second toe that's longer than the big toe..."

Rudy started laughing. He couldn't help it. "Well, Emie, I've heard of the big toe and the baby toe, but never the bossy toe..."

"Rudy, it's not funny. The bossy toe means that I'm bossy. In my family only Daddy has the bossy toe, but he's supposed to be the boss." She stopped, sat on the ground and started pulling off her shoes.

"Emie, what are you doin?"

"I'm showin' you what a bossy toe looks like. Mama told me when girls have bossy toes that they need to work extra hard at bein' nice, or no boy will want to marry 'um."

Still laughing, Rudy sat down next to Emie and began taking off his own shoes. If Emie was going to show her feet, he wanted to be part of the game. When she placed her foot close to him, he couldn't help but notice the deep scar running across the base of her big toe and second toe. He began to tickle her toes, bossy toes included. The two ended up lying in the grass, shoeless, howling with laughter.

When the laughter subsided, Rudy spoke softly to Emie, "I don't mind your bossy toes. In fact, I kind of like 'um."

"Why, thank you."

Rudy's thoughts began to wonder about the young woman next to him. He appreciated that she didn't hide her wounds, but at the same time, he worried that she was quick to diminish her pain. She had started to share her story of injury but hadn't addressed her own suffering. He began to pray silently, *"Lord, help Emie. Help her to grow in You. Touch the places in her life that hurt. Help Auntie Ada to soothe and comfort her."*

Emie was doing her own thinking. She reached over and pressed down on Rudy's forehead where his cowlick stood. When she released her hand, the tuft of hair popped back into the air. *It has a mind of its own, just like my friend*, Emie thought.

"What you doin', girlie?"

"Auntie Ada told me once that a cowlick meant that a person had a mind of his own and that his brain was so full of different ideas that the hair couldn't help but stand on end."

Rudy chuckled. "My mama told me that I was born in a barn just like Baby Jesus, and that Hannah, our big heifer, licked my forehead marking the spot where my hair would never lay right."

"Did she say anything about your red hair?" Emie asked light-heartedly.

"Mama said that a lick was like a kiss in Hannah's eyes, and that when the heifer kissed me, the angels in heaven gave me red hair."

Emie shyly looked at her friend, "I like your red hair and cowlick."

The two lay in the grass, eyes closed, enjoying the sunshine and slight breeze for a few more minutes before Emie continued her story. "My toes were cut bad, Rudy. I went into the house yellin' and cryin' like a baby. Mama was out back and came running. I could see the bone, but Daddy said to wrap my foot in rags and get back to work."

Rudy's heart ached. He wanted to cry for Emie. He wanted to give her daddy a punch in the mouth. He wanted to say something to comfort his friend, yet there were no words. He remembered his mama telling him once that with just a touch his daddy could comfort her, and set the world right. Rudy placed his hand on Emie's shoulder. He gazed over the meadow surrounding them and pondered life; there were always thorns among the roses.

After some time, the threesome continued their journey. When Rudy saw their destination ahead, he stopped briefly and looked at his friend once again. "Emie, may I come visit you at Auntie's?"

She embraced her childhood companion, "Ernest said that you would come, but I wasn't sure. Thanks for carin', Rudy. Come as often as you can."

Chapter Sixteen

"One cure for hiccups is to tickle the nose with a feather."
(Appalachian Folk Belief)

Rudy went to work right away helping Ernest and Doc Bright on the shed, which was now being referred to as "the little house," and Emie went in search of Auntie Ada. She found her in the small cabin kitchen preparing enough food to feed General Pershing's army! Emie had learned about the general in school. His actions during The Great War made him famous. In Emie's mind, Aunt Ada was just as famous; famous for her kind words and deeds. Auntie was in her element cooking and serving those the Lord brought into her life. She was singing hymns as she worked.

Emie's thoughts wandered, *Ernest sings when he's frustrated, and Auntie sings when she's happy. Maybe I'll sing my own song one day.*

Auntie greeted her with a firm, bosom-filled embrace. "Glad you're here, my darlin'. We're gonna get you right with the world again. Put your things on the back porch. That's your room."

"Auntie, I may be here for a long time. Mama and Daddy ain't wantin' me at home no more. I done shamed 'um."

"Nonsense. You ain't shamed a soul. The shame belongs to Eugene and his boy. This is your home now. We're a family – you and me, Emie."

While heading to her room, Emie soaked in Auntie Ada's words, "We're a family..." Auntie had always been family to Emie, but now more than ever she needed to live in the security a family should provide. She needed "good mornings" and "good nights" and all that fell in between. She felt celebrated with Auntie, not just tolerated – but celebrated. *Jesus, thank you. I'm takin' a bath in your mercy.*

Auntie had covered a cot with embroidered linens and a hand-sewn quilt, and placed it in the corner of the narrow room. There was even a soft pillow with crochet trim on the case. The room was decorated with willow baskets, dried flowers and herbs, and red clay pottery. The pottery had been fashioned by the hill people in the holler. It wasn't suitable for cooking or eating, but was beautiful to behold. Mama had always said, "Ain't no use for red pots. They just sit and gather dust. Can't be used for nothin'."

Emerald thought differently. Oh, she respected her mama's views, but things of beauty were important in the world. Sometimes just looking at something lovely is enough to make a person smile.

The porch had been covered for several years; Lester and Ernest, both in their teens at the time, had tackled Auntie's building project. Of course, Daddy had been consulted each evening about what should be done. The porch felt cozy to Emie. She wanted to lie down on her new bed and dream the rest of the day away, but at the same time she wanted to be with Auntie Ada. Her dreams weren't sweet anyway. They were of Charlie and what he had done. "Lord, help me to dream about beautiful things again," she softly prayed.

She placed her scarce personal belongs in two willow baskets that were on a tall, narrow stand in the opposite corner of her bed. The stand was also made from willow limbs. The baskets were among her favorite style that Auntie made. They were woven in an oval shape. Some of the willow saplings had been stripped of bark, while others remained dark in color. The contrast of color, along with the dried lavender stems and flowers that Auntie had included made such a display of artwork that Emie felt like she was muddying something beautiful with her raggedy hand-me-down clothing. Why, even her hair comb was missing half its teeth.

She turned to see Auntie Ada standing at the doorway. "Girlie, are you needin' a rest?"

"No, Auntie. I'm just admirin' my lovely room."

Emie and Ada spent the remainder of the afternoon cooking a feast. Auntie felt that Justice and his family should be welcomed in style. A table was set under the trees in the front yard and covered with a lace cloth. Emie gathered late spring wildflowers from the nearby field and placed them in Mason jars on the table and front porch. Auntie showed Emie her special jar that wasn't to be used. The young girl found her Aunt's instructions interesting, but with so much to be done, there wasn't time to ask questions.

Sometime during the late afternoon, MayLou arrived with her girls. They worked right alongside the men getting the little house ready.

By the time Sheriff Robbins arrived with Justice's wife and daughter, the shed had been transformed from a mere shack to a somewhat suitable home. The men had shored up the foundation and walls, and Auntie and Emie had decorated the two rooms with what furniture she could find and wild blooms and cones stuck into woven twigs from nature. Ernest put Rudy in charge of digging the new outhouse, which had made Emie laugh. Rudy, however, didn't seem to mind. Emie could see that he was happy working alongside Doc and Ernest. Each time she heard a raised pleasant voice or laughter from the little dwelling, she smiled.

Cece, who was Justice's wife, and Mercy, his daughter, were both lovely in form and heart. When Emie had thanked God earlier for His mercy, she had no idea that His wondrous gift would appear in body. Mercy was shy and spoke very little, while Cece babbled like a brook. Mercy reminded Emie of the willows that danced quietly in the breeze, and Cece brought reflections of Big Creek when it swelled under nature's watering. The flow would ripple and bubble over the rocks and limbs that dotted the creek.

When Justice arrived, just before dark, both Cece and Mercy ran to meet him. They clung to him like a vine growing up around the trunk of a tree. Emie thought they might squeeze the life from him. She couldn't help but stand and watch; she had never seen such affection among a family. They laughed, cried, jabbered and thanked the good Lord all at the same time. The kisses and hugs seemed a wonder. When Emie's heart became too wishful, she drug herself away from the reunion, and went to light the beeswax candles on the table.

At dinner, Emie sat between Rudy and Ernest. Auntie was right, she thought. Being here will set me right with the world and with heaven.

Emie went to sleep peacefully that night. Ada had insisted on tucking her in and saying prayers together. Emie felt like a small child. After Auntie kissed her forehead and turned down the oil lamp, Emie lay awake for only a few minutes listening to the crickets before sleep overcame her.

In the night, her rest was interrupted once again by dreams of Charlie. Only this time, it was Coral that Charlie was hurting. She noticed a flock of wood thrushes sat in their perches among the oaks and watched silently. Emie woke with a start, perspiration wetting her cotton gown. She lay awake praying for Coral, praying for all her sisters that God would be with them and take care of them. She thought of Coral smashed in the middle, and about the twins who would soon be married. She also thought about the little ones. What would the future hold for them?

It had always been extremely quiet at Auntie's cabin. So quiet at times that Emie could even hear her own heartbeat. When morning came, however, she woke to unfamiliar sounds. It seemed as if the whole holler was awake. She heard Ada and Justice talking outside her window, making plans on how to provide for their new community.

When Emie overheard that Ernest was bringing a couple hogs for Justice to tend, she jumped right out of bed. There were also supplies coming from Rudy's daddy's store. It seemed that Auntie wanted to add an extra room to the little house.

Emie found a robe and slippers that Auntie had placed at the foot of her bed. She had never owned a robe or night shoes before. The robe was cotton like her gown, and embroidered with bluebells. Emie was certain that Auntie had sown the robe, but the slippers were store bought. She almost hated to put them on. Mama had said that robes and slippers were for city girls and that they had no use in the holler.

While Emie hurriedly put on the robe and shoes, she heard Doc Bright's voice. He was insisting that he had little to do but help Ada today. He had brought an old weathered cart along with two mules for Justice to use. The two were named Amos and Andy, after the popular radio program. There was also an aged plow that the animals could pull. Justice planned to prepare the soil for a garden, and indicated that Cece and Mercy could do the planting. Doc promised to bring seeds on his next visit, which Emie knew would be soon, by the way the good doctor had been making cow eyes at Auntie.

Emie could tell by the sound of Aunt Ada's voice that she was enjoying every minute of her lively surroundings replacing her once quiet abode. Change was coming to Auntie's home, and she seemed to relish the new people and commotion. Emie quickly made her way to the outhouse. She noticed the warblers and swallows chirping like a sweet chorus in the surrounding oaks. She raced through her morning toiletries, dressed, and headed outside. She didn't want to miss any of the excitement, and was anxious to know her part in the grand scheme of things.

She was greeted by Ada first, "Girlie, go on and get your breakfast. I left some eggs on the stove. You and me has got business to tend to."

Justice nodded his good morning, and Doc Bright winked his greeting. Emie could see in the background that Cece was drawing water from the pump. It was quite early, maybe Mercy was still sleeping.

While Emie ate, Auntie discussed the needs of the day. "Now, darlin', I know you ain't much for workin' indoors, but today we got people we're needin' to feed. I've done made biscuit dough and started stew for lunch. Finish up what I started and then head to the fields and gather mustard greens. I know your mama taught you how to fix greens. I also got some apples in the cellar. I'm wantin' you to make a pie or two..."

Emie knew how to do all that Ada was asking. She'd just never done them all at once. On occasion, she would make a pie, and then on another occasion, she'd roll the biscuits, but what Auntie was asking her to do seemed too much to tackle in one morning. She started to question her Aunt's instructions, but before the words went from her mind to her mouth, Ada headed back outdoors.

Emie had no choice but to get busy. She punched the biscuit dough just like Mama had taught her. When the dough began to stick, she floured her hands. Mama had told her once, "Mess with the dough as little as possible, girlie. You don't want it too stiff. Your biscuits won't be good." But Emie couldn't help it. Every time she pounded the mixture on the flour board, she thought of Charlie.

When she started cutting the carrots, potatoes, onion, and celery for the stew, she thought of Pastor Eugene. She pictured herself telling Cousin Eugene what for. She thought about all his self-serving messages from the pulpit. She thought about how mean he had been to his wife, and how he'd taught his son lies. With her knife in hand, she felt like a Samurai. She had read about the Japanese fighters in her reader at school. She felt powerful. She just wished that her knife was longer. She had a small paring knife, but a Samurai used a sword with a length of two feet.

Right there in the kitchen, just for the joy of it, she started to dance the Charleston. "Take that, Charlie." When her leg kicked back for one of the steps, she shouted, "In your tallywacker..." She thought about what Charlie had said about her chest, and spoke her own insult out loud, "I've seen your thing, and it ain't much neither."

Even her walk through the field felt wonderful. With each step, she thought of Daddy and his manipulative ways. She felt she could trample all the lies that had been spoken to, and about, her.

When she found the patch of mustard greens, she made an effort to slow her movements; she didn't want to bruise the plants or damage the roots. She knew that Auntie Ada would pick greens all summer and into fall. She gathered what was needed for lunch, placed her bounty in a basket, and then twirled in the field. The sun was shining brightly. She felt the stirrings of freedom. She knew it would take time, but she felt hopeful today. She danced in circles and then fell to the ground dizzy. She sat and enjoyed the swirling of nature around her. When she regained her balance, Emie felt tears in her eyes. They were tears of grief, but also tears of expectation and tears of hope.

She watered the flowers next to her with tears. Ernest believed that God kept the tears of His children contained in bottles in heaven. If Ernest was right, she hoped when her life was through that the tears of joy outweighed the tears of sorrow.

Like the previous evening, lunch was shared under the large maple tree in the front yard. The day was warm and the tree offered needed shade. Emie was about to refill the water glasses, when Auntie asked Rudy to say grace. The water from the pump in the yard was cold. Auntie's well was deep. The day was hot, and everyone was thirsty. Rudy expressed thanks for the food and also for Emie's preparations. Emie blushed when Rudy mentioned her name in prayer. She was glad that everyone had their eyes closed in worship, so no one could witness her embarrassment.

As Emie refilled the glasses, the food was dished out. She enjoyed the sounds of silverware clinking on plates and the shared conversations that primarily centered around the morning's activities. Even shy Mercy smiled and added a few comments.

When the meal was winding down, Justice spoke. "Pastor Eugene says it ain't right for white and colored to eat together."

Doc Bright looked directly at Justice, "My friend, I disagree. I have certainly enjoyed sharing lunch with you and hope you feel likewise."

"I do," Justice answered. "Every few weeks the Pastor would travel up the holler and hold service just for the black folk. He said that the Lord's house in Big Creek was strictly for whites. He also said that we was the cursed people of Ham."

Emie could see that Auntie was winding up, but before she could speak, Ernest interjected. "Justice, did Eugene ever explain what he meant by the cursed people of Ham?"

"He said this and that. Mostly his opinions, I think. I can read some and I ain't never seen in the Bible nothin' about black folks bein' cursed."

Failing to hide her frustration, Auntie Ada glanced at Ernest. "Son, do you have any idea what Eugene would have been yammerin' about?"

"In the Bible, Ham was one of Noah's sons. He saw his daddy naked and brought his brothers to take a look."

Justice then added to Ernest's words, "Pastor Eugene said that Ham had dark skin. When the Good Lord punished him, he punished all black people makin' them less than the whites."

Auntie clicked her tongue in disgust. "My, my, my. I ain't never heard such nonsense. Punished 'em for what? And I ain't beholdin' to any of that foolishness. How would Pastor Eugene know if Ham was a different color from the rest? Was he there? I don't believe it's written as such. We're all a family now, and we'll eat together when and if we want."

Cece had talked all through lunch, but had become unusually quiet when Justice brought up Pastor Eugene. "Pastor Eugene also said that the colored ain't goin' to the same heaven as the whites because we ain't got a crown. Do you think that's true, Auntie?" Cece challenged.

"Now, I'm getting mad," Ada declared. "We're all goin' to the same heaven. None of us get our crowns till we get there, and then we throw 'em at Jesus' feet."

Doc Bright patted Ada's shoulder. He added his deep voice to the conversation. "Ignorant as his persuasions might be, I think Eugene could have been referring to a different type of crown. When babies are born, they all have a soft spot on their heads. It's doesn't matter if the baby is black or white. As the baby grows, the soft spot on the head comes together forming a crown. Every person is born with a crown on their head. Now with some people, depending on the way their hair grows the crown isn't as visible."

Ada stood up from the table. "We're a family now, and we ain't buyin' into any of this foolishness. Ernest, I'm wantin' you to lead us in a song, and then we're goin' take hands and pray. Around this table we're all equal like the good Lord intended."

Chapter Seventeen

"It's bad luck to bathe on your wedding day."
(Appalachian Folk Belief)

Emie couldn't believe that it was Sapphire and Ruby's wedding day. The past month had flown by like the ruby-throated humming birds that visited Auntie's lavender and black-eyed Susans, and royal blue lobilia in the flower and herb garden each afternoon. The extra room had been added to the little house. Though Amos and Andy proved difficult to handle, the garden had been tilled and planted. Ernest was even holding reading and writing lessons for Cece and Mercy. Cece had never been to school, and Mercy's prior lessons had been few and far between. Auntie's enlarged family was flourishing.

At times, Emie even felt like her old self. Auntie had taught her how to make jelly from the already ripe blackberries. She had also taught her how to make honey butter and candles from the bees' bounty. With each skill learned, there was a spiritual application. While separating the seeds from the berries, Auntie spoke about getting rid of sin in your life. Making honey butter included a lesson on how God's Word should be blended and part of everyday living. The candle making taught spiritual truths on being a witness for Christ. There were also lessons on making soap, kneading bread, and stitching finery.

Auntie even shared with Emie how to make the special willow baskets that she so admired. Emie wove the saplings until her fingers bled. Auntie moistened old rags for Emie to dab her fingers. "Girlie, you need tough skin to live in this world. People are gonna do and say things that hurt."

Auntie and Emie prayed while weaving their baskets. At first, they prayed for simple things of the heart, and then for more complex matters like Lester, Pastor Eugene, and even Charlie. During those times, when Emie could hardly voice her prayers, Aunt Ada patted her hand, "God listens to all prayers, darlin', even the ones too painful to be sayin' out loud."

Rudy often came to visit. His daddy was interested in selling the goods that she and Auntie made. Emie was excited about earning a little money. She wanted to contribute financially to her new family, but Auntie cautioned that time would tell what the good Lord had in mind.

As Emie dressed for the wedding, she thanked God for Auntie and her kindness. "Where would I be if Aunt Ada hadn't taken me in?"

Emie wasn't invited to the wedding. In fact, Ernest had brought word from Mama and Daddy that she wasn't to attend. Ernest wanted to boycott the wedding, but agreed with Emie that it wasn't fair to punish Sapphire and Ruby for their mama and daddy's hard-heartedness. Auntie and Ernest came up with a plan; Emie was to view the wedding camouflaged by a grove of trees. She wouldn't be able to hear Pastor Eugene's words, which suited her just fine. She was just happy to witness everything that took place. Emie sent a gift with Ernest for each sister, a new willow basket filled with the special things that Auntie had taught her to make. Aunt Ada made Emie a fancy dress for the wedding, and Ernest promised to bring her a piece of cake from the celebration following the ceremony. Emie hoped it was the white cake with the buttercream icing that she loved.

Emie slipped the new dress over her head, but struggled to fasten the buttons in the back. The dress had been dyed from the blackberry mush that wasn't suitable for making jelly. She went looking for Ada and found her in her room getting ready for the wedding.

Auntie helped Emie button her dress. "Emie, my darlin',

you've been eaten' good since you got here. You've put a little meat on your thin frame. You're a beauty, that's for sure."

Emie helped Auntie in turn with her zipper. Ada had a store-bought dress that Doc had gifted her. The ladies both looked exceptionally lovely when their escorts arrived.

Doc Bright was taking Auntie to the wedding, and Rudy was going with Emie to watch the ceremony from afar.

As the guests took their seats, Rudy and Emie watched from the trees. The service had yet to start when they heard a rustle behind them. Emie feared that Daddy had gotten word she was watching, and had sent someone to chase her and Rudy away. When the two friends turned toward the noise, they found Lester standing in the shadow of the trees. Emie jumped with fear, and Rudy bowed out his chest ready to fight, though Lester was one and again his size.

"Ain't no need to be afraid, sister. I ain't here to harm you or Rudy." Lester held his head down as he spoke. "I'm here to apologize and beg your forgiveness."

The eldest Ashby brother then approached Emie and knelt low before her, taking hold of her slender ankles. "I ain't much of a brother, and I don't deserve your forgiveness, but what I did was wrong. I'm full of shame, Emie. I lied about you, my own flesh and blood."

Emie was too stunned to answer, and Rudy stood back with his fists still clenched, ready to fight; neither one was able to grasp what was taking place.

Lester began to cry, not trickles of tears, but sobs of regret. "I'm full of sin. The shame won't leave me. Ernest said that God could help, but I guess I'm just too far gone."

Lester then began to confess his sins of drinking, carousing, hating, lying, and cheating. Emie remained silent, while Rudy knelt beside Lester, placing his arm around his shoulders. "Lester, tellin' your bad deeds is for the Lord to hear."

Lester grew quiet and then spoke softly, "Show me, Rudy. Show me how to be right with God."

Under the canopy of trees, with Emie watching, Rudy shared

the simple plan of salvation. "Lester, no one can forgive your sins but God. He sent His Son, Jesus, to die on the cross. His love and grace is greater than anythin' you ever done, includin' the way your hurt Emie. I'll be your witness, Lester. Just ask Him to forgive your sins, and tell Him that you will try and live right. Do you want to pray?"

When Lester nodded yes, the younger man, with a heart like David, prayed for the older boy who had once had a heart like Saul. When the two finished praying, Rudy took his treasured piece of scarlet cloth from his pocket, and placed it in Lester's hands. "This will remind you that the blood of Jesus took away your sins."

While Lester and Rudy sat among the trees talking, Emie watched the wedding ceremony. Her heart was divided in two. She wanted to hear what Rudy was telling Lester about God, yet she didn't want to miss this special moment in the lives of the twins. As soon as the kissing was over, she redirected her attention to her brother and friend, and went and sat with them under the shade of a tree.

Lester spoke first, "I already told you that I was sorry, Emie, but I'm needin' to tell you again. What I did with Charlie was wrong, but there were also other times when I didn't treat ya right. Please, sister, I'm begging to know, can you forgive me?"

Emie was moved by Lester's repentance. His tears of faith brought moisture to her own eyes. Tenderness for her brother crept into her astonished heart. She spoke no words, but embraced Lester long and hard. In her mind, she was living what she had witnessed between Justice and his family; there were tears, laughter, and prayers all exchanged at once.

Emie only let go of her brother when he told her that it was time for him to leave.

"Girlie, I'm needin' to leave the holler."

Emie raised her voice, "No, no, Lester, not now…"

"I have to. I've some things I'm needin' to make good. 'Sides I can't stay here and do right by God. Daddy, Eugene, and Charlie will pull me back into trouble."

"I'll help you. So will Ernest and Rudy," Emie pleaded.

"Sister, I know who I am. I can't stay. Sin will call me back, and I'm not strong enough to say 'no.' While everyone is celebratin' the wedding, I'm gonna plow the corn field under that Charlie and me planted. Then, I'm gonna visit Mrs. Randolph. Maybe her family in Charleston can help me get started new."

"What about me? What about Ernest and the girls?" Emie cried.

"God be with you, Emie, and with me. I'm trustin' your care to Ernest and Rudy. I promise in time we'll be together again." Lester turned to leave. "I'll try and find Ernest before I go. If not, please tell him what happened and thank him for bein' a good brother."

Emie didn't say a word. She couldn't. She simply nodded yes.

Rudy wiped her tears with his fingers, took her hand, and escorted her home. They sat together on the front porch of the cabin. "Emie, I'm thinkin' we need to give thanks for what just happened."

She bowed her head, while Rudy prayed. She was distraught at the thought of Lester leaving, but at the same time admired her brother's new found wisdom.

After their prayer, Emie excused herself. She went to her room and quickly found the piece of red cloth that MayLou had passed to Ernest. She tore it in two and returned to the front porch. She sat down next to Rudy on the steps and placed the torn piece in his hand. As Emie held his hand, she prayed her own words of thanksgiving, "Lord, thank you for saving Lester. Thank you also for my friend, Rudy."

After a bit, Justice joined them. Cece and Mercy were working on their lessons. When Justice heard about Lester calling on Jesus, he raised his hands and with his deep baritone voice also gave thanks to God.

Doc Bright and Ada arrived soon after. Auntie rejoiced in her own way with both words and tears. "What a day it's been!"

Rudy sat on one side of Emie and Auntie on the other. Ada kissed Emie on the cheek. "Darlin', God has answered our weaving prayers."

Emerald smiled and thought to herself, "Someday I need to tell

Coral that it's not so bad being sandwiched in the middle." She was enjoying the feel of Rudy on one side and Auntie on the other.

Ernest arrived just after dark. He found Emie and Ada sitting in the parlor. Ada was sipping tea and working on stitchery. Emie was writing in her journal. Auntie had encouraged Emie to keep a record of God's healing presence in her life, and in the lives of those living in the holler. Her entry for the day was long and detailed. She didn't want to forget a single moment.

Ernest bowed before his sister, presenting her with a piece of wedding cake. "The weddin' was nice, wasn't it? The twins send their thanks for the baskets and all…"

Emie saw a twinkle in Ernest's eye and the pleasure on his face. She knew he had visited with Lester. She also knew that Ernest would try to hold out on sharing just to tease her.

"How was your day, Emie?"

"Just fine, Ernest," she said, playing along with her brother's antics. "You looked mighty nice at the weddin'. Did it give you any ideas about findin' your own girl?"

"Now, Emie, you know I got all the girls I need in my life, between you and Auntie, my hands are full."

Ada looked back and forth between the two siblings, and smiled. "The two of you do my heart good, but I'm wantin' you to quit the banter. You're like two puppies yappin' and playin'. I'm wantin' to talk about Lester."

"I was just waitin' for someone to ask," Ernest spoke as he took a seat on the floor in front of the two ladies he loved, the braided rug acting as his cushion. "Lester found me right after the weddin'. When we were boys we had a special whistle. I heard the whistle and couldn't believe it. He was hidin' off to the side. I just followed the direction of the whistle."

Emie leaned closer to her brother anticipating what he would say next.

"He told me about Rudy prayin' with him. He then asked for my forgiveness. Said he hadn't been a good brother. He also told me about the mischief he and Charlie were doin'."

"Does he have to leave the holler?" Emie asked.

Ernest comforted his sister by placing his hand on her knee. "I don't want him to go neither, but it's best, Emie. Lester knows he's always been led astray by Charlie. There might be trouble brewin', girlie. He ain't wantin' no one to know where he is right now, especially Charlie, Eugene, and daddy. Lester promised to write us. He's gonna write to Doc Bright, who will pass along his letters to Auntie."

Ernest squeezed Emie's knee reassuringly, smiled, and turned toward Aunt Ada. "Now, Auntie, I am wantin' to know about them lightnin' bugs that keep showin' up on your front porch," Ernest jokingly asked.

"I love you both with all my heart, but some things are meant to be kept secret," Ada answered with a secretive twist to her face. "Now, why don't you two go out and gather us some of those showy white service berry branches to decorate our table?"

"Auntie, if you love us both with all your heart, tell me what's left for the good doctor?" Ernest replied.

Ada softly smiled and continued sipping her tea.

Chapter Eighteen

"Cut briars and trees when the moon is waning to kill them."
(Appalachian Folk Belief)

Toward the end of the following week, Ada called a family meeting. Everyone was to attend, including Doc Bright, Ernest, and Rudy. Though the three men didn't live at Auntie's, she considered them family and felt they should be included.

Emie's curiosity piqued as she assisted Auntie in preparing refreshments for the meeting, but despite her questions, Auntie remained close-lipped about what was to be discussed. "Emie, darlin', you're as curious as a kitten."

Emie smiled, "Aunt Ada, this ain't the first time someone's told me that."

While the small community gathered under the maple tree, Emie served cold tea sweetened with honey, and homemade oatmeal cookies sprinkled with cinnamon.

Doc Bright opened in prayer, and then Auntie began the discussion, "Justice talked with me yesterday evenin' about a difficulty. Along with Cece, we've come to an agreement, but still felt it best that each person have a say."

Justice then spoke up, "My sister is married to a mean man. He drinks and beats her. They have four boys: Adam, Beau, Claude, and Dean. I won't lie to ya, they is naughty boys. My sister gets so mad at 'um that she can't even remember their names. She's went to callin' 'um one, two, three, and four. A friend from further up the holler heard I was here and paid me a visit. Said my sister's husband done run off, and she's headed after him, leavin' them boys to fend for themselves. It ain't no good. The oldest is twelve and the littlest one six."

"They ain't never been to school and had no discipline. They's ornery. Stretch your patience for sure," Cece contributed.

"I'm worried. Yes, I am," Justice continued.

Auntie Ada waved her hand and got everyone's attention. Her fingers were clutched around a white handkerchief trimmed in blue crocheted lace that she delicately used to wipe the glisten from her brow. "I don't think we have a choice but to help these boys. I believe they're needin' to come and live here."

"Where they gonna sleep and how we gonna fed 'um?" Mercy quietly asked.

Justice put his arm around his daughter. "Now, sissy, your mama, me, and Auntie have some ideas. We're thinkin' we should add to the back of the little house again. Givin' you a room and a bedroom for the boys. Our garden's doin' good. We got plenty of berries and apples. We'll slaughter one of them pigs, and believe the Lord for the rest. You're a child yourself; you don't need to be worryin'."

Everyone seemed to get excited at once. Emie, who had been missing her little sisters, couldn't wait to meet the boys. Rudy thought his daddy might help with some supplies from the store, and Ernest was certain he could bring over a couple more piglets for raising, and even discussed teaching the boys basic schooling. Doc Bright was the only one who remained quiet.

"Christian, is there somethin' you're needin' to say?" Ada asked.

"It's not about the boys coming to stay, Ada. I'm worried about how Justice's friend knew that he and his family were living here." Doc Bright paused and then looked at Justice, "Did your friend say how he found you?"

"No, sir," Justice responded. "I didn't think much about it at the time, but Doc, you're right to be worried. Maybe we need to be callin' for the sheriff."

"I agree," Ada added. "But before we send for Sheriff Robbins, let's make a choice about them boys comin' to live here at least for a time."

A consensus was quickly reached that the four brothers should join their extended family. Rudy headed to town to get the sheriff, and Ernest quickly headed back to the Ashby residence to gather some grain that Justice needed for the pigs and Amos and Andy. He wanted to return to Auntie's before the sheriff arrived. He was concerned about the safety of those he loved. He hoped that Sheriff Robbins had an explanation for how Justice was so easily found.

Ernest was also thinking about paying a visit to Mrs. Randolph later in the day. He needed pencils, writing tablets, and hopefully readers to assist the boys in their learning.

While Auntie, Justice, and Cece were making plans, Doc Bright invited Emie and Mercy to take a stroll. The girls quickly responded to the doctor's invitation, and the threesome headed toward Big Creek.

"Girls, it's always a pleasure to visit with both of you, but the reason for our walk today has a greater meaning. I want to arrange something special for Ada and need your help," Doc Bright shared.

What he had in mind sounded very romantic to Emie: a small table under the maple tree covered with lace and adorned with candles and flower petals. The doctor also wanted jars of fireflies to light the pathway from the cabin to the tree canopy. Mercy agreed to gather the miracle insects and promised to poke holes in the lids of the jars.

"From the time Ada and I started courting, until I left for school, I would often leave a jar of lightening bugs near her front door, and then in the mornings, she would release them unharmed back to nature," Doc revealed. "God gave fireflies a special light to attract their mates. It was my way of telling Ada that I loved her, and believed that she was the one God gave me to marry."

Emie now understood the mystery surrounding Auntie's special jar.

Mercy and Emie helped Doc Bright with the final arrangements. Mercy was in charge of decorating and Emie preparing the meal.

When they arrived at the creek, Emie sighed. It felt good to visit the willows and water. She felt like the willows sighed with her, as if they shared her secret, and that the stream carried away her troubles. As excited as she was to help the good doctor, she worried that because of what Charlie had done to her that no one, if they knew the truth, would ever go to so much trouble for her.

Big Creek had a calming effect not only for Emie, but for Mercy and Doc as well. The doctor sat at the base of a willow lost in thought, and Mercy joined Emie in bathing her feet in the stream.

The trio could have enjoyed the remainder of the afternoon at the banks of Big Creek, but all were concerned about what Sheriff Robbins would have to say regarding Justice's visitor. The warmth of the day pulled them to rest and dream by the water, but worry called them back to Auntie Ada's meadow home.

"I was worried this would happen," Sheriff Robbins spoke up. "It ain't no secret that Emie's living with Auntie, so some commotion was expected, but there's been too much haulin' of goods and food for people not to notice there was more goin' on."

The sheriff drew in the dirt with his foot. "I made some inquiries before headin' your way. People are puttin' two and two together about Justice and his family. It's just a matter of time before Charlie and Eugene hear what's happened."

The sheriff then looked at Ernest, "It's my understandin' that your brother's left town. None too soon as far as I'm concerned."

Ernest wanted to defend Lester, but knew in his heart that the sheriff had every right to be relieved that his brother had left the holler. It always amazed him, even as a child, how news could spread through the hills. He had fallen out of a tree when he was ten. Lester had dared him that he couldn't reach the top. The fall had knocked him unconscious. Before the day was through, it seemed like half the town knew about his injury.

Ernest could tell by Sheriff Robbins' mannerisms that he was worried.

"I'm thinkin' we just need to be extra careful," the lawman spoke. "Everyone needs to stay close to home. If trouble comes this way, don't be foolish. Keep clear headed. If need be, fire some shots in the air, but don't be aimin' to hurt anybody."

Ernest considered all that the sheriff said. He knew if trouble came it would be in the form of the local pastor and his son. It was just a matter of time before someone with bad intentions showed up on Auntie's doorstep.

Ernest whispered "goodbye" to Emie and told Aunt Ada that he would be back before nightfall. He felt the need to pray. He also turned and waved to Mercy.

Ernest thought of her coy smile as he headed to his favorite praying spot, a group of trees on the other side of Lester and Charlie's cornfield. True to his word, Lester had tilled the field under. He had even taken a sledge hammer to the still.

The grove had been struck by lightning several years back. Some of the trees had burned to the ground, while others remained standing, singed on one side or the other. The grass below the trees was green and lush. Ernest thought that it was just like God to use fire from heaven to bring new growth.

The Lord had been speaking to Ernest about a number of issues lately. He hadn't heard an audible voice, but in his heart he recognized the workings of God. Like the trees burned to the ground, some of Ernest's plans had gone up in flames, others had been singed. His dreams didn't look the same any more. He knew he needed to draw near to God; he needed understanding on what he was to do next.

He had thought about seeking the advice of Auntie, Mrs. Randolph, or even Doc Bright, but also knew that the concerns of his heart could only be understood by his Creator. He longed to teach, to educate, but knew he couldn't leave Big Creek and head to Charleston. Mrs. Randolph had worked so hard to prepare him for teaching school, but how could he leave Emie, or any of his sisters for that matter? He was also worried about Mercy. He didn't want to discontinue their sessions together. She was so eager to learn. Her reading and writing skills had improved greatly. She was ready to explore science, history, and math, and what about the four new arrivals coming to Auntie's home?

He worried about his future, and also worried about the future of those he loved, the ones he had loved for years, and the new faces that he was growing to love.

When he came across a fallen log toward the center of the copse, he sat down. He felt surrounded by the presence of God. He began to pray, so much was on his heart. He struggled to express himself. He felt the Spirit of God rising up within him, a presence bubbling over from his inward being to his throat and then his mouth. He stood on his feet and raised his hands, all the while his voice of worship grew louder, seeming to echo through the hills.

Time lost all measure as Ernest worshipped and prayed. His body rocked in the wind. Though his eyes were closed, he saw a picture, a vision from God. Ernest was standing in the midst of colored children, teaching them how to read and write. He was laying his hands on them and telling them about Jesus.

Ernest began to question his Savior, "How, when, where?"

He sensed the Lord saying, *Peace; be still.*

Ernest lay face down on the ground. God had revealed a portion of what was to come, but for now the plans were for him and his Creator alone. He somehow understood that he wasn't to share with anyone, just yet, what the Lord had shown him.

Numbers one, two, three, and four arrived at Auntie's in the early afternoon. They were a rowdy group alright! Within an hour Ada had set boundaries that the boys were not permitted in her home without permission.

It was early summer and the nights were warm, so Justice spent the day setting up a canopy for the boys to sleep under. Cece and Mercy did their best to keep the boys corralled. Finally, Cece gave up and told the foursome to run wild through the hills, and if a bear or mountain lion ate one of 'em, the others should let her know.

When Ernest arrived back at Aunt Ada's, the boys were trying to ride Amos, or maybe Andy, he wasn't sure. Ernest quickly gathered the troublemakers, and worked with them on writing numbers in the dirt.

Mercy joined him, bringing sliced apples and brown bread for the boys to enjoy. "They're somethin', ain't they?"

"Your mama and daddy will get them right in no time, Mercy."

"Thanks for helpin' me with my lessons, Ernest," the younger woman quietly spoke.

"It's my pleasure. You're so far along that you can help me work with the boys."

Mercy looked surprised. "Really? I'm not sure I know enough to teach these naughty boys anything."

The two shared a moment of laughter before their attention was diverted back to Adam, Beau, Claude, and Dean and their mischief. Ernest was glad that their mama had seen fit to name them in alphabetical order. It would help when he started to teach them their letters, but it also made it easier for him to remember their names.

Chapter Nineteen

"If two people's hoes hit together, they will
work in the field together next year."
(Appalachian Folk Belief)

As summer pushed onward, the days and nights grew warmer. The boys were still sleeping under the canopy that Justice built, but soon the bedroom construction would be finished. God had been gracious to Auntie's extended family. The garden was bountiful.

MayLou had made new clothes for Emie, Mercy, and the boys. Rudy often brought goods from his daddy's store, and Mrs. Randolph had provided needed school supplies.

Emie was healing. She laughed daily at the antics of the four boys. Under Cece's watchful eye, and Justice's loving yet firm hand, Adam, Beau, Claude, and Dean were adjusting to their new home. Justice believed that a pat on the back was a mere few inches from a kick in the pants. With the extra mouths to feed, dirty clothes, and mothering of four rambunctious boys, Cece had been forced to cut back on her schooling. Faithful Ernest worked with Mercy and the foursome.

Ernest seemed to thrive during his school time with Mercy and the boys. He spent so much time at the cabin that Auntie wondered how he was keeping up with his chores at home.

Ernest had shared with her privately that things weren't going well at the Ashby residence. "Daddy knows that Lester has left the holler. He's takin' out his frustrations on Mama and the girls."

Auntie was concerned about Alma and the girls, but she was also worried about Ernest. "How's he treatin' you, my boy?"

"He's treadin' carefully. Daddy knows that he needs me to run the farm and tend the hogs. With Lester gone, I'm doin' the best I can. Rudy's been helpin' me some."

"Good. Rudy's a fine boy. Spends quite a bit of time with our girl. She's needin' friends right now. Between Rudy, Mercy, and them ornery boys, she's been busy." Auntie embraced Ernest. "I ain't told ya, but thank you for sleepin' on the porch each night."

Since the sheriff's warning, Ernest had been coming after dark and staying at Auntie's until just before sunrise. His love aunt made a pallet each night on the wooden porch slats. She wanted him to sleep inside, but if trouble came Ernest wanted to be aware sooner than later. He enjoyed the mornings that Doc delivered fireflies. The two men would always take a few minutes to visit.

Ernest held his aunt longer than what was necessary. "I'm just glad we ain't had problems. I'm wantin' to bring a pup over in a few weeks. Sadie dropped her litter. The puppies will keep the boys entertained, and in time, also let us know if trouble's comin.'"

Auntie agreed that it was a good idea. "Let's give one to the boys and one to our girl. She can keep the pup with her on the back porch at night."

"Why, Auntie Ada, I ain't never known you to have a dog inside."

"She's still havin' bad dreams, Ernest. Maybe a dog will soothe her."

As the end of July drew near, Ernest sensed that change was coming. He wasn't sure what all it entailed, but knew that something was amiss. He had fallen asleep the night before praying for Emie. Ernest knew her road to recovery would be long and difficult. The rape had stolen her innocence. Every once in a while he saw a glimpse of who she was before Charlie attacked her, but for the most part it seemed as if her childhood had gone missing. She enjoyed watching the boys play and laughed at their antics, but rarely joined in the foolery.

Ernest woke one morning to the sound of Doc's voice. "Sorry to wake you, son. Would you please give Emie and Mercy a message for me? Tell them that tonight is the night. They'll understand."

Ernest stretched and yawned.

"Are you awake enough to remember, Ernest?"

The young man sat up from his make-do bed. "I'll remember."

Ernest folded his blankets and laid them on the porch rocker. He also rolled the thin mat that served as his mattress and stuck it behind the rocker. He knew that Auntie would refresh his linens today. When he went to bed tonight, they would smell like the West Virginia sunshine. He also knew that Aunt Ada would be faithful in leaving him a nighttime snack. He was eating at home and at Auntie's. His arms and chest were filling out. It felt good to go to bed with a full stomach.

He headed around the back of the cabin and knocked gently on Emie's window. It was still early, and he didn't want to disturb Aunt Ada. He knocked repeatedly before Emie heard the soft taps.

His sister looked surprised and pulled back the curtain on the bedroom window. "Ernest, what are you doin'? The sun ain't even up."

"Wakin' my lazy sister."

Emie rolled her eyes.

Ernest couldn't help but smile. "Good mornin' to you too, grumpy."

"Good mornin'," she said with mild annoyance.

"Sorry to wake you, girlie, but Doc Bright wanted me to give you and Mercy a message: 'Tonight's the night.'" Ernest repeated.

Emie nodded, closed the window and climbed back in bed. Even with her beloved brother, it was too early to carry on a conversation.

As Ernest made his morning trek back to Daddy, Mama, and his little sisters, he prayed. He prayed in the meadow for Justice, Cece, and the boys. He prayed on the swinging bridge for Auntie and Emie. He prayed for Rudy and Doc in the apple orchard, and for Mercy as he approached the back door of the Ashby home.

His mama was already up and working in the kitchen. "All well at Ada's?"

"Seems so," Ernest responded.

"Your daddy is mighty upset about Lester. Do you know anything that might ease his mind?"

Ernest sighed, not a sigh of frustration, but a sigh of sorrow, sorrow for his mama, his sisters, and even for his daddy. Over the past few weeks, his heart had begun to shift. His anger toward his parents was subsiding, and as it diminished, he was experiencing a measure of compassion. He was also experiencing a newfound peace and freedom personally. He took the responsibility of caring for sisters to heart, but had reached the realization that his parents, who were adults, had to come to terms with their own lives. He couldn't protect his mama and he couldn't control his daddy. "Mama I don't know where Lester is. I told both you and Daddy all I know. I'm sorry that I can't be of more help."

Alma turned her attention back to the food on the stove. "Son, your dad is in a bad way. I'm keepin' the girls away and doin' the best I can, but I'm scared."

With her back still turned, Ernest hugged her. He had previously said all there was to say. He hoped that that his embrace brought her some degree of comfort.

Emie and Mercy spent the afternoon preparing for Aunt Ada and Doc's special evening. The table had been laid with Auntie's best dishes and silverware. Mercy had included the candles and flower petals that Doc Bright and the girls had agreed upon, and lined the walkway from the cabin porch to the maple tree with mason jars containing fireflies.

Emie, who had been placed in charge of the food, made Auntie's favorites: roasted chicken with new red potatoes, greens lightly dressed with apple cider vinegar, sugared carrots, and oatmeal cake for dessert. She had even convinced the foursome to help her churn ice cream. As thanks, each boy was served a small dish of vanilla sweetness.

Auntie donned her best dress; the one Doc had purchased for

her. She was anxiously waiting in the living room for what was to happen next. Emie and Mercy had been close-mouthed about the evening's events, only telling her that Doc was preparing a special surprise for her. Ernest had been instructed that Doc Bright would keep watch that evening, and Cece and Justice had promised to entertain the boys inside the small house, with hopes that the couple would have a quiet evening to themselves.

When Mercy gave the signal, three firm raps on the front door, Emie escorted Aunt Ada to the front porch. Christian met her with his arm extended and led her through the lighted walkway to the small table under the tree. There was a full moon. Auntie's gray head was illuminated by light from above. It looked like a halo was resting on her curls.

Emie and Mercy served the meal, and then retired to the kitchen with their own thoughts of moonlight, candlelight, and firefly light.

Outside the couple enjoyed the heavenly light, the glow of the candles, and the lightning bugs turning on and off like the light switches from the city that the people in the holler had heard about.

Ada took hold of her suitor's hand, "Christian, thank you for a lovely evening."

"My pleasure," the man replied. "Ada, I don't want to waste any more time courting you. I loved you long ago and still love you. I want you to be my wife."

She kissed his check.

"Am I to believe that with your kiss you're saying 'yes' to my proposal?" he inquired.

"I am wantin' to marry you, but I need to explain a couple things. I don't want there to be any secrets between us."

Christian nodded in agreement.

He was a patient man. He had waited this long for his bride, he could endure a little longer. Ada was taking her time in sharing her secrets. He knew that his intended was talking with God before she talked with him.

"All those years ago, when I turned from you, it was because I saw my mama layin' with another woman. I was frightened and confused. I've never told anyone what I saw…"

The doctor stood, lifted Ada to her feet, and then held her.

She whispered in his ear, "My mama saw me that day, and told my daddy the truth. Not long after that mama left the holler with her woman friend. After all these years, Christian, I still ain't sorted things through."

"Ada, you may never understand all that took place, but that shouldn't keep us from building a life together. We've wasted a lot of years, and I don't want another year to pass before we are living side-by-side as husband and wife."

She pulled back from their embrace. "I'm old and I've never been with a man."

"I assumed as much, and you're not that old, Ada."

"I'm sixty-two and you're a little older."

"I know our ages, sweetheart."

Christian helped Ada sit down, took the ring from his pocket and knelt before the woman he loved.

Before he could speak, Ada interrupted, "Christian, I have one more thing to tell you…"

Mildly frustrated, he took his seat once again.

"It's Emie," Ada spoke. "She hasn't had her menses since she got here."

"Are you sure, sweetheart?"

"I'm sure." Ada responded. "I would know. She'd be needin' some things to help."

"Are you saying she's pregnant, Ada?"

"I'm not sure. She's also put on some weight, and she got sick this mornin' when I was fryin' pork fat."

"Do you think she suspects anything?"

Ada shrugged her shoulders. "I don't think so. She don't know much, Christian. Sex is a mystery to her as much as it is to me."

"Not for long," the good doctor chuckled.

Ada blushed. "You won't just be marryin' me, but you'll also be marryin' Emie and a maybe a baby."

"She'll be the daughter we never had, and her baby will be our grandbaby to dote on and love."

The couple sealed their commitment to each other with a kiss and an engagement ring. The ring had belonged to Christian's grandmother. The slim gold band held a reddish yellow topaz that reminded Ada of the lightening bugs that she so dearly loved. As their evening drew to a close, Christian and Ada went jar to jar releasing the fireflies that Mercy had captured earlier.

Chapter Twenty

"For a good crop of watermelons, crawl through the patch backwards."
(Appalachian Folk Belief)

The following afternoon, Emie sat on her bed reading the Good Book. She often read her Bible, but especially on a day like today, when she was feeling out of sorts; the words brought her comfort.

In third grade each student had been presented with a Bible from Mrs. Randolph. The teacher had written in the front of every book, "When you read these ancient words, what you read becomes part of you." The third graders then spent the remainder of the year memorizing verses. At the end of the school year, the student with the most verses committed to memory won a plaque. Rudy won, and then Mimi and Emie tied for second place.

Rudy had memorized long, long passages. His grandpappy, who was a minister, had helped him. Mimi and Emie had looked for the shortest verses they could find. The first one they memorized was John 11:35, "Jesus wept."

Emie was drawn back from her memories by Aunt Ada's voice, "Darlin', where are you?"

As the young girl started to rise from her cot, Ada appeared at the back porch door.

"Are you needin' a lolly, girlie?" the love aunt asked.

"Lolly" was a unique and special word from Auntie's

childhood. Ada claimed that a lolly or an afternoon nap was a sweet and delicious as a lollipop from Rudy's daddy's store.

"I'm a little tired. I ain't feelin' quite like myself," Emie answered.

Out of concern, Ada pressed further, "Can you tell me what's ailin'?"

"I can't put my finger on it," Emie said, looking puzzled. "My tummy seems to be turnin' quite a bit, and smells are botherin' me. This mornin' the boys smelled a might bad. They'd been wrestling out by Amos and Andy and rolled in somethin'. I lost my breakfast out by the corral."

Ada took a seat next to Emie on the small bed. She silently prayed for wisdom. She wasn't sure what to say or how to say it.

Emie continued, "Mama always said that Ernest and Lester smelled like mules, but they never made me lose my insides."

Auntie patted Emie's leg. "Darlin', you know how babies is made, right?"

"Of course," Emie smiled. "I'm fifteen and grew up on a farm."

Ada paused for a moment. "Girlie…" was all she could get out before Emie began to shake her head and cry emphatically, "No, no, no…"

The older woman drew the young woman close and held her. Ada didn't say a thing. She allowed Emie time to cry and think.

After a few minutes, Emie withdrew from her aunt's embrace. "What Charlie did to me, Auntie, couldn't have made a sweet baby! He was rough and mean. He said ugly things to me. He was on me, then off quick like. No baby should be made that way. It ain't right."

"No, it ain't right, but sometimes babies come anyway, darlin'."

"I can't be havin' a baby, Auntie. I know I act like I want to be all growed up, but in my heart I'm not."

Emie knew that Aunt Ada loved Doc Bright and wouldn't keep secrets from him. "What does Doc think?"

Ada tried to comfort Emie with a smile. "You know, he asked me to marry him. I told him that he'd have to marry you and maybe a baby, too."

"Does he think there might be a baby?"

"He's not sure, my girl." Ada took Emie's small hand in her weathered, wrinkled one, and spoke to her in a soothing voice. "Emie, do you understand that a monthly menses is a body's way of sayin' there's no baby? I know you ain't had your bleedin' since you been here."

Emie pondered Ada's words before answering. "Auntie," Emie sighed. "I think my bleedin' will come back. It's like a friend that's gone away. Just takin' a break, lettin' me rest a little bit before we're reacquainted."

Emerald laid her head on the pillow and stared up at the ceiling. "I ain't wantin' to talk about this anymore, Auntie Ada. Please don't say anything, even to Ernest." After a minute or two, she rolled over on her side and faced the wall. She then curled her body into a tight ball.

"You have my word," Ada promised.

The love aunt remained at the end of bed. She said no more, but patted in a series of three the girl she loved. If Emie was expecting, soon enough there would be no denying that a baby was on the way. In her heart she prayed, *"Lord, I know that children are a gift from you, but somehow this don't seem right."*

Ernest arrived at the meadow cabin late in the afternoon. The sun was starting to turn westward. He had two male puppies in tow. He had tried to leash them, but when that didn't work he carried them from the Ashby home to Auntie's. The wiggly bundles were making his arms ache. The pups were of mixed breed, chubby and healthy. Their paws were large. Though they were young mutts, Ernest knew their bodies would eventually grow into their feet.

His sisters at home had been playmates with the puppies for several weeks. They all cried at their departure. It didn't seem to matter that there were four more little ones in the barn with their mama. Coral cried silently. There were no sounds, only tears running down her checks. Ernest sensed that her silent sorrow was more sincere than that of the little girls.

Coral was a mystery to Ernest. She was too quiet as far as he was concerned. Mama always said that being in the middle was rough. When Coral did smile it seemed to be over the simplest things: dandelion puffs blowing in the breeze, a fishing worm under a rock, one of the little girls making up a whopper of a story, even wrinkled toes and fingers after a swim in the creek. He longed to see her belly laugh. He wished that the little town of Big Creek had a movie theatre. Ernest had heard about the antics of Felix the Cat. Maybe the cartoon character could bring the sound of laughter to quiet Coral.

When Ernest saw Justice in the yard, he sat the puppies down and rubbed his aching arms. He watched in delight as Justice presented the larger of the two dogs to the four boys. Ernest and the older man had agreed that the stouter dog would be better for Adam, Beau, Claude and Dean. The larger dog also had a more curious disposition.

Ernest chuckled when he thought of the four boys. He hoped they would be preoccupied keeping their puppy out of mischief. The boys' antics could be exhausting. Ernest listened to Mercy instruct the foursome on the importance of treating their new pet with kindness and gentleness. She mentioned not pulling his tail, or tying his mouth closed.

Mercy was also a mystery to Ernest, in a different way than Coral, but a mystery none the less. As he headed toward the front of Aunt Ada's cabin, he overheard Mercy helping the boys decide on a name for their puppy.

Beau wanted to name the dog, "Dog." Adam thought "Rancid" would be nice. It appeared that earlier in the day, Emie had told the boys that they were "rancid." Obviously, Adam didn't have a clue what Emie had been talking about, Ernest thought.

Dean wanted to name the puppy after himself, "Dean, Jr.," and Claude thought that "Thunder" would be nice since the puppy had fat rolls on his tummy. Ernest made a mental note to teach the boys the difference between rolls of thunder, rolls for eating, and the rolls that were caused by eating too many rolls.

He didn't bother knocking on Ada's door. His aunt's home felt more like home to him than where he had been raised. He found

Auntie sitting quietly in her chair in the front room. As Ernest entered the room, she looked up from her stitchery.

"How are you, my boy?"

"Just fine. I brought Emie a gift."

"I can see that. She's in her room takin' a lolly."

Ernest was immediately concerned. It wasn't like Emie to take a nap. "Is she feelin' alright?"

"I think she'll be just fine. Why don't you head on back and give her that monster you're holdin'?"

Ernest smiled. "I gave the boys the bigger pup."

He tucked the squirming puppy inside the front of his shirt and headed toward the back porch. Emie was lying with her face toward the wall. Ernest couldn't tell if she was sleeping or not. He moved quickly before the pup had a chance to yap, and placed the ball of fur next to Emie's exposed neck.

She had recognized her brother's steps. "Ernest, I'm havin' a bad day. I don't feel like playin'. Quit tickling me."

When her brother started to laugh, Emie rolled over. The surprised look on her face made Ernest laugh even louder.

"Does Auntie know you brought a dog into her house?" Emie whispered.

He smiled knowingly, "She's the one who suggested this creature might make a good gift for you. I gave the boys a puppy, too. Theirs will be sleepin' outside, but Aunt Ada thought you needed a friend to dream with you."

"Thank you, brother."

"My pleasure. Now let's get you and that monster out of bed. He's lookin' like he needs to piddle."

"Ernest, since he's gonna be sleepin' in my bed, let me try somethin' first." Emie then opened her window and held the puppy outside. The dog squirmed, but the young girl held on tight. When the puppy piddled it sounded like sprinkles of rain. Emie laughed out loud.

Once again, Ernest was charmed by his sister.

Emie sat the puppy on the floor. When he rolled over she tenderly rubbed his belly. "Now, this puppy and I can dream longer. No need to be runnin' outside in the middle of the night."

"Have you thought of a name, Emie?" Ernest asked.

A melancholy looked passed over his sister's face. "I'm thinkin' about the name 'Rain.' You know the Bible says that rain falls on the just and the unjust."

"Sounds like a perfect name. The boys are thinkin' about namin' their puppy 'Thunder.' Two brothers, 'Thunder' and 'Rain,' what could be better?"

"Ernest, thank you for my gift, but he won't solve my struggles."

"I know, girlie." Ernest knelt on the floor next to his sister. "When Jesus was in the wilderness forty days being tested by the devil, the Bible says that the animals were His friends." He rubbed under Rain's chin, while Emie continued her belly pats.

"What if there's more trouble to come, Ernest?"

Panic started to rise in the young man. He could feel the presence of fear and doubt. He wanted to scream, *What more could happen?*

He swallowed hard, attempting to push away the awful feelings. He had to be strong for Emie. "I hope there's no more trouble, but if there is, God will help us. He's been good to us. Hasn't He?"

"So good," she softly spoke as she lifted Rain into her arms.

The brother and sister were interrupted by the sound of the four boys yelling. Ernest headed for the front door, and Emie followed holding Rain next to her heart.

"Auntie, what's all the commotion?" Emie asked.

"Just orneriness, I'm sure."

Auntie Ada stayed put in her chair, while Emie quickly followed Ernest outside. Thunder had gotten stuck between Amos and Andy's water trough and small loafing shed. Adam and Dean were pulling on one end of Thunder, and Claude and Beau had the poor puppy by the tail pulling on the other end. Mercy took two of the boys in hand and Emie the other two, while Ernest rescued the trapped dog.

When the boys requested to hold Rain, Emie, already feeling

protective, made excuses. "Boys, my puppy's just gettin' to know me. I don't want to confuse him with so many new faces. Maybe in a few days he'll be ready for your affections…"

Thunder took off running and the boys after him. Emie wanted to yell, "Run, Thunder. Run for your life."

Emie left Ernest and Mercy discussing how best to train the boys and Thunder, and started back toward the cabin when Rudy arrived.

As Rudy drew closer, Emie could tell that something was wrong. The look on her friend's face was a dead giveaway. His usual crooked smile had been replaced with downturned lips, and a wrinkled forehead had set his cowlick askew.

Rudy only nodded to Emie and Mercy, and then addressed Ernest, "You're needed back at home. I stopped by to help you with chores and something's wrong with the sows. They're peeing blood, and won't feed the piglets."

"All of 'um?" Ernest questioned.

"I'm thinkin' so," Rudy answered.

As the two headed past the maple tree in front of Ada's cabin, Ernest looked back toward his sister and Mercy. "Evenin' is drawing near. Tell Auntie if I can, I'll be back before dark."

Chapter Twenty One

"It's bad luck to burn wood from a tree struck by lightning."
(Appalachian Folk Belief)

Later that night trouble came to Auntie's cabin. The moon was only a sliver hanging in the sky. The clouds were thick and elongated, hiding the stars. The night was so dark that it was easy for the three men to slip through the meadow.

Two of the men headed toward the little house. There was no sound or light coming from the little dwelling. Justice and his family were fast asleep. The larger of the two men laid a bone on the ground for Thunder. Amos and Andy, sensing that something was out of place, rustled around a little bit, but not so much as to awaken the inhabitants of the house.

The third man had visited Ada's cabin before. He knew that a loose window pane could be jimmied, allowing access to the hook and eye lock on the front door.

Auntie was tired from the day. She had spent the daylight hours working on her niceties for the wedding and had retired early. Her soft rhythmic snoring could be heard throughout the cabin. Emie had written in her journal just before bed. Now, she was sound asleep with Rain by her side.

The puppy whimpered, waking Emie. Thinking that he needed to piddle, she rose from the bed. Rain followed her to the window. She pulled back the white curtains, trimmed in Auntie's handiwork, and opened the window. The curtains billowed in the breeze, reminding Emie of angel's wings. When she knelt to pick up Rain, she saw someone standing in the shadows of her small room. The man was almost invisible in the darkness; his hat and clothes blended with the night.

She thought to scream for help, but when she opened her mouth there was only silence. Fear had stolen her voice. Her heart raced and panic filled every pore of her being.

The man closed her bedroom door. He reached Emie in three long strides. With one hand he gripped her arm, and with the other hand he covered her mouth. She knew it was Charlie.

"Don't be thinkin' of yellin', Emie. I've got a couple friends waitin' out back. You don't want any harm comin' to the colored folk, do ya?"

She shook her head no.

"That's a good girl."

He ushered her to the bed and forced her to sit down. Charlie kept his hand over her mouth, but let go of her arm long enough to reach into his pocket. He laid a good sized bone on the floor for Rain.

"I can't abide what you're doin', girlie. Spreading lies and such."

Charlie smelled. His breath reeked of alcohol and his body of sweat. Emie thought she would vomit. He was foul in soul and body.

"Listen and listen good. Since I ain't wantin' you no more, your daddy has done promised me Coral."

Emie breathed in deeply and held her breath.

Charlie removed his hand from her mouth and sat down next to her on the bed. "You and me, Emie, we need to come to terms. Do you hear me, girlie?"

She released her breath, and again nodded in response.

"If you confess your lyin' ways, I'll keep visitin' the whores up the holler, and tell your daddy that Coral's too young."

Emie closed her eyes, willing Charlie to go away, hoping she would wake from the nightmare of his presence.

"I want you to tell the church on a Sunday morn that you were makin' things up. Do you understand?"

When Emie didn't answer, Charlie roughly grabbed her by the hair.

"Answer me, Emie."

She quietly answered, "I understand."

"If you don't do what I say, I'll take her just like I did you, and then I'll marry her and hurt her again and again. I'll also come back and burn out the Negro and his kin."

Charlie let go of her hair and rose from the bed, but leaned forward, keeping his face close to Emie.

His closeness demanded that she look at him. "I need to think," Emie softly spoke.

She saw him snarl his skinny upper lip, like a bad dog ready to bite.

"Three days, Emie. That's all. You hold their lives, girlie. Remember that."

As he readied to leave, she stood on her feet. Without realizing it she spoke her thoughts, "Don't come back here. Don't you ever come back here!"

Charlie looked at her like she was an ant that he could squash with his finger tip. "Three days. That's all I'm givin' you. Send word to my daddy."

Emie was dressed and sitting in the parlor when Aunt Ada entered the room the next morning. The young girl had been awake most of the night. Rain was lying at her feet gnawing on his bone. His tail thumped at Ada's presence.

The older woman patted Rain's head and noticed the bone. "What'd you make for breakfast, girlie? Half a side of beef…"

Simply staring into the air, and not making eye contact, Emie answered, "No, Auntie. I had a visitor last night. Charlie gave the bone to Rain to keep him quiet."

Ada hurried to Emie's side. "Oh, darlin', are you okay?"

Emerald's body began to shake. She wanted to be brave. She hadn't cried during the darkness. She had patted Rain, and remembered what Ernest had told her about the animals being Jesus' friends in the wilderness. She had also kept her bedroom window open, and saw the wind time and time again form the angel's wings with her curtains.

The sobs came. She couldn't help it. Rain abandoned his bone and placed his big paws on her knee, wanting up. He was pushed aside when Ada knelt before Emie's chair and hugged her about the waist, whispering soothing words of comfort.

When Emie's cries quieted, Aunt Ada began to ask questions. "Sweet girl, did he hurt you? How did he get in the house?" Filled with worry, the older woman began to ramble. "I know I locked the door. I didn't hear a thing. What was I thinkin' puttin' you in that back room? I should have kept you right by my side…."

Emie placed her arms around her aunt's neck. The older woman quieted. "I'm wantin' to talk with Sheriff Robbins. Charlie gave me an ultimatum. I tell the church people that I've been lyin', or else he's gonna do to Coral what he did to me."

"Hush now, my girl," Ada said lifting her head.

"I don't want to believe it either, Auntie, but we can't deny it. Daddy told Charlie he could marry Coral."

Ada released Emie and rose from her knees. "Let me get dressed. I'm comin' with ya. I'll see if Justice can run and get Ernest."

Emie stood. "I've been thinking some. Or tryin' to think. My brain seems all muddled, but Charlie told me to get word to his dad. If Eugene is helpin' Charlie make trouble then so is Daddy."

Auntie Ada nodded in agreement. "Maybe we should wait to tell Ernest what happened. If Justice runs to fetch your brother, your daddy might suspect somethin'."

"I'm thinking that's best. 'Sides, Ernest is busy with the ailin' sows."

"Emie, darlin', if you needed your brother, he'd come runnin'. Sows or no sows."

The two women walked hand in hand toward town with Rain following close behind. The puppy dawdled some, sniffing the ground and chasing squirrels, but Ada and Emie didn't seem to notice. Ada thought to leave the dog at home, but knew that Emie liked him near.

"He ain't much of a watch dog," Ada said, pointing toward Rain.

"Now, Auntie, he tried. He whimpered. I just didn't understand what he was sayin'. I thought he meant to piddle and here he was tellin' me that Charlie was in my room."

Their steps were slow and deliberate. Auntie had told her girl when they stepped off the front porch, "Walking is good for the soul. Sometimes God speaks to His children when they journey down the road."

They didn't go to Sheriff Robbin's office. Ada thought it best they meet with the sheriff in secret. There would be too many onlookers if they walked down the center of the little town to the sheriff's office. Instead they stopped at Doc Bright's clinic. They entered through the back door startling the good doctor, who was getting ready for his morning visits from patients. After minimal explanation, Christian ushered the ladies and corralled Rain into the back exam room.

"You ladies need to stay put. I agree that it's best that Charlie and Eugene don't see or hear anything about you meeting with the sheriff." He kissed Ada on the lips and Emie on the cheek, and left them and Rain in the clinic. He then headed down Main Street toward Sheriff Robbin's office.

While waiting, Emie and Ada said little to one another. They were both seemingly lost in their own worlds. Emie was pondering what to do. Her heart ached and her mind raced. She was worried about Coral. She noticed that Auntie's lips were moving, and felt strengthened knowing that her love aunt was visiting with the Savior.

Some time passed before Sheriff Robbins knocked quietly on the door and then entered the room. "Doc will join us when he's able. He's got a couple patients waitin'."

He took a seat in the chair next to Emie. "Now, girlie, we've done this before, and we both know it ain't pleasant, but I'm needin' you to tell me all of it."

Emie shook her head "yes" and then started in, "I was at my bedroom window tendin' to Rain…"

She paused when she saw the confused look on Sheriff Robbins' face. "Rain is my new puppy, Sheriff."

When Emie saw him glance toward Ada, who was holding Rain in check, she continued. "I looked back and saw someone standin' in the bedroom. It was Charlie. He shut the door and forced me to sit on the bed..."

The sheriff interrupted, "Did he rape you, Emie?"

She couldn't help but notice that Auntie was holding her breath, waiting for the answer.

Emie took her eyes off the sheriff and looked at her aunt. "No. It's okay, Aunt Ada, he didn't hurt me."

She then continued her conversation with the sheriff. "He just wanted to talk about Coral. Charlie told me if I didn't stand in front of the church and say I made up lies about him that he would hurt Coral. Daddy told Charlie that he could marry Coral. She's just a baby. She won't be thirteen till fall."

Just like before, Sheriff Robbins was taking notes in his book.

"He also told me that he would hurt Justice and his family," Emie continued.

Only when Emerald had given a full account of what Charlie had said and done, and shared her feelings on Pastor Eugene and her daddy's participation, did the sheriff speak.

"I'll head on up to your place, Ada, and have a look around. Hopefully, Charlie left somethin' behind that will connect him and his friends to their night visit."

Then he smiled at Emie. "You did good tellin' me what happened. For now, I want you to keep this quiet."

"I'll be needin' to tell Ernest and Rudy," Emie spoke. "Probably Justice too."

"I understand," the sheriff offered.

Sheriff Robbins then paused gathering his words, "MayLou doesn't like it that I play poker. She says that cards are of the devil and used for fortune tellin'. But poker's taught me a few things about bein' a sheriff: don't show your hand until it's time, and sometimes bluffing is the best way to win the game."

Chapter Twenty Two

"If your hand itches, it means someone will give you a present soon."
(Appalachian Folk Belief)

"Daddy, I don't understand," Ernest said, giving the nightly hog report. "The salt licks for the sows have done been moved."

"Well, boy, they're heavy and they don't move by themselves," Ahab spoke sarcastically. "You were neglectful. You're spendin' too much time at Ada's. Now you done brought trouble on us."

"Daddy, I told you. I placed the licks behind the feed troughs early spring. I can still see the residue. Someone's moved 'um."

"Enough of this nonsense, Ernest! Tell me how the mamas and babies are doin'," his daddy bellowed.

Ernest was so baffled that it was hard to answer his daddy's questions. "We only lost one mama, and her litter was almost weaned. The rest seem to be comin' around."

"We never had trouble like this when Lester was here. Any fool knows if you don't give sows salt their milk dries."

"Well, Daddy, Lester ain't here, and I'm doin' the best I can. It's a miracle we only lost one."

"Are they still peein' blood?"

Ernest sighed in frustration. "It's getting' better."

Ernest headed back to the barn. It would be another long night. He and Rudy had spent the previous night doctoring the sows and feeding the youngest of the piglets with bottled milk. He was thankful that most of the mamas had already weaned their young.

He was surprised to find Coral waiting for him in the barn. "Hey, girlie. I thought Mama had you watchin' the little ones."

"They're playin' out back. I can hear 'um from here."

"I'm sure they're old enough to be on their own for a few minutes," Ernest added.

Coral quietly spoke, her voice almost in a whisper. "Brother, I'm needin' to tell you somethin'."

Her words caught Ernest off guard. It was rare that Coral initiated a conversation with anyone.

"Charlie was here awhile back. I can't remember exactly when, but school was still goin' on. He and Pastor Eugene were talkin' to Daddy. I was outside with the little ones. We was playin' Red Rover. I saw Charlie head to the stinky, then he come into the barn. I couldn't see real clear, Ernest, but I think he carried off the salt licks."

Ernest knelt down next to Coral listening closely. "Sister, tell me exactly what you saw?"

"It was late evenin', Ernest. I was expectin' mama to call us in from play. The little ones was gettin' tired." Coral paused and then added, "I don't like Charlie much, brother."

"I don't like him much either, Coral," Ernest answered patiently. "I need you to try and describe what he carried from the barn."

"I'm not sure. He made three trips in and out of the barn. Whatever he carried was heavy. I could tell by the way he was walkin.'"

Like a puzzle, some pieces were coming together. There had been a large salt lick behind each of the three water troughs. Not wanting to move them again, he had placed them strategically. The licks didn't require any attention and knowing that they would last for quite some time, he hadn't given them any more thought. Charlie must have moved them after they had been placed.

"Girlie, did you see where he carried them?"

Coral pointed toward the hog pens. "I don't hear the little girls, Ernest. I better go and check on 'um."

The older sibling stood and patted her shoulder. "You've been a big help. Go on, now. It's gettin' dark; Mama will be calling for you soon."

When Rudy arrived a few minutes later, the two headed toward the pens. The sun was quickly setting. There was minimal light, but Ernest was determined to investigate Charlie's mischief.

When they reached the outdoor pens, Ernest headed one way and Rudy the other. It wasn't long before Rudy shouted for Ernest to come and look. Charlie had hidden the licks under a stack of warped wood. Lester had piled the wood there the previous spring.

"Do you want me carry the licks back to the barn?" Rudy questioned.

"It can wait till daylight," Ernest replied. "Lester saw a couple rattlers in this pile last summer. The evening's warm and they might be around."

As they walked back to the barn, Rudy and Ernest volleyed questions back and forth trying to understand Charlie's motives. As they entered the barn, Ernest shook his head in confusion, "It's nothin' but a mystery."

Just as mysterious was his mama's presence in the outdoor building. He couldn't remember the last time she'd visited the pigs. She had always told him and Lester, "When your daddy was in the war, I tended those rascals. Now that you boys are older, I'll tend the garden, the children, and the chickens. The pigs is all yours."

Rudy glanced at Ernest and excused himself, "I think I'll head to Aunt Ada's and check on things."

Ernest nodded and looked toward his mama, "Is everythin' alright?"

"Right as can be," she answered. "I'm just checkin' on the sows and babies. Your daddy said that one of the sows passed."

"Coral saw Charlie move the salt licks. When the sows don't get enough salt they quit givin' milk."

"I know, son. In case you've forgotten, I've tended pigs."

"I ain't forgotten. I'm just wonderin' why you're showing an interest now."

Ernest knew that his mama was hiding something. Her head was down and she was wringing her hands. She was standing under one of the barn lanterns. Her face looked old in the light, and

Ernest could see that her head was sprouting gray hairs.

"I'm worried is all, Ernest."

"I know you're hidin' something from me. Tell me why Charlie moved the licks."

His mother didn't answer.

"I'm tired. I've been at it all night and day. Now, it's night again. I'm doin' my best to take care of you and the girls. I need to know the truth. I deserve to know the truth."

Alma's eyes lifted to Ernest's face. "Son, look around. Can't you see that no one deserves nothin' in this holler?"

"You're right. This holler gives very little in the way of comfort, but I'm your boy, your son." Holding out his hands, Ernest continued. "Look at my hands. They're bleedin' and raw from work on this farm. Tell me, Mama."

When she didn't answer, Ernest started to walk away.

"Don't leave me, boy."

"I ain't leavin'. I'm just checking on the babies in the back."

She sighed. "But you will leave, if I tell you what I know."

He turned and faced her. "I won't leave the girls." He knew his words stung, like the bees when he gathered honey, but he couldn't bring himself to say that he would stay for her sake. His mother had made her choices. The girls, on the other hand, had no choice.

"Yesterday, your daddy sent me to town to tell Pastor Eugene the pigs were ailin'. I didn't know about the salt licks."

"Why would Eugene care if the sows were peein' blood?"

"Maybe your daddy was askin' for prayer."

He huffed in disgust. "You and me both know that ain't true. He and Eugene were scheming. Tell me why."

Ernest could see the guilt on his mother's face. She knew more than she was telling him. He was angry and frustrated, but he knew expressing those emotions right now would get him nowhere. So he waited, hoping if he remained quiet long enough that his mother would spill the beans.

"It had to do with Charlie and Emie. Your daddy and Eugene was always worried that Emie might not go along with marryin' Charlie. The boy moved the salt licks soon after you put them in place. Your daddy knew it would take time for the sows to get sick, but if confusion was needed it would be there. You have to believe me, Ernest. I didn't know…"

Ernest bit his tongue to keep from saying, *"But if you had known, would you have told me?"*

Ernest wanted to rant, rage, and rail but instead, he simply said, "Thank you for tellin' me."

"You won't be thankin' me later," she quietly spoke and then left the barn, heading in the dimness back to the house.

Ernest was still confused. Some of his mama's story made sense, but other parts just didn't add up. He decided to check the sows and piglets one more time, and then make a trip to Ada's. He wouldn't be able to stay the night. The small piglets would need fed and the sows tending, but right now he needed peace of mind that Auntie, Emie, and Justice and his family were fine. His thoughts also turned toward Mercy. He hoped that she was in good hands. He knew that God's hands were big. He just wished that his own hands were larger and stronger.

Ernest headed through the orchard toward the creek. The trees were laden with immature fruit. He was reminded of his mama's words about the people in the holler being undeserving. He understood what his mama meant; life was hard for the mountain folk, but at the same time God's bounty was rich in the Appalachians. He supposed that his mama's struggles overshadowed the goodness of the holler.

It was growing dark when he walked across the swinging bridge and headed toward the woods. The path to Auntie's was well worn. Just as the woods gave way to the meadow expanse, he recognized Mercy standing among the grasses. Her hands were raised in worship. He could hear her softly singing. *"There is a fountain filled with blood drawn from Emmanuel's veins. And sinners plunged beneath that flood lose all their guilty stains. Lose all their guilty stains, lose all their guilty stains; and sinners plunged beneath that flood lose all their guilty stains."*

Ernest was reminded that the hymn had been written by a man who was experiencing severe mental anguish. Mrs. Randolph had explained to him that the writer had lost his mother at a young age, and never seemed to quite recover. Ernest understood a measure of the man's grief. Though he hadn't lost his mother physically, he knew the pain of being abandoned by the one who had birthed him, and from whose breast he had nursed.

Ernest stood and listened. Mercy's voice was soothing and beautiful, and her worship so sincere that he was moved to tears. He had never heard her sing before. They had spent time together reading and studying, but never singing. When she came to the fourth verse, he stepped forward from the shadows of the trees, and raised his voice with hers.

At first she was startled, but then reached for his hand, welcoming him to join her. *"E'er since, by faith, I saw the stream thy flowing wounds supply, redeeming love has been my theme, and shall be till I die. And shall be till I die, and shall be till I die; redeeming love has been my theme, and shall be till I die."*

Their voices flowed together for several songs, at times both singing the melody and exchanging verses one to another, at other times their voices harmonizing. In the midst of their singing, Ernest's heart of worry shifted to a heart of worship.

With unspoken agreement, when their songs were finished, they each prayed, blessing their families and community.

They walked to Auntie's together, Mercy's arm looped through Ernest's bent elbow. He had been physically close to Mercy before. He had stood over her shoulder explaining school lessons. They had sat closely sharing a book. Ernest couldn't explain why, yet somehow this felt different, like the two of them were traveling to a distant, unexplored land.

Chapter Twenty Three

"To ward off evil, carry drinking water across a running stream."
(Appalachian Folk Belief)

Ernest sat on the edge of the worn chair in Auntie's parlor. He couldn't believe the audacity of Charlie. If ever there was evil in a person, it was present in Charlie, also in Eugene and Daddy. All three were schemers. They planned their evil deeds in advance. The salt licks were originally moved in case chaos was needed down the road. The ailing sows and piglets created the perfect cover for Charlie to visit Auntie's cabin.

Ernest knew that prayer was the answer, but his fists were clenched. He wanted to take matters into his own hands. Auntie had passed by the back of his chair twice, each time patting his shoulder. He knew the love pats were intended to calm him, yet he remained angry, worried, frustrated, and fearful.

Earlier in the day, much to Thunder and Rain's dismay, Sheriff Robbins had confiscated the dog bones for evidence, and had located the loose window pane. Charlie had been neglectful in putting the glass back in place. Justice had already made the repair, and placed a bar latch on the door.

"I'm going to do what Charlie wants," Emie told the small group, which included Ernest, Rudy, Doc, and Aunt Ada. "I talked with Sheriff Robbins and we have a plan." She held her hand up, encouraging those present to be still until she finished what was on her mind. "The sheriff and I agreed to keep our plan secret. I know none of you like that, but it's better that way. The sheriff said this way an element of surprise is on our side."

When Emie paused, everyone started talking at once. Ernest couldn't discern who was saying what, but knew all the messages were the same. When the voices in the small room finally faded, he stood and spoke quietly. He would have rather yelled at his sister, *"Are you crazy?"* but he knew that Emie wouldn't respond to a raised voice. She would shut down and withdrawal into a shell. They had all learned the protective response from their daddy's abuse. His best approach was kindness and reason.

"Emie, we all love you and only want what's best. Are you sure that givin' Charlie his way will make a difference?"

"I'm not sure of anything, Ernest. But I have to do something. I can't let Charlie hurt Coral. Talkin' to Mama and Daddy won't help, and Eugene is beyond hearing anyone but himself. I don't think I have a choice."

While Ernest was trying to gather his words, Emie walked the few steps to where he stood. She placed her hand on his arm, "Brother, thank you for understandin' and not fightin' me on this."

Emie stood on the front porch of Aunt Ada's cabin. She was surprised that no one had followed her outside. The moon was bright and the heavenly stars twinkled. *Lord, please guide me. Like the wise men who followed the star to baby Jesus, show me the way.*

Her thoughts were interrupted by Rudy. "I suppose you're wantin' to be alone," Rudy spoke. He had slipped around the back of the house, avoiding the parlor door that led to the front porch.

"I was just wonderin' when someone would come and check on me," Emie answered.

"It was hard for me to wait this long." As he moved from the shadows, he explained his actions. "I came around back hopin' no one would notice. I wanted a moment alone with you, Emie." Rudy took the porch steps in one stride. "I have no right, but if I did, I would tell you to do this different…"

Emie placed her hand on Rudy's familiar arm. "It'll be okay.

Wait and see."

"I'm afraid for you."

"Don't be. I'm afraid enough for both of us."

"I wanna help. I wish I could make all of this go away. We could leave together. I know that my grandpappy would help us. He'd take us in. Think about it. No Charlie. You wouldn't have to be afraid…"

Emie squeezed Rudy's arm, silencing her friend. "Rudy, if it was only 'bout me, right now, I would pack my bag and off we'd go, but what about Coral? I couldn't leave her in Charlie's hands! I know what he's capable of. He'd hurt her and hurt her bad."

Rudy, resigned, turned and placed his arms around Emie. "If I can help, just ask."

She enjoyed the feel of her friend's embrace, yet she didn't allow herself to linger there. "Rudy, there is something that you can do for me."

When she hesitated, Rudy spoke up. "Anything, Emie. Just say it."

Putting her hand in her skirt pocket she pulled out a small folded piece of paper. She had torn the page earlier from her journal. "Please deliver this to Pastor Eugene this evenin' on your way home."

"This is what you want?"

"I don't know, Rudy. I hope I'm doing the right thing."

In the weeks that followed, the members of the small community each took a turn at trying to convince Emerald to change her mind. Ada tried to persuade with words and when that didn't work, she resorted to tears. Ernest stayed patient and calm in his approach, but Emie knew that he was seething inside. Even Doc Bright took a turn. He was logical and talked about hiring an investigator and then an attorney to prevent Charlie from marrying Coral. Rudy said very little, but Emie knew he was worried. His cowlick was a dead giveaway. It was off kilter each time he visited. Justice brought his whole family over to Auntie's cabin one evening. The four boys sat quietly for once, while Justice presented his argument. Emie knew that Cece must have threatened the boys but good.

Even Mercy joined in the persuasive talk. "We're like sisters, Emie. Please don't do this. Don't shame yourself by standing in front of the church and givin' into Charlie's lies. There has to be a better way."

Emie held fast. She had met with Sheriff Robbins periodically to review and update their plan. Now, as she stood before the congregation, satchel in hand, she wasn't so sure that she was doing the right thing. Her knees felt weak. She had already vomited once that morning and again felt bile rising in her throat.

The church was packed. There was standing room only. People were even standing in the yard between the church and school house. She knew that Justice and his family were somewhere outside. Eugene didn't allow colored folk in the church or they would have been sitting among the congregation. The pastor had gotten the word out that Emie would be at church that morning confessing her sins. The mountain folk were curious by nature, but even Pastor Eugene appeared befuddled by the large turnout.

Her parents were sitting in the front row. Charlie and Pastor Eugene were sitting beside them. Charlie looked smug. It was hot in the sanctuary, and both Eugene and her daddy were sweating profusely. The twins were sitting in the back with their new husbands, the little girls were sitting with Ernest, and Rudy was sitting somewhere in the middle. She knew that Ernest had an aisle seat. She had watched him pace up and down the center aisle twice already. Aunt Ada and MayLou Robbins were sitting in the second row directly behind Pastor Eugene and Charlie.

Before Eugene introduced her, he shared from God's Word about liars going to hell.

The sheriff had previously coached Emie to look at him and him alone. "Emerald, when you stand in front of the church, it'll be hard. I won't be tellin' you different. Look at me, girlie. Don't look at all the other faces. We'll get this done together."

She needed to concentrate. Sheriff Robbins was exactly where he told her he would be, standing in the back on her right side. Emie cleared her throat and started in. "Thank you, Pastor Eugene, for reminding us that liars go to hell." She glanced at Eugene and saw a proud look on his face and then quickly looked back at Sheriff Robbins. She needed to focus.

"I've been asked this mornin' to confess my sins. Well, my sins are many, includin' lying on occasion. I am thankful this mornin' that Jesus died to take away my sins. I don't have to go to hell."

Emie heard a couple of "amens" from the congregation, but kept her eyes fixed on the sheriff.

"In the Bible, there was a valley of dry bones. The bones were dry because of sin."

Emie put her hand in the satchel and removed one by one the bones that Charlie and his friends had given to Thunder and Rain.

"The bones may have looked like these two bones. All dried up."

She desperately wanted to look at Charlie. She wanted to see the smug look wiped from his face, but she stayed focused on the sheriff. Emie paused in her delivery, just like Sheriff Robbins had instructed.

She then heard a loud voice from the back of the sanctuary. It was Rudy's daddy. "Why, Emie, those bones aren't like in the Bible. They're cow knuckles, I usually throw them away, but a few weeks back Charlie bought the pair for a few pennies. He said his daddy wanted to make soup. Well, I knew that wasn't true. They aren't good for making soup, and we all know that Eugene doesn't cook. He relies on the good women of our church to bring him meals."

There were more "amens" from the congregation and few "a hums" from the women in the church.

Emie picked up the bones and pretended that she was examining them real close. The sheriff had told her for dramatic effect to pause and take her time.

"Well, folks," she continued. "In the Book Ezekiel, God asked the prophet if he thought the bones could live."

Again there was a voice from the congregation, toward the middle left side of the building. This time it was Granny Smith, who lived not far from Aunt Ada. "Emerald Ashby, I'm tellin' ya now those bones you're holdin' ain't gonna live. Why, Charlie and two of his friends passed through my yard a few weeks back and had them bones in a poke. My dogs went crazy sniffin' and chasin' around. I finally had to pen them so Charlie could pass."

Emie waited for the sheriff's nod before she continued. "When Ezekiel prophesied to the bones and told them to live, the Bible says that the bones began to rattle." She picked up the bones again and began to shake them.

Now it was Sheriff Robbin's turn to interrupt. He walked swiftly from the back of the church to the platform where Emie stood. He took the bones from her hands and held them high. "I found these bones in Ada's yard. You can see teeth marks from the dogs chewin' on 'um."

Out of the corner of her eye, she saw Eugene rise to his feet. When she looked closer, both MayLou and Aunt Ada had their hands on Eugene pushing him back down on his chair.

The sheriff then descended from the platform and showed the bones to those sitting closest to the front of the church. Heads began to nod in agreement that the teeth marks were present.

Sheriff Robbin's voice grew louder, "Now, I know we're not in a court of law, but we're in church where God's law is taught and truth should be upheld."

Eugene began to struggle against MayLou and Aunt Ada, and Charlie, being a coward, rose to his feet and headed for the back door of the church.

The sheriff drew the congregation's attention to Pastor Eugene. "Eugene, what's wrong? MayLou and Ada are just tryin' to love on you a little bit, and here you are fightin' like a mean ol' polecat."

Snickers could be heard from the congregation.

"Take a seat, Pastor, and let me expound a bit on lyin'. I'm just addin' to what you talked about earlier," the sheriff continued.

Eugene began to squirm like the piglets when Emie gave them a bath. When he finally broke free, he headed for the platform squealing nonsense about the sheriff not being a preacher.

Rudy's daddy spoke up once again. "Pastor Eugene, let the sheriff talk. I'm interested in hearing about the bones."

Then Rudy, Ernest, Doc, and a number of others began to yell out. "Take a seat, Pastor. Let's hear from the sheriff. I want Emie to finish the story about the dry bones rattlin'."

When Eugene had been sufficiently shouted down, he had no choice but to return to his seat. Emie saw Charlie trying to sneak out the back door. The sheriff, in his wisdom, had placed two large farmhands in front of the door blocking Charlie's exit.

That day at Big Creek Church the truth was told. Eugene couldn't deny the many testimonies shared about his corruption. When Emie talked about Charlie's abuse, there wasn't a dry eye in the place. No one rose to the duo's defense except Ahab, who was booed and ridiculed for giving both Emie and Coral into Charlie's defiled hands.

The sheriff moderated the service like a skilled poker player using keen insights to win the game. Before the day was through, the parsonage was cleared of Eugene and Charlie's personal belongings, and the two were taken to the train station in Charleston. Sheriff Robbins threatened them with prison if they ever returned to Big Creek or the surrounding areas.

The sheriff and MayLou paid a visit to Ada and Emie that night. MayLou brought a bounty of celebratory food, and the sheriff offered his own treasure. "Emie, you're a brave soul. They won't be back. I wish I had enough evidence to lock 'um up. But you and I both know for every witness I have they'll produce two. Rest now, girlie. You done good."

Chapter Twenty Four

"If you see enough blue sky to patch a jacket, the rain is passing."
(Appalachian Folk Belief)

Summer was turning to fall. The mornings and evenings were getting cooler. The leaves were giving a glimpse of the magnificent colors that would soon come. Emie thought it interesting that the leaves had to die to nourish the trees through the winter. She had read all about it in her reader at school. It's like life, she pondered. Somehow the death of one thing brings good to another.

School had started once again in Big Creek. Mrs. Randolph was working with Rudy on his schooling in the evenings. Emie knew that during the day, he was helping his daddy at the store and working the hogs with Ernest.

Rudy was doing his best to convince her to join him in attending school. The two were sitting along the banks of Big Creek, lazily soaking their feet in the cool water.

"Emie, come on. You're smart. There ain't no rule that says a girl has to quit school after eighth grade."

Emie enjoyed learning. She was tempted to join Rudy, but knew in the long run it simply wouldn't work.

"Just tell me why you won't come," Rudy asked. "Mrs. Randolph said it would be fine."

The two friends had been gently splashing each other's legs and feet, when Rudy, having a wild red hair, decided to wade in the stream. He, of course, pulled Emie in with him. The water soaked her light-weight shift, revealing the small mound of her tummy. Emie tried to pull the dress away from her skin, but it was too late; she was certain Rudy had witnessed what she'd been hiding. She'd known for a number of weeks that a baby was coming. It wasn't just that her menses hadn't visited; she had also felt her body changing. The nausea had subsided somewhat, but in return her breasts had grown tender, and her emotions were often out of sorts.

She hadn't talked any further with Aunt Ada about the baby, but she knew that her aunt's earlier suspicions had been confirmed. Ada had to have witnessed the too-tight clothes, the tears that flowed easily, and the afternoon lollies.

"Rudy, now you know why I can't go to school. I need to work. Your daddy's sellin' my wares and even askin' for more. I need things for the baby. I can't take handouts forever from Auntie Ada. I have to find my own way for myself and the baby."

Rudy touched Emie's slightly rounded tummy. He held his hand there for a moment, and then, without a word, took her hand and walked with her from the stream to where their shoes lay under one of the willows.

While lacing his shoes, Rudy finally spoke. "Why didn't you tell me?"

"I'm sorry. I haven't wanted to tell anyone. It's been my secret."

Rudy took Emie's shoes and tried to put them on her feet.

"I'm not helpless, Rudy."

"I don't know what to do, Emie. I had a plan, a plan for us."

"If you had a plan and it involved me, then you should have told me. Now, who's keepin' secrets?"

Rudy struggled to find the right words, "You weren't ready, Emie. I was waitin' till the time was right. Plus, we're talkin' about your secrets, not mine."

"Rudy, there ain't no time like the present."

It made Emie mad, but he helped her with her shoes anyway.

When he finished, he looked up at her face. "I've loved you since we were little. I've known all of my life that I wanted to marry you..."

Before he could continue, she interrupted, "Rudy, you're only fourteen..."

"Almost fifteen."

"Alright, almost fifteen. What you want now won't be what you want later."

"You're wrong, Emie. I know I could take care of you and the baby."

Emie sighed. "Rudy, I don't doubt that you would work hard and make us a family, but it wouldn't be fair. You need time to grow up. Time to finish high school and go to college. I know you're wantin' to be a pastor. It won't help to have a wife with a baby that ain't yours."

Rudy couldn't hold back his emotions. "Emie, you hurt me. I would love that baby like it was mine, no different than the other children we would have. Tell me that you love me. Tell me that you'll marry me."

"I do love you. I love you like a friend, like a brother, and maybe someday like a husband. I love you and that's why I'm tellin' you that I won't marry you."

He hung his head. "Not now, or not ever?"

Emie touched his face with the palm of her hand. She had tears in her eyes. "Not now, but I'm not sayin' 'not ever.' I want us to grow up a bit. I've been through a lot with Charlie and all, and I want us to be sure. I want you to experience your dreams. I don't want to hold you back, Rudy."

"Emie, you don't understand, you and now the baby, are my dreams."

The two sat under the willow tree for the remainder of the morning. Emie understood that she couldn't hide her secret any longer. Now that Rudy knew, it was time to tell Ernest, Mercy, and Justice and Cece. She figured that Auntie and Doc had already talked. She was comforted that she and the baby would have a home, but scared about what others would think. She had told the truth about Charlie and the rape, but in her telling would the bundle she now carried be received by the holler folk with joy or judgment?

"Granny Smith came to visit yesterday."

"Really, Grandpappy," Rudy answered. "Does she have eyes for you?"

The older gentleman chuckled. "It doesn't matter if she does. I ain't got eyes for any woman but your grandma. God rest her soul."

Rudy's grandma had passed away more than a year ago. At the time, his grandpappy was pastoring a church outside of Spencer. When she left this earth and went on to heaven, Pappy left his pastorate. Rudy had worried that his grandfather was angry with God and leaving the ministry for good.

"Rudy, my boy," his grandfather had told him. "I ain't mad with the good Lord, but if I was, I am certain that He could still manage. I'm grievin'. Your grandma was the love of my life. I just want to be alone. I don't want to stand in the pulpit each Sunday, and tell the good people that everythin' is alright, when I don't feel it's alright."

After Eugene was run out of town, the church leaders contacted Rex, Rudy's grandpappy, about pastoring the congregation at Big Creek. Rudy guessed that his grandfather's grieving had subsided some, because upon invitation he quickly arrived and settled in at the parsonage behind the church building.

Grandpappy was tall and gangly. Rudy had inherited his red hair and cowlick from the kindly gentleman. He was soft-spoken, yet firm. Rudy's ma said that Grandpappy had a way about him, and Rudy agreed. From the time he was little, he had confided in Pappy. They had talked about broken toys, broken bones, and broken hearts. On more than one occasion, those confidences had included Emerald Ashby.

"Rudy, Granny Smith was out walkin' by the creek yesterday when she saw you and Emie wadin'."

"It was a fine day, Pappy, for wadin' in the cool water."

"I'm sure it was, son."

Grandpappy only called Rudy "son" when a conversation was turning serious. Rudy thought about Emie's dress clinging to her rounded tummy, and wondered exactly what Granny Smith had reported.

"Granny Smith is a nice woman. She stuck up for Emie at church," Rudy responded.

"She's a God-fearin' woman. That she is. Rudy, is Emie expectin'?"

"Expectin' what?" He didn't mean to be disrespectful. He loved his grandfather. It was just hard to talk about the baby.

"Son..."

Rudy hung his head. "I'm sorry. I'm just worried about what people will think." He looked up at his grandfather. "She's havin' a baby. Emie's dress clung while we were wadin' in the creek. Granny must have been close enough to see her growin' belly."

"No. She saw your hand on her belly. She thought you were actin' too familiar."

"In truth, I'd like to be more familiar," Rudy spoke.

Pastor Rex couldn't help but laugh. "I bet you would. Most boys your age think a lot about bein' familiar with girls."

Rudy rolled his eyes. "Not like that." Then he paused and joined his grandfather in laughing. "Well, I guess like that," he said honestly. "But more so, Pappy, I love her."

He was worried that his grandfather would make light of his affections for Emie. After all, like Emerald had declared earlier, he was only fourteen, almost fifteen.

"Son, I suspect that you do love her."

Rudy chided himself. He should have known better. Pappy never made light of anything he shared. "Thank you for not makin' fun."

"I fell in love with your grandma when I was about your age. I knew even then that she was the one for me. I sure miss that gal."

Rudy was wrong. His grandpappy's grief was still very raw. Maybe grief was like the seasons of the holler, changing with the passing of time.

"Granny Smith thinks the baby must be yours."

"The baby's Charlie's," Rudy answered. "I ain't been with her like that, Pappy. I wish he or she was mine though, then Emie would have to marry me."

"You don't want Emie to have to marry you. You want her to choose to marry you."

"Well, she ain't choosin'. She says that we're too young and need to grow a bit. She also says that she and the baby will hinder God's plans."

Pappy placed his hand on Rudy's shoulder. "Your grandma loved the song, 'Someone to Watch Over Me.' I would sing it to her at night when we were fallin' asleep in bed."

Rudy smiled.

The older gentleman smiled in return. "Now, don't be laughin'. You and I both know that I can't sing a lick, but your grandma didn't seem to care. My favorite part was and still is *Tell me, where is the shepherd for this lost lamb?"* And her favorite, *"I'm a lamb who's lost in the wood."*

"Don't mind an old man, Rudy," his grandfather finally spoke. "I know you think Emie's a lost lamb, and you're just the shepherd who can find her, but it don't work that way. Your grandma and me shared a special song, but we both knew that Jesus, the Good Shepherd, was the only one who could help lost lambs. Give Emie time, son. Don't rush her."

Emie had said the same thing, but had used different words. Rudy wondered why it was easier to hear "wait" from his Grandpappy than from the girl he loved. He supposed it was a matter of the heart.

As Rudy readied to exit the church and head home, his Pappy patted his back, "If Emie's the one God has for you, don't worry what others will think. Ministry is mighty fine, son, but it can't replace a good woman holdin' you at night."

Chapter Twenty Five

*"It's bad luck to watch a friend leaving if you continue watching
until the person is out of sight."
(Appalachian Folk Belief)*

Emie knew it was time to talk with Ernest. It was bothering her to
keep the baby a secret from her brother. In fact, she had asked
Justice a short time ago, to take her brother a message. She would
have gone to see Ernest herself, but knew she wouldn't be
welcomed at the Ashby homestead.

As she sat on the front porch steps, shelling beans for Auntie,
Emie recalled when her aunt had first suggested that a baby was on
the way. *I was so frightened*, she thought.

Now, she was growing accustomed to the idea. She had fought
with God just like Jacob. She'd wrestled with her thoughts, going
to dark places, trying to understand about Charlie and the baby. In
the end, though she didn't understand, God performed a miracle.
She was still scared, but she was falling in love more and more
each day with the baby growing inside her, and on most days, love
overshadowed her fear.

She needed her brother. She needed her friend, Rudy, and she
also needed Aunt Ada and her small community. She knew they
would all help in the days to come.

Before she knew it, the beans were shelled and soaking in the
clay bowl next to her. She was ready to begin work on her willow
baskets. She was thankful for Rudy's daddy's help in selling her

wares. Mr. Blessman encouraged her to grow in her craftsmanship and to develop what he called "business savvy."

During her last visit to the store, he had been very complimentary, "Emerald, you're a talented young woman. I have two stores in Charleston that are interested in showin' your goods."

Emie enjoyed talking with Rudy's dad. He was thoughtful, fair, and honest. Mr. Blessman had grown up in the holler, and like Doc, had left for college and then returned to his roots. When he came back to Big Creek, he brought Rudy's mother with him. After spending time with the couple, it was easy for Emie to understand Rudy's kind nature. On an especially difficult day, Mr. Blessman had encouraged Emie, "I can see why Rudy enjoys his friendship with you." On her way back to Auntie's that afternoon, Emie had felt like she was floating in the air, like the red balloon that Mimi had once brought to school for "show me and tell me."

Her thoughts were interrupted by Ernest, who was running through the meadow yelling and waving his hands like a madman. Worried, Emie quickly rose from the wooden porch steps and sprinted toward her brother. They met just past the maple tree.

Ernest was so out of breath that it took Emie a minute to understand what he was saying, "What's wrong, sister? Justice said you were needin' to see me."

"Ernest, nothing's wrong. I asked Justice to have you come callin' when you had opportunity. Didn't he tell you that?"

Ernest had run all the way from the Ashby barn to Auntie's cabin. "Yes…that's what he said…but you've never sent Justice to get me before."

"Brother, let's take a walk."

Ernest took a couple deep breaths. "Emie, can't you see I'm out of breath? I ran the whole way. I ain't wantin' to take a walk."

"And you ain't wantin' to be too friendly neither," she teased.

Emie took her brother's elbow and led him to the front porch where Rain was sniffing her bowl of beans. She sat down and put the growing puppy in her lap, and then motioned for Ernest to sit as well. Soon Rain would be too big for her to cradle, but another treasure would take his place.

It was obvious that her brother was frustrated. "Emie, don't be messin' with me. I wanna know what's goin' on."

She was nervous. "Rain's doin' good with his potty trainin'. Auntie says that he's a quick study…"

"Emie…"

"Mercy made a new dress. It's mighty nice. By the way, do you think Mercy's pretty?"

"Emerald…"

"Well, do you?"

Ernest was momentarily caught off guard. "Why, of course I think Mercy is pretty."

"I thought so," Emie giggled. "I've seen you lookin' at her. Is it her beautiful skin or the graceful way that she walks that you like so much?"

Ernest's face reddened with embarrassment. When he composed himself, he sternly asked his sister again, "What is goin' on?"

"Let me get you some lemonade. Auntie says that it's always nice to offer refreshments to visitors…"

"Sister, I ain't a visitor. I practically live here, but I'll take some lemonade. I'm a might dry, and it'll give you a chance to gather your words."

She headed to the kitchen and poured two glasses of the sweet mixture. Lemons were hard to come by. Rudy had brought them to the cabin several days ago as a special gift for Aunt Ada.

Auntie had showed Emie how to roll the lemons on the counter and then how to squeeze the fruit to release the precious juice. "Emie, if you roll the lemons hard, they'll release their sweetness. Just like the good Lord pressures us and in that pressin' we learn how to be sweet and kind." Auntie had then sweetened the juice with sugar and added water. The end result was both delicious and refreshing.

It was time to tell Ernest about the baby. She felt intimidated. She knew in the end that Ernest would be loving and kind, but she also knew that initially he would be very angry – not angry at her, but angry at Charlie, Eugene, and, of course, Daddy. She didn't like it when people were angry. Emie was tired of all the madness. She wanted peace: peace for herself and peace for her baby.

The expectant mom began to hum as she thanked God for the peace He had given; but in this moment she desperately needed more peace: peace for herself, peace for Auntie, peace for her friends, and, right now, especially, peace for Ernest.

As she headed back to the porch, her brother recognized her humming and started to sing, *"Peace, perfect peace, in this dark world of sin? The blood of Jesus whispers peace within. Peace, perfect peace, our future all unknown? Jesus we know and He is on the throne."*

Ernest sighed and Emie knew he was praying.

He took his glass of refreshment from his sister's hand and drank it down in one gulp. Emie then handed Ernest her glass, and he did the same. "Thank you. I'm feelin' better. I've heard about lemonade, but ain't never drank it. It's a might good, sweet and tart at the same time." Ernest looked directly at his sister, "Reminds me of someone I know. Now, girlie, are you ready to talk?"

She hung her head.

"Sister, I love you and nothin' can change that. Whatever is wrong, I'll do my best to help."

Emie knew that Ernest was worried, but she didn't know how to start their conversation, so she blurted out the first thing that came to mind, "Rudy wants to marry me."

"That's it, Emie! I raced over here for that?" Ernest couldn't help but laugh. "Rudy's been makin' cow eyes at you since you were all of five or six. Of course, he wants to marry you! I'm just surprised he waited this long to ask."

"Well, he did ask me once before, in the third grade…"

The brother and sister were laughing loudly when Auntie joined them on the porch.

"Well, Aunt Ada, Emie here is gettin' married. Rudy done asked." Ernest chuckled. "Maybe you all could have a double weddin'." Still teasing, he continued, "Well, girlie, did you say 'yes' or 'no?'"

"I said, 'Wait and see.'"

Ernest smiled, "Good answer, sister."

Auntie took a seat on her rocker. "Now, tell us, darlin', what prompted Rudy's proposal?"

"That's the hard part of the tellin'," the young woman answered.

Ernest, sensing that the foolery was over, turned to his sister and waited.

As she recounted what happened at the creek, Emie could see Ernest's shoulders tense. "Brother, please don't be angry."

"I'm not angry at you, I'm angry at what Charlie did to you."

"I understand that, Ernest. But I'm tired of everyone bein' mad all the time. I just want peace. Like you sang about."

Ernest placed his arm around her, "I'll try, Emie. Truly, I will."

"I want you to love my baby, Ernest."

"Girlie, what's there not to love? This baby is part of you. He or she will be a blessin', God's Word says so."

"The baby is also part of Charlie."

He gently squeezed his sister's shoulder, "I know that, but it won't make a difference."

Tears were rolling down Emie's cheeks as she shared her fear. "I want a girl. A boy might be like Charlie, and I couldn't bear it."

Aunt Ada rose from her chair and sat down on the opposite side of Emie. "Life is hard to understand, darlin'. What Charlie did to you was a horrible thing, and I wish your sufferin' were over. God's doin' a work, Emie. He loves you and loves your baby."

"We've wrestled some, but I know He's doin' a work. I can feel it. Maybe I'm like Jacob; God's wantin' to change my name," Emie answered.

Chapter Twenty Six

"If you say something three times, it must be true."
(Appalachian Folk Belief)

Ernest was on his way to meet with Mrs. Randolph. He had met with her several weeks before to discuss the teacher's college in Charleston. The visit had been difficult. He had known all summer that he wouldn't be able to leave the holler. He had also known that his decision to stay wouldn't surprise his beloved teacher. Auntie Ada often visited with Mrs. Randolph. He was certain that his aunt kept the teacher apprised of the hardships the Ashby family was facing.

Throughout the years, Mrs. Randolph had always been gracious and kind to Ernest. She had been dedicated in helping him graduate from high school and then prepare for college. He didn't want to disappoint her; he also didn't want her to feel that all her time and hard work had been for naught.

To thank Mrs. Randolph for all her kindness, Ernest was taking her a bouquet of fresh-picked daisies and a package of recently rendered bacon. *What a combination,* he thought, as he traveled down the dusty road to the schoolhouse.

He had picked the fall daisies himself, just moments after leaving the Ashby residence. Daisies littered the holler fields during the late summer and early fall. Auntie referred to them as Black-eyed Susans. Doc Bright had told Ernest that the name came from a sad song about a young woman with dark eyes, who was searching for Sweet William, the man she loved. The good doctor had even quoted the song. Ernest couldn't recall all the lyrics, but he did remember the final line, *Adieu, Susan, adieu, as she waved her lily hand.*

The bacon had been separated from the lot yesterday afternoon. His mama hadn't asked where the bacon was intended; she had simply followed Ernest's request that it be wrapped in old newspaper and set aside. Maybe in his mother's eyes, he was finally becoming a man, no longer a child where every decision had to be questioned and discussed at length.

Even through the newspaper, the smell of the bacon overpowered the delicately scented daisies. Ernest had half a mind to throw the flowers in the roadside ditch. Then he remembered Mercy gathering daisies after school yesterday. She had put some in a Mason jar with water and had also woven two rings of daisies and carefully placed them around Amos' and Andy's necks. He had laughed right along with the four boys at Mercy's clever idea. The usual ornery mules had peacefully stood side by side, nibbling at each other. Auntie considered the daisies weeds, but since Mercy seemed to enjoy them so much, Ernest figured that Mrs. Randolph might like them as well.

Lessons were drawing to a close when Ernest arrived at the schoolyard. He saw his sisters exit the schoolhouse; in fun, he nonchalantly sat on one of the swings on the playground, and waited to see if they would notice him. Opal was the first to spot her brother. She ran toward him, yelling with glee. She instantly climbed onto his lap, wanting to be hugged. Coral greeted him, but as usual, she stood back, always the observer.

Ernest had plenty on his mind with the hogs, schooling, Emie, and the baby, but lately it seemed that Coral was never too far from his thoughts. She'd grown even quieter since learning about what Charlie had done to Emie. Ernest had been naïve to hope that Coral wouldn't understand the concept of rape. He had also hoped to protect Coral from learning about their daddy's decision to marry her off to Charlie. He'd been wrong on both counts. Even at the age of twelve, Coral understood about violence and the backwoods ways of the holler.

Opal began talking a mile a minute about the day's activities. Ernest let her ramble before he looked to Coral for an answer.

"I wrote a poem about bumblebees," she replied.

He was eager to visit with Mrs. Randolph, but it was so rare for Coral to share something personal that he waited while she recited her poem.

"Nice job, sister. Did you know that words like buzz are called 'onomatopoeias'?"

Coral replied in an adult-like voice, "Yes, I did brother."

Ernest smiled proudly, "I need to talk with Mrs. Randolph. If my two favorite sisters would like to wait for me, I would be delighted to walk them home."

Opal spoke up, "You tell every sister that she's your favorite, Ernest."

"No, I don't," he responded with a gleam in his eye.

Opal then answered for the two sisters, "Yes, you do, but we'll wait for you anyway. Won't we, Coral?"

Coral merely nodded "yes" and then picked up Mrs. Randolph's gifts that he had sat on the merry-go-round. Ernest winked at Coral as he took the gifts from her hands.

Mrs. Randolph was waiting for him by the flagpole. "Ernest, it's so nice to see you."

He hesitated in giving her his gifts; he felt like a young school lad bringing his teacher an apple. When he stepped forward, the kindly teacher sensed his awkwardness. "Are those for me?" she asked.

His face flushed. "Yes, to offer thanks for all you've done."

She smiled and invited Ernest into the schoolhouse. "I'm so glad that you stopped by. I have wonderful news. When I told the college administration about your work with colored children, they agreed to sponsor you..."

"I'm sorry, Mrs. Randolph," Ernest interrupted. "But I don't understand. What do you mean by 'sponsor me'?"

"Each year the college selects a future educator and provides the resources to help him or her succeed. The school administration has agreed to assist you with curriculum, desks, school supplies, and minimal funding for a school building for the colored children in the holler. They will even provide you with a small salary."

"Mrs. Randolph, do they know I only have five students?"

"Yes, but with their support, Ernest, you can add a number of additional students."

He starting thinking about the vision God had given him. He hesitated to share the experience with his teacher. He didn't want her to think of him as odd or strange. "Mrs. Randolph, I don't want you to think I'm crazy, but God showed me that I would teach Negro children. He gave me a vision of sorts. I was teachin' the children the basics, and also tellin' them about Jesus."

"Ernest, I don't think you're crazy. God speaks to us each and every day. We just need to listen." The teacher smiled and continued, "The best part is that you don't need to travel to Charleston to get your teaching credentials. Because of the work you are already doing, the school has agreed to let you take correspondence courses. The courses will have to be completed in a timely manner, and it will be my job to oversee your studies. The tuition is minimal, and, as you know, Ada has set aside funds to help you."

Ernest could hardly believe the good news. Once again, God had shown Himself faithful.

Ernest danced from the schoolhouse to the playground. He picked up a sister in each arm and spun around until they were all dizzy. He could hardly contain himself.

Chapter Twenty Seven

"Name a fishing hook after the person you love. If you catch a fish with the hook, it means the love is true."
(Appalachian Folk Belief)

Rudy had worked with Ernest all morning. He was debating whether to head to Auntie Ada's and see Emie or not. He was hot and sweaty and was worried that his odor might be offensive. He'd been working with the hogs and was certain he smelled like one. Ernest had caught him sniffing his own armpits.

"Wantin' to walk over and see Emie, are ya?" Ernest laughed.

Rudy replied, "Yes," then paused. Exasperated he continued, "You know I asked her to marry me."

"She told me about it," Ernest answered.

"I love her."

"I know you do, Rudy. Just give her time."

"Grandpappy told me the same thing. I don't understand what she's thinkin'. It would be much simpler to just get married. She could tell everyone that the baby was mine. We'd settle down here in the holler…"

Ernest's chuckles interrupted his friend's words. "You got it all figured out, Rudy."

"I thought I had it figured out, but she won't cooperate."

"Women are like that at times," the older of the two responded. "Not that I know that much about women folk," Ernest continued.

"You know more than I do," Rudy answered. "You got all them sisters."

"Sisters ain't the same, that I do know." Ernest handed Rudy a bucket. "Fill it with water from the pump. There's a piece of soap and rag in the barn."

Rudy quickly washed and headed toward Aunt Ada's. He found Emie sitting on the front porch peeling apples. It warmed his heart to see her smile as he approached.

"I'm helpin' Auntie make pies. We got one on the fire, and I'm makin' ready for a second one. I hope you ain't in a hurry."

"No. I worked with Ernest this mornin' and wanted to stop by and visit."

She smiled again and then turned back to her work. She seemed content to sit quietly and focus on coring and peeling her apples.

After a few minutes of silence, Rudy thought of the perfect way to get his girl's attention. "I saw Mimi yesterday."

Emie looked up and waited eagerly for Rudy to expound. When he didn't say anything more she fired a series of questions his way. "How is she? What's she been doin', Rudy? What was she wearin'? Did you tell her about the baby?"

"Whoa, whoa, Emerald! Not so many questions at once! I didn't quiz her. We just shared a few words outside my daddy's store," Rudy laughed.

"You're bein' mean, Rudy. Tell me everything. Every detail."

"She's just fine, Emie. Been spendin' time with her family in Spencer. And no, I didn't tell her about the baby. Wasn't my place. If and when you see her, you can tell her what you want."

"Did she look pretty, Rudy? What was she wearin'? Somethin' nice, I bet."

Rudy was puzzled. He wasn't quite sure how to answer. "I don't know, Emie, she looked like she always looks. Was wearin' something pink, I think, and frilly."

Tears welled up in Emie's eyes. "Rudy, I know you've always liked her. You think she's pretty. I know you do. You even remembered what she was wearin'."

"Emie, you asked me what she was wearin'!"

"I saw you push her on the swings at school. You're sweet on her. Tell me the truth."

Rudy was stunned. He'd never seen Emie like this before.

"Admit it, Rudy. You pushed her on the swings…"

"Emie, we went to school together. I pushed you on the swings, too."

"She's pretty, and I look like a blimp. You do know what a blimp is, don't you? We read about it at school," she continued sarcastically.

"Emie, ain't I always told you that you're the prettiest girl in the holler? I ain't changed my mind. "

"Mimi is so sophisticated, and I'm some homely holler girl. She can dance the Charleston and sing like a lark. In my family only Ernest can sing. Did she dance or sing for you, Rudy?"

"I already told you, Emie, we were standin' in front of my daddy's store. Of course, she didn't dance or sing." Rudy shook his head in frustration.

"And don't be shakin' your head at me, Rudy. It makes me mad."

"Seems like you're plenty mad, and I ain't done nothin', Emie. I'm gonna head on home. When you're back to normal, let me know. I'll come callin' again." Rudy stood up to leave. "And by the way, I do know what a blimp is!"

Emie knew she was being unreasonable. According to Doc, her hormones were out of whack. She wasn't exactly sure what that meant, but never in her life had she been so unkind to Rudy.

She was also experiencing a new emotion – jealousy. She was worried that Rudy liked Mimi. What happened if he wanted to marry Mimi instead of her? What would she do? Just the thought squeezed her heart so tight that she struggled to form words in her mouth. She needed to apologize.

Emie stood to her feet. "Rudy," she yelled. "I'm sorry."

He turned back toward her and without thinking, she blew him a kiss.

Rudy ran his fingers through his red tufts of hair, making his cowlick even more pronounced, then he sighed. "Emie, I'm frustrated, but it does my heart good to see you jealous."

When he finally smiled, Emie knew that all would be well.

"And by the way, Emerald Ashby, next time you kiss me, it won't be your sweet breath carried to me by the wind. It will be your lips on mine, and not just one little smooch, neither."

She felt her face grow hot, and was glad that Rudy was some distance away. "That's naughty talk, Rudy."

"It ain't naughty talk when two people care for each other like we do. I'm needin' to do some thinkin', Emie. I'll be back later for apple pie."

Emie looked down at her bowl of apple slices. There seemed to be more than enough for a second pie. Rain came around the side of the house and nuzzled her hand. The same hand she had used to blow Rudy a kiss. She stooped to pick up the worn enamel bowl filled with apple slices. She placed the paring knife and extra apples on top the bowl and headed into the house.

Aunt Ada, Doc, Emie, and Ernest were gathered in the cabin's small sitting room. There weren't enough chairs, so Ernest was stretched out on the floor. Rain was sitting beside him. Generally Rain paid no attention to anyone else if Emie was present. Ernest wondered what he had done to deserve the dog's affections, then he remembered the piece of dried meat in his pocket that Mercy had wrapped and given him earlier. Justice was quite the hunter. He kept the small community supplied with fresh game and often dried the meat.

Emie said it reminded her of the vaqueros who would place meat under their saddles and let it dry out in the heat. Ernest had told his sister that he'd yet to see Justice sitting on Amos or Andy with meat between his bottom and their backs.

The foursome had enjoyed dinner together. Ada was a fine cook. Ernest had eaten more than his share of venison. The backstrap had been prepared just right, seasoned with onions and herbs from the garden behind the cabin. The potatoes had been harvested a week earlier. Ernest understood that Emie had retrieved them from their place of rest in the root cellar. The potatoes had been seasoned with rosemary and then roasted on the fire. Ada had even made yeast rolls. She had made more than enough rolls and had put Ernest in charge of delivering the extras to Justice and his family.

Ernest had been embarrassed when he arrived back at Auntie's from his errand. The others were waiting for him at the table. What should have been a quick errand ended up in a nice conversation with Mercy. *She is so unassuming, gentle, and soft spoken, yet such a distraction,* Ernest secretly chided himself.

After dinner, the small family enjoyed slices of apple pie served with fresh cream. A portion of the large orange harvest moon could be seen from the front window. Ernest enjoyed the heavily treed areas of the holler, but just for tonight, he wished he could see the singing moon in its fullness. He knew from Mrs. Randolph that the term singing moon was based on folklore; it had something to do with wolves singing to keep the farmers awake as they hurried to harvest their fall crops under the light of the harvest moon. He didn't think much of the tale; he simply liked the idea of the moon singing in worship to God.

Ernest's thoughts were interrupted by Auntie's praise for Emie's apple pie, "You done good, my girl. The apples are seasoned just right, and the crust is nice and flakey. Just like I taught you."

He nodded along with Doc in agreement with Ada's compliment. Ernest's heart swelled with pride. Emie was becoming a fine young woman. He worried some about the baby, but was working on disciplining his mind. Worry was like the darkness of night. It crept in slowly. He knew that thinking about the light of God would drive away the darkness of worry.

The group began discussing wedding plans. Ada and Christian's wedding was a mere few days away. Emie and Ernest were to stand beside the couple as they exchanged their vows. Rudy's grandpappy would do the honor of performing the wedding. Ada's and Emie's dresses were readied. Doc had purchased himself a new suit and a suit for Ernest. The menu was planned. The church ladies would be making and serving the food. Ada had woven a canopy of willow branches that the couple planned to stand under for their first kiss as husband and wife. All seemed to be in good order.

The conversation shifted again when Doc brought up the subject of Lester. He addressed Ernest and Emie. "I received a letter from your brother yesterday."

"Where is he, and how is he?" Ernest anxiously asked.

"He's in Charleston. Mrs. Randolph's family helped him get settled. Charleston is a big city, but Lester doesn't want me to pass along any more information about where he is living. He made some enemies here in the holler and is worried that the two of you might be pressed for his whereabouts. He's working hard and going to church. He even has a side job making extra money."

Ada wanted to know where he was going to church. Emie seemed curious for more details about everything, and Ernest wanted to know where Lester was working and what his side job entailed.

Doc answered the best he could but didn't seem interested in expounding about Lester's additional source of income. Ernest couldn't help himself. He pressed Doctor Bright for more information. Finally, the doctor had no choice but to answer, "He's driving in the stock car races."

Before the good doctor could respond to Emie and Ada's puzzled looks, Ernest spoke up, "I read about the races. Some of them moonshiners soup up their cars tryin' to outrun the law. Then they'll go up in the hills and race each other. Sometimes there's gamblin' to see who wins." Ernest couldn't help but laugh, "It's just like Lester to get involved in some dare-devil craziness. Heck, I didn't even know he could drive a car."

Auntie Ada shook her head in concern, "Oh, my. He's playin' with the devil again."

"Now, Ada," Christian spoke, "Lester seems to be doing just fine. He's attending church and growing in his faith. Give him time. I think he's even sweet on a girl. She's going to church with him."

Ernest, still laughing, added his own opinion, "Ah, come on, Doc Bright. Just 'cause you're in love doesn't mean that Lester's been bitten."

After the goodbyes were said, Emie gathered water from the pump in the kitchen. She brushed her teeth and washed her face. She changed into her gown and then snuggled under the covers. Sleep wouldn't come. Her thoughts were racing like the moonshiners' cars that Lester drove.

Her initial thoughts were of Rudy. True to his word, he had stopped by in the early evening just before dinner. The sun was starting to hang low in the sky. He didn't stay very long, which was well and good, since Auntie had put her in charge of setting the table and making the final preparations for the evening meal. When invited for dinner, Rudy explained that his mama was waiting supper for him at home. Of course, that didn't stop the young man from eating a large piece of apple pie. When Aunt Ada served the slice to Rudy, Emie could hardly believe the size of it. *Who could eat that much pie in one sitting,* she had pondered. Well, Rudy ate it all and then complimented Emie on its goodness. Rudy had also winked at her, when Auntie wasn't looking, and had whispered "darlin'" in her ear, which she found very unnerving.

Who knew that blowing a kiss would have this effect, she thought. Why, she'd even seen Mercy blow kisses at Amos and Andy. Of course, Mercy had been teasing the boys, and Emie wasn't sure it was proper to compare Rudy to a mule, but there was definitely something not right with him.

"Lord, please have mercy on me," she prayed. There was a part of her that wanted to laugh, and a part of her that wanted to cry. She wanted to understand the change in her friend. Maybe if the wind carried her kiss to Rudy, it could carry it right back, and return things to the way they were.

She also thought about Ernest discussing the "love bite" with Doc Bright. What kind of bite did love entail? Was it a gentle nibble or did it draw blood? Or maybe it was both?

Next her mind traveled to the snake handlers that had visited Big Creek Church last summer. The congregation was mesmerized by the two men who picked up rattlers and wrapped them around their necks and limbs. Neither of the men were bitten by the venomous snakes. Auntie had said that it was plumb foolishness, and that God's people shouldn't test their Maker.

Emie wasn't sure about the snake handlers, whether their actions were foolish or not; she just wanted to understand what it meant to be bitten by love. She had wanted to ask Ernest, but then thought better of it. Maybe Aunt Ada was a better choice on the questions of romance.

Rain started to whine. She'd completely forgotten about his nighttime piddle. Emie rose from under the covers, picked up the puppy, and held him outside her bedroom window. Soon he would be too heavy for their nightly ritual.

That night with Rain by her side, she dreamed about Rudy. He was standing in Auntie's garden eating the biggest piece of apple pie imaginable. A small garter snake was crawling around his feet. Rudy picked up the snake, examined it closely, and with a big smile put it in his overall pocket.

Chapter Twenty Eight

"If a cricket chirps in your fireplace, all will go well."
(Appalachian Folk Belief)

Ernest arrived at Aunt Ada's early the next morning. When he had left the Ashby household, it was completely dark. No one was awake yet from their night's slumber; he was hoping that Auntie and Emie were still dreaming as well. He knew Justice's morning routine and wanted to visit the gentle giant in private. Just as Ernest suspected, he found his friend feeding Amos and Andy. Thunder was close by, sniffing the grass and wetting his muzzle with the morning dew. A mist hung in the air that would soon dissipate with the morning light.

Just as Ernest readied to announce his arrival, Justice offered his greetings. "Good mornin', Ernest." The man chuckled. "I know your footsteps, plus you were hummin'."

Justice didn't look up from his chores, but Ernest wasn't offended. He knew that the mules could get ornery in a flash. It was always best to be on the lookout for Amos and Andy's antics.

"Do you have a few minutes before the troops are up?" Ernest asked.

"I think we got a little time before the commotion starts," Justice answered. "Them boys sound like a troop of soldiers, don't they? Runnin', yellin', and fightin'. Wouldn't trade 'em for nothin' though. Cece and I love 'em like they was our own."

The older man finished with the mules and sat down on a log next to the lean-to. Thunder, wanting attention, placed his wet muzzle on the man's lap. Justice didn't seem to mind the wetness and patted Thunder's head and rubbed his ears. Ernest joined the man and his dog, and started right in; he knew his time was limited. Soon the small community would be up and about and all privacy would be lost.

"I've been burstin' to tell you some news, Justice. Mrs. Randolph talked to the college in Charleston about me teachin' the boys and Mercy. The college wants to help us with a school for the colored children in the holler."

"God be praised, Ernest! I been praying about those children." Justice responded. "I'll help any way I can."

"I was hopin' you would say that. I'll be needin' your guidance. I think the first thing is to find a schoolhouse. Anything come to mind?"

"Let me think on it a bit. I know that Cece's cousin has a good size buildin' on the land he works. Don't know what the landowner would think about havin' a school there. It's a few miles up the holler, just past the hogback. Close to where a lot of colored folk live."

"Should I call on Cece's cousin and see what he thinks?" Ernest asked.

"Now, Ernest, I think I best do the callin'. Ain't too many white folk come visitin' up there."

"Alright, Justice. Let's keep this between you and me for now. I'm needin' to settle a couple things."

As Ernest stood to leave, Justice suggested that they share a moment of prayer. The teacher was moved by his friend's prayer. The words were stitched together with humility and sincerity. Ernest also appreciated Justice's insight. His friend prayed for him to have the courage to do what was right. He needed courage, especially today. It was time to tell Mama and Daddy about his plans.

Ernest arrived back at home as his mama was finishing breakfast preparations. She had just taken the buttermilk biscuits from the oven. The tops were golden brown. The sausage gravy was thickening on the stove, and the fried potatoes smelled of onion and green pepper.

"Where you been this early?" his mama asked.

"I had a quick errand at Aunt Ada's."

His mother shook her head in response and turned back to the stove.

Ernest put the plates and silverware on the table. Lester and Daddy believed that kitchen work was only for women, but Ernest felt differently. Work was work and if it needed done, why not help? He could hear his sisters chatting in the other room. "Is daddy awake?" he inquired.

"He's waitin' for his breakfast," his mother answered.

"I'm needin' to have a moment with the two of you this mornin'."

"Let him eat his breakfast in peace. You may as well have a bite yourself before the trouble starts."

"Mama, who says I'm wantin' to make trouble?"

"Are you forgettin' that I'm the one who birthed you? You're a man now, son, but I can still read your face. You got somethin' that needs said and whatever it is, you know your daddy ain't gonna like it."

His mama took his plate, filled it from the stove, and motioned for him to sit. She then prepared his daddy's plate and headed into the other room. A few minutes later, the girls joined him at the breakfast table. While Coral helped the smaller girls with their food, Ernest filled the glasses with milk. Thanks to Garnett and Ruby, the Ashby household had an abundance of milk these days.

When the older sisters married, he worried that they would forget the little ones, but just the opposite seemed true. Garnett and Ruby were happy to share what they had with the youngsters. He wished they'd take an interest in Emie, but he understood why they didn't. Plain and simple, Daddy wouldn't like it. To embrace Emie meant sacrificing Coral, Opal, Pearl, and Sapphire. The married sisters knew that the next-in-line sister was in good hands at Aunt

Ada's, while the wellbeing of the youngest siblings depended on Daddy's mood.

The morning drew to a close before opportunity made way for Ernest to talk with his parents. "Mrs. Randolph and I had a visit a few days ago," he began. "The teacher's college in Charleston wants to help me start a school here in the holler for the colored children."

"Why that's nice, son," his mama interjected.

Always the peacemaker, Ernest thought. She's spent her life tryin' to appease, and it's brought her nothin' but heartache.

Ahab looked at his wife in a condescending way. "There ain't nothin' nice about it, Alma. Can't you see the boy ain't done sharin' his news! Teachin' school means not workin' the hogs."

"You're right, Daddy. For me to teach school means changin' how things is done."

His mama sighed and his daddy huffed.

Ernest waited a mere moment and then continued, "I don't have it all worked out, but I'm thinkin' that Rudy will be willin' to help in the mornings and evenings. I'm hopin' he'll take meat for his daddy's store in payment for his work. Dependin' on where the school's located, I may or may not be here durin' the week, but I'll work the hogs on the weekends."

He could see his daddy's face flame up with anger. The red color started at his neck and worked its way up to his chin, ears, cheeks, and forehead. His blue eyes also bulged. "I've lost both my boys, Alma! One's disappeared and the other's chosen colored folk over his family." Ahab harshly grabbed his wife's forearm. "It's your fault, woman…"

Before his daddy's aggression could continue, Ernest stepped in. He gripped his daddy's hand. When the older of the two gave way, Ernest put his daddy's hand back in his lap. "Daddy, nobody's done nothin'. This is my decision. The college will be payin' me for teaching. It won't be much, but it'll help our family."

"That money will be comin' to me, Ernest. It'll be payment for leavin' your family," his father spoke.

"I'll be usin' the money to help my sisters with clothes, food, and such," Ernest declared boldly. "I think I can manage what the college gives me myself. I'm grown now, Daddy."

"You're grown when I say you're grown."

Ernest raised his shoulders and stood taller. "Really, Daddy. I don't want to disrespect you, but you can't keep me under your thumb. In this family there are some things that even you can't control."

His daddy started to argue, but then stopped. His voice grew quiet. "You said what you needed to say, now leave me be."

The change was like the sails on a ship when the wind died. All the bluster was gone. Ahab began to mumble. The mutterings were about his sons leaving, but Ernest couldn't understand much more. His mama started to move toward his daddy, but Ernest motioned for her to stop. He helped his daddy from the wheelchair to the bed. As Ahab struggled to turn himself toward the wall, his leg blanket rose and Ernest caught a glimpse of his daddy's badly scarred legs. When Ernest attempted to pull the blanket down, the older man only pushed his hands away.

His mama silently left the bedroom. Ernest followed her into the kitchen. He wondered if she tasted the salt from her tears as they rolled down her cheeks, touching the outline of her lips. He wanted to offer her comfort and encouragement, but the words were gone. They'd all been said at one time or another, and, after being unheeded, were carried off by the wind; they were lost now. They had gone to places unknown and couldn't be found. He noticed that the woodpile by the stove was low. He walked out the kitchen door toward the barn. He made three trips back and forth from the woodpile to the kitchen. He carried fuel for the day's remaining meals and probably enough for the following day as well. Though words escaped him, perhaps his actions would offer solace.

Chapter Twenty Nine

"It's bad luck to bathe on your wedding day."
(Appalachian Folk Belief)

It was a glorious day for a wedding. The afternoon sun was shining brightly in the sky. The fall breeze cooled the air enough for the guests to be comfortable in the wooden chairs that had been borrowed from the schoolhouse. Justice had used his cart, pulled by Amos and Andy, to haul the chairs from town, and Emie and Mercy, under Ada's direction, had placed the seats in the meadow for the service. Nature had decorated the meadow with fall wildflowers. Red, orange, and golden leaves from the heavily treed woods behind the meadow made the perfect backdrop. Bouquets of dried lavender tied with burlap twine hung from the chairs located at the end of the rows. Every detail had been attended to.

Most of the guests had arrived when Doc and Ernest took their place in front of the congregation. Ada and Emie stood at the back, out of view, under a small cluster of trees. Emie could tell that her aunt was slightly nervous. She wondered if Aunt Ada's nervousness stemmed from thoughts about the honeymoon more than the ceremony. Emie had overheard a conversation between her aunt and Mrs. Randolph that suggested such.

Ada and Christian were going to a fancy hotel in Spencer for their honeymoon. The couple didn't want to travel the distance to

Charleston, and also preferred the quaintness of Spencer over the big city. At Ada's request, Ernest would be keeping Emie company at night. It didn't seem to matter that Justice and his family were a stone's throw away. Auntie wanted to be sure that her girlie was safe and sound.

Emie looked for Rudy in the crowd. She spotted his red locks and smiled. Rudy had started calling her "darlin'"; maybe she should start calling him "Red." It had a nice ring to it. If he had a special name for her, then she wanted a special name for him. Maybe she would write a letter to Mimi and ask her friend.

Emie saw her little sisters sitting with the twins and their husbands toward the back of the meadow. She then noticed her parents sitting toward the front. Her mama was sitting at the outside end of a row with her daddy in his wheelchair right beside. Looking at them brought back painful memories to Emie, and she turned away. Today was a day of celebration, not sorrow.

As Pastor Rex called the guests to attention, Ada and Emie moved from the shadows toward the back row of chairs, and waited for their cue. When Mercy started singing "The Man I Love," Emie began to walk slowly down the aisle in front of Ada. Auntie said that the song rang true for her; she had waited a long time for Christian to come her way.

Someday he'll come along, the man I love. And he'll be big and strong, the man I love. And when he comes my way, I'll do my best to make him stay. He'll look at me and smile, I'll understand. And in a little while, he'll take my hand.

Emie smiled at Mercy. Her voice was lovely. Both Auntie and Doc thought it absurd that in the holler colored people and white people didn't mix much. Emie agreed. She loved Mercy like she was one of her own sisters. Emie then focused her eyes on Ernest and Uncle Christian, what Doc Bright now insisted that she call him. When she reached the front, she turned to look at her love aunt. Ada's face was beaming. Christian stepped forward, taking Ada's hand in his much larger, broader hand.

The ceremony was lovely. Emie caught herself dreaming about marrying Rudy one day. Maybe they'd marry on a fall day in the meadow just like her aunt and uncle. The vows were said and the rings exchanged. Emie knew that Pastor Rex was ready to pronounce the couple "husband and wife." Then the couple would move to the vine canopy that Auntie had labored over, and exchange their first kiss as husband and wife.

Before the pronouncement began, Rudy's grandpappy was interrupted by her daddy's bombastic voice, "I object."

Everyone in the congregation grew quiet. Even the babies seemed to quit fussing. Emie knew that the holler people would be talking about this ceremony for years to come.

"Ahab, I didn't ask if there were any objections," Pastor Rex spoke.

"Well, I object nonetheless."

"There's nothin' to object to," the pastor answered. "I think the bride and groom are old enough to know what they're doin'."

Pastor Rex's words brought a chuckle from the congregation. Emie was relieved that the minister was making light of her daddy's words and attempting to continue the ceremony. She glanced at Ernest, who was shaking his head in disbelief. He looked like he was trying to wake himself up from a bad dream. Emie understood exactly how he felt. She hung her head. She was embarrassed and ashamed to be her daddy's daughter.

"I ain't objectin' to the couple marryin'," Ahab declared loudly. "I'm objectin' to a harlot standin' as a witness."

When Emie looked up from the crushed meadow grass by her feet, all eyes were upon her. At first she was confused by her daddy's words, but slowly, understanding came. Ernest walked toward her, stood by her side, and then placed his arm around her shoulders. She saw Rudy leave his seat. Everything and everyone seemed to be moving in slow motion. Rudy came and stood by her other side, his hand grasping her trembling one.

Her daddy continued his onslaughts, "Her mama suspects that the girlie's havin' a baby. She ain't married. She admitted to sexin' with Charlie. There might be others. She ain't fit to be here!"

Emie wanted to melt like the wicked witch in the book, "The Wonderful Wizard of Oz." Or better yet, maybe if she clicked her shoes together and said, "There's no place like home," she would be magically transported somewhere else. Then again, this was home, at least her earthly home.

Ernest tightened his grip on her shoulder. She could feel his anger. When he started to step forward, Pastor Rex put his arm out and held him in place.

"Ahab, I'm askin' you to be still," Pastor Rex spoke sternly. "This ain't the time or place. We got a weddin' to finish…"

Ahab ignored the pastor and continued his rantings. The congregation, now recovered from their initial shock, began murmuring one to another. As their voices grew stronger, Emie felt herself grow weaker. She wished that God would take her to heaven, like Enoch, who was and then was no more.

Suddenly, Emie felt Rudy raise their hands in the air, like two champions linked side-by-side crossing a finish line. "The baby's mine," he declared. "I've asked Emie to marry me and don't see a reason not to exchange our promises right here and now along with Auntie and Doc."

Pastor Rex looked directly at Rudy, "Son, did Emie say 'yes' to marryin' you?"

Rudy released Emie's hand gently. It fell limply to her side. She was too stunned for words. Rudy then got down on one knee and proposed in front of the entire holler. When she didn't immediately respond, he addressed her in a soft voice, "Emie, when a fella asks for your hand, it's nice to answer. Even if it's the third time he's askin'.'"

Words didn't come, but she shook her head "yes" in response. Her heart was pounding. Was she doing the right thing? The wrong thing? Who knew? God knew, but He seemed so far away. Somehow His voice couldn't be heard above her daddy's.

Rudy rose to his feet, took her hand, and led her to where Auntie and Christian were standing. She looked at Aunt Ada. Emie was looking for answers, but Ada's eyes showed the same confusion that was clouding her own thoughts. When Emie looked closer, she could see her aunt's lips moving slightly. Aunt Ada was praying. Emie felt a sense of relief wash over her.

Out of the corner of her eye, Emie saw Sheriff Robbins stand to his feet. "Now, Pastor," the sheriff spoke. "The laws of West

Virginia say that if a person is under the age of fifteen that he or she can't marry unless the parents give permission."

Pastor Rex looked in the direction of where Rudy's parents were sitting. Rudy's mama was crying, and his daddy looked as dazed as Emie felt.

When Rudy's father stood to his feet, Emie's heart skipped a beat. Rudy wasn't quite fifteen. What if his parents didn't approve? Not only would she be a harlot, like Daddy said, but a jilted bride to boot.

All eyes were on the young man's parents. Rudy squeezed her hand gently and smiled. Emie wished that she shared his confidence.

"I think they're a might young," Rudy's daddy spoke out. "But his mama and I are committed to helping them. My son loves Emerald Ashby and now with a baby on the way, it seems best."

"I object," Ahab yelled once again.

"What are you objectin' to now?" Pastor Rex asked sarcastically.

"I ain't ready to give my permission. At least not now. I'm needin' to think on it a bit," Ahab added.

"Well, Ahab, how much time are we talkin'?" Pastor Rex questioned.

"I ain't rightly sure, but it won't be today!"

Pastor Rex shook his head, Emie supposed in frustration. He then stepped aside and motioned for the sheriff to join him. Before he headed to the front, MayLou patted her husband's arm reassuringly.

Emie strained to hear what the man of the cloth and the man of the law were saying, but she couldn't make out the words. Her eyes were puddled with tears. She'd endured more humiliation than anyone ought to bear. She looked around. People were shaking their heads, waging their fingers, and nudging one another. She was never leaving her back porch room again. She would live out the remainder of her days alone. But then again, she wouldn't be living alone, she'd agreed to marry Rudy, and a baby was on the way. Well, they would all live in her small bedroom together with

Rain. That's how it would have to be. She and Rudy, along with the baby, would become a hermit family.

She felt Rudy squeeze her hand again. She looked at his face. He smiled at her and softly spoke, "You said, 'yes,' Emie. I can't believe you said, 'yes'! We belong to each other now."

"Rudy, I'm dying."

"No, you're not."

"I want you to dig a grave and bury me right here…"

Her words were stopped short when she saw Ernest move from the front and head toward where her parents were seated. She stared. She couldn't help it. This was like a tragic novel. She was the main character, yet she couldn't fathom what would happen next.

It was hard to tell, but she didn't think Ernest spoke at all to her daddy. He simply grabbed the back of the wheelchair, turned the chair around, and headed out from the meadow. Her mama rose to her feet and followed. Emie wished she could see her daddy's face. She wished she could see Ernest's face. She could hear her daddy cussing at Ernest, but couldn't make out much more.

Pastor Rex and Sheriff Robbins approached her and Rudy. The sheriff spoke first, "I'm sorry, Emie, Rudy, but the law's the law."

The pastor placed his arms in a semi-circle and gathered her and Rudy close. "You can't marry today, but God willin', you'll marry soon, and hopefully I'll be the one to lead you in your vows. Don't be grievin' for what you don't have, but be happy for what you do have. You've made a promise to each other and that's important." The good pastor reached into his left pant pocket, the side closest to his heart. "Emie this is the ring my wife wore. I've carried it with me every day since her death. I'm hopin' that you'll take it as a promise from and to my grandson."

"Emie, let me help you," Rudy whispered. He took the ring and placed it on her finger. "This means that we're engaged, Emerald. Not today, but someday soon we'll be together, you, me, and the baby."

Emie had things that she wanted say, but now wasn't the time. They were private things meant for Rudy only.

Pastor Rex called the congregation to order. "Well, this has been quite the day. Ain't never seen a weddin' quite like it." He chuckled and the congregation joined in. "I'm thinkin' we need to pray…"

Emie knew that Rudy's grandpappy was dulling the sharp edge that had cut and confused today, and refocusing the thoughts of everyone present on God and His goodness. When the prayer concluded, Pastor Rex graciously instructed the people, "Today we're celebratin' the marriage of two dear friends. When our thoughts come back to this weddin', we need to remember Ada and Christian, and the love they have for each other."

The wedding reception was a blur to Emerald. She and Rudy stayed close to one another. They held hands and twice he kissed her cheek. Rudy's parents and several others approached the young couple with congratulations, but for the most part, the holler people responded to Pastor Rex's direction and seemed to focus on Ada and Christian.

When Ernest returned, Emie tried to question him, but his answer was short and to the point. "It don't matter, sister. They ain't here. Let's celebrate the weddin'."

When it was time for Aunt Ada and Uncle Christian to leave for their honeymoon, her sweet aunt approached her with concern, "Emie, I'll be stayin' if you need me. Christian said it would be alright. I ain't wantin' you to worry none. We'll sort this out with your daddy and mama…"

"Auntie," Emie interrupted. "Go. Enjoy your honeymoon. Ernest will stay the nights with me like we planned. Rudy will come and visit. I'll also have Justice and his family. I'll be fine. I've got some thinkin' to do, and it'll do me good to have some time by myself."

Aunt Ada kissed Emie's check, and then turned toward her husband. The newlyweds left the meadow at dusk as the fireflies started their nightly dance.

When Emie began to help the church ladies clean up, Rudy winked at them and requested that his fiancée be relieved of KP duty. The ladies surprised Emie with their smiles and giggles.

"My hair might be a little gray, Rudy," MayLou spoke, "but I ain't so old that I can't remember young love. Walk your girl home and enjoy the evenin'."

The other ladies nodded in agreement, and Rudy lost no time in taking Emie's hand and leading her away from the crowd. Ernest waved and said that he'd see her shortly.

They were barely out of earshot when Rudy said, "Emie, I love you. Thank you for agreein' to marry me."

"Now, Rudy, I'm wantin' to talk about that…"

"You promised, Emerald, and my ring is on your finger."

"I know I promised, and I'm planning on keepin' my promise." She heard Rudy sigh with relief. "I'm just glad that we're waitin' a bit. Are you mad that we didn't marry today?"

"Emie, darlin', how could I be mad? You said, 'yes' to me. I don't mind waitin'. I want us both to feel ready."

"Rudy, with what my daddy said today, I don't want you to be ashamed of me."

"I could never be ashamed of you, Emie. Your daddy's the one who should be ashamed. Not you. You're lovely. I'm proud you're mine."

"Thank you. I don't want you to be judged because of me."

"No one's judgin' me, Emie. And they ain't judgin' you, neither. You heard my parents and Grandpappy give their blessing. Others also offered congratulations. The church ladies were kind, weren't they?"

"Yes."

"Don't let your daddy rain on our joy, darlin'. We got a lifetime of dreams to talk about."

"Rudy, why would you say that the baby was yours? What will your family think? What will the people in the holler say?"

Rudy placed his hands on her growing belly. "This baby is mine because he or she is yours. We share everything, Emie. My family knows exactly what Charlie did to you, but they will love this baby. They already love our baby. My mama's even workin' on diapers and clothes. And the people in the holler – well, I don't know what they'll say. Maybe that you're so beautiful that I couldn't keep my hands to myself." Rudy then kissed her soundly on the mouth.

Emie had worried about their first kiss. Would it bring back awful memories? Rudy's kiss was sweet and gentle. Tender. Auntie said that chicken was tender to the bone when it tasted so good that it almost melted in your mouth. Emie wanted to melt. Not like earlier, when she wanted to melt and disappear like the wicked witch. Now she just wanted to melt into Rudy's arms.

When they arrived at Ada's cabin, the couple sat on the front porch steps. They had sat there together on numerous occasions, but this time it felt different. They had crossed a bridge today. She thought of the other bridge they had crossed together: the bridge over Big Creek when Rudy carried her away from the nightmare of Charlie, that same bridge when she moved to Auntie's. Previously she knew where the bridges would take them, but this time the destination felt unknown.

Rudy interrupted her thoughts, "How many pieces of white cake did you eat, Emie?"

"I ain't tellin', but remember I'm eatin' for two," she answered.

"Darlin', I won't rush you to marry me. I promise."

Emie smiled. "We'll marry. It just may take some time. I'm wonderin' what my daddy was thinkin'. Maybe Ernest can shed some light."

"I'll sit here with you until he comes home. I want us to hear together what he has to say."

Now it was her turn to reassure Rudy. Their fingers were already entwined together, so she gently squeezed his hand.

"Rudy, have you ever kissed a girl before?"

"Why are you askin'? You didn't like my kiss?"

Emie could hear the insecurity in Rudy's voice. "It ain't that. I was just wonderin'."

"So you did like my kiss?"

"Yes."

"Emie, have no worries. I've been savin' all my kisses for you," he laughed good-naturedly.

"Who said I was worried?"

Rudy, still smiling, shook his head in response. "You amaze me, darlin'."

"And why are you callin' me 'darlin' all of a sudden?"

He turned and faced her. She could see the puzzled look on his face. "Emie, are you sayin' you don't like that neither?"

"I like it fine, and I already told you I like your kisses. I'm just curious."

"It just feels right. I've thought of you as 'darlin' for a long time, Emie. It just seems okay to say it now."

"Do you shave?"

"This is a strange conversation, Emerald Ashby."

"I'm just wonderin?"

"Yes, I shave."

"Every day?"

Emie knew that shaving was a sensitive issue when it came to boys. Ernest had talked with her about it once. He said that shaving was a rite of passage from boyhood to manhood. Of course, Ernest had said nothing about the frequency of shaving. Lester was hairy like Daddy, but Ernest not so much. Her thoughts returned to Rudy. Did he have chest hair? Should she ask?

"Emie, can we talk about something else?"

"Sure, Rudy. I'll stop askin' so many questions."

"It's not that, Emie, I like your questions, but things like kissin', endearments, and shavin' all remind me of our youth, and I know where you're headed. You think we're too young for a promise."

She hadn't realized until Rudy spoke it out loud that even on this special night, she was worried. Worried that Rudy loved her now, but wouldn't love her so much when the weight of being an adult rested on his shoulders.

"Rudy, just one more question."

"Alright, one more."

"Will you always love me?"

Without hesitation, Rudy answered, "Yes, Emie. I will always love you. In the good and the bad, I will stay faithful to God and to you."

She smiled at Rudy and then rested her head on his shoulder.

Rudy whispered in her ear, "Emie, when I say 'I love you,' I need you to say it back."

"I love you too, Red."

Ernest hoped that he had given Emie and Rudy enough time alone. It wasn't every day that a couple got engaged. He wanted his sister and her beau to enjoy some privacy before he joined them.

Well, Rudy, Ernest thought, *you got the answer you wished for – albeit not the way you expected. Welcome to the Ashby family!*

He knew that Emie would have a number of questions for him, but he wouldn't have any answers. His daddy cussed some, but other than that he didn't say a word. It was hard telling what he was up to. Even his mama had remained silent on the trek home.

He saw Rudy and Emie before they saw him. The two were sitting on the front porch steps holding hands. Emie's head was rested on Rudy's shoulder. It did his heart good to see Emie enjoying the affections of someone. He had worried that her mind and heart were tainted by Charlie.

When Emie saw him, she lifted her head and offered a greeting. "Well, brother, come join us. How are you?"

"I'm just fine, girlie. And you?"

"Fine as well."

Ernest couldn't help but notice Rudy looking back and forth between him and his sister. It was hard not to laugh. They were playing a sibling game. Emie generally initiated the game, albeit unawares, and sometimes Ernest, if not too eager to share his information, played along. From the time Emie was little, Ernest had teased her about her propensity for questions. She was like a curious kitten exploring her world. He had talked with her time and time again about the niceties of conversation. She needed to make polite talk before beginning her curious onslaughts.

Emie continued her pleasantries, "You know I'm engaged. I was just wonderin', did you see any young ladies that might interest you at the weddin'?"

"Not a one, sister."

"Not a one. Why, brother, I saw a number of eligible girls present; some with dirty feet, others with stinky breath, and one had a wart on the tip of her nose."

"Why, Emie, you know just the kind of woman I'm lookin' for…"

"Okay, Ernest, I'm done bein' nice, tell me everythin'…"

"Emerald, that was bein' nice. Talkin' about stink and warts," Ernest laughed.

"Come on, brother. Rudy and I have been waitin'. What did Daddy say?"

Ernest grew serious. "He didn't say anythin'."

"Nothin'?" Rudy asked. "Not a word?"

"Well, he cussed a little, but that was it," Ernest answered. "I couldn't even get Mama to talk."

"What'll we do now?" Emie wanted to know.

"I'm not sure," Ernest responded. "Any ideas, Rudy?"

"None," Rudy answered.

"I guess we wait. At least for a couple days and see what happens. Daddy sometimes goes silent after his fits of anger. He's devious, but Mama ain't. If she knows what he's up to, we might get wind of it," Ernest shared.

Chapter Thirty

"For a snake bite, cut up the snake that bit you and press its flesh to the
wound. This will draw out the poison."
(Appalachian Folk Belief)

Her mama arrived at Auntie's late the next morning, just as she
was finishing her letter to Mimi. When Emie heard the knock on
the door, somehow she knew it would be her mother calling. Emie
put away her letter and opened the door cautiously. She hadn't
spoken to her mama since the day she and Rudy moved her things
to Aunt Ada's. Emie felt nervous. Whatever news her mama
carried wouldn't be good. She knew that Ernest's arrival at the
Ashby homestead had signaled to Mama that it was time to visit.
Whatever needed to be said wasn't meant for Ernest to hear.

"Good mornin', Emie."

"Mama."

"Aren't you gonna invite me in?"

Emie opened the door further, allowing room for her mother to
enter.

Her mama took a seat on the worn rocker. "I taught you
manners, girlie, are you gonna offer me somethin' to drink?"

"What would you like? Milk? Tea? I also have fresh cider."

"Cider might be nice. Ada does a good job pressin' the apples."

"I made the cider, Mama."

"I'm glad you're bein' useful to Ada."

Emie walked the few steps to the kitchen and poured herself and her mama a glass of the partially hardened apple juice.

"I got young ones at home, so I can't stay long, Emie."

Emerald didn't answer with words, but nodded in response.

"I'm needin' you to come on home. I think you might be havin' a boy and your daddy's wantin' another son. All's forgiven, girlie. Your daddy and I will raise the boy as our own."

Emie was stunned. She hadn't known what to expect, but this was beyond even her wildest imaginings. She wished that Ernest would come back to the cabin, or that Rudy would stop by for a visit. She needed someone to help her; someone to tell her what to do and say.

"Mama, I…can't come home," she stammered.

"Emie, your daddy needs this. His sons have left him. Lester's taken off, and Ernest is headin' on up the holler to teach the coloreds. Rudy's gonna tend the hogs some but that won't last long. We'll have to hire a hand until the boy's old enough to work the pigs."

"No, Mama…"

"Emie, hear me out. You got a whole life ahead of you. You should be grateful that your daddy's willin' to take this baby."

"I'm not comin' back…," she spoke softly. Like a bouquet of wild roses without water, Emie felt herself wilting.

Her mama rose from the chair and pulled a threaded needle from her apron pocket. From the time she was little, Emie remembered the apron her mother now wore. The colors were bright at one time. Now they were faded. The apron was worn and torn. Emie felt like she was fading. She'd been worn and torn by Charlie and Daddy, but she'd always hoped that her mama would come around.

"I believe it's a boy because of the way you're carryin', but we're needin' to make sure. Give me your right arm, girlie," her mother commanded.

When Emie hesitated, her mama took hold of the young woman's arm and held it out straight with her palm side up. "Don't fight me, Emie. This will only take a minute."

Didn't her mama know that there was no fight left in her daughter? Bit by bit the fight had been taken.

Mama held the needle just above the pulse point on Emie's wrist. Emie knew the old wives' tale, if the needle moved up and down, it meant the baby was a boy, and if the needle moved side to side, it meant the baby was a girl. She didn't know if her mama willed it so or not, but the needle moved up toward her palm and back toward her elbow.

"I knew it," her mama declared. "Get your things."

Emie didn't know what to do, so she did nothing. She didn't move, and she didn't speak. She sat and waited. She wasn't sure what she was waiting for, but it seemed right to stay still and silent.

Her mama chided her to get moving, but Emie sat quietly. Time seemed to suspend for a few minutes. She knew the story in the Bible about God holding back time; the Lord stopped the sun from setting, so His children could defeat their enemy.

She continued to wait, and in her waiting, God began to strengthen her. She felt the sprinkle of His presence, then the rain of His grace.

Her mama attempted to pull her from the chair, but Emie wouldn't budge. She waited still. Her mother, looking puzzled, sat back down in the worn rocker. "Emie, I ain't got time for this. Your daddy might be needin' me..."

Finally Emie spoke, and when she voiced her words they were with power and authority. "This baby isn't livestock that's given or sold. I love my child. He or SHE isn't yours to take."

"Girlie, I know this baby don't belong to Rudy. It's Charlie's. If you don't come home, your daddy will get in touch with Eugene and who knows what he'll do. Charlie might even take the baby from you."

How could her mother say those things? Why didn't she rise to her daughter's defense? Why didn't her mother protect her? Emie felt fearful. *What if Charlie did come? What if he took the baby? What would she do? Give me strength, Lord. Help me be like Sampson,* she prayed.

"Let him come, Mama. Let him come! Comin' for this baby is admittin' that he raped me, and he'll go to prison!"

"Who are you, Emie? Talkin' to your mother this way…"

"I'm a mother myself. Fightin' for my baby to have what's good."

At first her mama seemed stunned. Then she slowly stood. "I'm takin' my leave now."

Emie stayed seated and watched her mother exit through the door and close it behind her. She remembered her earlier thought about wilted roses. Emie had felt herself wilting, yet God in His mercy had helped her. She needed to be strong for her baby. Throughout Emie's childhood, she had witnessed her mother wilting bit by bit. *How long could her mama survive without water? And how long could her baby sisters survive without a strong mother to tend to their care?*

Rudy had worked all morning at his daddy's store. The work was fine, but he enjoyed the outdoors so much more than being cooped up inside. His daddy had fussed with him earlier for keeping the front door to the store open, but Rudy couldn't help it. He needed to feel the breeze on his face. Ernest had asked him last night to help with the pigs, so he was anxious to be on his way up the holler. The cool autumn day would make for nice walking weather.

Just as he exited the store, he noticed Coral standing at the corner of the building. She was looking the other direction. He started to yell out a greeting, but remembered Emie and Ernest sharing with him about Coral's extreme shyness. In fact, he had tried to talk with Coral a couple times, but found it difficult. She was so quiet. He knew it wasn't right to compare sisters, but he couldn't help it. She and Emie looked alike, but beyond that they were so different.

He cleared his throat as he approached. "Hello, Coral."

"Hello, Rudy."

He waited for Coral to say something more, but when she didn't, he spoke up, "What are you doin' in town today?"

"Rudy, I'm surprised that you even know my name," she spoke softly.

"Of course, I know it. You're unforgettable, Coral."

She smiled slightly, "I can see why Emie has takin' to you."

He waited for her to answer his original question, and when she didn't respond, he asked again, "What are you doin' in town?"

"Daddy sent me on an errand. He wants to visit with you."

"Thanks, Coral. I'm headed up the holler to help Ernest; I'll stop by the house and see your daddy."

Coral surprised him by touching his arm. Her touch was so gentle that he barely felt it through his shirt sleeve. "Rudy, my daddy ain't a nice man. Be careful."

"I'll be fine. Come on. We'll walk up the road together."

"I can't." Coral then hung her head. "Old Man James paid Daddy $5 for me to go to his house. I'm supposed to cook him food."

Immediately the hair on the back of Rudy's neck stood on end. Mr. James was an odd man, repulsive yet strangely interesting. Children generally stared, but didn't want to talk or visit with him. Mothers who knew him, or knew about him, often requested that their children stay away. In fact, his own mama had given him such instructions.

"Coral, Mr. James has lived alone for years. He can certainly cook for himself."

Nervously she bit her lip. "I don't want to, but Daddy said he'd get the switch if I didn't go. He also said that I'd better be nice and do what Mr. James asked."

Rudy knew that this was bad, real bad. "Coral, I'll be right back. Wait here."

Rudy went back to the store, opened the till and took $5. His daddy was busy waiting on customers, so he quickly wrote an I.O.U. for the money and included a sentence saying that he would explain later. He hurried back outside. He looked for Coral at the building corner, but she was gone. He started to panic. Emie would never forgive him if something happened to her sister, and he could have helped. He would never forgive himself if harm came to quiet, innocent Coral. He walked hurriedly up the street. She couldn't have gone far; he had left her for only a couple minutes. *The Ashby girls are going to be the death of me*, he thought. His heart raced as he franticly continued his search. Finally he spotted her across the street talking with Grandpappy.

He felt like his heart was beating out of his chest when he approached the two. "Coral, why didn't you wait for me?"

"I'm sorry, Rudy. Don't be mad at me. I saw Pastor Rex and wanted to say 'hello.' I was gonna head right back."

"I'm not mad at you. I was just worried that Old Man James might have spotted you."

"Son, what's going on here?" Grandpappy asked.

Rudy explained about the odd man and the $5. "I'm planning on goin' to Mr. James' house, givin' him back his $5, and also givin' him a piece of my mind."

Rudy could see the apprehension on Coral's face. He was certain that Grandpappy also noticed her nervousness.

"Son, why don't you and Coral take the back way up the holler? Leave Coral to visit Emie a bit, I know you're needin' to help Ernest. I'll talk with Mr. James and take the sheriff with me. I don't think we need to worry any more about food makin'.'"

Coral's voice was so soft that Rudy had to strain to hear her. He noticed that Grandpappy was bending low and cupping his ear to hear her words. "Pastor Rex, my daddy's wantin' to visit with Rudy, and I got some concerns."

"Ahab's a sly one, Rudy," his grandfather knowingly shared. "The Bible says that we need to be as clever as a serpent and as harmless as a dove. The snake in the Garden of Eden tricked Adam and Eve. Snakes are shrewd. Doves on the other hand… well, they're fragile. First cold spell, and they're gone. "

"Pastor, Rudy shouldn't go," Coral spoke up.

"I don't like it either, Coral, but Rudy needs to do what he thinks is best for him and Emie."

Rudy was humbled. Earlier he had wanted to tell both Coral and Pappy that there was no need to be concerned. He could handle Ahab Ashby, but when Grandpappy spoke, Rudy was humbled. Rudy realized that his youthful pride and zealousness needed to be surrendered to God. He needed the Lord's strength every day in every way; meeting with Ahab should be a matter of prayer.

Grandpappy knew him so well. The kindly man knew that Rudy's pride and his love for Emie wouldn't allow him to ignore Ahab's summons. Rudy thanked God for the special bond he enjoyed with Pappy and for the teaching moments they often shared. He wouldn't forget the lesson about snakes and doves.

As Rudy and Coral started to walk away, Rudy remembered the $5 in his pocket. "Pappy, here's $5 to pay back Mr. James."

"I won't be needin' the money, son. He ain't gettin' a refund. You head on up the holler to see your girl. And, Rudy, you be careful today." Pappy then winked at Coral and headed toward the sheriff's office.

Rudy and Coral took the path at the far end of town that wound up the hillside toward Aunt Ada's. It really wasn't much more than an animal trail, but the way was very familiar to Rudy. These days, he spent more time in the hills than he did at home.

He and Coral exchanged only a few words on their walk. Coral seemed content with the solitude, and it gave Rudy time to think. He thought about what might have happened to Coral and thanked God for divine intervention. Next, his mind wandered to where he, Emie, and the baby should live. His parents had offered the small house that they owned next to the store, but Rudy couldn't see Emie as a city dweller. Not that Big Creek was a thriving town, but he knew his girl loved the creek and the willows. Rudy's thoughts then shifted to his upcoming meeting with Ahab.

When the cabin came in sight, Coral thanked Rudy for his kindness. He smiled and nodded. "Coral, I think it's best we don't mention my meeting with your daddy. I'll talk to Emie about it later. I don't want her worryin' none."

"Okay, Rudy," she answered. "I know I talk quiet like. Mrs. Randolph tells me at school that I need to speak up. I saw Pastor Rex leanin' close and cuppin' his ear to hear me. I'm gonna pray for you today, Rudy, and then I'm gonna cup my ear and listen close to what God has to say."

"Thank you, Coral."

Emie's younger sister was a puzzle. Of course, most women, young and old, were puzzles to Rudy – Emie for sure, and at times even his own mama. Ernest had agreed with him that girls were mysteries. When it came to Emie, Rudy was determined to put the pieces together and see the beautiful picture that formed.

Standing outside the store earlier, Coral had seemed so fragile, like a bent flower. She was small in stature, but brave in heart. She had shown extreme courage today, and Rudy was proud of her. He wondered if he should tell her so. He didn't want to embarrass her, yet, he knew that her life was hard and being told she had courage might strengthen her in a time of need.

"Coral..."

"Yes, Rudy."

"I'm proud of you. You showed great courage today. You're a very brave young woman."

Coral dipped her head and then softly spoke, "Thank you."

Emie and Rain were sitting under the maple tree. Emie was working on her wares for his daddy's store. Rain trotted to meet Rudy and Coral. Wanting his belly rubbed, the puppy rolled on his back in front of Rudy. He knew that Rain shared Emie's bed, but in the not too distant future, Rain would be lying on the floor, and he would be beside his girl. Emie looked up from her crafts and waved. Her lap was covered with willow vines, so Rudy motioned for her to stay seated.

"Good afternoon, darlin'."

"Hello, Red. Hi, Coral."

"Emie, Rudy was my hero today."

"He was?" Emie smiled. "Tell me more..."

Rudy interrupted the sisters. "Ernest is waitin' on me. I got more heroic deeds to do today." He couldn't help but laugh. "I got piglets to castrate, sows to bathe, and a couple hogs that need my attention. I'll leave you sisters to gossip about me."

He bent low and kissed Emie on the cheek and then surprised Coral by kissing her cheek as well. As he headed toward the meadow, he could hear the girls giggling.

On his jaunt to the Ashby homestead, Rudy tried to pray, but his thoughts kept racing to and fro. Mostly he was thinking about

Emie. She was lovely in spirit and in form. It was the thinking about her form that kept his mind preoccupied. In an attempt to redirect his thinking, he stopped walking and shook his head. When that didn't work, he began praying out loud, which seemed to help. He talked to the Lord about all kinds of matters; the things that were racing through his head and the things that were weighing on his shoulders. Marrying Emie was a big responsibility. How would he provide for his new family? How would he work, finish school, and still have time for his wife and baby? And what about the future?

He also prayed for Coral, and thanked God for his grandpappy. He tried to pray about Old Man James, but couldn't seem to get past his anger; so Rudy prayed about his anger, and then about his pride, asking the Lord to forgive him for thinking he could meet with Ahab in his own strength.

As the Ashby home came into view, the thought occurred to Rudy that he should invite Ernest to join the meeting with Ahab. Again, his pride rose up. He could handle this on his own. Or could he? It seemed that pride became an issue when situations involved Emie. He wanted to prove to his fiancée and to himself that he was ready for marriage. *Lord, help me be humble. There are times when I need others to advise and guide me. I don't want to harm myself or my wife and baby because of pride.*

Grandpappy had told him once that pride and insecurity were kissing cousins. At the time, Rudy didn't understand, but now he was beginning to get the gist of it. His insecurities about becoming a new husband played games with his emotions, then pride would swell to the point where he wanted to handle things on his own.

Rudy bypassed the Ashby home and found Ernest in the barn. "Hey, Ernest, sorry I'm late."

"Not a problem, Rudy. Family comes first. I know your daddy needs help."

"You are my family, Ernest. Emie's family is my family, and that's not why I'm late," Rudy answered. He then told Ernest about Coral and Mr. James.

Ernest's fists were clenched when he spoke, "My daddy done hurt Emie, and now he's workin' on Coral. Old Man James is a pervert, Rudy. Everyone knows it. It just cain't be proved."

Rudy shook his head in agreement.

"Do you know where the word "pervert" comes from? Mrs. Randolph's been teachin' me a little Latin. It means 'pee pot,' Rudy. The man's just like an outhouse hole!"

Rudy stayed quiet. He knew that his friend was angry and rightfully so. When Ernest started to leave the barn, Rudy spoke up. "God is faithful. He took care of Coral today."

Ernest grunted in response. Rudy didn't blame him. It would take time to think through, pray through, and follow through what his friend had just learned.

"Ernest, Coral was also in town today bringin' me a message from your daddy. He's wantin' to visit with me."

"I ain't surprised, Rudy. I saw my mama head across the meadow this mornin'. I'm bettin' she went to see Emie. I wanted to follow, but felt like the good Lord said to stay put. My daddy's schemin' and my mama's doin' his biddin' once again."

Rudy patted Ernest on the back. "Put me to work. When we've sweated out our frustrations, we'll come up with a plan to deal with your daddy."

The two worked tirelessly for the remainder of the afternoon. Rudy prayed and Ernest sang. Sometimes so loudly that Rudy thought the clouds had rolled back and that the Lord had returned.

As if on cue, they both ended up in the barn in the late afternoon.

Rudy's stomach growled.

"I guess we missed lunch," Ernest spoke.

"My body might be hungry, but my mind is not thinkin' about food. I'm nervous about talkin' with your daddy." Rudy then confessed about his insecurities and how they had taken the form of pride. "I need your help, Ernest."

"Rudy, my dad is wily like a coyote. I once saw a coyote chase down a doe and her fawn. The coyote ran back and forth, tirin' out the mama who was protecting her baby. Eventually the doe collapsed from exhaustion, and the fawn was left alone. I don't need to tell ya what happened next. My daddy will try to divide and conquer. He'll trick and deceive. He'll run back and forth with his words tryin' to confuse and wear us out."

Rudy could only shake his head in amazement. "Are we cleanin' up before we head to the house?"

Ernest couldn't help but laugh. "Rudy, this here is a hog farm. Hogs stink and since we've been workin' the hogs, we stink, but there ain't no need for washin' right now. If we smell bad enough maybe Daddy will keep his words brief."

Chapter Thirty One

"Flowers which bloom out of season are evil."
(Appalachian Folk Belief)

Rudy noted that Ernest wasted no time in greeting his mama or the girls. He headed immediately to his daddy's tiny, sparse, worn-out room. Rudy followed Ernest's lead and stayed focused on the task at hand.

Ahab was lying on a sagging double bed with his face turned toward the wall. He wasn't snoring, but Rudy could tell he was asleep by his deep rhythmic breathing.

Ernest paid no mind to his daddy's slumber. "Wake up, Daddy."

When Ahab didn't immediately respond, Ernest roused him by shaking his shoulder. The older man woke up fumbling with his thread-bare covers muttering cuss words.

"Daddy, I know about Coral," Ernest spoke sharply.

"Well, I'm sure you do know Coral. She's your sister, ain't she?" Ahab answered, trying to shake off his sleep.

Alma came to the door of the room. Her face was pale − paler than the faded, neglected grayish-white walls of the bedroom. "Ahab, are you needin' me?"

He simply shoed her away like a mean-hearted man would a stray dog that was hungry, frightened, and alone. The man couldn't even respond to his wife with words, Rudy thought.

Ernest stayed determined. "Daddy, Coral's with Emie. Pastor Rex and the sheriff are meetin' with Mr. James. How could you do it? How could you sell your daughter?"

"I did nothin' of the sort. The man is old, Ernest, and he needed help makin' supper. Coral can cook a little. Was I supposed to let a fellow man go hungry…?"

"He's a pervert. You know it, and I know it. You sent her to the lion's den. You knew what Mr. James would try and do…"

"Stop it, Ernest. Stop it right now! You're talkin' nonsense, and nonsense in front of Rudy here. He ain't family yet. We'll discuss this later."

Rudy was surprised Ahab was even aware of his presence. The young man didn't know what to do. Should he greet Emie's daddy? He didn't want to; he had never been particularly fond of Ahab, but now the older man seemed just downright repulsive. He knew the role that Ahab had played in Emie's rape, and to think what might have happened to Coral today gave him shivers.

Rudy didn't have to think for very long about whether to speak up or not because Ernest's momentum didn't wane. "You sent your baby girl to the nasty outhouse hole…"

Ahab, now fully awake, was shaking with anger. His face was red and his nostrils were flared. If he was a dragon that breathed fire, Rudy knew they would all be consumed.

"Get out! Get out of my room! Get out of my house and don't come back!"

"I ain't leavin', Daddy. I already sleep at Ada's, and you know I'm headin' up the holler. I'm barely here, but I know what's goin' on, and I ain't leavin' the little ones to your doin'."

"Your mama takes care of them girls."

"Mama only does what you ask of her."

"I can't make ya leave. I ain't able, but I'll have your mama fetch the sheriff. He'll dismiss you fine and proper! Now, leave me. Rudy and me got business."

"Daddy, it would give me pleasure for Mama to fetch the sheriff. I'll help him push your chair up the road to the jailhouse!"

Rudy had never experienced the likes of what was happening. He was nervous and intimidated. He knew that his future with

Emie depended on what would take place in the next few minutes. He wanted to be a good husband, a good father, and yet he felt like a little boy ready to wet himself. He had no choice but to face Ahab. He wondered if the Prophet Elijah felt the same way when facing his Ahab; well, maybe not the part about wetting himself. *Lord, give me strength to face this Prophet of Baal*, Rudy prayed silently. He took a deep breath, squared his shoulders, and stepped forward.

"Mr. Ashby, I've asked Ernest to join in our meetin'. I love your daughter and our baby, and I need Ernest's ears and eyes to help me."

Rudy's confidence grew a little when he saw Ernest's nod of approval.

Ahab's defensive body language spoke louder and clearer than his words. "Fine by me, as long as he sits quiet. Let's talk man-to-man."

Grandpappy was right. Ahab was a snake. Rudy could see the change in the man's posture and tone. If allowed, Emie's daddy would manipulate and deceive. He thought about the prophets of Baal. They shouted and cut themselves, hoping that their god would answer and bring fire from heaven. Elijah told the false prophets that their god was on vacation, maybe asleep, or even in the stinky. Baal never showed up. Elijah then soaked his sacrifice with water, stood next to the altar he'd build, and ask God for a sign. Fire rained down from heaven. *Lord, I'm the sacrifice today,* Rudy prayed. *Wash over me with the water of the Spirit. Bring down fire from heaven. Let Ahab know that he's not just messin' with a young boy, but with a powerful God.*

There was only one chair in the room, and it was located right next to the bed. Ernest motioned for Rudy to take a seat, and then sat himself down on the floor with his back against the door frame.

Ahab began, "I've been thinkin' some on you marryin' my girl. Emie's a special one, dear to my heart."

Rudy didn't know if he should punch Ahab or strangle him with the quilt that was tightly wrapped around the older man's legs. Rudy clenched his fists and prayed silently. He could feel Ernest praying as well.

"I have something for you to think on," the older man continued. "It's fine if you marry my girlie. With Lester gone and Ernest headin' off to teach them coloreds, I'm needin' help with my hogs. We'll see if your daddy and pappy will help us build you and Emie a little house of your own out by the barn. The two of you and the baby can live here. We'll work the hogs together, as a family."

When Rudy didn't immediately respond, Ahab put his hand on the young man's arm. The hand was ghostly white, and the fingers were slightly atrophied. He thought about the coyote and the fawn. He could see in his mind the coyote devouring the fawn. If allowed, Ahab would run him in circles, wear him out, and then devour Emie. Part of his privilege, as her soon-to-be husband, was to protect her from the evils in the world, to make sure that she and the baby were safe from harm. Emerald would never be safe near her daddy. She would be run ragged from dawn to dusk, and when given the opportunity, Ahab would use and abuse. Living with Ahab would be no life for Emie or their child.

"Mr. Ashby, Emie and I won't be livin' here. We need to build a peaceable life of our own. With Ernest gone some, I'm willin' to help. I won't leave Emie's sisters for lack."

Rudy could feel Ahab's body tense. "I think you need to be reconsiderin'. I need you to live here. There's too much work to be done. Think long and hard now, boy. Emie's needed here to help her mama, and I'm needin' you to run the farm. I'll pay ya a little and won't be chargin' any rent. It's what God would want, a young man helpin' his family."

Grandpappy had a taught him from the time he was young to never use the name of the Lord to manipulate another man. Pappy said that it was witchcraft to twist and turn God's words.

Rudy felt Ahab lift his hand. It was bound to happen, but Rudy didn't think the niceties would be over so quickly. "I am willing to help, but on Emie's and my terms. We'll be buildin' our own life together." Rudy looked at Ahab. The man looked like he was ready to explode.

"I won't let you marry, and then I'll take that baby from her. I'll raise the boy as my own. If need be I'll go to court and talk about Emie's sinful ways. Hell, I'll put a notice in the newspaper, and she'll be run out of town!"

Ernest started to stand, but Rudy motioned for him to stay seated. Emie would soon be his wife. He wouldn't tolerate anyone, not even Emie's daddy, speaking in such a way.

"Stop right there, Ahab…"

"So it's no more 'Mr. Ashby', is it?"

"I don't see the need to address you by a title. I respect that you're Emie's daddy, but I don't respect what you're doin.' I'll marry Emie. Without your permission, it will take a little more time, but I'm a patient man."

"You're just a boy. We both know it."

"A boy becomin' a man, who knows a liar when he sees one. I think Emie would welcome a day in court to tell all about you, Eugene, and Charlie. No judge would give you a baby after what you did to Emie, and now to Coral. And put your notice in the newspaper. If a BOY like me can recognize your lies, so will the good people of Big Creek."

Rudy looked at Ernest and stood. "Ernest, I'll be takin' my leave now."

This time it was Ernest's turn to follow Rudy's lead.

Rudy headed directly across the meadow. He couldn't be bothered with the swinging bridge and walked through the creek. The water was low and barely reached his knees. He pointed himself toward Aunt Ada's. He needed to see Emie. He wanted to tell her everything that happened. He glanced back; Ernest was right behind him.

He saw Emie before she saw him. Emie and Coral were sitting on the porch. His girl was laughing. He knew her blue eyes were shining; they always did when she was happy. Seeing her calmed him. Hoping that it took her a minute or two to notice him, he stopped and stared. She was beautiful. So was Coral. They both seemed so innocent. How could such purity exist with Ahab as their father?

Ernest was trailing close behind, so it only took him a minute to reach Rudy. He placed his arm around the younger man's shoulder. "What are you thinkin'?"

"I'm thinkin' I stink like a hog."

Ernest smiled. "You did good, Rudy. Real good. Emie will be proud."

"I've never seen the likes of anythin' or anyone like your daddy. Thanks for standin' with me."

"Emie's lookin' our way."

Rudy turned back toward Auntie's house and saw both girls waving. "We better get up there, or they'll be runnin' our way with Rain between 'em."

Emie stood as the boys approached. "Well, if it ain't two handsome lads comin' to call on us, Coral."

Coral giggled. "Yes, sister, they are mighty handsome and strong…"

"And smell like pigpens," Emie added, holding her nose.

"Are we that bad?" Rudy asked.

Both girls nodded "yes" in unison.

"Well, darlin', you best get me a bucket of water, a rag, and some soap. I'm gonna take a bucket bath."

"I'll set you up in my room, Rudy. That way it'll be private," Emie said.

As Emie left to make preparations, Ernest helped Coral to her feet. "Come on, sister, let's head home. I bet mama's workin' on dinner."

"How did it go with Daddy?" Coral timidly asked.

"We'll talk about it on the way home, girlie."

"I'm a little scared, brother."

"Don't worry, girlie. I won't leave until Daddy's sound asleep."

"Snorin' like an old ornery dog."

"Worse – a grizzly hibernatin' for winter."

Coral smiled and placed her arm through her brother's. The two turned and headed back toward the creek just as Emie appeared at the front door and motioned for Rudy to join her.

"I put everything in my room. I'll wait for you on the porch, Rudy."

"If I didn't stink so bad, I'd give my best girl a kiss."

"Best girl? I'd better be your only girl!"

Rudy took her hand and squeezed gently. "I'll be right back."

He'd never been in Emie's room before. He had glanced back there a couple times, but had never set foot in her domain. He first looked at the bed. It was small. Rudy wondered how he and Emie would both fit. Never mind, he chided himself, I'll just hold her close all night long. The room was definitely girly, but at the same time simple and clean. Emie's nightgown was hanging on a hook behind the wooden plank door. He touched the pink bow that held the neckline together. It was soft and sweet, just like Emie.

He bathed in a rush and then looked at the mess he'd made on the floor. *She doesn't know what she's gettin' into,* Rudy thought.

Kind Emie had even left him clean clothes. Rudy could tell by the way they fit that they probably belonged to Ernest. The trousers were long and the shirt hung on his shoulders. He was anxious to talk with Emie and quickly headed to the front porch where she was waiting.

He sat down next to her on the steps, placed his arm around her shoulders, and gently kissed her cheek. "Hey, darlin', did you have a good day with your sister?"

"I had a hard time gettin' over the shock of what my daddy tried to do. Rudy, what will become of Coral and the little ones?"

"I don't know. For right now all we can do is pray. I'm thinkin' as soon as Auntie and Doc get back that we need to have another family meetin'. Like you, I'm concerned."

It was early evening and the sun was casting cloud shadows in the meadow. It was beautiful. Though Rudy was anxious to share his news, he took a moment to enjoy the scenery. It was as if God has laid a banquet of beauty before him and Emie, and then called them to come and dine. He was reminded of the greatness of God. *Surely, the Creator of the World, the Magnificent One who walks on the bottom of the sea and whose name is whispered by alligators, can take care of Coral and the sisters.*

Just as Rudy started to share his thoughts, Rain came bounding from the side of the house. He practically knocked Emie over with his affections. Rudy couldn't help but laugh at his antics. Emie pretended to chide him, but kissed his head and rubbed his ears nonetheless.

"Rudy, my mama paid me a visit this mornin'."

"Ernest thought as much when he saw your mama headin' out early."

"She wants me to come home."

"Emie, you can't go home," Rudy spoke firmly.

Tears welled in Emie's light blue eyes. "I told her I wasn't comin'. I was so scared. I prayed that you or Ernest would come and help me."

"Emie, I wish I could have been there. I will always try and protect you, but there will be times when only God can be at your side."

"I felt His presence, Rudy. I truly did. He helped me and gave me just the right words to say."

"Are you worried?"

"I'm worried about Coral, but not about my mama comin' back. She even brought a string and needle with her. She's convinced the baby is a boy."

Rudy shook his head. "She believes that old wives' tale?"

"I guess."

Rudy took his arm from around Emie's shoulders and held her hand. "I've some news as well."

Emie looked into his eyes and waited for him to continue.

"Coral was also in town today bringing me a message from your daddy. He was wantin' me to visit."

"No!" she emphatically responded.

"Emie, I've already seen your daddy."

She jerked her hand away and stood up. "You shoulda told me, Rudy. You shoulda talked with me before callin' on him."

"Now, Emie, I can tell you're mad, but let me explain."

"You knew when you brought Coral here you were gonna talk with him, and you didn't tell me. What's to explain?"

Rudy's heart skipped a beat. Emie was right. He should have talked with her. He should have gotten her opinion. As a couple, they should have prayed together and asked the Lord for guidance.

As a young boy, Rudy's mama had taught him the proper way to apologize. It wasn't enough to say, "I'm sorry." He stood on his feet next to Emerald. When he tried to take her hand, she pulled away. *Oh, boy,* he thought. *This is new territory. How do I make her understand? Will she forgive me?*

"Emie, please hear me out. I'm sorry. You're right. I should have talked with you. Forgive me. I know that I'll make mistakes as a new husband, but I promise to try and do what's right."

Emie sighed and reached for his hand.

"Do you forgive me?"

"I'm thinkin' on it," she answered. "Tell me everythin' and don't leave nothin' out."

Rudy started at the beginning from the time he told Coral not to mention the meeting to Emie. He could tell by the look in his girl's eyes that it didn't set too well that he'd brought Coral into his deception. Emie's eyes sparkled when she was happy and clouded over when she was upset. When he finished, she didn't say a word. In fact, she left him standing on the porch and entered the cabin by herself. He wasn't sure what to do. Should he follow her, or stay put? What was she doin'? Was she still angry? He decided to take a seat and simply wait for a few minutes.

Emie returned shortly with apple cider and cookies in hand. "We're gonna celebrate, Rudy."

"What are we celebratin'?"

"We're celebratin' you, Rudy. We're celebratin' that you stood up to my daddy and made a good choice for us and the baby today."

Emie waited up for Ernest. Generally he was at Auntie's around dark, but tonight he was delayed. She hoped everything was alright. She sat in the worn rocker in the small parlor room. Ada sometimes referred to the space as the "everthin' room." Emie guessed it was because most everythin' that took place in the cabin seemed to happen in the small room.

Her mind wandered as she watched for Ernest. Auntie and Uncle Christian would be back in a couple days. It seemed like so much had happened while they were gone: Mama came calling, Coral was rescued from who knows what, Rudy stood up to Daddy, and then there was Ernest's big secret.

The secret was why she was sitting by candlelight waiting for her brother. Rain was at her feet. He was tired. The boys had worn him out earlier in the evening. Emie sometimes worried that their roughhousing would hurt her precious pup, but Rain seemed to enjoy all the running, fetching, and wrestling.

She probably should have lit the oil lamps, but the candlelight somehow soothed her. It felt like a love-light bringing her brother home. She heard Ernest's footsteps on the porch, and rose to greet him.

"Good evenin', girlie. Was you gettin' worried?"

"Only a little, Ernest."

"No need to worry. I waited to leave until Daddy was sleepin'. Thank goodness he had an early night. Probably tired from meetin' with Rudy. You would have been proud, Emie. Right proud."

"I was mad at Rudy earlier. Upset he didn't talk with me before meetin' with Daddy."

Ernest nodded with understanding. "I can see why you'd be grieved, Emie, but a man's got his pride, and Rudy wanted to handle things his way."

"I don't like secret keepin', brother."

When Ernest didn't respond, Emie continued, "Are you keepin' any secrets?"

"Was it Mama or Rudy that mentioned my teachin'?"

"Rudy knew beforehand and didn't tell me!"

"Emie, now don't get all riled. Daddy said somethin' about it today, but I'm not sure that Rudy was in a place to pay any mind."

"Why didn't you say that you were leavin' me, brother?"

"I'm not leavin' you, or any of my sisters. I'm just movin' a little ways up the holler. Justice is checkin' on a location for the school. It won't be too far. I'll be at Auntie's on the weekends.

You'll be fine. Doc will be livin' here, and Rudy visits almost every day. In fact, he'll be visitin' even more. I think he's gonna check on the pigs some durin' the week."

Tears rolled down her checks. She didn't want to cry in front of Ernest, but she couldn't help it. "I want you to be happy, Ernest, but I'm selfish. I want you with me."

"You'll be fine. We're growin' up, girlie. Life's bringin' changes. Good ones. Soon you and Rudy will be wed with a new baby."

"I love you, brother."

"I know you do."

Emie smiled, "Ernest, Rudy says that when someone says 'I love you' that you need to say it back."

"I was just makin' you wait a minute. I love you, too." Ernest paused and then added, "Girlie, I hear what Rudy's sayin', but what happens if you don't love the person? Are you supposed to say it anyway?"

"I don't know. Rudy's the love expert, not me."

Ernest couldn't help but laugh. "Where did his expertise came from? I don't recall learnin' such things at school."

Emie could only shake her head. "Well, he knows names of endearment, and has taken to kissin' and such."

"He's a regular Romeo, is he?"

"I don't know about being a Romeo, but Coral thinks he's a hero."

"He was a hero today, Emie, in more ways than one."

Chapter Thirty Two

*"Make a wish on a load of hay, but don't look until the load
is out of sight, and the wish will come true."*
(Appalachian Folk Belief)

For the past couple weeks, Emie and Mercy had worked secretly on their evening of entertainment for Rudy and Ernest. It was Rudy's birthday, and Emie wanted to celebrate in a big way.

At first Mercy had been reluctant to participate. "Emie, I don't know. I ain't ever danced the Charleston, and I don't know the song, 'Ain't Misbehavin'.'" Emie remembered how Mimi had taught her to dance.

She persisted. She unashamedly acted just like Adam, Beau, Claude, and Dean, who wrestled and strong-armed each another until someone gave in. She hadn't used physical force, but had certainly resorted to emotional persuasion. Emie was determined to make sure that Rudy never took notice of her old schoolmate, Mimi, again. She knew it was jealousy, plain and simple, and that she was using Red's birthday celebration for her own purposes. It was Rudy noticing Mimi's pink and frilly outfit that kept her goading Mercy, and the two practicing untold hours. She was acting like a spoiled child. Jealousy had taken her. Now Mercy was accompanying her misbehavin', but she couldn't help herself.

Not that she didn't appreciate Rudy's fifteen years — she couldn't wait to sing "Happy Birthday" and present him with the vine basket she'd made. She had woven two baskets into one to represent their upcoming life together. For the basket trim, she'd used a portion of the scarlet thread that her beau had presented to her not so long ago. It some ways that awful time seemed so distant, but in other ways it was fresh as the morning breeze she felt each day when she opened her window for Rain's start of the day tinkle. She had also recruited MayLou to help her sew a shirt for Rudy. She was embarrassed by her stiches, but knew that Rudy would treasure her efforts. MayLou said that Emie would improve with practice. Auntie had said the same, but Emie wasn't so sure. Only time would tell.

As she and Mercy waited for the boys to arrive, her stomach was all atwitter. She didn't want to look foolish in front of Rudy. The girls were using the front porch as their stage and the "everythin' room" as their dressing area. They had placed Auntie's two porch chairs on the lawn. Ernest and Rudy would have prime seats for the girls' performance. Emie and Mercy had even decorated the chairs with wildflowers and ribbon. Rudy's chair also included a sign expressing birthday wishes. She had removed the stand by her bed and put it between the two seats. The small table held hot milk tea for the boys to enjoy. Rain, curious as always, was eyeing the stoneware cups, and Emie was eyeing Rain, making sure that he minded his manners. The tea would warm them. The evening was slightly chilly. Ernest arrived first, dressed in his finest. Then a couple minutes later Rudy joined the party. Emie had heard him whistling before she saw his handsome face.

He greeted her with his usual, "Hello, darlin'," and a kiss on the check.

It was obvious to Emie that, just like Ernest, Rudy had put some time in on his appearance. His cowlick was unusually tame. She wondered how long it would stay in place and wanted to tease him, but was too nervous about her upcoming performance.

The boys were directed to their seats. Emie thought to warm their tea, but the two were already gulping the mixture down. Emie guessed that sipping slowly wasn't a male tendency. She and Mercy headed into the cabin to change into their first costume of the evening. Emie had traded baskets with Rudy's daddy for black material which had been fashioned into flapper outfits. When Emie had explained her plans, Rudy's daddy had belly laughed, and his wife had volunteered to help make the outfits. Emie had worried that her soon-to-be in-laws would think her scandalous for wanting to dance and sing for their son's birthday, but instead they thought her idea was great fun and couldn't wait to hear the rave reviews.

Emie and Mercy giggled as they changed clothes. They helped each other adjust their feathered headbands and shared a quick embrace before heading to the stage.

The evening began with the girls dancing the Charleston. Emie had taught the steps to Mercy, who was a quick study. The boys clapped and cheered. When the dance drew to a close, both Ernest and Rudy stood on their feet whistling and shouting accolades.

Next, the showgirls sang a popular song. Auntie didn't have a radio, but Doc did and Emie had heard the song one afternoon in his office. To her surprise, Uncle Christian had the lyrics memorized and was able to help her transcribe them. The tune was simple and easily remembered.

Mercy sweetly sang the first verse. *No one to talk with, all by myself. No one to walk with, I'm happy on the shelf, babe. Ain't misbehavin', savin' my love for you.*

Next, it was Emie's turn. She was so nervous that she stumbled over the first couple of words, but as she continued her confidence grew, and her alto voice carried the lyrics like a meadowlark singing in the wind. *I know for certain the one I love. I'm through flirtin', you that I'm thinkin' of. Ain't misbehavin', oh savin' my love, oh baby, love for you.*

The girls sang the remaining verses together. Emie sang the melody and Mercy harmonized. Their rendition was unique. The original plan was for Mercy to carry the melody, but Emie had worried that her nerves would get the best of her during the performance, and the melody was easier to follow than the second part. *Like Jack Horner in a corner, don't go nowhere and I don't care. Oh your kisses worth waitin for, babe. I don't stay out late, don't care to go. I'm home about eight, me and my radio, babe. Ain't misbehaving', savin' all my love for you.*

When the song was finished, Rudy and Ernest again stood on their feet and clapped enthusiastically. The girls bowed in unison and held up their right index fingers indicating that they would quickly return. They entered their so-called dressing room, removed their headbands and added a white button-down shirt to their costumes. They were going to end their performance by singing a hymn and felt that more appropriate attire was required. Each girl held a bouquet of wildflowers at her waist. They had chosen to sing a worshipful song that was dear to both of them, "Tell Me the Story of Jesus." They planned for Mercy to sing the chorus and Emie the verses, but when they began, both boys joined in wholeheartedly. When the song was finished, Mercy and Emie stepped down from their stage and presented their bouquets to Ernest and Rudy. Rudy instantly hugged his girl and thanked her over and over again for the evening's performance. Without thought, Ernest did the same. At first Mercy was startled by Ernest's embrace but quickly found herself caught up in the celebratory moment.

The evening followed with birthday wishes and a chocolate cake made by Emie. Rudy's mama had shared her son's favorite recipe.

Ernest lay in bed that night thinking of Mercy. He couldn't help but laugh at the girls' antics. He knew the idea had been Emie's, and was certain it had taken quite a bit of persuasion for Mercy to participate. She was generally shy. Sometimes it was hard to even engage her in conversation. It did his heart good to see her dance, sing, and laugh so freely. He also couldn't help but remember their embrace. It felt right. She seemed to fit perfectly in his arms. He had known for some time that he was developing feelings for the lovely young woman. He just wasn't sure what to do with those feelings. The world could be a cruel place. It didn't matter to him that his skin was fair and that Mercy's was the color of cream-laced coffee, but he knew it mattered to others. If he really cared for her, would he create a scenario that might hurt and harm?

Auntie's bed felt wonderful. He had spent the last couple months sleeping on the front porch, but with Ada out of town he'd moved indoors. The evenings were also getting nippy. Ada and Christian would be home in a couple days. His protection would no longer be needed. He didn't enjoy the idea of slumbering at his parents' home, but it didn't appear, at least for now, that he had a choice.

He and Justice were scheduled to travel up the hill tomorrow. Justice had visited with Cece's cousin, who in turn had talked with the landowner, Mr. Carpenter. Tomorrow they would be meeting the owner to discuss using a vacant building for the new school.

Ernest was excited; in fact, too excited to fall asleep. His thoughts drifted from teaching school to Mercy. He smiled when he thought of her sweet soprano voice. His favorite part of the evening was when the two couples sang "Tell Me the Story of Jesus."

Tell me the story of Jesus. Write on my heart every word. Tell me the story most precious. Sweetest that ever was heard...

Ernest knew that the hymn had been written by Fannie Crosby. Mrs. Randolph had shared a book with him about Fannie's life. Her story was amazing. Due to an eye infection as an infant, she was blind, yet a prolific poet who loved God above all else. He thought about all the lives that Fannie continued to impact, and prayed that his own life would touch others for Christ.

Ernest's eyes grew heavy as he sang over and over again about the story of Jesus.

It was barely dawn when Ernest met Justice by the barn. The older man was determined that they ride Amos and Andy up the hillside. Ernest thought that walking was a better idea. Amos and Andy were double trouble. The mules were often uncooperative. Justice said the distance was far for walking and they'd make better time with the troublesome duo.

"Pick your mule, Ernest, and let's get started."

Amos and Andy were already bucking a little and their backs were still bare.

"Justice, I've only ridden a horse a dozen or so times, and now you're wantin' to put me on a mule."

"Here, take hold of Amos. He's Mercy's favorite, and it'll do her heart good to know you rode on his back."

Justice kept the mule as still as possible, while Ernest climbed aboard. The mule had a make-do harness, but no saddle or bit. Ernest was surprised when Amos took his weight without too much of a fuss.

Justice threw his leg over Andy and directed Ernest to follow. "Andy usually takes the lead, so Amos should come along nice-like."

Amos had two speeds, standing still and running. He kept stopping to nibble at the fall foliage; then, he would run to catch up to Andy.

They hadn't traveled far when Ernest's backside and the interior of his legs began to hurt. Yet he couldn't discount Justice's idea of taking the mules; they were able to plod along the steep hillside without any trouble.

With Amos following Andy, conversation among the two men was nearly impossible. They had traveled about an hour when Justice suggested they stop. Cece had packed breakfast for them to enjoy. Justice attached lead ropes to the harnesses and tied the mules to a massive oak. The rope was long enough that Amos and Andy could enjoy the grass beneath the towering tree.

Justice and Ernest, wanting to distance themselves from the mules and any stink or folly, walked up the hill a little ways and took a seat on the soft ground. Cece had sent buttermilk biscuits with homemade blackberry jam, sausage patties, and fried potatoes mixed with onions and peppers.

"Ernest, I've been thinkin' about the school and the best way for me to help. I'd like to move my family up the holler with ya."

Ernest couldn't help but look surprised.

"Things ain't the same up there as Ada's," the older man continued. "You're gonna need day-to-day help understandin' the people. They may not take to you right off. It don't matter if you're helpin' their children or not."

"Justice, are you sure about this?"

"As sure as I can be. We'll know more when the day is through. I'm hopin' there's lodgin' for my family and a place for you as well. Won't work for you to be travelin' back and forth every day."

"I figured as much," Ernest answered. "I'm hopin' to check on my sisters durin' the weekends, and my daddy will also be needin' help with the hogs. Rudy's gonna work 'um some during the week."

"We'll see what the good Lord has in store," Justice wisely spoke. "The Bible says that man plans and God laughs. I've been plannin' and so have you."

As they headed back toward Amos and Andy, Ernest felt prompted to talk with Justice about Mercy. His heart was racing. A part of him just wanted to keep his affections for the attractive young woman a secret, but he knew with them being neighbors, it would never work. He also wanted Mercy to help him with the school. Even with Mercy living next to Auntie, Emie had begun to wonder about his feelings for the sweet girl. He also knew that when something lived in your heart it would eventually show through in other ways. He had tried to guard his speech and actions, but last night was a perfect example of his heart shining through. When Mercy presented him with her flowers, without thought or even intention, his arms had reached for her, and he knew, unless he purposefully distanced himself, it would happen again. Besides, the thought of not seeing her or talking with her caused a deep ache in his soul.

"Justice, I need to visit with you about Mercy," Ernest began.

The older man stopped and waited.

"I don't know how to say this, and in truth, I'm a little nervous."

"Whatever it is, son, we'll talk it through and talk to God. It'll be alright," Justice spoke reassuringly.

"I like your daughter," Ernest blurted out.

Justice laughed, "I thought you were gonna tell me somethin' I didn't know."

"I'm not sure you understand. I mean I really like her. I have strong feelings for her."

"I understand just fine, Ernest. And if you're worried about her feelings, don't be. I can see it in her eyes, and so can her mama."

"I'm not sure this is gonna work, Justice, but I wanna try. You're her daddy, would you consider me visitin' with her?"

"I say you best make your claim. Once we get back up this holler, others'll be thinkin' she's fine."

"I'm white."

"I can see that."

"I know it will be a problem."

"Yes 'um, it will for some."

Ernest took a moment to think. He wasn't sure if he wanted to ask Justice his question or not. He needed to know, but what if Justice didn't answer the way he wanted? "Will me seein' Mercy be a problem for you and Cece?"

Justice put his hand on Ernest's shoulder. "It ain't a problem for me, and I know Cece feels the same. I ain't sayin' it won't be hard, though. There might be struggles in it for all of us. You got my blessin', Ernest, but make sure you're truth tellin' with my daughter. Don't be givin' promises that you can't keep."

"Thank you, Justice."

"Time will tell if you'll be thankin' me or not. We live in a fallen world. People don't act and say what they should."

The two traveled for the next hour up the hillside. When they arrived at the property, Mr. Carpenter and Cece's cousin, Lewis, were already waiting.

Ernest shared his hopes for teaching the children and talked about the college in Charleston helping with the finances. Mr. Carpenter was a broad-shouldered, stern-looking man, but when he spoke, Ernest could see the kindness in his heart. He professed to believe in Jesus and agreed that it was important for all children to receive an education.

The building being offered was actually an old barn. The structure was sound; with minimal repairs, the facility would work. There was an outhouse behind the school and a small three room house that Ernest could use as his personal quarters.

Justice and Lewis agreed that the building would be fine and were already making plans for the needed repairs. While the two wandered off to examine closely the lay of the land, Ernest took the opportunity to speak with Mr. Carpenter privately.

"Sir, I wanna thank you for your kindness. I'll be doin' my best to teach the children in these parts what I can. I'm new at teachin', but my work will be overseen by Mrs. Randolph in Big Creek and the people at the college."

"I appreciate your honesty, Ernest, and believe that you're the man for the job."

"One more thing, Mr. Carpenter, my friend Justice is wantin' to move his family back up here. His daughter is my assistant, but more than that, I'll be needin' his help and advice."

The older man nodded his head in agreement."I'm hatin' to ask, but do you have housin' for Justice and his family?"

Mr. Carpenter took a moment to think. Ernest worried that the man would decline any further assistance. He was already providing a schoolhouse and quarters for Ernest. How much could he be expected to give?

"I think I have just the place. Let's get Justice and Lewis and take a look."

The four men walked a little distance from the soon-to-be schoolyard. When they approached a treed area toward the back of the property, Ernest could see a small house nestled among the pines. Ernest and Lewis held back while Mr. Carpenter showed Justice the home and discussed rental fees.

Ernest thought about the verse that Justice had shared with him earlier, "Man makes plans and God laughs." He and Justice had both made plans, yet the Lord's plans were so much better.

When they arrived back at the homestead, Ernest saw that Mercy was washing clothes. Sometimes he felt sorry for the women in the holler. There was always so much work to be done. As a child, he had wondered why his mama never rested, and now as a grown man, he worried about his sisters and Mercy. Would the holler rob them of the pleasure of living?

Ernest knew that doing laundry was an all-day process. The water was hauled from the yard pump and then heated in a large cast iron pot over an open fire. The pot was heavy; a pole was placed through the handles for carrying. Ernest was certain that the boys must have helped Mercy. The two older boys probably carried one end and Mercy the other. The clothes were washed with handmade soap and stirred with the same long and heavy wooden pole used for hauling.

He saw Mercy struggling with the washboard as the boys and two dogs raced around her skirts. Ernest couldn't help but come to her rescue, "Boys, take them pups and play elsewhere. Your sister's got work to do."

The boys ran off with the dogs following, and Ernest set to work helping Mercy. He rolled up his shirtsleeves and took the scrub board. He removed clothes from the pot, item by item, scrubbed them on the board, and handed them to Mercy for rinsing, wringing, and hanging to dry. The two worked in unison – humming and harmonizing.

Ernest knew that most holler men felt washing clothes was only women's work, but Ernest felt that doing laundry was just another chore. If he could help, why not lend a hand? He wasn't sure what the future held for him or for Mercy, but he wanted the kind young woman to know that he would never stand for someone he cared about to work hard and not feel appreciated.

"Thank you, Ernest. I'm enjoyin' your help," Mercy spoke shyly.

"The pleasure is mine. When I tend the piglets, they'll be wonderin' how my hands got so red and chapped," he joked.

Mercy smiled in response. Ernest thought of the scripture in Song of Songs where the young lover described the teeth of his object of affection. He had always laughed at the verse, but now he understood. Mercy's teeth were beautiful, so white and perfect. The lovely young woman blushed. Of all things, he had stared at her teeth too long.

As the last of the clothes were hung on the line to dry, Ernest suggested that the two of them enjoy a walk together.

"You don't want to ride the mules?" Mercy asked jokingly.

"Amos is a rascal, and we've parted ways," Ernest responded with a smile. He wondered if Mercy was staring at his teeth but didn't think so.

Mercy turned toward the small house, "Let me tell Mama where I'm goin' so she don't worry."

When Adam, Beau, Claude, and Dean wanted to join them, Ernest was insistent that they stay behind and tend to the mules. He didn't even know what tending to the mules entailed; he just knew that he wanted Mercy to himself.

"I had a talk with your daddy on our way up the hill," Ernest shared, as he and Mercy headed toward the meadow. "I'm needin' to make my claim."

When he looked at Mercy, he saw confusion in her eyes. "I'm sorry. I'm makin' a mess of this. Rudy says that I should know all about girls with havin' so many sisters, but I keep tellin' him that it's not the same..."

Mercy held up her hand, silently asking Ernest to pause and take a breath. "I think you need to start over, Ernest. I'm a little befuddled. I ain't certain what we're talkin' about."

Ernest directed them to a fallen log where they both sat down. "Let me explain," he began. He talked about the new school and moving further up the holler. He also talked with Mercy about needing her help with the children. Ernest was thrilled when she responded wholeheartedly about working with him.

"I have feelings for you," he continued. "The kind of feelings a man has for a woman, Mercy, and I need to know if you share those feelings."

She smiled, "So you want to know if I have feelings for a woman? Well, I enjoy spendin' time with Emie, and I think Auntie Ada is a might special. I also love my mama..."

Ernest shook his head in frustration.

"I'm teasing you," Mercy laughed and then softly spoke. "I have those same feelings."

Ernest hesitantly took her hand. "I don't know how this will work. I'm not sure others will understand. I don't want you to be hurt, Mercy."

"I don't want you to be hurt neither, but people are people, white people or brown people. Some won't understand. We'll have to decide, Ernest, is it more important what others are thinkin', or what we think?"

The two spent the remainder of the late afternoon and early evening discussing plans for the school and the move higher into the hills. They also discussed their friendship. Mercy wanted to take things slowly. Ernest agreed but was insistent that when school began, their new community understand his pursuit of her affections.

Toward the end of the day, it occurred to Mercy what Ernest had meant about making his claim. She couldn't help but smile. *He's worried that some other handsome lad will win my heart.*

Chapter Thirty Three

"It's bad luck to look in a mirror at midnight."
(Appalachian Folk Belief)

The family meeting hadn't been called to order yet. The participants were too busy eating, talking, and laughing. Auntie's parlor was too small for the gathering, so sawhorses and wooden planks were set up outside. The evening was cool. Ada and Cece wrapped shawls around their shoulders. Rudy and Ernest even built a bonfire to keep the large group warm.

Ernest, always the teacher, was telling the group that bonfire actually meant bone fire. The four boys were intrigued to learn that animal bones were burnt during the Middle Ages to ward off evil spirits. In an effort to scare his younger brothers, Adam began to howl, which brought Thunder and Rain to attention.

The small community was glad to be together. There was so much to celebrate and discuss. God's blessings were abundant. There were also changes coming to the extended family. The group agreed that it was best to talk openly about the future. They understood that when things remained hidden there was room for offense.

Uncle Christian called everyone to attention by loudly clearing his voice. It was dusk and the evening star could be seen in the sky. "I think we should start our meeting with everyone sharing important events that have taken place over the past couple weeks. Ada, why don't you and I begin?"

On cue, Auntie talked about their beautiful wedding day and with flushed cheeks shared about their honeymoon in Spencer.

Rudy went next. He took Emie's hand and pulled her to her feet. He thanked God for their engagement and the upcoming birth of the baby. He also talked about his time with Ahab and his appreciation for Ernest's support.

Emie, still standing next to Rudy, shared with tear-filled eyes about her mama's visit.

Ernest talked about the new school and God's provision for a building and personal residence. He then openly told the group that he and Mercy were exploring their future together. Ernest's heart swelled with appreciation when the small community cheered. Shy Mercy didn't offer any words but smiled at Ernest, which was enough to make his heart race.

The four boys, not wanting to be excluded, each shared about their lives. Adam mentioned a snake he had found; Beau talked about stepping in Thunder's business; Claude said that he saw Rudy and Emie kiss and not just on the cheek; and Dean talked about bones and evil spirits.

Auntie and Emie cried when Justice shared about his family's move further up the holler but understood that Ernest would need assistance. Once emotions were settled, Ada suggested that Rudy and Emie take the small house as their home.

Ernest noticed the smiles exchanged between the engaged couple. He could almost feel Rudy's relief at knowing where his young family would reside.

Ernest also added his two cents to the conversation, "I think the little house will be perfect for Emie and Rudy." Then he looked at Auntie and Doc, "I appreciate all that you've done for my family. If Emie's movin', would you be willin' to let Coral stay on the back porch?" Ernest then shared about Old Man James and Coral's near brush with tragedy.

"Just like Emie, we'll take her as our own," Uncle Christian responded.

Ada, who was once again overcome with emotion, could only nod her head "yes" in response. Justice, Cece, and Mercy were also stunned to hear about what almost happened to Coral.

Mercy rose from her seat and made her way to Ernest's side. She didn't say anything, but placed her hand over his. Her touch spoke volumes, and Ernest found comfort in her fingers resting on his own.

The group readied to conclude their time in prayer, when Ernest noticed billows of smoke in the distance. He stood to his feet, and motioned for those gathered to look upward.

"It's a big one," Aunt Ada spoke under her breath. "Lord, help us..."

Ernest, along with Rudy and Justice, headed in the direction of the smoke. Doc grabbed his medical bag from the cabin and hurried to join them.

Ernest could hear Auntie leading the rest of the family in prayer. He was moving too fast to pray aloud, but in his head and heart he began to intercede.

It was fall. The grass and vegetation, for the most part, were dry and brittle. It was too late in the year for afternoon summer rains and too early for snow. The fire could easily spread across the mountain. Homes were few and far between in the holler, but Ernest had read stories about flames jumping from tree top to tree top, and he was worried.

He knew in big cities that there were paid firemen, and that the horse-drawn pump had been replaced by the red fire engine, red to stand apart from Henry Ford's black cars. But in the Appalachians, fires were fought by the hands of mountain men and water came from the nearest stream or yard pump.

From a distance it was hard to tell where the fire was located. The men, knowing their help would be needed, ran toward the general direction of the smoke clouds. When they reached the swinging bridge at Big Creek, there was no doubt in anyone's mind that the Ashby home was ablaze.

Ernest felt panicked. His first thoughts were of his sisters. He and Rudy quickly rushed toward the house. When they found the three youngest girls in the orchard roped together and tied loosely to a tree, Rudy yelled back for Doc to make sure that the little ones were alright. Doc and Justice were doing their best to keep up with the younger men.

The fire had spread to every room of the house. The flames were like arrows shooting toward the sky. Ernest found Coral standing in their mama's garden. She was barefoot and clothed only in her step-ins. He couldn't tell if she was hurt or not. Her face and body were black from smoke, and she was coughing so hard that she couldn't speak.

When Ernest asked if she was all right, she nodded and pointed toward the house. He ran as far as the flames and heat would allow. There was nothing to be done; the entire home was engulfed in fire.

He yelled for his mama, then for his daddy. There was no answer. He circled the house, coming as close as he dared. His parents were nowhere to be found. The wind had caught a few flames and carried them to the field across the road, but for the most part the dirt road had created a barrier. He headed back toward the garden. The small ditch that lay between the house and barn had delayed the fire from spreading, but Ernest could see that the flames wouldn't be contained for long. Rudy had already released the sows and piglets, and with Justice's help was carrying water bucket-by-bucket toward the barn. It was understood that the house was too far gone for saving.

He turned back toward Coral, removed his shirt and covered her. He already knew the answer, but still needed to ask, "Mama, Daddy?"

"I tried," she whispered between bouts of coughing.

He nodded slightly and motioned for her to stay put. He then rushed to help Rudy and Justice. By then others were arriving to join the fight.

When dawn came, the house sat smoldering. There were only charred remains. The barn had burned as well, and two lives had been lost.

Rudy approached Ernest with news that several of the local farmers were rounding up the sows and piglets. Thank goodness it hadn't been necessary to release the boars from their pens.

Ernest saw his sisters sitting on the small hillside up from his mama's garden. He counted and all seven of them were there. The youngest girls were wrapped in blankets. The older girls were fussing over the younger ones. The grass was covered in dew, and he thought all of them must be chilled. He and Rudy walked from what was left of the barn to where the girls were sitting.

Emie stood first. She quickly hugged Ernest and then ran into Rudy's arms. It did Ernest's heart good to see his sister looking for comfort from her fiancé. Ruby and Garnett surrounded Ernest with an embrace. Somewhere in the night, Ernest remembered seeing their husbands fighting the fire in the barn.

He wanted to be strong, but the physical and emotional warmth that his sisters were giving him made him cry. His body shuddered with exhaustion and emotion. The girls held on, and when Ernest opened his eyes he was surrounded by his seven sisters and Rudy.

Church ladies appeared with hot drinks and food. They placed quilts on the ground and the Ashby children, save Lester, sat together as the sun continued to rise seemingly inch-by-inch over the burned rubble. Auntie Ada was helping with the food, but Ernest knew that her eyes were constantly on his sisters. She was ready to step in when needed.

At first no one talked. Some of the sisters held hands and others linked arms. Emie sat on one side of Ernest and Coral on the other. Ernest noticed that Coral was wearing more than her step-ins and his shirt. He was thankful that someone had provided for her. He looked down at his undershirt. It was black from smoke and soot.

Not much was eaten, yet Ernest was grateful for the nourishment provided by the holler neighbors. They were good folk who readied themselves when tragedy struck. The three youngest sisters, who Mama had called the babies, were obviously overwrought. They weren't crying or fussing, but Ernest couldn't help but notice their glazed eyes and dazed bodies.

It was decided that Opal, Pearl, and Sapphire would go home with the twins and their husbands. Ernest was so thankful for the Houston boys. His sisters had married good men. Coral would go with Emie to Auntie's for the time being. Ernest didn't know how everything would work in the end, but he felt relief that his sisters all had places of refuge.

Sheriff Robbins approached the family. He had also worked throughout the night. Ernest had noticed him just before daybreak carefully walking around what was left of the Ashby home. He had worried that the lawman would be injured by a hot spot. He wasn't surprised when the sheriff requested to talk with Coral.

Ernest asked to join them. The sheriff agreed but insisted that Ernest allow him to ask all the questions. Emie indicated that she would wait with Rudy until Coral was finished. The other sisters headed to the Houston homestead.

"Now, Coral," Sheriff Robbins began. "We've only talked a couple times, but I know you're an honest, straight-up girl. I'm needin' you to tell me what happened last night."

Ernest, who was holding his sister's hand, squeezed her fingers slightly. He wanted to reassure Coral that it was fine to tell her story to the sheriff.

"Daddy and Mama were fightin'," Coral began. "Daddy was yellin' real loud, and I think Mama was cryin'."

"What were they arguing about?" the sheriff asked.

"Daddy was mad that Ernest was leavin' to teach the colored children. He was also yellin' about Lester."

"Was there anything else?" the sheriff continued.

"Yes, about Emie."

Ernest couldn't help himself. "What about Emie?"

The sheriff looked at Ernest. "Now, son, you know our arrangement."

Ernest nodded his head and pursed his lips together.

"Daddy told Mama that she was to head to town the next mornin' and call Pastor Eugene. He wanted Charlie to know that the baby was a boy..."

Tears welled up in Coral's eyes and then rolled down her cheeks.

Ernest took Coral in his arms and held her tight. "It's okay, girlie, I'm right here. I ain't goin' nowhere."

Through her tears Coral turned to face the sheriff and continued, "Daddy said if Charlie was willin', that he would trade the baby for me."

The sheriff was puzzled, "Coral, do you know what your daddy meant?"

"Yes."

"Would you please tell me?"

"It pains me, Sheriff. What my Daddy wanted to do wasn't nice."

"I'm sorry, but Coral, I need to know."

Coral began to wring her hands. Her actions reminded Ernest of their mama. He took a deep breath and fought back his emotions. He needed to be strong for Coral. He knew exactly what their daddy had meant and was ready to step in and answer the sheriff's question, when his sister started talking.

"My Daddy and Uncle Eugene was workin' on plans to take Emie's baby. Charlie wanted the baby if it was a boy. My Daddy was hopin' that Charlie would take me and leave the baby with him and my mama."

Ernest closed his eyes and shook his head. He felt like his heart was being held in a vice. He put his hands on Coral's shoulders and drew her near. "I'm sorry, Coral. You know I would have never let that happen."

"I know you would have tried to help me, but I was scared, Ernest."

Before redirecting the conversation back to the incidents of the previous evening, the sheriff paused for a couple minutes. Ernest knew that the lawman was giving opportunity for him to comfort Coral.

After waiting, the sheriff asked his next question, "Now, Coral, do you remember what happened next?"

"Well, Sheriff Robbins, I was in the other room, so I could only hear. I couldn't see what happened."

"What did you hear?"

"My mama was talkin' real quiet and then I heard her cry. I think my daddy hit her."

"Do you know how the fire started?"

"I ain't quite sure. I was with the babies in our room. The little ones were playin' with a couple dolls. I was watchin' them, but at the same time tryin' to hear what was happenin' in the next room."

"Coral, how did you know there was a fire?"

"I heard Mama yellin'. She was yellin' at Daddy sayin' 'What have you done?' and Daddy was sayin', 'Leave me be, woman.'"

Coral grew quiet. Ernest was anxious to hear the entire story and was relieved when the sheriff encouraged his sister to continue.

"A few minutes later," Coral recounted, "Mama came runnin' into the girls' bedroom talkin' real loud, sayin' that the house was on fire. She told me to take the babies to a safe place."

Coral took a deep breath. "I took the little ones and hurried toward the kitchen. When I passed Mama and Daddy's room, I could see the curtains was on fire, and there was flames runnin' up the wall. I only got a glimpse. I didn't look too close. I wanted my sisters to be safe. I ran with them to one of the apple trees in the orchard. We'd picked apples from there earlier in the day. I took off my dress and ripped it in two. With one strip I tied the girls together, and with the other I tied them to the tree."

Coral shook her head. Ernest knew that it must have bothered her to have roped the girls. "I didn't tie them very tight. I didn't want 'um hurtin', but at the same time I was worried that they would try and follow me back to the house."

Ernest patted his sister's shoulders, and when she turned and looked at him, he softly spoke, "You did real good, Coral. You did just fine keepin' the little ones safe."

"Coral, can you please tell me what you saw when you got back to the house?" Sheriff Robbins requested.

"It was hot, real hot. Doc looked me over last night. He said I got some burns. Not real bad ones, but they'll be hurtin' some."

"I'm sorry you were hurt, and I hope you'll be better soon," the sheriff patiently commented.

Ernest had always liked Sheriff Robbins and his wife, and now his appreciation for the officer grew even more. He was extremely kind and compassionate when talking with Coral. Ernest imagined that he had been the same with Emie not that long ago.

"Sheriff," Coral spoke, "I made it to the kitchen but couldn't get no further. There was flames around the bedroom door. My mama was pleadin' with Daddy to get in his chair, but I don't think he was movin'. He told her, 'My sons done left me and now you ain't willin' to do my biddin'. I might as well die. Hell's waitin' for me.'"

The young girl turned to Ernest, "Brother, do you think hell was waitin' for Mama and Daddy?"

Ernest wasn't sure how to answer and paused before responding. "Coral, Jesus was prayin' to His Father that Mama and Daddy would ask for help. The Lord doesn't want anyone goin' to hell."

"Ernest, I think Mama prayed for God to help her, but I don't know about Daddy. Do you think he prayed?"

"I don't know, girlie. I'm sure hopin' he did."

Sheriff Robbins looked at Coral, "We're almost finished. You've been very brave. Can you remember anything else?"

Coral answered quietly, "I can't remember much else. I was real scared. I think my mama tried to leave the room, but I ain't sure. I couldn't see much. The fire was growin'. It was hot. Real hot. I didn't wanna die. I'm only twelve."

"I'm glad you didn't die," the sheriff spoke. "Someone as courageous as you needs to have a long life. Coral, when you left the house, did you go back to your sisters?"

"No, sir. I stood in Mama's garden. I wasn't ready to say 'good-bye.' I just stayed there, hopin' to see her run out the back door." Coral turned and faced Ernest once again. "She didn't come. I just heard her screamin'. It was terrible, Ernest. My heart felt all broke up inside. I just stayed there in the garden 'til you found me."

"Coral, is there anything else you're wantin' to tell me?"

She thought for a moment. "Sheriff, after I heard Mama, I heard another noise comin' from the house. It sounded sort of like thunder, a rumblin' noise."

Sheriff Robbins knelt down. "I'm not sure what that would have been, Coral. Maybe some type of noise made by the fire." He looked directly into young girl's pale blue eyes. "Thank you for tellin' me what happened. I'm very proud of you, and I know your brother is proud as well." He then motioned for his wife, who was standing a short distance away, to join them. As MayLou approached, he requested that she take Coral for a few minutes while he and Ernest talked.

Speaking softly to the young girl, MayLou took Coral by the hand and led her away. Out of the corner of his eye, Ernest saw Auntie join them.

"Ernest," the sheriff spoke, "Your sister's story lines up with what little evidence I've been able to find. I'm thinkin' that your daddy threw a lit oil lamp at the wall. The oil fueled the fire. Just like Coral said, the curtains started to burn and her recollection of fire running on the wall makes sense. The oil would have splattered, creating lines and patterns. I also think the oil was somehow spread to the bedroom doorway. Maybe your daddy threw a second lamp, or the first one didn't break completely and perhaps rolled toward the door. I'm not sure, but from what little is left of the house, it would seem that the charring is worse by the where the window and door was located."

"Sheriff, did you find their bodies?"

"What was left. I'm sorry, Ernest. I don't know if this helps or not, but I think Coral was right – your mama was tryin' to leave the bedroom. Her body was found close by what I believe was the doorway. The fire surrounded your parents – the curtains and wall on one side, and the blocked doorway on the other."

Sheriff Robbins placed his right hand on Ernest's shoulder. "I'm sorry for your loss. Doc Bright is also the county coroner. He'll let you know what happens next."

"Thank you, Sheriff."

"I don't think I'll have any more questions for your sister, but if I do, where will she be stayin'?"

"She's headed to Aunt Ada's."

"Ernest, you're a good brother. I know you been lookin' out for your sisters for some time. I won't speak ill of your mama or daddy, but them girls was needin' your help. God will give you strength for what lies ahead. MayLou and I will be prayin'. I'm here to help, and so are others."

Ernest was exhausted. He'd been awake for over twenty-four hours. Most of the day had been spent putting out hot spots. Once the ashes were cold, he would dig through what little was left of the house and barn.

Rudy and Justice had spent most of the day building pens for the sows and their babies; all but two of the young boars had been found. He hoped that the lost boars had been castrated. A wild hog living in the woods was dangerous, but one that was looking for love was even more threatening.

Aunt Ada and Doc had made sure that his four young sisters were fine. Coral had some burns on her torso, arms, and legs, but the others were in good physical health.

All of his siblings were in a state of shock. Ernest had worried over Emie and the baby. Doc had examined her as well. He wanted her to take things easy for a couple days but was confident that both she and the baby would be fine. Ernest knew that Aunt Ada would take good care of them.

By late morning, his parents' bodies had been removed from the house. His sisters had already gone, and Doc and Sheriff Robbins had shielded him from watching. The mountain people were curious by nature, but the removal had been handled discretely with as few onlookers as possible.

Auntie had told Ernest that tomorrow would be soon enough to think about the sending home service. He believed that his mama was in heaven singing with the angels but was worried about his daddy. He knew there was no sense in worrying. There was nothing to be done. Not even prayer helped the dead.

It was dusk, and everyone had left for home. Rudy and Justice had departed for Auntie's a few minutes earlier. Rudy was anxious to check on Emie, and Justice always worried when he left Cece with the four boys for too long.

Ernest wanted a few moments by himself before heading to Aunt Ada's. He mustered what strength he had left and began the trek across the orchard. Just as he crossed the swinging bridge, he saw Mercy waiting at the end of the expanse.

"Mercy, what are you doin' here? It's gettin' late. Are you okay?"

"I've been waitin' for you."

"Just how long have you been waitin?"

"Since last night."

Ernest couldn't help but embrace her.

"I wanted to be by your side, Ernest. I wanted you to know that I felt your grief, but it didn't seem right for everyone to see us together."

"I would have been proud to have you by my side, but you're probably right. The people of Big Creek are good folks, but they're talkers. They'll be enough tongues waggin' about the fire. I think we'd just plain wear 'um out if they had to talk about a white boy and pretty girl with lovely brown skin."

Mercy stepped from Ernest's embrace, looked at his face and smiled. "Let's get you to Auntie's. I'm sure she's got food on the table waitin' for her boy."

"Do you mind if we sit? Just for a minute."

Ernest sat down at the end of the bridge. Mercy didn't sit, but stood behind him. She placed her long slender fingers on his shoulders and began to rub out the knots and stress. Ernest put his chin to his chest, and she massaged his neck. His heart ached with grief; grief for the death of his parents, but more so for what could have been but wasn't.

Along with her ministering hands, Mercy started to sing. She began with a lullaby. *She comes in through the skylight, for the door is not allowed. Her eyes are bright as little stars. Her dress is like a cloud. She holds me very kind and tight, and talks about her land where all the flowers are boys and girls, and the mothers are at hand.*

Next she sang one his mama's favorite hymns. *There's a place, in Heaven prepared for me. When the toils o this life is over, where the saints are clothed in white, before the throne singin' praises forever, forever more. In my Father's house there are mansions bright. If he said it, then I know it's true, there's a place for me beyond, beyond the sky. Brothers and sisters there's one for you. Jesus promised me a home over there. Jesus promised me a home over there. No more sickness, sorrow, pain because He promised me a home over there…*

Ernest felt like God Himself was singing over him.

Chapter Thirty Four

"Lots of nuts and berries means that the winter will be severe."
(Appalachian Folk Belief)

Coral was sharing Emie's small bed. Ernest was certain that his sisters didn't mind. They were accustomed to sleeping in close quarters. In fact, when Ernest looked in on them, Coral was curled up against Emie. Ernest sighed. He hoped his sisters found comfort in their closeness.

Rain was lying on the floor next to the bed. He lifted his head when Ernest entered the room, thumped his tail, and laid back down. Ernest thought it strange the puppy hadn't greeted him with the usual fanfare, but then realized Rain probably didn't like being relegated to the floor. He usually slept by his mistress in the small bed. *Better get used to it, buddy,* Ernest thought. *Soon it will be Rudy cuddled up next to Emie, and you'll be on the floor each and every night.*

Aunt Ada and Uncle Christian had heard Ernest enter the cabin. They were waiting for him in the "everythin' room". Before he ate and talked about the day, he had wanted to check on his sisters.

Auntie prepared him a large plate of food: fried pork chops, mashed potatoes, greens, and berry pie. Ernest surprised himself by eating the plate clean. He especially enjoyed the blackberry pie. He knew that Emie and Mercy had spent several summer days picking gallons of berries. Auntie and Cece had canned the berries and also made jam. While he was eating, there was a sense that things were normal, but with his plate finished and his belly full, the tragedy he and his siblings were facing came again to roost on his shoulders. It was like a large swooping black crow that cawed over and over again.

"My boy, can I get you more?" Ada asked.

"I think I've had plenty. Didn't realize I was so hungry," Ernest said.

"I tried to get in touch with Lester," Doc said. "I left a message with someone at the number he gave me. I'm hoping he stops by there within the next couple days."

"Thank you, Doc."

"We want to help, Ernest. What can we do?" Aunt Ada asked.

"I'm meetin' with the older girls tomorrow to talk about the sendin' home service," Ernest replied. "Beyond that, I don't know."

"I'll make sure everything is in order," Doc responded.

"I know you will." Ernest looked first at Doc, then at Ada. "Where would I be? Where would my sisters be without your help?" His eyes clouded over once again with tears. *Grief is a strange thing,* he thought. *My heart hurts with a depth that can't be measured, yet I continue to breathe, talk, and even eat.*

Ernest knew Auntie and Doc would want to know what happened. He just wasn't sure that he had the strength to tell the story. "I'm tired," he finally spoke. "But I don't want to go to bed without tellin' ya a little bit of what took place."

"If you're up to it, Ernest," Aunt Ada spoke. "If not, we'll wait till mornin'."

"I know you won't sleep without knowin', Auntie."

Ernest recounted Coral's story and the sheriff's conclusions. When Ada started to ask questions, his new uncle stepped in and said everything else could wait.

"He's exhausted, sweetheart. Let's let him rest. The girls have been sleeping for some time, and they'll be up early wanting their brother." Doc stood and took Ada's hand, helping her from the rocker.

The newlyweds headed to their bedroom, and Ernest prepared his pallet on the floor from the blankets and pillow that Ada had left for him. He desperately needed sleep, but each time he started to doze, his body would jerk him awake. He laid there for quite some time; then he gathered his bedding and headed to the back porch bedroom. Quietly he entered the room, not wanting to wake his sisters. He laid the linens down, as close as possible to Emie's bed, and with Rain beside him, joined his sisters in deep slumber.

Ernest woke the following morning to the sound of braying mules. He was in the bedroom by himself and wondered about the time. He was ready to get up when Rain's nose pushed open the door. The young dog headed straight to Ernest and greeted him properly with a wagging tail and a lick on the face.

Ernest heard light footsteps. He knew it was probably Emie and pretended to be asleep.

"Rain, come," the mistress whispered.

Ernest held the dog tightly.

"Rain, you naughty boy, come here," Emie quietly spoke.

Ernest waited another moment and jumped to his feet. He held the overgrown puppy in front of his face and snarled like a rabid dog. Rain barked and wiggled from Ernest's arms.

Emie squealed like a little girl, and then started to laugh. "Now who's naughty?"

Ernest rewarded her with a big smile.

"Brother, do you think it's wrong to laugh? Mama and Daddy are gone."

"Emie, we need to laugh. Grief and laughter are a two-sided coin. I'm thinkin' we'll be flippin' the coin a lot. Sometimes we'll cry and sometimes we'll laugh. It's the way of life, girlie."

His sister nodded her head.

Ernest heard the mules again. He closed his eyes and shook his head. He didn't know what Justice saw in the two ornery creatures.

"Justice is wantin' to help us, Ernest. The mules are pullin' their cart over walnuts the boys gathered. Rudy's daddy is gonna buy the nuts once they're cracked and shelled," Emie explained.

Ernest smiled again. "It's nice to have friends, ain't it?"

Late morning Emie and Coral headed outside. Auntie felt that the sunshine would do them good.

"Emie, how come we ain't helpin' plan the service?" Coral asked.

Emie didn't want to reveal that Ernest thought it would be too much for the younger sister. He'd said it wasn't fair to make Coral tell her story over and over again. Coral had already told what happened enough times − first to the sheriff, then to others who asked questions at the homestead, and finally to Emie lying in bed the previous night. She had also talked with Uncle Christian and Aunt Ada some. Emie also knew Ernest was worried about her and the baby's wellbeing. She was doing what Uncle Christian suggested and was taking things easy.

"It's how it works with the middles in the family," Emie answered. "We're not old enough to be thought of as adults, and we're too old to be pampered and fussed over like the babies."

"I'm guessin' you're right."

"Don't worry, Coral. Ernest will be askin' about our thoughts when he gets back."

It wasn't long before Ernest returned to Auntie's cabin. Emie and Coral were full of questions about the other sisters, especially the young ones. They also wanted to know what had been decided about the sending home service.

"The little ones are doin' fine," Ernest shared. "I'm thinkin' they don't rightly understand what's happened. Ruby and Garnett are takin' good care of them." Ernest also talked about the service.

"If you two agree, we'd like to ask Rudy's grandpappy to handle things. Ruby and Garnett asked if I would sing a hymn. I'd like Mercy to join me. We agreed to honor to Mama and Daddy. This ain't the time to be speakin' about things we wish was different."

Emie bit her tongue but then couldn't constrain herself. "Ernest, I don't think we should be sayin' bad things, but I don't think we should be lyin' neither. It ain't right, brother. Things is what they is. Daddy was a mean man. Mama did her best, but to keep the peace, she allowed his meanness."

Ernest nodded in agreement. "Ruby and Garnett and I talked about such. We'll do our best to not speak ill, but not to lie."

Coral remained quiet, too quiet. Finally, Ernest asked if she had any thoughts on the service.

"No, brother," she softly answered.

"Coral, are you alright?" Emie asked.

"Right as I can be. I'm worried about what will happen with Mama and Daddy gone. Where will me and the little ones live? I maybe could try and take care of myself, but not the babies. I'm also wonderin' why they had to die, 'specially in a fire. If I think on it too much, I can still hear Mama…"

Emie wrapped her arm around Coral and drew her near.

Emie could tell that Ernest was waiting to see if she had something to say. She needed to think a moment before answering Coral. While she gathered her thoughts, her sweet brother once again comforted their younger sister.

"Girlie, you have no need to be worryin'. Aunt Ada and Uncle Christian are wantin' you to stay right here, and the twins and their husbands are wantin' to keep the little ones."

"Sister," Emie added, "I ain't rightly sure why Mama and Daddy died, and you're right, a fire is a bad way to leave this world. I'm sorry you keep hearin' Mama in her final moments. I'm gonna pray the Lord helps you. I don't want you hearin' that."

Just then Adam, Beau, Claude, and Dean came running from the meadow with Thunder and Rain in close pursuit. The four boys were talking loudly and all at once about walnuts and mules. Thunder chased his tail, and Rain joined in the conversation by whining for attention at Emie's feet. Mercy heard the commotion and came from behind the cabin. She tried to quiet the boys and corral them toward the small house.

Mercy looked shyly at Ernest. "I'm sorry. The boys have been waitin' to tell you all about their walnut pickin'."

Emie was frustrated by the interruption, but when she saw Coral smile, she realized the intrusion was a welcomed distraction. Anything that brought pleasure to her sister was a blessing.

The boys settled down when Justice told them that Cece had lunch ready. Emie and Coral headed to the cabin to visit with Aunt Ada. The older sisters had wondered if their sweet aunt would work with the church ladies on some of the arrangements for the service.

Ernest and Mercy were left alone. Ernest knew that their relationship was new, but he couldn't help reaching for her hand.

"How are you?" Mercy sweetly asked.

"Better when I'm with you."

Mercy blushed. Ernest enjoyed seeing her flushed cheeks.

"I talked with the older girls this mornin' about the service for Mama and Daddy. They'd like me to sing, and I'm wantin' you to join me."

"Are you sure, Ernest?"

"I'm sure. I like how we harmonize, and not just with our singin'."

Mercy smiled in response, but, in short order, the look on her face turned serious. "There aren't any colored folks that attend Big Creek Church."

"So you and your family will be the first."

"Ernest, the service is about rememberin' your mama and daddy. Me bein' there will create a commotion."

"I need you there. I'm hurtin', Mercy. I need your strength."

When she didn't answer right away, Ernest grew worried. He released her hand. "I'm sorry. We're just startin' out, and I'm talkin' like we've been together a long piece. I'm not thinkin' clearly. We agreed to move slow like…"

"Ernest, it's not your talk that's botherin' me. I ain't wantin' to take anythin' away from your family. Your sisters are grievin'. You're grievin'. I can be your strength even if I'm not standin' right beside you. You're in my heart and in my prayers."

"If my sisters all agree, will you sing with me? And if it makes you feel better, I'll also talk with Pastor Rex."

He stayed quiet and waited for her answer. Her response was worth the wait.

Chapter Thirty Five

*"If your ears are ringing, you are hearing the death bell, and
someone will pass away."*
(Appalachian Folk Belief)

Emie was beside herself. Rain had tangled with a porcupine. Uncle Christian had used pliers and pulled out the quills, while she had done her best to hold the overgrown puppy still. The quills had backward facing barbs, and she worried that if pieces left inside Rain could get an infection or even worse. Her new uncle thought the puppy would be fine. Emie felt comforted by his words, until she overheard Auntie remind Doc that he was trained to treat humans, not dogs; especially naughty dogs who slept on beds and played with quilled rodents. She heard her uncle laugh in response and then saw him, out of the corner of her eye, pat Auntie's bottom.

Love was in the air, she guessed, first Auntie and Doc, then she and Rudy, and now Mercy and Ernest. In all her eighth grade learning, love was shown to be a peculiar thing in the animal kingdom. Her McGuffey Reader said a male porcupine urinated on his would-be partner prior to mating. Thinkin' of it turned her mouth sour. And then there were baboons. The male apparently showed off his red bottom when he was interested in a female.

Emie hoped that love among people was very different than animal sex.

Emie headed to the back porch bedroom with Rain walking by her side. He looked pitiful. His gold-colored eyes were droopy, and his tail stood still. She patted his head, and his tail thumped once against the wall.

The sending home service for her parents was this afternoon. Rudy planned to walk with her to the church. She hoped that she didn't have to go naked. She was five months into her pregnancy, and her little pooch was growing; none of her clothes fit properly. She stood in her panties and camisole in the small bedroom she and Coral now shared. She guessed that Ernest shared the bedroom as well. Every morning, since their parents' death, she woke to find him lying on the floor next to her and Coral's bed. The nights were growing cold, and she worried that her brother was chilled. She hoped Ernest snuggled with Rain. She knew from experience that her puppy emitted enough body heat to melt a glacier.

Emie didn't want to cry, but yet the tears came. Her step-ins were tight and her camisole barely covered her growing breasts, but that didn't matter much, no one would see her underclothes. It just didn't seem right to wear a too-tight dress to her parents' send off. What would happen if all the buttons popped; it occurred to her if her dress came open that everyone would see her snug panties that were now rolling down past her belly button. She cried even harder.

"Emie, are you alright?" She heard Rudy's voice from outside her bedroom door.

"Don't come in!"

"I ain't comin' in the bedroom with you 'til we're married."

"We won't be stayin' in this room once we're married!"

"Emie, what's wrong? Why are you cryin'?"

"Nothin' is wrong."

"I can't help if you don't tell me."

"Rudy, you can't help with this."

"Let me try, Emie. You know I love you and would do anythin' I could."

He waited for his girl to answer, then he waited some more. Finally he sat down next to the bedroom door. "Darlin', pretend I'm Charlie Chan and a least give me some clues about why you're upset."

"I'm worried. Did you know that boy porcupines pee on the girls they love, and boy baboons show off their red bottoms when they're likin' a girl?"

"And this is makin' you cry?"

"No, Rudy. I ain't cryin' about porcupines and baboons. Well, I'm kinda cryin' about porcupines. Rain's hurtin'. A porcupine got him good."

"Emie, the porcupine didn't get Rain; Rain got the porcupine. The quills don't fly through the air like darts."

"I know, Rudy!"

"Alright, Emie, I'm not sure what's wrong, but I don't think I'm helpin'. Do you want me to get Auntie or Ernest?"

"No, Red. You're helpin' just fine," she sighed.

Rudy's chest puffed out a little bit. He knew he wasn't really helping Emie, but at the same time he wanted to be her hero.

"I'm cryin' cause this baby is growin', and my belly's too big, and I ain't got nothin' to wear. My mama is gonna look down from heaven and be ashamed."

"Well, darlin', maybe I can help you after all. My mama sent a special package for you, and I'm thinkin' it just might be a new dress." Rudy felt like Buck Rogers. Ernest had told him about the serial book character who explored outer space. Rudy felt like he and Buck had something in common; they had both traveled to places unknown by the common man. Rudy was convinced that Emerald Ashby was unexplored territory, not of this world.

"Red, I'm not dressed."

"Okay," he responded, trying not to picture his beloved.

"Would you leave your mama's gift by my door?"

Rudy sat the gift down, but didn't move.

"Rudy?"

"Yes, darlin'," he chuckled.

Emie smiled at Rudy's antics and also with relief at being given a new dress. "You need to be leavin' now," she instructed.

"Say 'Please, Red, and thank you for being Buck Rogers today.'"

"Who's Buck Rogers?"

"Never mind, Emie," he laughed. "I'll see you once you got your clothes on."

She heard Rudy walk away, waited a moment, and then opened the door just wide enough to reach out and take her gift. The package contained not only a new dress, but new shoes and new underthings as well. *Bless Rudy's mama,* Emie thought. Everything was a bit big, but Emie didn't mind. She needed room for growing. The dress was dark blue with a cream colored lace collar and sleeve cuffs. The shoes were black and also a bit big. She knew her feet would swell by the end of the day, but for now she stuffed some of the package wrapping into the toes of the shoes.

Mid-morning, Emie and Rudy were greeted at the church door by Sheriff Robbins. "I've been waitin' for you," the sheriff spoke. "Charlie's here. I received a call a couple hours ago from a lawyer outside of Charleston sayin' that Charlie would be attendin' the service for his aunt and uncle."

Rudy spoke up, "Did you tell the lawyer Charlie wasn't welcome?"

"I did, son," the sheriff answered, "but, right now, legally I can't keep him from bein' here."

Emie started shaking. She wanted to be brave, but Charlie still frightened her. Rudy drew her close and placed his arm around her waist.

"The lawyer assured me that he'd be gone as soon as the service was over. He won't even go to the gravesite. I've got him sittin' in a far back corner with a couple of the holler men keepin' a close eye on him. He won't be creatin' mischief."

She could feel tears rolling down her right check. Rudy removed his arm from her waist, reached into his pocket and withdrew the torn piece of cloth that Emie had shared with him so long ago. He used the remnant to gently wipe away her tears.

"Thank you, Sheriff, for the warnin'," Rudy spoke.

He guided Emie into the foyer, stopped, and looked around. She knew he was looking for Charlie. Emie couldn't bring herself to look. She focused instead on the morning sunrays streaming over the pews. Fairy dust seemed to float lightly throughout the church. She could tell when Rudy spotted him, though. Her fiancé's entire body stiffened. Rudy placed his hand on the small of her back and guided her up the narrow far-right aisle between the pews and the whitewashed wall. She assumed that Charlie was sitting on the opposite side of the sanctuary.

Emie took a seat on the front row beside her sisters. The two youngest babies were sitting on the laps of the older sisters. The twins had their husbands sitting along with them. Emie's nerves were on end. Coral gripped her hand, and the twins smiled sweetly. The little girls seemed too overwhelmed to say or do anything. She noticed Ernest standing on the platform with Mercy. They were talking with the piano player. Her brother was focused on matters at hand. Emie didn't think her siblings were aware that Charlie was present. She motioned for Rudy to join her.

"I'll be back in just a minute, darlin'."

She knew that Rudy was headed toward Charlie. Earlier she had willed herself to look and couldn't find the courage, but now her eyes followed her beloved. The look on Rudy's face was unfamiliar to Emie. Charlie was seated on the far left hand side in the back row. Rudy bent low and spoke directly into Charlie's ear. He then pulled something long and narrow from his coat sleeve and placed the tip of it at Charlie's neck. Her cousin flinched. Emie's heart raced faster. She worried that Charlie would jump from his seat and attack Rudy. When Sheriff Robbins approached the two, she breathed a small sigh of relief. Rudy discretely put the weapon back up his coat sleeve. The sheriff motioned for Rudy to step away from Charlie. When Rudy headed her way, she shifted to face the front, her body collapsing against the back of the pew.

Emie felt Coral move as well and knew her younger sister had also witnessed the interaction between Rudy and Charlie. She looked down the row at the rest of her sisters; everyone was facing the front. She then looked at Ernest, who was still intent on his music.

She didn't want the day to be about Charlie. The service was about her mama and daddy. She whispered to Coral, "Let's not tell the others that Charlie is here."

Coral shook her head yes and scooted over to make room for Rudy.

When Rudy sat down, Emie didn't ask what happened. Instead she placed her thumb and forefinger up Rudy's coat sleeve and pulled out the mystery weapon. It was a porcupine quill − pointed and sharp at the end.

Rudy took the quill from Emie's hand and placed it back up his sleeve. "Darlin', I want to hurt him bad, but I just drew a prick of blood, that's all. I told 'em if he didn't behave, I'd put out an eye or maybe puncture an eardrum."

Emie turned. She looked shocked and puzzled.

"The quills are like needles, Emie." Rudy hissed. "They can *hurt*. Maybe I'm young, but he best not be be thinkin' that I won't protect what's mine."

She'd never seen this side of Rudy. She had only known him to be sweet and kind. Rudy's testosterone was flaming!

"Doc left the quills layin' on the small table in the parlor and I took one," Rudy continued. "It wouldn't fit in my pocket, so I put it up my sleeve." He took Emie's hand. "Now don't be worryin' none. It ain't good for you or the baby. The sheriff's watchin' Charlie, and he won't come near."

Ernest and Mercy left the platform. Ernest took a seat almost at the very end of the sibling row, and motioned for Mercy to join him. Mercy smiled, patted Ernest's shoulder, and then took a seat directly behind him. Just as the service started, Justice and Cece, the four boys, Aunt Ada, and Uncle Christian all joined Mercy in the second row.

Given the type of service, the congregation was quiet and all eyes were looking toward the front when Rudy's sizable, but wisened, grandpappy took his place behind the wooden pulpit dressed in a black suit. As a little girl, Emie's mama had told her the history behind the oak pulpit. It had been made years and years ago, even before her mama was born, by an old man who lived far up the holler. He had used oak to represent the great strength of

God. A single oak tree produced both male and female flowers. Emie thought about her parents and the blending of their lives; instead of the two becoming one and creating something beautiful; the two had mixed like oil and water. Her mama was the water, and her daddy the oil that always lay at the top — smothering and hiding the goodness underneath. Emie wanted her life with Rudy to be different. She wanted their marriage to be like the oak tree with both types of flowers blooming together and creating something beautiful.

"On behalf of the family of Ahab Elijah and Alma Lynn Ashby, I want to thank you for bein' here today," Pastor Rex began. Emie suddenly trusted him to say the right thing.

The kindly pastor shared her parents' dates of birth and dates of death. He also talked about those left behind. She was thankful Grandpappy included Rudy, mentioning him as her fiancé. He also included Aunt Ada, Uncle Christian, and Justice and his family.

Ernest and Mercy stood on cue. Her brother took Mercy's elbow and escorted her to the platform. Emie could tell her friend was nervous. She was close enough to see the slight tremble in Mercy's hands. The pair sang a hymn that Emie loved. Her Mama had often hummed the melody as she worked in the garden or kitchen. *Face to face with Christ, my Savior. Face to face, what will it be. When with rapture I behold Him, Jesus Christ who died for me. Face to face I shall behold Him, far beyond the starry sky. Face to face in all His glory, I shall see Him by and by. Only faintly now I see Him with the darkened veil between. A bless'd day is coming when His glory shall be seen. What a rejoicing in His presence, when are banished grief and pain, when the crooked ways are straightened, and the dark things shall be plain. Face to face, oh, blissful moment. Face to face, to see and know. Face to face with my Redeemer, Jesus Christ, who loves me so.*

Ernest and Mercy's voices blended like the willows on the creek banks, perfect harmony from two of God's amazing creations. Tears filled Emie's eyes. *This is a day for cryin'.* Her tears weren't just for bereavement, but also for hope. What she, her sisters, and brothers had lost with the death of their parents was confusing. She yearned to know the Redeemer had claimed them.

Pastor Rex began his sermon with 1 Corinthians 13:12, *Now we see but a poor reflection, then we shall see face to face.* Toward the end of the service, Grandpappy asked if anyone would like to share a personal thought regarding Ahab or Alma. Aunt Ada approached the small platform. Pastor Rex helped her up the two narrow steps. She shared how Ahab and Alma had both grown up in the holler. She also talked about their age difference and how Ahab had waited until Alma was old enough to marry. Ada also told a funny story about Emie's mama falling in the mud and her daddy trying to help, only to fall himself.

It was hard for Emie to imagine her parents laughing and rolling in the mud together. She had no recollection of her daddy ever belly laughing. Tears pooled in Emie's eyes. She found herself wishing she had known her daddy before the war, before bitterness took hold and stole away his jaunty strength. Auntie talked about Ahab being a war hero, and how Alma was a hero too, tending her babies and running the farm in her husband's absence. Emie was thankful that Aunt Ada talked about the days of old, and not the present where heroes became cowards, where people afraid of living as God made them, found no pleasure in work or in play.

When Auntie finished, Pastor Rex asked if anyone else had something to say. An elderly man that Emie didn't know walked from the back of the church.

"My name is Doyle Blanchard. I was in the 'war to end all wars' with Ahab. He was a friend, a companion in the trenches, and a comrade in the fields. He was a fighter; he hurt his legs fightin' for his country. He wanted a better world for his wife and children. May he and his wife rest in peace."

When Mr. Blanchard stepped down off the platform, he walked over to Ernest. Emie saw him hand her brother a picture. Ernest stared at the old photo and passed it down the row. When the picture reached Emie, it was wet with both Ernest and Coral's tears. Her daddy's face was circled, and the caption "Companion in the Trenches, Comrade in the Fields," had been added.

A few others shared on her parents' behalf. They spoke of days gone by. No one from the front row talked about their mama and daddy. There were few kind words to speak, and what could have been said was overshadowed, like the clouds covering the moon at night, by years of harshness.

Near the end, Rudy shared a poem. He seemed more handsome introducing his reading by talking about the importance of grieving with, and for, the children of Ahab and Alma. Emie wasn't surprised by Rudy's selection. Mrs. Randolph had been teaching her and Rudy about famous poets, including William Blake.

> *Can I see another's woe, and not be in sorrow too?*
> *Can I see another's grief, and not seek for kind*
> *relief? Can I see a falling tear, and not feel my*
> *sorrow's share?*

Pastor Rex ended the service with prayer and an invitation for the congregation to join the family at the schoolhouse for a late lunch. Ernest and the older sisters had agreed that the gravesite service would be brief and for family only – family by blood and family by choice. Emie and Coral had wanted it that way as well.

The cemetery was located behind the church next to the parsonage. Uncle Christian had ordered the caskets be absent at the sendin' home service. Ernest knew very little was left of his parents' bodies. He didn't want to see their remains and didn't want his sisters to see them either. It was hard enough to say goodbye without adding horror to heartache. In the noonday sun, the pine caskets were set in place, ready to be lowered by ropes into the ground. The Ashby family and closest of friends stood in a circle around the gravesites. Ahab and Alma would be buried side by side.

The weather had cooled from earlier in the day. The sun was hidden by large, gray ominous-looking clouds that gave welcomed shade to the mourners. Ernest thought it might even spit snow. He would welcome some moisture. It seemed right the heavenly wetness would mix with his tears.

Each person in attendance held a slender stem of dried lavender. Auntie Ada had laid the fall spike-like flowers, on top of cut willow branches, as arrangements on the caskets. She had fashioned the bouquets herself, tied with lace. She had also explained to the Ashby children that the tiny purple florets were thought to soothe headaches and comfort grief. Emie thought she'd never smelled anything so wonderful. She crushed a few bud between her thumb and fingers to savor the fragrance. A raindrop fell into her hand.

As everyone settled into place, Pastor Rex asked permission to speak freely from his heart. Ernest answered on behalf of himself and his sisters, "Please, Pastor, share what's needed."

"I'm puzzled by your daddy's name," Pastor Rex began. "Ahab Elijah is an unusual combination. In the Good Book, Ahab and Elijah were at odds with each other. Ahab had a dark heart, and Elijah was a man seekin' God. I'm thinkin' your Daddy's name describes the struggle he had within. I'm sorry he's gone and left his children wonderin' about where he is in eternity, but I'm believin' the best – hopin' he called to God with his last breath."

Rudy's grandpappy then prayed and shared a few verses of comfort.

Ernest led the family in singing, 'In the Sweet By and By' as sprinkles of rain descended. He selected the song hoping his sisters would find comfort in the lyrics. At the end of the last stanza, a baritone voice joined in the singing. Ernest turned to see Lester walking toward the gravesite, holding the hand of a petite blonde woman. He couldn't help but sigh in relief. He needed his older brother and so did his sisters.

The singing ceased and greetings were quickly but solomly exchanged. Emie immediately embraced Lester's damp shoulders. Ernest was touched by his older brother's display of emotion. He openly wept as Emie held him in her arms. The other sisters held back. Unlike Emie, they hadn't witnessed Lester's transformation.

Lester and Ernest shook hands. Lester's hands were just the same, large and strong, rough and scarred. The brothers then hugged. Ernest welcomed his brother's arms around him. It felt good to know he would have someone share the load. The fighting with Daddy, the needs of his sisters, and the troubles of his mama had all taken their toll. Since the death of his parents, Ernest at times felt like a millstone was hung around his neck. Lester hugged like a bear, albeit a wet bear. Ernest felt the weight of responsibility and sorrow lift in some measure. A millstone had two parts: the bed stone and the runner stone. Ernest wasn't sure what lifted from his shoulders, the stone that held everything in place, or the stone that did most of the work. He just welcomed the relief like the scents of damp earth, goldenrod and ironweed rising to his nostrils.

Lester put forward the attractive woman who stood near him, introducing her as his new wife. Wisps of hair hung in ringlets in the humidity along her cheeks and neck. Then Lester apologized for missing the goin' home service. "I didn't mean to interrupt the singin'. Let's finish sayin' our goodbyes to Mama and Daddy, and then start our hellos to each other."

Ernest wanted to laugh out loud but thought it inappropriate. Lester was back only a few minutes and already taking charge.

In the sweet by and by, we shall meet on that beautiful shore.
In the sweet by and by, we shall meet on that beautiful shore…

Auntie was the first to approach the caskets. She kissed the casket of Alma and patted gently the casket of Ahab. Ernest expected her to place the lavender stem on one of the caskets. Instead, she stripped the stem of its flowers and crushed the blossoms between her fingers. The bruised florets fell among the pine boxes, and the scent seemed to rise like spirits rising in the air. Auntie then tossed the stem aside.

Family and friends followed Ada's example. Ernest stood back. He wanted to be the last to place his flowers. As he watched, he thought about Jesus being prepared for burial with spikenard placed on his body by his own mother, Mary. Ernest wept in remembering Jesus and his mother had also experienced the confusion and loss of death. He recalled that spikenard and lavender were the same fragrant spice.

Chapter Thirty Six

"Cobs from seed corn should be placed in running water and not burned."
(Appalachian Folk Belief)

Just after sunrise the following morning, Lester and Ernest met at the Ashby homestead. They hadn't arranged a meeting, but years of working together and an unspoken understanding between brothers brought them to the same place. They spent most of the morning digging through the ashes. The ashes were heaped into large piles and would later be used for laundry soap and compost for gardening. The material would also melt ice and break down the outhouse matter. Ernest wanted the ashes blown to the wind. It felt morbid somehow to mound the remains of the farm and cover them for later use but, even in tragedy, it wasn't the Appalachian way to waste.

Most everything in the house had been taken by the fire. Some remnants remained in the barn. Ernest hated the task at hand but enjoyed working side by side once again with Lester. His brother was a hard worker. Their combined efforts reminded him of a verse in Ecclesiastes, *"Two are better than one because they have a good reward for their labor."*

The brothers also checked on the pigs. Fresh water and feed were given. The livestock seemed fine. Ernest worried some about the piglets being exposed to the elements, but Lester assured him that they were old enough to survive. "They're Ashby stock, bred mean and tough."

"I guess that's good if you're a hog," Ernest responded, and then shared his concerns about the young pigs that were missing. The fleeting look of concern on Lester's face didn't go unnoticed by the younger brother. A piglet wasn't a problem, but piglets became boars, and a grown boar roaming free meant trouble.

The boys took a break at lunch time. Charlotte, Lester's wife, had packed lunch for her new husband. The food was delicious and plentiful. When Ernest asked Lester how he met his bride, Lester seemed hesitant to share. Ernest was curious and pressed him, but the older brother either changed the subject or ignored his brother's promptings. Finally, Ernest had had enough of Lester's pussy footing around.

"Spill the beans, brother. How did you meet Charlotte?" While Lester hemmed and hawed, Ernest couldn't help but laugh. "This story has got to be a doozy."

"It's more than a doozy."

"Well, brother, I've always enjoyed a good story."

Lester paused, and Ernest could see that he was struggling. Generally his brother was bold and brash and had no problems expressing himself.

"Charlotte's stage name is Lottie Legend."

"Stage name?" Ernest questioned.

"Let's just say that Lottie has some special talents."

"Brother, I'm thinkin' you otta give a few more details about your sweet Charlotte. What kind of talents? Singin'? Dancin'? Other things that I don't think I should be mentionin'?"

"Ernest, ain't nothin' like that! What do you know about such things anyways?"

"I don't know nothin', but I know you know about such things."

"Brother, I'm a changed man."

"I know that, but it doesn't mean you don't know about you know…"

"It's shameful, but I've had my share of lovin'."

"Lester, I'm not sure that sexin' and lovin' are the same thing."

"I'm squirmin' like a worm here, Ernest, and you're enjoying it!"

"I won't be lyin', brother; I'm havin' a little fun at your expense."

"Ernest, there really ain't much to the story. I'm a might proud of my wife. I just met her in an unusual way – while I was workin' at the races."

Ernest shook his head in bewilderment. "Doc told me about your newly acquired drivin' skills. Was Charlotte watchin' the races?"

"Not really." Lester waved his hand like he wished his younger sibling would disappear. "Brother, you're not gonna believe this but Lottie's a modern day Annie Oakley. She has a natural gift for shootin', especially a bow and arrow. While the crowd was lookin' on, the organizers was wantin' to have some fun with the drivers. Charlotte came out all dressed like a cowgirl. She was asked to select a driver and shoot an apple off his head. She picked me."

"Was it your charmin' ways or good looks?" Ernest smiled. "First you're racin' cars when you don't even know how to drive and next a pretty little lady is shootin' at you."

"At the time, I was none too pleased. Plenty of people were watchin', and I was a might uncomfortable."

"Well, brother, did you duck, or did Lottie hit her target?"

"I ain't known her to miss."

The brothers went back to work. Others stopped by and offered help, which eased not only the brothers' physical strain but the emotional one as well. Late afternoon, when the boys found themselves alone again, Lester shared how he met Lottie a second time at church. The couple briefly courted and then married. Ernest talked about his feelings for Mercy and his fears about their future.

"Only the Good Lord knows the best woman for you," Lester responded. "I'll be here if you need me, and I know the sisters will help."

Ernest was relieved by his brother's response. A part of him expected Lester to speak out against Mercy. Like Daddy, Lester had always been prone to talk ill of people whose skin color was darker. There was no place in a Christian's heart for prejudices of any kind, but Ernest understood that spiritual growth took time. The heart was like a home filled with rooms; it took time for the rooms to be filled with good and pleasant things.

Ernest also talked about teaching the colored children, and Lester talked about returning to the family farm.

Lester and Charlotte had spent the night at Rudy's parents' guest house. Lester had already talked with them about living there until a home could be rebuilt on the Ashby property.

Ernest thought to himself, *It's just like Lester to have a plan and not include anyone else in the plannin'*, yet he couldn't find fault with his brother. He supposed that was the way of the oldest child in most families. In the midst of heartache, God was moving among his siblings. He whispered a prayer of thanksgiving to the Lord for His goodness.

"Ernest, Charlotte and I are wantin' the babies to live with us."

When Ernest didn't answer right away, Lester gave him "the look." The same look that Daddy had always given when he wanted information. The look wasn't quite like the stink eye, but close enough.

"Are you wantin' my thoughts?" Ernest asked.

"Yes, brother, I am."

"You love them babies; I love 'em too," Ernest began. "Do you love them enough to leave 'em be? They're doin' good with the twins. Sapphire and Ruby have always been like second mamas."

"I want 'em with me," Lester interrupted. "I'm the eldest."

"Lester, them babies is scared of you. In fact, all the sisters are scared, except maybe Emie. They don't know the new you. They haven't spent time with you since Jesus came into your life, and it ain't gonna help if you start pushin' your weight around."

The eldest brother hung his head. "Charlotte told me the same. She said I need to be lovin' on my sisters and not bossin'."

Ernest smiled. "She's right."

"Lottie told me that I was born to boss and that it ain't always the best way."

Ernest laughed. The more he heard about his brother's wife, the more he liked her.

"It's not that funny, brother. I'm tryin', but it ain't easy. Charlotte's a good woman, and she keeps me in my place. She claims I'm a bit of a challenge."

Ernest couldn't help but nod in agreement.

"I'm guessin' you feel the same," Lester added. "Since I'm workin' on my bossy ways, I probably should be talkin' with the sisters before makin' plans to build a home and live here."

"I don't think they'll be mindin', Lester, but just the same you should talk with 'em."

"Pray for me, Ernest. I'm tryin' to do right."

"You ain't alone, brother. We all should be tryin' to do right."

Late afternoon, as their work day drew to a close, Ernest could tell that something was bothering Lester; his brother who was usually vagarious now seemed pensive. At first, Ernest thought Lester might be anxious to get home to Charlotte and suggested such to his older sibling. Lester agreed he missed his new wife, but added there was something on his mind.

"I did some bad things before I left here for Charleston. I owe a couple of people money, brother. Bad people who would just as soon kill me as take what's due."

Ernest wasn't surprised.

"Sin always has a price. It always takes you further down the road than ya wanna go," Lester spoke.

"Mama used to say that."

Lester nodded in response. "I've got the money to pay my debts. That's why I drove them cars in the races. It was good money, and I saved most of it."

"What are you thinkin' to do?"

"I'm gonna parley with the bad boys and pay what's due. Remember, I'm Ashby stock, bred mean and tough."

Ernest raised his eyebrows at Lester's last statement, then smiled. "Don't be comparin' yourself to the hogs. It ain't becomin'." He continued on a more serious note. "I wanna help."

"I ain't sure you should be gettin' involved. I don't scare easy, but I'm scared. Mostly I'm worried about Charlotte and the sisters. These men will do anything to get even."

Ernest wanted to say or do something that would make everything right but knew it wasn't within his power to fix his brother's predicament. He was worried for Lester, for Charlotte, and the girls. Yet he knew that worry didn't change anything. He felt drawn to pray for his brother. Ernest placed his hand on Lester's shoulder and began to beseech the Father above.

Chapter Thirty Seven

"Wood cut on light nights will burn hotter."
(Appalachian Folk Belief)

Emie spent part of the day visiting with Charlotte and was anxious to tell Rudy all about her new sister and friend. Lester could be mean as a pole cat. Emie wondered how he'd gotten such a sweet wife. Auntie had told her once that opposites attract. Maybe the newlyweds were like sweet and savory dishes where there was an element of sugar and an element of spice.

There was also Lester's new found faith. Charlotte talked about her husband's love for Jesus and also shared how they courted. Emie could hardly fathom the gentleness her brother had shown by bringing flowers, whispering sweet nothings, holding hands in church, and proposing on one knee. None of the gestures Charlotte mentioned seemed like the brother she knew.

Emie didn't believe that you could truly serve Jesus and be mean. She knew from experience when meanness was in her heart, God had a way of calling it to her attention. She also knew whatever was in her heart would eventually come out her mouth. Lately she felt a little mean, but, so far, she'd been able to keep her words in check. She was praying daily that the Lord would help her to have a right heart and attitude.

She knew some of the struggle was due to her pregnancy, but she didn't want to make excuses. Sometimes she felt just plain tired − tired in body, spirit and soul, but mostly body and soul. Coral said Emie slept like a log at night, never even moving in her sleep. Emie knew, however, that her sleep patterns were starting to change. The baby was moving more, and he or she seemed to be most active in the night hours.

The previous night Emie had enjoyed rubbing her tummy and singing quietly to the baby. Coral slept through her lullabies but once or twice she heard Ernest humming along. Of course who knew if Ernest was asleep or awake? Emie had heard him on more than one occasion sing in his sleep.

She wondered if Mercy knew what she was in for. Ernest said he and Mercy were beginning their journey together. Emie was convinced they were further along in their courtship than Ernest or Mercy wanted to admit. Ernest had eyes for his lovely girl.

Just as she readied to open the door to Rudy's parents' store, her handsome fiancé exited. Rudy's smile did her heart good. Somehow his lamb's lick and full lips always brought joy to her heart.

"Hey, Red, I was just comin' to see you."

"What a pleasant surprise, darlin'! I was thinkin' about headin' up the hill to see you."

"Rudy, let's go on a date."

"Emie, we have a date together almost every day."

"I know, but a real date - like you take me somewhere."

When Rudy hestitated, she could feel her meanness rising up. "Unless you're ashamed of me?"

"Emerald…"

"I know I'm big, pregnant, and not even married."

"Darlin'…"

"Rudy, have you seen Mimi lately? She ain't answered my letter!"

Rudy placed his hands on Emie's shoulders. "Stop. Stop right now, Emie. We agreed that Mimi wasn't part of us, and that you weren't gonna talk like that again."

He ran his fingers through his cowlick and sighed. "I would gladly take you somewhere, but we're in Big Creek. Emie, there's no place to go. We ain't got a restaurant, a movie house, nothin'."

"You're right, Red. I'm sorry. I don't know what's gotten into me."

"Sweetheart, your parents just passed. You're carryin' a baby. Life is changin' and racin' by. I'm thinkin' you're just plain tired of runnin' the hills."Rudy knew her so well. Emie took his hand and gently squeezed. "I got an idea, Emerald Ashby. My Mama churned ice cream last night. Let's grab us a dish, find a quiet spot, and have a date."

Before she could answer, Rudy headed back inside the store. His parents lived just behind their place of business. Emie sat down on the bench outside the establishment and thought some more about her meanness. *Lord, give me sweet words for my sweet man,* she prayed.

Later as the two sat under a tree just on the outskirts of town, Emie began her apologies.

"There's no need, darlin'," Rudy spoke.

When she started to explain, he heaped her spoon with the sweet, creamy mixture hand-churned with love and filled her mouth. Emie couldn't help but giggle.

Rudy had brought one bowl and two spoons. Emie liked sharing. Ernest had told her once that sharing food was a sign of affection. When Emie questioned him about the pigs eating from the same trough, he told her that food sharing affection only applied to humans. "We ain't animals, girlie. The wild will take food even from each other's mouths. We're humans with a soul. We're meant for helpin' one another. Sharin' is part of life, part of expressin' love to each other and to God."

She loved Rudy. She was scared yet anxious to begin their life together. *With Mama and Daddy gone, there was no one to give permission for marryin',* she thought. Yet, it felt wrong to be movin' ahead with living. How did one live when life had ended for someone else?

301

Coral and Ernest were still asleep when Emie exited the bedroom. Rain prodded after her. He needed to tinkle. He was getting too big to lift out the window, or maybe she was getting too big to lift him out the window. She stopped their potty ritual several nights ago. Ernest offered to do the lifting, but she knew it was time for her big-eyed, bushy-tailed puppy to exit through the cabin door for his business. As she opened the front door for Rain, she heard Ada in the kitchen. Emie hurried to help her aunt start the morning fire. "Auntie, I think I'm ready to marry Rudy," Emerald declared.

"Well, I'll be. Christian and I was bettin' you'd wait until after the baby came."

"I had been thinkin' that way, but changed my mind."

"Do tell," her aunt encouraged.

"Last night, I had a dream about my mama. She was tellin' me that love was hard to find and even harder to keep. She smiled sweetly and said that babies was always needin' love and tendin'. She said it was hard to care for someone so tiny by yourself."

"A dream's a dream, my girl. Don't be lookin' for answers in your sleep. If you're ready to marry Rudy, Christian and I will help as much as we can. But don't be thinkin' you're ever gonna be alone in carin' for this baby. You're surrounded by people who love on you. More importantly, God's love for you is without measure."

"I'm scared and bewildered," Emie confessed.

"I know, and I wish I had your answers but this is something you're needin' to decide by yourself. It's hard to grow and make choices, my girl, but I have faith in you, and more importantly, faith in God to help you."

"I love Rudy. I'm not afraid of marryin' him. I am afraid of some of the things that go along with bein' married. I ain't ready for such stuff. I ain't fit right now for Rudy to be lookin' at me without my clothes. I want it to be different when we start out."

"Have you talked with Rudy?"

"No, Auntie, it don't seem proper."

"What's proper changes when you're gettin' married, Emie. Christian and I had to talk about such things."

"Weren't you ashamed?"

302

"Not ashamed. I felt shy and a little outside myself, but Christian made it right, and I'm thinkin' that Rudy will do the same."

Emerald headed to the creek; she wanted to hear the willows whisper. She often found comfort in the sighing of the trees. Like her life, the trees looked and sounded different these days. Most of the leaves had fallen from the willow branches – some were lying on the ground, while others had been blown away in the wind. She needed to make a decision about when to marry Rudy. It wasn't fair to leave him not knowing. She thought about the clothesline that hung behind Auntie's cabin. It often sagged under the heavy weight of wetness. When full it didn't even sway in the breeze. She wanted Rudy to sway and not sag. She didn't want him over-burdened; she knew he carried a heavy weight while he waited for her decision.

Her time with Jesus was precious. She sang songs of praise, not as sweetly as Ernest, but she didn't think the Lord minded. She read her Bible and wrote in her journal. She talked with the Lord about the baby and about Rudy. She also talked about Ernest and Mercy, Lester and Charlotte. In fact, she mentioned all of her siblings in prayer. She still didn't have answers, but had a measure of peace knowing that the answers would come.

She was drawn and driven away at the same time to cross the swinging bridge, walk through the meadow, and view the burned remains of her childhood home. She needed to grieve. It would be hard to move forward with the heavy load of grief hanging about her shoulders. She thought again about the line filled with wet clothes. She had felt weighed down for far too long. She was changing and things were better in her mind and heart, but she want to experience true freedom. She'd forgotten what it was like to sway in the breeze.

It was obvious that someone had been working at the homestead. Emerald assumed the cleanup was the result of Lester and Ernest's efforts. The house was completely gone. She walked through what little rubble remained and remembered where the rooms and furnishings had once been present. The tears came. Auntie was right: some things had to be experienced without the presence or help of other humans. She knelt among the remaining ashes, not caring about soot or grime, and wept for the loss of her mama and daddy. She grieved not just for the loss of her parents, but for the loss of her own innocence – what Charlie had taken and what her parents hadn't been able to give.

When she headed back across the bridge, a breeze began to blow. She was alone, yet not alone. The wind increased and the swinging bridge began to sway. Her freedom was coming in measures – sometimes an inch at a time, sometimes a foot at a time.

Chapter Thirty Eight

"If your hand itches, it means that someone will give you a present soon."
(Appalachian Folk Belief)

Ernest was nervous. He had spent untold hours in the hills and hollers that surrounded Big Creek, but the path Lester was taking was unfamiliar. The going was steep and rocky. His brother said they were taking the back way in hopes of not being detected. There was a shorter and friendlier route which Lester and his cohorts had used to haul their moonshine and stolen wares. Lester was hesitant to let Ernest join him for the parley, but the younger brother insisted. "Two are better than one, Lester. If somethin' happens, I want to help you."

Lester argued. "It won't do if somethin' happens to both of us. Who'll care for Charlotte, Mercy and the sisters?"

Ernest was touched that his older brother remembered Mercy in his cautionary statement, yet he couldn't help but insist on making the trek into the hills. The two finally compromised. Ernest would travel with his brother to just before the meeting place. He would then find cover and wait for Lester. Hopefully, trouble wouldn't come. If it did, however, Ernest would be ready to help. The goal was a peaceable meeting with his brother's former business partners and the payment of the funds owed without either of the Ashby brothers being stabbed or shot.

"Does Lottie know what you're up to?" Ernest asked.

"Does Mercy know what you're up to?" Lester responded.

"I'll take that as a no."

"Charlotte and I have an understandin' that we don't keep secrets, but I couldn't tell her what we're doin', brother. She'd worry the day away. I'm askin' the Good Lord to bring us both home safe. It won't be long now; we're almost there."

When the older brother grew quiet, Ernest knew the moonshine operation was close at hand. The landscape opened up to a treed area, and Ernest could hear the faint ripple of a small stream. Lester motioned him toward the trees and continued the course. Ernest watched his brother round a slight bend and quietly followed.

Lester held his hands high in the air. "I ain't armed."

Two men came into view. The bigger and uglier of the two was the first to talk. "Look who's back! We've been searchin' high and low. Thought you mighta died. But then, maybe today's a good day for dyin'."

The other man pulled a small gun from his waistband. A five shot .38 wasn't a very powerful weapon, but with Lester standing so close, if shot he would certainly suffer and experience possible death. The hair stood up on the back of Ernest's neck. His years of hunting in the hills told him someone or something else was present. He looked around and didn't see anyone or anything. He turned back toward his brother and the two men just in time to see an arrow hit the gun bearer's right foot. The man yelled out in pain and began to wave the gun frantically. A second arrow hit the man's shooting hand, and he dropped the gun.

Lester drew the money from his faded work overalls and quickly handed it to the uninjured party. "You best take this. It ain't my intention to cause any more harm. Our business is done and we're partin' ways for good."

Lester walked toward Ernest shaking his head. The younger brother was surprised that the older brother didn't immediately begin his chastisement. In fact, Lester didn't say a word. He grabbed Ernest by the arm, albeit a little roughly, and started down the hillside. When the two were out of earshot, Lester began to call softly for Charlotte. The brother's voice was soft in volume but loud with emotion.

"Lottie," Lester spoke intently. "Charlotte, where are you? I'm needin' to see you, heart."

Ernest heard his sister-in-law's voice before he saw her. "Now, Lester, don't be sayin' 'heart' if you don't mean it. I know you're angry, and I'm prepared for harsh words."

When Charlotte stepped into view, Lester reached for her and held her close. "Harsh words are racin' through my mind, but I'm more relieved that we're all fine." He then drew Ernest into their embrace.

As the trio headed home through tall autumn grasses of rust and browns and yellows, towards the taller green willows on Big Creek, Ernest considered the Ebenezer stone, the stone of help. In the Bible, Samuel put the stone in place of remembrance on behalf of the Lord's victory.

Chapter Thirty Nine

"It's bad luck to sew on Saturday unless you finish the job."
(Appalachian Folk Belief)

It was moving day for Justice and his family. Amos and Andy were harnessed to a wagon loaded with the family's belongings. The two mules were biting and nipping at each other. Emie's eyes were brimming with moisture.

"Look at the Lord's bounty," Ada spoke as she pointed to the overloaded cart. "You came here with nothin' and look what the Lord's given."

Emie would miss Mercy. She'd also miss the boys, Justice, and Cece. Even Rain looked downhearted. Her brown-eyed puppy knew that something was amiss. The gold flecks in his eyes that were usually bright with curiosity and mischief were dim.

While Ernest and Justice finished securing the load, hugs were given and given again by the rest of the family. When everything was in place, Justice moved from behind the wagon. "I ain't good with words," he began. "We built a life here, a good life, and it pains me to be leavin', yet I know it's time." He looked toward Ada and Emie, "How can I thank you for all you've done? I can't, but I'm asking God to rain His blessings down on you."

Rain, hearing his name, approached Justice, who patted the dog's large head and rubbed his ears. The puppy took great pleasure in having his ears massaged. Rain partially closed his eyes and looked like he was in a trance. Emie wished that she could join Rain. Maybe in his far off place time stood still.

Ernest helped Justice get Amos and Andy moving and motioned for his friend to continue up the hillside. He looked at Mercy and smiled, "I'll be along in a few minutes." She nodded in return, understanding that Ernest needed a little time with his sisters.

"Girlies, I won't be far away. Send Rudy if you need me. I told Lester that I'd help him with the hogs on Saturday. I'll stop by on my wanderings to the old homestead."

Coral hugged her brother. "I'll miss you, Ernest. Mrs. Randolph told me that it takes thirteen days by car to get from New York to California. It'll only take you three hours of hard walkin' to see me and Emie and shorter still if you ride one of those rotten mules."

"I'll miss you too, Coral." Ernest then reached for Emie. "I'm proud of you…" Ernest began.

Emerald silenced her brother with a tight squeeze. "Ernest, it's you who I'm proud of. I'm used to bein' with you each day, and it's selfish wantin' you to stay. You have big dreams, and I'm wishin' they all come true."

Emie was nesting. At least that's what Uncle Christian called her frantic efforts to prepare the little house for herself, Rudy, and the baby. Coral worked just as hard as Emie in cleaning, organizing, and decorating. Rudy's parents were also a big help. With the Christmas season approaching, Red's daddy had stocked up on Emie's wares. He also sent numerous willow baskets to fellow shopkeepers in the surrounding areas. The soon-to-be bride was able to purchase things for both her home and baby. MayLou also helped Emie make curtains and bed linens. The older woman told Emerald that what her stiches lacked in skill they made up in love. Emie recalled the weaving prayers she and Aunt Ada once shared. They still prayed and worshipped as they made their crafts, but the prayers were now different. Emie was thankful for God's strength and provision.

Rudy knew very little about Emie's preparations. Thanksgiving was approaching, and the young woman planned to propose to her beau and set a wedding date. Emie hoped to be married and settled in the little house by Christmas. Rudy had already asked for her hand in marriage. The two were officially engaged, but she wanted to kneel before Red just as he'd done before her and confess her love and longing. She only hoped that Rudy would be willing to help her get up once she knelt. Her belly seemed to get bigger every day. Her decision to marry before the baby's birth had been difficult to make. In the end, she knew that sharing the last few weeks of her pregnancy with Rudy would endear them to one another and to the baby. The baby recognized Rudy's voice; he or she often kicked when Rudy was present, and Emie had taken to privately addressing Rudy as "papa" to her unborn child.

Emie had debated back and forth in her mind about what the baby should call her and Rudy. The words "mama" and "daddy" didn't hold endearments in her heart. They were just words. Words she once called the people who made her. The same people who didn't really love and nurture her like they should have. "Papa" seemed like a natural name for Rudy and maybe "mommy" for herself. She wasn't quite sure.

"Well, Coral, what do you think? Is the little house ready?" Emerald asked.

"The bigger question, sister, is are you ready?"

"I think so. I'm not plannin' to move until Rudy and I marry. I want us to move together."

"I'll miss you, Emie."

"I'll miss sharing our back porch bedroom and dreamin' together each night, but I'll be right close. We can visit every day. Especially when the baby comes, I'll be needin' you and Auntie."

The little house was beautiful. The decorations from nature made everything cozy. Along with dried lavender and herbs, willow baskets graced the kitchen. Enamel bowls filled with apples and nuts sat on a small corner table. A wooden shelf held canned vegetables that Emie and Auntie had grown and preserved. There were even jars of honey and jam. Emie had woven a large wreath from willow saplings that served as a headboard. Rudy's parents gifted a bed and two oak rockers that rested in the small sitting room. The knotted quilt on the bed had been made by her mama and given to Auntie a number of years back. When Ada presented Emie with the bed covering, the young woman cried. She even recognized some of the swatches – worn clothing that had been cut into squares and stitched together. She'd been angry at her mama for such a long time, even before she'd moved to Auntie's cabin. Somehow, her anger had begun to fade. Emie gave credit to the dream she'd had about her mother. The dream prompted her to pray and find the answers for starting her life with Red. She was working at forgiving her mama and her daddy. Ernest had told her once that forgiving didn't mean forgetting. She had pondered her brother's words but hadn't reached a conclusion her mind. She worried that if she didn't forget, at least in some measure, the heartache would never fade.

Emie decided she needed a cat. A family of mice moved into her new home. She found their nest behind the wood stove. She knew that vacant places were perfect homes for field mice, but she didn't want them taking up residence in the little house. She was also frustrated with Rain. He seemed to enjoy the companionship of the rodents. It didn't bother him, in the least, to see them run across the floor. In fact, his tail would thump, almost encouraging them to play, breed, and multiply.

"Coral, I can't abide these mice. They'll be nibblin' at my food and fabric, and what will Rudy think? We worked hard to make things nice. Nice for humans, not for mice. I'm thinkin' I need a cat."

"I'm not so sure, sister. Dogs and cats fight."

Emie sighed. "Well, Rain ain't much of a mouser, and since he likes mice maybe he'll like a cat as well."

When Coral shared Emie's plan with Aunt Ada, the older woman chuckled. "Good luck with keepin' them mice outdoors where they belong. They're sneaky things. Some say their little ears and noses that twitch make 'em cute, but I ain't one for sayin' a rodent is attractive. If needed, I would be like the farmer's wife who chased the three mice into the bramble bush and made 'em go blind, or the butcher's wife who cut their tails off with a carvin' knife."

"Auntie, do you remember the rest of the story?" Coral asked. "Them mice took a special tonic. They grew new tails and recovered their sight. They even bought a house and lived happily ever after."

Chapter Forty

*"If a black cat crosses your path, it's bad luck, unless the cat crosses
from right to left."
(Appalachian Folk Belief)*

"Emie, I think I hear a cat."

"Really, Rudy, I don't hear a thing. Maybe it's the wind in the willows."

"Since when does the wind sound like a cat meowing? Maybe a stray's wondered in."

Emerald couldn't help it. She started to giggle. "Red, I've got something to show you." She took his hand and led him to the little house. It wasn't quite Thanksgiving, but close enough to the planned time for her proposal. She opened the door decorated with cattails she had gathered in the marshy places along Big Creek and ushered Rudy inside.

"Emie, my, my, you have been workin' hard. It's lovely, darlin'."

Her heart swelled at Red's compliments. The couple walked through the small rooms. When they got to the bedroom at the back of the house, Red seemed distracted by the big bed, so Emie seized the moment to kneel and begin her proposal. "Rudy, we've known each other most of our lives. I love you and want to know if you'll have me for your wife."

Red grinned. "Emie, in case you've forgotten, I've done proposed and we're already engaged. 'Sides since when does the girl do the askin'? I thought it was the man's job to do the proposin'."

"Generally the man does do the proposin', but I was also wantin' to declare my love and ask you."

Rudy bent over and kissed her forehead. "In that case, the answer is 'yes.'"

"Help me up, Red."

"Gladly." Rudy used their nearness as an opportunity to embrace Emie and passionately kiss the girl he loved. "Darlin', I'm gonna like sharin' this bed with you, but you best know that Rain, and that yellow ball of fluff that just ran across the floor, won't be sleepin' with us. I need you all to myself."

"Her name is 'Daffodil.'"

"Cute. Now, let the cat out of bag. Where did she come from?"

"Granny Smith. Some mice are likin' our home."

"I ain't surprised. I like it pretty fine myself," Rudy joked. "You done real good. I'm a might proud to think I'll be sharin' this home with you. Emie, did you know in times back sellers would put a piglet in a poke for their buyers to take home? The sellers would tell the new owners to wait until they got home to check on the pig. They used the excuse that the piglet might escape. Not so smart men and women would heed the advice, and when they got home, a cat would climb out of the bag rather than a piglet – lettin' the cat out of the bag."

Emie laughed. "Well, Daffodil, didn't come home in a poke. Coral and I took turns carryin' her. She fussed a little at first, but was mostly content to snuggle and purr."

Rudy was anxious to talk with Pappy. When he left Emie, he immediately headed to the parsonage where he hoped to find the elderly gentleman at home. No such luck. Rudy was in a hurry, yet he couldn't help but notice the fallen leaves covering the front porch. He found a broom and swept the bracts into a pile. He knew in the fall that trees sealed the places where the leaves were attached. When the fluids from the trees no longer nourished the leaves, they would change color and eventually fall to the ground. The process helped the trees survive the cold winter.

His girl loved the willows by the creek. They were also letting go of their leaves. In fact, some of the trees were already bare. Rudy knew Emie was healing from invisible wounds. He also knew that like the trees, she was sealing the places in her life that were robbing her of precious nutrients. She was mending, and he was thankful.

He found his pappy at the church house. "I hope I ain't interrupting."

"I always have time for my favorite grandson."

"Pappy, we both know, I'm your only grandson."

"Still my favorite," the kindly man smiled.

"I've got news. Emie's ready to get married."

"I'll be. When's the special occasion?"

"That's why I came callin'. With the baby comin', she's hopin to wed by Christmas. She's wantin' a simple ceremony – which is fine by me. Nobody, not even Mimi, will want to come to church in the snow!" Rudy looked directly into his grandpappy's light blue eyes. "Will you marry us?"

"It would be my pleasure," the pastor replied.

Rudy grew quiet. He was overcome with thoughts of the upcoming wedding and was also pondering another concern.

"Son, you said you're fine with a simple weddin', but I'm thinkin' there's something goin' on that's not fine, and that's part of why you came callin'."

Grandpappy knew him so well. "It's not the weddin'. It's what happens after the weddin' that's bothering me."

"You love your girl and she loves you. I'm thinking what happens after the weddin' will be fine as well, and if it ain't, we can talk a spell and see if I can help."

"She wants to wait, Pappy."

"Because she's expectin'?"

"Yes. She said that she's not ready for me to see her naked. I told her we could stay under the covers, but she still wants to wait."

"I can see your line of reasonin', son, but I ain't surprised that she's wanting to wait a spell. Rudy, patience is a virtue, especially for a new husband." Pappy paused for a moment and then asked, "When's the baby supposed to come?"

"Toward the middle of February. Doc told me awhile back when a baby comes a couple's got to stay quiet-like for a few weeks. I worked it out, Pappy, that puts me and Emie close to spring."

"Did you tell her your concerns?"

"No. I didn't want her to know I was disappointed. Plus, she started talkin' about bein' naked, and I got distracted."

"I can see why you'd be distracted."

"She wanted to know which was correct 'butt naked' or 'buck naked?'"

Pappy shook his head and smiled. "She's some girl, Rudy."

The young man headed home. He didn't have answers to his concerns, but was determined to remember his grandfather's words, *Patience is a virtue, especially for a young husband.*

Chapter Forty One

"If you swallow a chicken heart you will win the hand of the one you love."
(Appalachian Folk Belief)

Ernest had worked hard the past couple weeks: teaching supplies and children's desks were ordered, the schoolhouse was repaired and painted, even his personal living quarters were organized and comfortable. In the setting sun, all these quarters seemed like gold. It was the first time he had ever lived by himself. In some ways, he enjoyed the solitude, but in other ways, he missed his brother and sisters. It wasn't appropriate for Mercy to visit his home alone, so he spent a great deal of time at her family's residence. The two would also meet at the schoolhouse and work together on making preparations for school to begin. With Mercy as his companion, he visited a number of families. Before school started in January, he was hoping to have some idea of the age and number of students who would be attending the school. He had already discussed with Mrs. Randolph the best way to evaluate the students academically. He had also scheduled an open house for the children to see the new facility. He knew some learners were anxious about attending school. He hoped that if they familiarized themselves with the outlay of what used to be an old barn and became better acquainted with him and Mercy, their fears would be squelched, and, in turn, they would be better scholars.

Most of the people were surprised that a white man came to the area to teach their children. Ernest remained firm in his conviction that God made people of all different shades to make the world interesting. Most of the children he met had never attended school. They had limited understanding of numbers and letters, but were smart and curious. Ernest could hardly wait for the school doors to open.

God was faithful to the new teacher. Everywhere he went he was welcomed, at times more cautiously than others, but greeted and welcomed nonetheless. He was a stranger, and it would take time to win the hearts of the community and his students.

It would also take time to completely win Mercy's heart. He adored her and thought the feelings were mutual, yet there was a problem that continued to plague them as a couple. Mercy wasn't willing to acknowledge their relationship publicly. They had talked prior to the move about the need to be forthright regarding their courtship. Yet, when they arrived further up the holler, Mercy had second thoughts. She made it clear she wasn't ready to let the community know about their feelings for each other. Ernest was frustrated. Like Justice suggested, Ernest wanted to stake his claim. It exasperated him to watch other young men smile and flirt with his girl. He wasn't sure what to do. He was trying to be patient and respect Mercy's wishes, but he also knew that if she was ashamed and couldn't work through her feelings, their relationship had no future.

He looked out the window of the schoolhouse to see his girl walking with yet another young man. He knew the would-be suitor probably joined Mercy as she journeyed to the school, but he didn't like it – not one bit.

Mercy addressed him as she entered the building. "Hello, Ernest."

He nodded her direction, but didn't return her greeting with words.

"Is everything alright?"

"Not really."

"Do you want to talk about it?"

"I'm not sure I can without gettin' angry. Do you mind if we work a little bit, then have our discussion?"

This time it was Mercy's turn to nod and remain silent. Ernest was certain she already knew what was bothering him.

The two worked for the next couple hours getting ready for the upcoming open house. An alphabet train was hung and a number chart put in place. Ernest also created a map of the world. It was important to the new teacher that the classroom look warm and inviting. Mercy displayed the books that had already arrived from Charleston. Amos and Andy had been busy hauling supplies and would continue to do so for the next few weeks. Ernest hoped the weather held until everything arrived. If a heavy snow fell, the two mules would have trouble pulling the wagon through the snow, slush, and ice.

"Mercy, do you mind if we take a break?" Ernest asked.

The young woman sat down at her desk. Ernest then sat down at his desk. The two were side by side, yet Ernest felt like they were miles apart.

"I care about you," he began. "I think you care about me, yet I'm puzzled. You don't seem to want anyone to know about our special friendship."

"Now, Ernest, that ain't exactly true. Those that are important to us know how we feel, just not strangers."

"Mercy, are you afraid?"

The young woman hung her head and mumbled. "Yes."

He knew what she was afraid of but wanted her to say the words. Maybe if she spoke her fears out loud they would diminish. "Afraid of what?"

"We're different. I'm not sure others will understand. There ain't nothin' wrong with keepin' secrets."

"True, some secrets need to be kept. But I don't want our courtin' to be a secret. I'm a grown man. I ain't wantin' to be part of a secret club. I'm proud of you, and I want you to be proud of me. Keepin' things a secret is like sayin' our friendship is wrong." When Mercy didn't respond, Ernest grew worried. "Do you think our love is wrong, Mercy?"

"I ain't sure. It doesn't feel wrong, but others may think different," she answered quietly.

At first, he wanted to grip his heart in pain then he wanted to scream in anger. He began humming softly and willed himself to stay calm. "Mercy, we've done talked about what the Bible says, and we've also talk with our families. I ain't gonna try and convince you of somethin' you don't want. We can't control what others think. I love you, but one-sided affection just means heartache."

"It's not the lovin' part that botherin' me − it's the tellin' part."

Ernest rose from his chair. "I understand what you're sayin', but it grieves me."

"Please. Can't we just keep things as is?"

"We'll see," he softly spoke and then headed toward the door. "I'm needin' to go for a walk."

He exited quietly, leaving Mercy to her own thoughts.

It was Thanksgiving weekend, and Ernest was headed to Big Creek. He was anxious to enjoy extended time with his family. He had let Mercy know several days earlier that he was leaving and would return on Monday morning. Since that day at the schoolhouse, their conversations had been a little stilted. He was trying to give her time and distance to make up her mind. He knew the saying *absence makes the heart grow fonder*, but wondered if absence could also make the heart grow fonder of someone else. Mercy had told him time and time again how much she cared for him, but he didn't want to be a secret − someone hidden away and only brought to light in front of those near and dear. It simply wasn't his way. Mercy had also told him that being secretive brought an air of mystery to their relationship. Ernest enjoyed a good mystery. In fact, mysteries were his favorite reading genre. He wasn't interested, however, in a clandestine romance.

He arrived at Auntie's mid-day. From the yard, he could smell the pies baking: pumpkin, apple, and an unrecognizable, yet delightful, additional scent. His mouth started to water. Tomorrow was a day for feasting and thanksgiving. He found Emie sitting on the porch. Rain was by her side with his overgrown head in her lap. "Girlie, ain't it a little chilly for sittin' outdoors?"

Emie pushed the puppy aside. The look on Rain's face was priceless. He seemed shocked that his mistress would shove him off her lap. Emie raced the few steps to her brother. "I've been waitin' for ya. Auntie sent me outside because I was pacin' the floor."

"Are you cold? Where's Rudy? I'm sure he'd enjoy keepin' you warm," Ernest teased.

"Brother, I'm bundled. I ain't cold. Before we go inside, I want to show you the little house."

Ernest was just as surprised as Rudy to see the transformation. "When are you movin' in?"

"Not 'til me and Rudy marry."

"I thought that bed looked a might big for just you and Rain."

"Rudy says that Rain and Daffodil can't sleep with us."

"Daffodil?"

"My new kitten. She's supposed to be handlin' the mice."

"Mmm…"

"What's that supposed to mean, brother?"

"'Mmm' as in how long your beau's gotta wait to share that big bed? And 'mmm' as in kittens ain't generally good mousers."

"She's as worthless as Rain in dealin' with the mice, but I'm hopin' when she grows things'll change. Also, she and Rain fight. They're fussin' all the time. I ain't told Rudy yet, but there won't be much sleepin' takin' place in that big bed with Rain barkin' and growlin' and Daffodil hissin' and clawin' all night long."

"Emie, Rudy don't care about sleepin' in that bed."

His sister blushed. "That is shameful, Ernest."

"Not shameful when you're married."

Looking embarrassed, Emie headed toward the front door of the little house. Just as she started to step over the threshold, she turned and faced her brother. "And by the way, Rudy and me are gettin' married in two weeks. I'm hoping you can make it!"

Ernest was so sleepy. He'd eaten more than his share of turkey and all the fixings. Aunt Ada was a wonderful cook, and it appeared that Emie and Coral were following in her footsteps. Lester and Charlotte had spent the majority of the day at Ada's. His brother had always been full of mischief, and Ernest had enjoyed recounting the older brother's antics to Lottie. Ernest couldn't remember when he laughed so hard. Charlotte was fun loving. It was good to see his sister-in-law tease and have fun with the rest of the family. It was as if Charlotte had always been an Ashby.

It was nearing bedtime before Ernest had a few minutes alone with Emie and Rudy. The two seemed very content. Though the sun had rested, and the oil lamps were burning, the white cotton curtains in the parlor windows hadn't been closed. The moon was shining through the glass panes, making Ernest feel melancholy. He was reminded of Reginald Heber's poetry. *I see them on their winding way, about their ranks the moonbeams play.* The poem was about men at war going home to see their Maker. The stanzas were both heartbreaking and heart rejoicing at the same time.

He knew the moon was also shining on Mercy's side of the mountain. Maybe moon beams were dancing in her hair. He hoped she was thinking of him. Then, he thought better. *Maybe she's praying and asking the Lord for help, just like I am.*

His thoughts were interrupted by Rudy. "Ernest, I would like you to stand with me at the weddin'."

Without hesitation Ernest answered. "I would be honored, Rudy."

"And, Ernest," Emie spoke, "I want Mercy to stand with me. I was hopin' she'd be with you, so I could ask her in person, but would you please let her know my wishes?"

"Of course, sister."

"Brother, are you alright?"

It was just like Emie to sense his melancholy mood. "I'm fine."

"You don't sound fine."

"I ate too much and feel sleepy."

"That ain't all," Rudy added. "Somethin' is troublin' you. Maybe Emie and me can help."

Ernest hesitated. He wanted to confide in his sister and her beau, but at the same time he didn't want to burden them or take anything away from their upcoming special day.

"The Bible says each person should carry his own load, but we should be helpin' each other with burdens — loads that are too big to carry alone." Rudy spoke.

"Mercy and me is havin' a problem," Ernest began.

When Emie started firing questions, Rudy interrupted his beloved. "Darlin', we need to let Ernest gather his words. Don't be pressin' for information he may not be ready to share."

Emie stopped and apologized. "I'm sorry, brother. Rudy is right. I'm anxious and want to help, but I'll do my best to stay quiet and listen."

My sister is growin' up, Ernest thought. When curiosity struck Emie, it wasn't like her to stay silent and hear another's thoughts. "Mercy and I both care for each other, but she ain't ready to tell anyone up the holler about our courtship. She wants to keep our friendship a secret."

"I'm sorry." Rudy spoke.

"It's painin' me, and I ain't quite sure what to do."

"I'm young in the ways of love, but lovin' someone in secret just don't seem right." Rudy paused, and then continued his line of thinking. "Secret lovin' generally means that somethin' is wrong."

"Maybe she just needs time," Emie added.

"That's what I'm hopin', but I ain't sure how much time to give, and it don't help that others are comin' round seekin' her affections."

"I just had a talk with Pappy about me and Emie," Rudy shared. "He told me that patience is virtue, especially for a new husband. I'm thinkin' that applies to any man in love."

"Patience is the last thing I want right now." Ernest said. "But I'll do my best to keep the pastor's good words in mind."

The three concluded their time together with prayer. It was a blessing for Ernest to receive the prayers of his sister and Rudy, and it was also a blessing to offer prayers on their behalf. Ernest then excused himself. He wanted to give Emie and Rudy a few minutes alone to say good night. He was also tired. He headed to the back porch bedroom where Coral had long been asleep.

Emie walked Rudy the few steps to the door. "So you've been talkin' with Pappy about me again."

Rudy smiled. "Now darlin', you're all I talk about these days."

"Nice try, Rudy. You're clever, but I'm thinkin', given Pappy's words, that somewhere along the line I've tried your patience."

"It ain't nothin', Emie. Kiss me goodnight and let me be on my way." When he stepped forward for a smooch, Emie pulled back slightly. *This ain't good*, Rudy thought. *Give me the right words, Lord.*

"Rudy, I don't want secrets between us."

"I don't neither…"

"I know you're tired, Red, and the way home ain't quick. If you wanna wait, we can visit tomorrow."

Rudy knew if he waited, he wouldn't sleep and his girl would toss and turn as well. "It's about sharin' our love, Emie. It's hard for me to think about waitin'. I ain't gonna pressure you, and I'll respect what you're wantin'. You don't need to be worryin' none…"

"Rudy," Emie interrupted. "I've been thinkin' about that same. I don't feel ready, but if I change my mind would that be okay?"

"That'd be fine."

"I'm a little shy about these things, Red. How should I tell you if I feel different?"

"Emie, just tell me that you're ready for lovin' all night long, and I will clearly understand." His girl turned bright red, and he couldn't help but laugh.

"Rudy," Emie stammered. "I think I need to be communicatin' in a different way. How about sign language?"

During their evening lessons, Mrs. Randolph had been teaching them some basics about American Sign Language.

"Darlin', we haven't learned the sign for matin', and I'm not sure I wanna be askin' Mrs. Randolph for instruction."

"Red, I'm thinkin' about using the sign for dirty rat." As a joke, the elderly teacher had demonstrated the gestures. The pointer and middle finger were intertwined and swiped the end of the nose – the symbol for dirty. The hand was placed under the chin with the fingers pointing out. The fingers wiggled – the symbol for rat. Emie reminded Red of the combined sign.

"Emie, there ain't nothin' dirty about our lovin', and I don't want you to be thinkin' of me as a rat." *Of all things*, Rudy thought.

"It ain't like that. We have mice livin' in our home and I don't like it none. As far as I'm concerned, mice and rats are about the same, and I want them gone. I also want all my fears gone. I think it's a good sign."

"This is downright embarassin', Emie, but I'm agreein' nonetheless."

"I love you, too, Red." Emie then gently kissed her beau on the cheek.

Chapter Forty Two

"If you dream about muddy water, you will have bad luck."
(Appalachian Folk Belief)

Ernest spent a portion of the weekend working on the farm with Lester. He could hardly believe the progress his brother had made in such a short time. "Amazing, brother, simply amazing…"

"Thank you, Ernest, I'm tryin'. Lottie and I are settled at the house in town, but I'm missin' my country roots. I never thought I'd be lonesome for this place, but I am. I'm wantin' to be moved back up here by early spring. The sows will need round the clock tendin' when they're givin' birth."

"Lester, did you talk with the girls about your move?"

"Yes, I did. None of 'em seemed to mind. And before you ask, I didn't mention the baby girls to the twins. You were right, them babies are doing' just fine. Lottie and I are tryin' to visit all the sisters each week. I've apologized to each one of them for my meanness. I love 'em and want 'em to know I'm a changed man."

"Glad to know, Lester. By the way, I'm likin' your wife. She's good for you."

Lester started to answer and then quickly motioned for Ernest to be quiet. "Shush…someone's comin'," he whispered.

Lester is sure acting odd, Ernest thought. Casual visitors were commonplace in the hills. There was no need for shushing.

Ernest looked around and spotted Rudy passing through the meadow. He recognized the young man's gait. "Lester, it's Rudy comin'. When I told him we were workin' today, he offered to help."

Lester breathed a sigh of relief. "Sorry, brother. I'm nervous about them old partners of mine. I saw one of 'em in town. He didn't say a word, just gave me a look. I've also been a tad concerned about Charlie. I know he's left the holler, but he's wiley. He was caught up in all this mischief as well."

"I'm prayin', Lester, every day, askin' the Lord to keep you safe."

"I ain't worried about me. It's Lottie and the girls." Lester started to relax, "Course, why should I be worryin' about my darlin' wife? She can hit a man quick as pullin' as arrow from the quiver."

The three men worked the remainder of the day. With a picnic basket in hand, Emie and Lottie joined them late in the afternoon. The boys fashioned a table and two benches from building lumber that had been hauled up the dirt road from Big Creek. As the sun set, the family remained seated at the make-do dinner table talking and laughing. The camaraderie touched Ernest. He wished Mercy was by his side.

It was too cloudy to see the stars. The canopy varied greatly in color: white, grey, pink and orange. All the shades were mesmerizingly beautiful. If Mercy were present, he would talk with her about the cloud colors and how they complimented one another. He would also hold her close; the evening was cold.

He had reached a decision about the girl he loved. Emie and Rudy's wedding was two weeks away and the open house for the school shortly after. He would wait until after the open house to approach Mercy about their relationship. In the meantime, he hoped to win her heart.

"Ernest, I'm gonna be missin' you," Emie declared. It was early Monday morning and her brother was leaving.

"Girlie, I'll see you in a couple weeks at the weddin'."

"I can't believe I'm gettin' married! Do you think I'm doin' the right thing?"

"Emie, it ain't for me to decide. I know Rudy's a good man; he loves you and the baby."

Rudy is a good man, well not quite a man, but headin' that direction. He's good and kind. Emie thought. "I'm still worried that we're a might young. What happens if we can't take care of the baby?"

"I wouldn't be worrin', girlie. You live right next door to a doctor."

"Did you know, brother, that God created ostriches without common sense?"

"I vaguely remember that from the Book of Job." Ernest was having trouble following his sister's line of thinking.

"An ostrich lays her eggs in the sand. The mommy sits on the eggs during the day, and the papa sits on the eggs at night."

"Okay, sister."

"Well, the Bible says that the mama ostrich doesn't think about how her babies could be hurt. Someone could step on 'em, or an animal could eat 'em. Then, when the chicks hatch, the mama ain't even nice. The Bible says that she's mean to her little ones."

"Now, Emie, that's right interesting, but why are we talkin' about ostriches?"

"Pay attention, brother."

"I am payin' attention!"

"What happens if I'm like an ostrich mama?"

Ernest sighed. "Emie, I don't see that happenin'. By the way, have you ever seen an ostrich?"

"No, I read about 'em in my school reader. They don't really bury their heads in the sand. Someone made that up."

"Good to know, girlie." Ernest couldn't help but smile.

"Brother, this is serious business. I don't wanna be a mean mommy."

"You're gonna be a great mother, Emie. Don't be worryin'."

"Ernest, the boy ostrich can make a boomin' noise. He inflates his neck and uses air to make the sound. It's real loud – almost sounds like a lion roarin'. He does it to attract a wife."

"Are you thinkin' that Rudy's gonna start roarin'?" Ernest laughed.

"No! Ernest, I don't wanna be a mean wife neither."

"Sister, quite your worryin'. You're about as sweet as they come. Now, Emie, I'm sorry to cut our talk short, but I need to get movin'. Tell Coral that I love her and not to be mad that I didn't wake her up to say goodbye. Tell her she was lookin' too pretty and peaceful to disturb." Ernest started to walk away, turned back, and embraced his sister. "You do my heart good, Emie."

On the trek up the hillside, he thought about Mercy. He remembered Rudy telling him how he had a plan for his relationship with Emie, but she wasn't cooperating. He now understood what his young friend meant. Ernest was hurt and disappointed. Yet when he saw the schoolhouse in the distance, he willed himself to think differently. God had been and would continue to be faithful. The teacher began to worship. *Great is thy faithfulness, O God my Father! There is no shadow of turning with Thee. Though changest not, Thy compassions, they fail not. As Thou hast been Thou forever will be…*

Ernest didn't see Mercy until the following morning. He was chopping wood outside the schoolhouse. Justice, with the help of Amos and Andy, had hauled fallen trees to the renovated barn. Ernest knew once school started that the majority of his daylight hours would be spent with his students, leaving precious time for wood cutting. It was downright cold outside, yet he was sweating beneath his coat and hat. Splitting wood was hard work. Pine was the easiest to split. Justice had also brought dried oak and cottonwood. Ernest's axe head had bounced off the hard oak more than once. It also didn't help that the blade needed sharpened. He knew using a dull axe was not only ineffective, but dangerous. A bastard file was needed for sharpening the head. Ernest knew the term "bastard" was used because the file size was unusual, but he had never liked the word. In Christ there were no bastards, whosoever called upon the name of Jesus became the son or daughter of God.

He had one cord of wood cut and was hoping to have two more in place by the time school started. A cord measured four feet high, eight feet long and four feet deep. The newly installed stove in the school seemed to be in good working order. His students would be accustomed to chilly surroundings, but he wanted them to be as comfortable as possible. It would be hard for a learner to hold a pencil if his or her hand was gloved or shaking from the cold.

He didn't hear Mercy approach, and her greeting startled him, "Well, I'm glad you're home safe."

"You scared me, Mercy. I didn't hear you comin'."

"Well, your axe was flyin'. It's early and you're already hard at work."

"I missed you. Wish you could have been with me for Thanksgiving."

The lovely woman smiled. "We had a nice celebration here. Some of the community got together for a sing."

"Did you sing for the good people?"

"Mama and Daddy pressured me."

"I'm sure it was lovely. I'm plannin' to call on a couple families today. Are you wantin' to join me?"

"I ain't sure. I'm a little nervous."

"Nervous about what?"

"Us. Things ain't right between us."

"No, they ain't, Mercy. I'm tryin' to be patient."

Ernest could see she was fighting back tears. She dropped her head slightly, and he wanted to comfort her. He even thought to reach out and touch her hair. Her chocolate colored curls intrigued him. Instead, he removed the work glove from his right hand and lifted her chin. "Mercy, it pains me to see you cry. We're both hurtin' right now. We need to give things a little more time and see."

"Ernest, there was a fuss at the sing."

"What kind of fuss?"

"A couple of the young men started makin' comments about me not likin' my own kind."

His heart started to race. "Are you hurt? Did anyone touch you?"

"I'm fine. My daddy stepped in and stopped the nonsense, but I was frightened."

"I'm sorry that happened, Mercy."

"Me, too."

Chapter Forty Three

"Eating parched corn or parched coffee will cure stomach ailments."
(Appalachian Folk Belief)

Emie couldn't believe that her and Rudy's wedding was just two days away. She felt overwhelmed, and it didn't help that with the baby she tired easily. Aunt Ada kept telling her all would be well and to quit worrying. Thankfully, her wedding dress was finished. Rudy's mom had made it as a gift. The dress was pale blue like the West Virginia sky in the springtime. It was trimmed in white lace like the billowy clouds that made shadows in the meadows during the summer. This time of year, the sky was gray, and the sun hid from the hill people. Doc said there was snow in the air. Emerald knew that the moisture was needed. If snow drifted down from above on her and Rudy's special day, she wouldn't mind. Rudy's mama had also made a matching blue shirt for the groom. Tomorrow Emie and her sisters would spend a portion of the day decorating the church. MayLou and Auntie had helped Emie with her niceties. Auntie was also helping Mrs. Randolph with the wedding cake.

Rudy had told Emie the night before that the focus of the wedding should be on their vows to one another and to the Lord – not on all the other stuff. Ashamedly, she had responded to her beau with her mean voice. "Do you want the church to look plain?

Do you want me to be naked at my own weddin'? And you naked as well? Also, Rudy, I'm wantin' cake, white wedding cake." *Poor Red*, Emie thought. She really was trying to handle her meanness.

Auntie had insisted that Emie take a lolly. She couldn't rest because her mind kept racing. She had multiple thoughts going on all at once. There were also emotions connected with the thoughts. She found herself crying, then laughing, smiling, then frowning.

She and Rudy were studying the writings of Shakespeare with Mrs. Randolph. Emie's mind drifted to Hamlet. *If thou dost marry, I'll give thee this plague for thy dowry. Be thou as chaste as ice, as pure as snow, thou shalt not escape calumny. Get thee to a nunnery, go.* She wasn't going to a nunnery, she was marrying Rudy, and they were going to build a wonderful life together.

Rain was lying next to her on the bed snoring softly. She closed her eyes and willed herself to relax. It didn't really work, but at least Auntie would be happy knowing that her girl's head was resting on a pillow.

When Rain sat up and whined, Emie thought that something might be amiss. It wasn't the puppy's piddle time. Then, she heard a funny noise, a rattle of sorts, outside the bedroom window. When she looked out the curtain, she saw Rudy dancing like a crazy person; he was also shaking something in his right hand. Out of curiosity Emie opened the window and called to Red. Rain was, of course, close by. He was just as curious and stood on his back legs, putting his front paws on the window ledge. *My puppy has gotten big, way too big*, she thought.

"Hey, darlin', I brought the baby a gift."

"What is it?"

"A porcupine rattle. Granny Smith killed her a thorn-swine. It was livin' under her porch. She sent you some quills and the rattle."

"And why are you dancin'?"

"Just for fun. Hopin' to make you smile."

She couldn't help but laugh. "I didn't know that the oversized rodents had rattlers. I thought snakes was the only ones who rattled."

"It's part of their quills. They shake their hindquarters to scare things off."

"Maybe Granny Smith got the porcupine that attacked Rain."

"Emie, we talked about this. The porcupine wasn't the aggressor."

She could feel Rain's tail wagging against her leg. "How did Granny Smith kill the thing?"

"With a piece of wood. She knew it was livin' under her porch. So last night she bundled herself in a blanket and sat quiet-like until the thing came out to explore. She wacked it on the head and rendered it unconscious. I'm not sure what happened next, but today she's cookin' herself a porcupine feast."

"How do you cook it?"

"Darlin', I ain't sure. All I know is that she had a fire goin' and a big stew pot."

Emerald started gagging. She couldn't help it. The contents of her tummy spilt out the window. She was still vomiting when she faintly heard the front door open and Rudy's heavy steps coming her way.

"Emie, I'm sorry for foolin'. I wasn't thinking about how squeamish your tummy is these days. Forgive me."

"I'm okay," she mumbled. "Just give me a minute, and I'll meet you in the front room."

"Are you sure, darlin'? You're lookin' a might pale."

"Go on, Red, I'll be right there."

Emie's hand was over her mouth, so the words were muffled, but Rudy got the general idea. His girl was needin' a few minutes alone. Rain was pressed against Emie's side. Rudy called the puppy to join him, but the faithful pet didn't want to leave his faithful owner.

It was lightly snowing; the dark clouds in the distance looked ominous. Even though Rudy wasn't supposed to see his bride until the wedding ceremony, he was standing outside the back porch bedroom. "Emie, I need to talk with you."

"Rudy, don't come in."

He sighed, "I ain't comin' in darlin'. We won't be sharin' a bedroom until tonight."

"What are you doin' here? I don't think we're supposed to even be talkin'."

"We got a little problem, girlie."

When the bride didn't answer, Rudy grew worried. "Emie, are you in there?"

"No, Red, I climbed out the window in my weddin' gown. Rain went with me. He's wantin' to marry Daffodil today…"

"Alright, so you're still in there. Why didn't you answer me?"

"There was nothin' to answer. You didn't ask me a question. What's the little problem, Rudy?"

"It's snowin'."

"I can see that."

"A storm's comin'. Grandpappy is worried if we don't move the weddin' time up our families won't be able to make it to the church. Or after the cake and such, we'll all be stranded. I ain't wantin' to spend my weddin' night that way."

"It's a big cake, Rudy, and I like cake." Emie giggled.

"I know you do, darlin'."

"Rudy, I ain't quite ready, and Ernest and Mercy ain't here yet."

"Well, girlie, as soon as they arrive, come to the church, and, by the way, I can't wait to marry you."

"Bye, Rudy."

"Emie, are you alright?"

"Yes."

"You don't sound alright."

"I'm just thinkin'."

Rudy grew nervous. Too much thinkin' on Emie's part might mean trouble. It would break his heart if she postponed the wedding. "What are you thinkin' about?"

"That I ain't goin' to a nunnery."

The groom sighed with relief and then laughed outloud.

Emie finished getting ready. She looked around the back porch bedroom and smiled. The tiny room had been a place of healing for her. She had wept and laughed in the small space she'd called home. Within the walls, she'd acted like a warrior and a coward, sometimes within minutes of each other. She would miss sharing a room with Coral, but was excited to share a sleeping place with her husband. Hopefully Rudy liked to talk in bed. She had always dreamt beside her sisters and talking and sharing about the day had been part of their nightly ritual.

Emie's thoughts were interrupted by the braying of mules. She could hear Ernest fussing at the ornery critters. She took one last look and readied herself to leave when she heard a soft knock on the door. She recognized the gentle taps of her aunt. "Come in, Auntie."

"Emie, my girl, you look so beautiful."

"I'm takin' it all in, Aunt Ada. This has been my home, my only real home. With Mama and Daddy there was a place to live, but it was never a home."

"You're only gonna be a stone's throw away."

"Dependin' on who's throwin' the stone."

"I got a good arm, and so do you."

"I know, but it won't be the same."

Ada smiled. "Your brother's here. Everyone's waitin' to take us to the church. Hopefully you'll be sayin' 'I do' before the storm gets too bad."

The wind had kicked up a bit, but so far everyone's concern seemed for naught. The softly falling snow was lovely. Ernest helped her climb into the wagon and whispered in her ear she looked pretty. Her brother and Justice sat on the front bench. With the wind blowing, Amos and Andy were especially flighty. Their ears were back, and they were bucking a bit. It would take the two men to keep the two mules in line. She noticed several wrinkled apples lying on the floor by Ernest and Justice's feet. Emie knew the Bible spoke against bribery, but in the case of mules, she was confident God made allowances. Emie sat with Mercy, and Cece and Auntie on the second bench. It was crowded, but the closeness kept them warm. The men had thought to bring a tarp, so the ladies draped themselves hoping to keep as dry as possible. Emie knew if it wasn't her wedding day, the cover would be put aside and she'd enjoy the dampness of the falling snow on her face. She might have even put her tongue out to catch a few flakes. The four boys sat in the back of the wagon. She complimented them on how handsome they looked. Although they seemed embarrassed by her words, they thanked her just the same. Emie wondered about Uncle Christian, but Aunt Ada assured her that he would meet them at the church. He had traveled to town earlier to check on a patient.

All the way to the church the boys prattled about this and that. Ernest and Justice spoke very little. They were attentive to Amos and Andy. Mercy, who was dressed in her finest, smiled and squeezed Emie's hand a number of times.

"Thank you, Mercy, for standin' with me. I'm so proud to have you as my friend."

"I'm the one who's proud, Emie."

Mercy leaned close and began to sing softly in her friend's ear. *Oh, we ain't got a barrel of money. Maybe we're ragged and funny. But we travel along, singin' our song, side by side. Don't know what's comin' tomorrow. Maybe it's trouble or sorrow. But we travel the road, sharin' our load, side by side. Through all kinds of weather – what if the sky should fall. Just as long as we're together, it doesn't matter at all. When they've all had their quarrels and parted. We'll be the same as we started. Just travelin' along, singin' our song, side by side. Through all kinds of weather – what if the sky should fall. Just as long as we're together, it doesn't matter at all. When they've all had their quarrels and parted. We'll be the same as we started. Just travelin' along, singin' our song, side by side."*

Emie started to laugh and then started to cry. She loved her friend, and, on this special day, she was so pleased to have Mercy by her side.

Emie and Rudy had agreed to keep the guest list short and the ceremony simple, but even with just family and close friends present, the little church seemed full. Emie stood at the back of the sanctuary with Uncle Christian by her side. When the music changed, the guests stood and looked back at the bride. With her arm entwined with her uncle's and holding a single Christmas lily, she walked slowly down the aisle. Ada thought the lily was a miracle. The plants behind the cabin had blossomed in October; the white petals had been tipped in red with the pollen tube and stigma bright yellow. The flowers had been sweet and ambrosial. After the first frost, the flowers wilted. A single bud protected by the foliage opened to the world a couple days ago. Emerald knew Jesus was the Lily of Valley. He was sweet and fragrant, pure and innocent.

When Pastor Rex posed the question, "Who gives this woman in marriage?" Emie was surprised to hear her siblings respond with one voice, "We do." Uncle Christian kissed her cheek, and Rudy took her hand, ushering her onto the platform with Grandpappy. Rudy was standing to her right. He had told her that it was tradition for the groom to stand to the right of his bride in case he needed to fight off any would-be suitors. Emie laughed and told him she didn't think it would be a problem.

Pastor Rex was a wonderful orator. He told stories about the conversations he'd shared with Rudy regarding Emie, and talked about the two being destined to become one.

"Will you, Randal, take Emerald to be your wife?"

"With pleasure."

"Will you, Emerald, take Randal to be your husband?"

"With pleasure."

Chapter Forty Four

"There will be a winter snow for every August fog."
(Appalachian Folk Belief)

The couple didn't linger at their celebration. Rudy allowed time for Emie to enjoy a piece of cake, but then hurried her along. "Darlin', it's really snowin' out there. I want to enjoy our first night as husband and wife in the little house. I don't want to share our precious time with anyone else."

Ernest chauffeured them home. The wind had kicked up even more, and the snow was rapidly accumulating. The storm seemed to be increasing in ferocity and moisture. Even with the remaining apples as bribery, Amos and Andy fought with Ernest. The goal was to get the newlyweds safely home and return to the church for Mercy, her family, Aunt Ada, and Uncle Christian. Emie wanted them all to travel together, but her brother insisted that it wasn't proper and that the newly married couple needed to journey to their home alone. Emie was fairly certain that Ernest now felt differently; she was concerned about him making it back to the church.

"Brother, dream at Auntie's tonight. The weather's too bad for travelin."

"I hear you, girlie, but everyone will worry. I best head back to the church."

Ernest laughed when Rudy struggled to carry his pregnant bride over the threshold. Rain also joined in the fun — barking and running to and fro.

"Well, darlin', we're home!"

"Yes, we are."

Rudy held her close and kissed his bride.

Kindhearted Aunt Ada had prepared a hamper of food for the couple to enjoy. As they sat at the table for the first time as husband and wife, Rudy offered thanks to the Lord.

The snowstorm was quickly turning into a blizzard. Ernest felt like he had experienced more than one blizzard recently. He had certainly been blindsided by Mercy's change of heart. Like the weather, he wondered if she had been suddenly struck by something large and overwhelming, or if her hesitation had happened bit by bit.

The return trip to the church was slow going. Amos and Andy were frightened by the storm, and he didn't blame them. He talked and sang to them along the way. He rambled about this and that. The mules seemed to enjoy his conversation. They settled down some when he spoke. He was talking loudly, but over the wind he wasn't sure how much Amos and Andy understood. Of course, what did it matter? It wasn't like they could really understand and answer in return. It was his tone, not his words that soothed them. He remembered the story in Scripture about the donkey that spoke to Balaam. The donkey was trying to warn Balaam of upcoming trouble. If Amos and Andy could speak, Ernest was confident they would be doing the same. He should have listened to Emie. It wasn't wise to be out in a snowstorm of this magnitude.

Ernest knew that once he arrived at the church, he would be staying. It was no longer safe to travel. He remembered a time or two when Daddy had told him and Lester to tie a rope to the barn door and run it to attach to the house. In the midst of a bad storm, the rope would guide them to and from the livestock that still needed their attention.

Lord, I need your care now, Ernest prayed. *Guide me and bring me safely to your house.* He thought to clarify which house, but knew it wasn't necessary. The Lord understood his thoughts and words. Ernest wasn't ready to die. He was looking for the church house, not his home in heaven.

It was hard to see the dirt road. Ernest held the reins loosely. Amos and Andy seemed to have a better understanding of where the road began and ended. Ernest knew they were headed in the right direction. He understood in his mind it was just a matter of time before they arrived at the church. His heart, however, seemed to have a mind of its own. Like the mules, he was nervous. The weather was playing tricks with his senses.

He sighed with relief when he saw the building come into view. Ernest wasn't sure what to do with Amos and Andy. They needed shelter from the storm, but the church property only included a school, parsonage and worship house. There wasn't a barn or lean-to. Hopefully, Justice would have an idea. Ernest was surprised by the compassion he felt for the mules. Normally, he barely tolerated the pair, but in the midst of the storm they had been his only companions, and he somehow felt indebted and endeared to them.

Mercy was waiting for him in the foyer. "I've been so worried, Ernest. Are you alright?"

"I'm just fine."

"Some of the men folk are makin' plans. Most of 'em think it's not safe to travel."

"I agree," Ernest added as he headed into the sanctuary.

He was both relieved and concerned to learn that shortly after he'd left to transport the bride and groom, most of the wedding attendees headed home. He was relieved because it would be difficult to accommodate too many people in the church house, but also concerned about the wellbeing of friends and family traveling in the storm. He said a quick prayer that everyone made it home safely. Since both residences were in town and only a short distance from the church, Lester and Lottie, as well as Rudy's parents, thought they could make it home. The men planned to return to the church with supplies for the remaining dozen or so guests who were forced to stay overnight at the worship house – food, water, and blankets would be needed for the evening and long night ahead. Justice suggested Amos and Andy be called into service for hauling the supplies. When Ernest approached Justice about food and shelter for the mules, his friend seemed distant and worried; Ernest assumed Justice to be distracted and concerned about his family.

Once Ernest was warmed, he thought about the hours to come. He hoped to share some special time with Mercy. The thought of resting by his sweetheart and holding her hand through the night warmed him even more. Then he thought again, others would have a watchful eye, and it wouldn't be appropriate for him and Mercy to stay side by side. He felt lonely for his girl. He also felt desperate about the future. Both were feelings that he didn't enjoy. His worries for the future revealed his struggle for control. His daddy had controlled his mama. He didn't want that kind of relationship with Mercy. He needed her to love him on her terms. Love wasn't something to be forced or demanded. If Mercy didn't freely love him and want to share a life with him, he knew they would need to part ways.

It wasn't until later in the evening that he had the opportunity to speak with Mercy. Like Justice, she seemed distant and distracted. Ernest was concerned and questioned his girl. When she looked away and wouldn't make eye contact, his heart sank. Something was wrong.

"Mercy, what is it?"

"Maybe this should wait 'til later," she answered.

"There's no time like the present."

She motioned him to a quiet place in the corner of the sanctuary. "Adam fought with another boy at the weddin'."

"Is that why your daddy was upset earlier?"

"Partly."

"Mercy, I wouldn't worry none. Boys are boys and fightin' and rough housin' is sometimes what they do."

"Ernest, they was fightin' about colored and white people. The boy told Adam that dark skinned people didn't belong at the church. That colored people were supposed to go to one church and white people another. He called Adam awful names."

Ernest tried to put off what he knew was coming. "People have been fightin' about their differences since the beginning of time. Look at Cain and Abel."

"Cain killed Abel, and I ain't wantin' anyone hurt or harmed."

Ernest realized he'd put forth a bad example and tried to backtrack, but Mercy wouldn't let him.

"Ernest, I also talked with Mrs. Randolph today. I know we ain't discussed marriage, but it's illegal for a colored and a white to wed. Some have been put in jail."

"Mercy, we live in the hills. If we wed, Sheriff Robbins ain't gonna be puttin' us in jail."

When his girl grew silent, he knew it was over. He started to raise his hand indicating he didn't want hear any more, but also knew he needed to hear plainly from her lips that there was no hope for the future. If he didn't hear the words, he might hold onto something that would never be. "Just say it, Mercy. Say what you're thinkin'."

"I can't be with you, Ernest. Not now, not ever! I'm needin' you to take my words to heart, and leave me be."

He wanted to convince her. He wanted to persuade her with a touch. He wanted to beg and plead, but knew it wouldn't change anything. He shocked himself when he even thought to whisk Mercy away to seduce her. Then she'd *have* to marry him. He was plotting and planning on how to accomplish this sin behind the back of the law and against timing and Mercy's own wishes...

Ernest shook his head to clear his mind. When it came to Mercy, he was walking a tightrope of his faith – to think sin would solve his problems now only showed how desperate he'd become.

"I'll honor your wishes," he finally spoke. He stood, gathered his coat, left the sanctuary, and walked through the front door.

Justice was a dark figure in the churchyard tending to the mules. Amos and Andy looked as distraught as Ernest felt. Their ears were pinned, their nostrils flared, and their tails were swishing madly. This wasn't their home. There wasn't any shelter. The blowing snow and loud wind frightened them. Justice, who was trying to soothe the duo, heard the church door slam. The wind had carried the door, pushing it hard against the building; the loud noise had startled both the men and the mules. Justice looked up from his ministrations. "She told ya, didn't she?" he asked.

"Plain as can be," Ernest answered and kept walking. Even when Justice yelled for him to come back, he kept his face forward, the snow blinding him as he went.

Chapter Forty Five

"Dreaming of thorns is bad luck."
(Appalachian Folk Belief)

"Emie, I'm thinkin' it's time for bed. I'm done talked out and you're noddin' off. It's been a full day." The two were sitting in chairs by the wood stove recounting their wedding day. The warmth from the stove added to the couple's sleepiness.

"Alright, Red. How does this work?"

"What do you mean, 'How does this work?'"

"I ain't never been married before. What do we do? Do I go into the bedroom and put on one of my niceties while you wait? Then I come back out and wait for you."

Rudy smiled. "Darlin', I'll wait here if you'd like, but just call me when you're ready. I don't have any niceties."

"What do you wear for sleepin'?"

"Drawers."

"Oh."

"What do your brothers wear?"

"An undershirt and drawers."

"I ain't wearin' an undershirt. Drawers is just fine."

His beautiful wife rose from the chair and headed to the back bedroom. He waited, then waited some more. He thought to call out to Emie, but remembered Pappy's words about being patient. Finally, he heard his beloved. "Red, I'm ready."

When he entered the room, Rudy couldn't help but shake his head. The covers were pulled to her chin.

"Red, you know I don't like it when you shake your head at me like that."

"I'm sorry, Emie, but you look like one of them mummy pictures from our school reader. Let me at least see your pretty gown. I know you worked hard makin' it special."

She slowly uncovered herself and rose from the bed.

"You look beautiful, darlin'."

"Thank you, Red."

As he quickly removed his shirt and pants, he was surprised that Emie didn't look away. "Now, girlie, I know our agreement, and I'm plannin' to honor what we said, but I am also plannin' on huggin' and kissin' on you."

His bride blushed as she crawled back into bed.

Though the kissing and caressing was delightful, it didn't take Emie long to fall asleep. Rudy sighed. He knew she tired easily these days. When he turned on his side, she surprisingly did likewise. Her belly was pressed up against his back and he felt the baby move. Rudy couldn't help but smile as he began to whisper sweet nothings into his pillow for bride and child.

In the middle of the night, he woke to find Emie's arm around his shoulders and her leg draped over his hip. The air was chilly, but his wife was doing a good job of keeping him warm. Sleeping with Emie was nice, yet it was going to be an adjustment. He thought it strange that he was so close to the edge of the bed. Then, he noticed Rain sprawled out on the other side of Emerald. Daffodil was lying at their feet.

He didn't want to wake his bride, but wasn't happy about sleeping with a big dog and yellow ball of fur. He wiggled his toes, and Daffodil jumped from the bed. He turned slightly, reached across Emie, and gently pushed Rain. The puppy thumped his tail a couple times but didn't move. He pushed a little harder. Finally, Rain moved from the bed to the floor rug. Emie had explained to Rain earlier about his sleeping spot. At the time, knowing the puppy couldn't understand a word that his mistress spoke, Rudy had chuckled. Now he didn't think it quite so humorous. Each time he started to doze the duo woke him up with their mischief. Daffodil hissed, and Rain whined. The cat swiped the dog's tail, and the puppy growled.

Their antics reminded him of Mrs. Randolph's account of "Our Gang," a movie short. The children in the series were always getting into some type of trouble. He worried that the "gang" living in his house would disturb his wife's sleep. When Emie opened her eyes and mumbled, he had enough. He held his wife close and kissed her cheek. When she quickly closed her eyes and returned to slumber, he put the kitten back on the bed. Rain immediately followed suit. Rudy slept soundly until early morning when he heard Emie singing to the baby. He loved his wife's alto voice.

Lullaby and good night, thy mother's delight. Bright angels around, my darling shall guard. They will guide thee from harm, thou art safe in my arms. They will guide thee from harm, thou art safe in my arms.

Ernest headed to Lester and Lottie's home. The normally short walk from the church to his brother's took quite some time. He couldn't tell if it was tears or the blowing snow that stung his cheeks in the cold. Ernest wasn't prone to cry, but the heartache he felt just seemed to seep from his eyes. Eskimos had special words for blowing snow and snow that accumulated quickly. He didn't know any of the words. He just knew they existed in another language in a faraway place. He also knew Eskimos had a special word for the snow they sculpted into corsages and gave to sweethearts on special occasions. He tried not to think of the beauty of such a thing, or the affection represented by such an unusual gift.

In order to be heard above the wind, he pounded loudly with his fist on his brother's door. He was surprised when Lottie answered the door and not Lester. Ernest was swiftly ushered into the small house and seated by the fireplace. Lottie made hot tea. She also filled a basin with warmed water and insisted he first soak his hands and his feet. His extremities tingled when placed in the bath. The night was early, but his brother was already fast asleep. Lottie offered to wake Lester, but Ernest insisted that his slumber go undisturbed. "I know my brother. If you touch him in his sleep, he'll wake up swingin'. I've been clipped by him once or twice."

Charlotte smiled and made him laugh at her description of throwing pillows from across the room to wake her sleeping husband.

His gracious sister-in-law was dressed in night clothes. A shawl was also wrapped around her shoulders. Charlotte was lovely on the inside and the outside, and Ernest wondered how his brother, who was such a rough diamond, had found such a polished gem. Ernest knew she was probably curious about his presence, but she didn't ask any questions. When he was sufficiently warmed, he began to talk. He started at the beginning when he first met Mercy. He talked about her lovely brown skin and chocolate colored hair. He also shared about her beautiful voice and the times they had enjoyed singing and praying together. He choked up when he talked about their mutual love for teaching children. Charlotte remained silent, permitting him to talk uninterrupted. Ernest talked the night away, Lottie comforting him with looks of concern, her own tears, and gentle pats on his arm or leg.

In order to tend the hogs, both brothers were accustomed to rising before dawn. Ernest wasn't surprised that his brother woke while it was still dark. The old Adage *early to bed, early to rise* certainly applied to the Ashby boys. The rest of the proverb *makes a man healthy, wealthy and wise* didn't seem descriptive of himself or Lester, or, for that matter, anyone who lived in the hills. He heard Lester before he saw him enter the small sitting room. The older brother was obviously surprised by the younger brother's presence. Before any questions could be asked, Lottie rose from the seat next to Ernest, embraced her husband, told him she was sleepy, and headed to the bedroom. Ernest started to apologize for keeping her awake, but when Charlotte placed her index finger over her lips, he quieted.

Taking his wife's seat, Lester spoke, "This has gotta be a doozy, and you know how I love a good story."

Ernest smiled, remembering he'd spoken those exact words to Lester not long ago. His brother's teasing did his heart good. Ernest didn't want to talk further about his affections for Mercy. Instead, he wanted to discuss what he should do next, and, in that vein, he quickly gave his brother an overview of what happened at the church. When Ernest mentioned Mercy's parting words, his brother responded by pressing his lips together and pulling his chin down. Ernest thought it strange how in the midst of personal struggle the most unusual things randomly came to mind – like, Lester's stubbled chin. It looked like sandpaper, and he wondered how Lottie felt about early morning hugs and kisses from her man.

Ernest told Lester about his desire to keep Mercy by enjoying sexual pleasures with her. He was thankful Lester responded with compassion and not judgment. The older brother was sitting close enough to place his hand on Ernest's shoulder.

"Love'll make a man do crazy things, Ernest. I'm truly sorry to hear about you and Mercy partin' ways."

"I'm sorry to be sharin' the news. I need to decide what happens next."

"You sure it's over?"

Ernest nodded his head yes. "Even if she was wantin' to try again. I ain't willin'. In the struggle, I don't like who I've become. I've been angry, mean at times. I've tried to manipulate and control her feelings, and wantin' to take her down against her will just to keep her. That ain't something I thought I would ever do. I was plannin' it all in my mind, Lester, where to take her, what to do and what to say!"

Lester raised his eyebrows. "Situations involvin' love can draw the good and bad from a man."

"I love Mercy like no other woman, but I love God more. I can't go down this destroyin' path. It ain't right."

"Are you sure? Things might look different in the mornin'."

"It *is* mornin', and I'm sure."

"Do you think she'll be changin' her mind?"

"No. Between the prejudices in the hills and here in Big Creek, I don't see that happenin'. Sides, I think knowin' it's illegal for white people and brown people to marry was too much. She was just sure they'd put one of us in jail, or both! *Yet straw upon straw was laid till the last straw broke the camel's back...* figure that's what had happened to Mercy. Straw upon straw was laid by the words and deeds of others, and when her own fears were added to the load, it just became too much."

"What broke your back, Ernest?"

"Knowin' what I was wantin' to do to Mercy to keep her!" He paused and added, "Not that she was ever truly mine."

"Any ideas about what you're gonna do?"

"I'm thinkin' of headin' to the church house. I'm gonna tell Justice I won't be joinin' him and his family on the journey up the hill, and I'm gonna spend a couple days on my knees talkin' to Jesus."

"Then..."

"I ain't rightly sure. I ain't wantin' to abandon the children I've been called to teach. Too much has been invested in me and the school, but, at the same time, I don't think I've the strength to work beside Mercy each day."

Ernest knew that the storm outside was over. Sometime during the night, the wind had died down. He was curious to know how much snow had accumulated but thought it best to wait until the sun was up to go outside. An oil lamp would only give him a limited picture of the conditions outdoors. He was tired of viewing the world through spectacles with the wrong prescription. He wanted to see clearly. When he did finally venture beyond the house, the sun was shining, but the air was cold.

Lester wanted to take Ernest's message to Justice. "It will be hard, brother, to face Mercy."

"I ain't a coward. She asked me to 'leave her be', and I have every intention of doin' what she asked."

"There ain't nothin' cowardly about protectin' your heart."

"In time my heart will be just fine."

"It ain't fine right now. I'm comin' with you, baby brother., Lester said.

Ernest in turn encouraged Lester to stay with his beautiful wife. "She's sleepin'. Crawl back into bed and keep her warm." The younger brother then smiled. "You might wanna shave off them whiskers first. I can't imagine any woman wantin' your chin stubble next to her face."

Lester chuckled. "You don't know my Lottie."

In the end, they both headed toward the church building.

The brothers had spent many mornings bundled in layers of clothing for warmth walking side by side.

Just as they exited town and went round the bend toward the church, Ernest sensed that something wasn't quite right. He started to voice his concerns to Lester, when several rifle shots were fired from the trees between the turn in the road and the school house. A bullet hit Lester in the chest.

The older brother instantly fell to the earth, his crumpled body sinking into the almost foot of snow that had fallen the day before. Ernest instinctively dove to the ground as well. Lester's wound was bleeding profusely; the snow blanket surrounding him quickly turned from white to crimson. Ernest wasn't sure what to do. The only cover was yards away. If he tried to drag his brother to safety, they would both be easy targets. He stayed as close to the ground as he could while still examining Lester's body. His brother was badly wounded.

Ernest began to yell as loudly as he could for help.

Chapter Forty Six

"If you burn potato peelings, your crops won't grow the next year."
(Appalachian Folk Belief)

Ernest stood next to Lester's bed; he didn't want to leave his brother. Doc had sent someone with Ada to get Charlotte. Lester opened his eyes and tried to speak, but Ernest quieted him.

Lester grabbled Ernest's hand and then barely above a whisper spoke one word, "Lottie."

When Ernest started to shush his brother again, Doc interrupted. "Let him speak, Ernest. He needs to tell you..."

"Lottie," Lester mumbled.

"She's on her way, brother."

Ernest could hardly hear his sibling. His voice was so soft. "Take care of her."

At this, the younger brother worked to stay composed. It wouldn't help Lester if he broke down in front of him.

"Promise," Lester whispered. Lester's eyes remained open, but his breathing changed. Doctor Bright continued his ministrations, but Ernest could tell death was near. His brother was leaving earth for heaven.

"I promise, Lester, I'll take care of her. She won't lack for nothin' if I can help it." He then began to sing his brother home.

I am a poor wayfaring stranger, traveling through this world of woe. There's no sickness, toil nor danger in that fair land to which

I go. I'm going there to see my Father. I'm going there, no more to roam. I'm just a-going over Jordan. I'm just a-going over home...

Lester was gone. His brother was gone. Ernest moved to the head of the bed, bent down, placed his forehead on top of Lester's forehead, and wept. He sobbed aloud for his losses at both ends of his soul and wondered how he would ever tell Charlotte that her young beloved had already left this earth. The pain he felt was like no other – so deep and profound that it was hard to breathe. He didn't know so much sorrow could take the form of physical pain; he hurt to the core of his being.

Ernest felt Doc's hand on his shoulder steadying his shuddering sobs. "Son, Charlotte's here. She's with Ada in the outer room. I can tell her if you would like."

Ernest stood, wiping his eyes on his sleave. "No. I'll go." When he opened the door, Charlotte was standing bracing herself by the post, her back to him. She swung round, blotched faced, tears pooling in worried eyes, she wrung her hands. Ernest's own bloodshot eyes met Charlotte's. He swallowed hard and reached for his sister-in-law. "His last words were of you..."

"No! No! Lester! No! Not yet!" Charlotte used Ernest's chest for a hay bale to punch. "Why, why, why?!" He finally caught her in his arms. The pair embraced for several minutes, tears mingling as they each grieved for the loss of the earthly treasure, Lester, now flown to heaven above. How could it be?

Emie was beside herself. What did Rudy mean that Lester was gone? He'd just come *home*. At first, she had paced the floor inside, then she sat outside in the cold and snow.

Something seemed wrong with the baby inside her. Now, Rudy insisted she lie on their bed. He wasn't even putting up a fuss that Rain and Daffodil lay beside her. She wasn't sure it was possible to endure more. The past few months had dealt blow after blow. It was like she was in a boxing ring where the loser was so far gone that he couldn't even lift his arms to fight back. Ernest once told her about the fight between Dempsey and Tunney. It was called *The Long Count Fight.* In round seven, Tunney, who was trapped against the ropes, in a corner, experienced combination punches that put him down. He took two rights and two lefts on the chin. He staggered, and then four more punches from Dempsey laid him on the mat. He was dizzy and disoriented. Dempsey was ordered into a neutral corner, but Dempsey just stood there looking at his opponent. This delay gave Tunney additional seconds to recuperate. The referee wouldn't start the count until Dempsey followed his instructions, and, in the end, Tunney *won*.

Emie could practically hear the clamber and clatter of those fight bells. She was defeated. There hadn't been enough time between rounds for her to recover. Unlike Dempsey, her opponent hadn't given her time to recuperate before his next blow.

Now, she thought she heard voices in the other room. She believed it was Aunt Ada and Uncle Christian. She started to get up, but her strength failed her. Rain jumped off the bed and pushed the door open with his nose. Daffodil yawned and stretched, but seemed content to continue her rest.

When she heard the gentle taps on the door, she knew it was Aunt Ada. Her aunt entered the room quietly and sat down in a chair next to the bed. Emie felt a cool wet cloth laid on her forehead, then on her cheek. No words were spoken. Ada simply took her girl's hand, and the two cried together. Emerald thought her aunt so wise for saying nothin'. Her school friend, Mimi, with good intentions, had offered platitudes to her in town for the loss of her parents. When Emie's parents died, she learned there were times in loss when it was just best to be silent.

After a few minutes, Rudy entered with Doctor Bright following close behind. The kindly doctor spoke, "Emie, dear, I know the timing isn't good, but Rudy called me over here sayin' it seems that something might be wrong. Do you mind if I give you a quick examination? I want to be sure that both you and the baby are fine."

Red! But, she closed her eyes and nodded in agreement. She knew things weren't right. Auntie squeezed her hand and rose from the chair, taking the cool cloth with her.Using the cloth, Aunt Ada wiped the tears from her own eyes. She then used her fingertips to gently swipe the new tears from her girl's cheeks.

As soon as Auntie moved, Rudy was by Emie's side. "Darlin', may I stay with you while Uncle Christian does his work?"

She smiled slightly at her husband. How could such joy and such sorrow occur at the same time? How she loved Red. She'd enjoyed their first evening and night sleeping with her arms around him. Husband and wife. Yet, this morning when Aunt Ada and Uncle Christian brought news of Lester being shot and his sudden passing the sorrow came down – sorrow so overwhelming that all other emotions were taken from her heart and placed among the icy layered snow. There was nothing but grief now, everything else was numb, frozen with the ice crystals. Sitting outside, she hadn't felt the cold. Though Rudy had escorted her to bed, rubbing her hands and feet to warm them, she felt chilled and damp. Would her husband's sincerity be able to separate her from her losses?

As Doc listened to the baby's heart, Rudy held her hand. She pictured herself lying in the snow, trusting her beloved to stay by her side. Rudy would respect her privacy, but little worries began to prick like roughed up slivers slicing into her heart.

"Emerald, my dear," Uncle Christian began. "You're leaking fluid from your womb. It's not much, but enough that you need to stay in bed for a few days. I don't want you up and moving. I know Rudy will see to your needs. I'll be here to help, and so will Ada."

"The baby…" Emie began.

"Right now, the baby is fine, just fine, and we want to *keep* him or her that way. Try your best to stay still and rest, my dear."

Rudy began to rub her arm. "Doc, just tell me what to do."

"Comfort her as best you can. Stay by her side. Make sure that she eats and drinks. Keep her in bed to rest as much as possible."

She closed her eyes and sighed. "Red, I'm scared."

"It'll be alright, Emie. Please just rest. Listen to Doc. I'll get you whatever you need."

"I wanna see Ernest. That's what I want. If I knew more about what happened it would give me peace."

"I don't know, darlin'." Rudy responded. "Sometimes it's best not to know."

Her spirit arched against this. "Please, Red. When you see Ernest, ask him to *come* to me."

"Emie, there ain't no need to be askin' Ernest to come. When he hears that you're ailin', he'll be here right quick."

Uncle Christian gathered his supplies. "Girlie, your auntie and I'll be back tomorrow. In the meantime, if you need me, please send Rudy. I'm sure that Ada will be over later with dinner."

"Thank you," she paused to think. "She's hurtin' too. Watch over her."

"It will be my honor." The doctor indicated to Rudy.

"Darlin', I'll be right back. I'm wantin' to walk Uncle Christian to the door."

"How bad is she?" Ernest asked in the yellow afternoon snow.

"Doc says if she gets rest and takes care of herself that she should be fine." Rudy answered.

"And the baby?"

"Right now, the baby's fine. We need to keep Emie as calm as possible." Rudy sighed. "She's been askin' for you."

"I came as soon as I heard. I've been with Lottie."

"I'm sure she's beside herself."

"In a bad way. Once I speak with Emie, I'm gonna head back over to Big Creek. Your mama and Mrs. Randolph are with her right now. Pastor Rex offered to stop by. It probably ain't proper, but I'm gonna sleep on her settee tonight."

"In times like this, Ernest, who cares what's proper? She's like one of your sisters."

Ernest's eyes swelled with tears. "He asked me to take care of her, Rudy."

"Ain't surprised. He loved and trusted you."

"How do I take care of her? What do I know about takin' care of a woman? Look at the mess I made with Mercy."

"Now ain't the time for blamin', Ernest. Mercy also helped make the mess."

"It's not her fault, but now it's over between us, you know?"

"I ain't surprised. A man wants the world to know he loves his girl. Secret loves are for when something's wrong, not right."

"Someday, I wanna tell ya what happened. I was sore-tempted to sin, Rudy. Now ain't the time of tellin' though. I'm needin' to see my sister."

"Ernest, you came."

"Of course, did you think I wouldn't, girlie?"

"No, I knew you would visit. Tell me everythin', brother. I need to know how it happened? Did he suffer?" Emerald broke.

Rudy pushed Rain off the bed, crawled in next to his wife, and cradled her in his arms. Over Emie's honey tresses, he shook his head "no" at Ernest. "Emie, it ain't good for you to be askin' all these questions. Now, I know that Rudy told you some. I'm wantin' to spare you, but I think you're needin' to know that he didn't suffer. His last words were of his wife. He's with Jesus, girlie. I sang him home to heaven."

"What did you sing, Ernest?" She then lifted her head from Rudy's shoulder and looked at her husband's face. "Red, please let him sing for me." Emie knew he was being protective not to worry her or the baby's well-being. "Red, I'll be fine. Ernest's voice will soothe me like the lavender and make me think of Lester's reunion with Mama and Daddy."

"Go on, Ernest. What did you sing?" Rudy asked.

I am a poor wayfaring stranger, traveling through this world of woe. There's no sickness, toil nor danger in that fair land to which I go. I'm going there to see my Father. I'm going there, no more to roam. I'm just a-going over Jordan. I'm just a-going over home. I know dark clouds will gather 'round me. I know my way is rough and steep. Yet beauteous fields lie out before me, where God's redeemer, their vigils keep. I'm going there to see my mother. She said she'd meet me when I come. I'm just a-going over Jordan. I'm just a-going over home...

"Thank you, Ernest. I know your words brought our brother peace. They brought me peace. I'm gonna rest now. I'm gonna think about them beauteous fields."

Chapter Forty Seven

"It's good luck to steal herbs."
(Appalachian Folk Belief)

Ernest had spent the last two weeks with Charlotte. His body ached from sleeping on the much too small settee. Lottie wanted to change places, but he couldn't displace his sister-in-law from the bed she once shared with her husband. He often heard her crying in the night. During the day, he comforted her with warmhearted words and thoughtful touch but at night he let her be. It would take time and often solace was needed in grieving.

He had organized the going home service for Lester. He was proud of Charlotte. She had insisted on sharing with the mourners about her husband's new found faith. The service had been a nice tribute to his brother. On Doc's orders, Emie didn't attend, but Ernest, along with Rudy, had filled her in on the details, and had patiently answered question after question. He was also proud that Charlotte had put aside her own grief to call on Emerald. The young women had hugged and cried together. They had laughed when reminiscing about Lester's mischievousness.

Ernest had met with Sheriff Robbins on several occasions. The sheriff agreed that Lester's killer was more than likely one of his previous partners, but there was no evidence to prove as much. The sheriff had interviewed the two men. Both had alibis for the time of the shooting. Together Ernest, Rudy, and the sheriff had located the spot where the shots had been fired. The shooter had obviously left in a hurry. No attempt had been made to conceal his footprints. The prints were extremely large and the shoe tread unusual. Sheriff Robbins had even measured the shoe size, which didn't appear to match either of the possible suspects. Several casings had also been left on the ground. Both men claimed not to own a rifle, which Ernest couldn't believe. He didn't think there was a single man in Big Creek, or in close proximity, who didn't own a rifle. A gun was needed for hunting, and the men obviously ate. The sheriff had told Ernest to be patient, but he was tired of being patient – look at where it had gotten him with Mercy.

Justice and Cece attended Lester's service, but Mercy and the boys weren't present. Ernest was glad. He felt responsible to help Charlotte and didn't need the distraction Mercy would have provided. In some ways, he appreciated that she let him be with his grief; yet, on the other hand, it hurt that Mercy, even in a subtle way, hadn't bothered to offer her sympathies. Justice later sent word that he would oversee the remainder of the schoolhouse deliveries and preparations. His message also said that Mercy would gather everything for the open house, but, just before the scheduled date, she would be leaving for an extended visit with a cousin who lived near Elkins.

Ernest and Charlotte were on their way to Rudy and Emie's for dinner. At first, Charlotte had declined the invitation. "Ernest, it ain't been three weeks since Lester's passin'. I ain't ready for socializing."

"Charlotte, we ain't socializing. We're seein' family. We're needin' them, and they're needin' us."

It has taken some persuasion on Ernest's part, but Charlotte was now sitting behind him bundled in a blanket. The two were riding Rudy's mare. When they arrived, Ernest tied the horse by the corral where the mules used to reside. Ernest thought fondly of the ornery pair and wondered what trouble they were creating up the holler. He also thought about the four boys: Adam, Beau, Claude and Dean, who were certainly creating mischief. Ernest

THE WHISPERING OF THE WILLOWS

missed the boys. He also surprisingly missed Amos and Andy. When he chuckled out loud, Charlotte patted his arm and asked what was so funny. He smiled in return, "Naughty boys and ornery mules."

On the walk to the little house, Charlotte requested that Ernest not make the evening about Lester. "Ernest, you've been good to me, but I'm knowin' you need to head on up the holler. Your students are waitin'. Please, let's remember this evenin' that God has a plan and will take care of each of us. Let's encourage Emie and Rudy to enjoy themselves as newlyweds. I want us to talk about better days to come."

Ernest took her hand and gently squeezed.

Rudy had outdone himself with dinner preparations. He insisted the credit go to Emie and Aunt Ada, but Emerald gave praise where praise was due and chimed right in on complimenting her husband's culinary skills. "Now that Doc says I can be up and about a little bit, I'll admit I made the table pretty and prepared the pie, but the meal's goodness is a tribute to my handsome and talented husband. I may never cook again."

Rudy rose from his chair and kissed Emie's cheek. "Now, darlin', if you continue gettin' better, Uncle Christian says you'll be back to your regular chores next week and cookin' up a storm." Rudy then looked toward Ernest and Charlotte. "The deer steaks were fresh. My daddy's started sellin' wild meat at his store, and I'm helpin'."

"What a wonderful idea," Charlotte added.

"Well, with Emie needin' to rest and not makin' her wares, my daddy was lookin' for some new ideas."

"Ernest didn't you tell me that some of the ladies by the schoolhouse are talented at craftin'?" Lottie asked. "Maybe their wares could also be sold."

"I'll talk with Rudy's daddy and see what he thinks, Ernest answered. "I've been prayin' for a way to help the families. The people are poor; if it's possible, poorer than the people in Big Creek. Children wear rags and have no shoes. I know it's the same for some here, but the further you go up the hill, the harder it is for people to squeak out a meager livin'."

The conversation continued about the students and families Ernest would be serving. The teacher was in awe of the support Emie and Rudy were willing to give. Emie talked about working with the ladies on how to prepare their wares for selling, and Rudy suggested that he and Ernest work with the men on harvesting game. Some of the longer and straighter pieces of wood Ernest had behind the schoolhouse would certainly work.

Ernest admired Charlotte's insights. "I think it's important we help, but help in a way that creates plans for people to help themselves. Even here in Big Creek, people need a hand in gettin' on their feet, but once they're up and movin', they need to keep walkin'."

Ernest was grateful his sister was recovering. Each day Emie grew stronger. She was now resting only a small portion of the day. He was also thankful for Rudy's help with the pigs. Rudy took the morning shift and Ernest the evening shift. This time of year, the animals mostly required a quick look over and fresh food and water. Rudy wanted to supplement his income by overseeing the hog operation. Ernest thought it was a good idea. He had also agreed with Rudy that the new husband should wait a few more days before approaching Emie with his plans. Ernest knew his sister only too well. "She'll be asking questions and more questions. She'll wear herself out and you, too."

Ernest could tell Emie was getting tired and suggested that he and Charlotte head back to Big Creek. As they prepared to leave, his sister spoke up, "Brother, your open house is in a couple days. With Mercy gone, how will you manage?" Before he could answer, Emie continued without stopping for a breath. "If I wasn't concerned for the baby, I'd go with you and assist. I was thinkin' you could take Coral, but I don't think she should leave Auntie right now. She's bein' such a help. Ernest, I'm a might worried…"

"Emie," Rudy interrupted. "Ernest is a trained teacher. He'll be able to manage. I don't think you should be worryin' none."

"Red, I can't help it. I just lost one brother, and I want the other one to be happy and healthy."

Before Emie and Rudy could continue their verbal back and forths, Ernest started to speak up, only to be interrupted by

Charlotte. "Emie, I ain't at my best, but maybe I can help with the open house. I've been dreadin' Ernest leavin', but if he thinks I can assist, I wanna try."

Ernest was overwhelmed by everyone's concern. He was also slightly frustrated that all the ladies were planning his life, doubting his abilities, and not letting him get a word in edgewise.

On the way home, Charlotte continued the conversation. Ernest didn't want to hurt her feelings, but was certain he could manage on his own. Yet, it was the first time since Lester's death that Lottie had expressed even the slightest pleasure in doing something. How could he refuse his sister-in-law's request to help?

"Ernest, this is so lovely. I'm nothin' but impressed. When your students and their families visit tonight, everyone will be excited for school to start." Lottie declared.

The schoolhouse did look amazing. Everything was arranged. True to form, Justice had kept his word. The renovations were completed. Ernest could also see Mercy's handiwork. The schoolhouse was orderly, and the curriculum and supplies were displayed for the learners and parents to preview.

Charlotte also proved invaluable. For the past couple days, she had worked side-by-side with Ernest in putting the final touches in place. She had prepared the evening's refreshments and even suggested Ernest use the opportunity to talk with the families about selling their crafts and wares. She also had the ingenious idea that the project could be a learning experience for the students. "Think about it, brother. You can teach 'em all about sellin' and pricin'. The lessons could include instruction on math and writin'. Some of the students might even have talents of their own."

Lottie had taken to calling him "brother." He supposed she was following the pattern of his sisters. He didn't mind. In fact, it was a blessing. He wanted to be sure that the people in the community viewed his relationships among females with all propriety. At the back of the school-house, Ernest had added make-do sleeping quarters for himself. He had also quickly constructed a primitive divider; he hoped the area wouldn't be too much of an eyesore. It was okay to briefly share living quarters with Lottie in Big Creek, but he didn't want the same arrangement further up the holler.

He was thankful Charlotte hadn't questioned him about his makeshift bedroom. He was also thankful for Charlotte in a number of other ways. She was going to provide the evening's entertainment by shooting an apple off the teacher's head. She had insisted that it would be great fun. When Ernest had expressed concern that the activity might remind her of Lester, she had agreed, but wanted nonetheless to put the bow in her hand, aim at the apple, and draw the string.

When the students and parents started to arrive, Ernest could hardly contain himself. At first it had felt awkward to be addressed as "Mr. Ashby," now he relished the words. He was finally a teacher. He encouraged everyone to tour the room and to ask questions about the materials on display. When Justice and the boys arrived, Adam, Beau, Claude and Dean raced to his side and began talking all at once. At first, Ernest thought to settle them down, but, just like a young boy himself, he joined in their talking and laughter. He also did his best to discretely deflect any of the boys' chatter about Mercy.

After the group received refreshments, Ernest requested that everyone take a seat. He discussed the upcoming school year. When he introduced Lottie Legend to the audience, there were looks of confusion and curiosity. In such a small community, where everyone knew everyone, to have a stranger present seemed odd, especially a beautiful light-skinned woman carrying a bow and arrow.

Ernest was impressed by Charlotte's obvious experience in entertaining crowds. The two had created a mini drama for the learners and their families. First, Ernest pretended to faint with fear, which didn't require much acting on his part. Although he had witnessed firsthand Lottie Legend's skill, he was still very nervous. As he fell to the floor, Charlotte shot the apple mid-air. Everyone shouted and those who weren't standing, stood to peer over shoulders.

Next, Ernest stood firmly in place and Lottie shot an apple clean off his head. People crowded in crowing like a circus. Lottie refused to pull her bow until they all moved back again. Finally, with two small apples resting on his scalp, his sister-in-law shot the first apple, reloaded and shot again, knocking the second apple off of Ernest's head.

The open house was a tremendous success. The students were captivated by Charlotte. Ernest was certain the evening would be etched on the heart of every learner.

When the last family exited the schoolhouse, Ernest embraced Lottie. "Thank you!"

"Brother, it's me who should be thankin' you. It felt good to perform again and laugh."

"Charlotte, I've so many ideas floatin' in my head," Ernest shared. "Would you consider comin' back up here in January? I'm thinkin' you'd be a great help to me and the students."

"You warm my heart, brother."

Ernest knew she was trying to hold back her tears.

"I've no family, Ernest. With Lester gone, you and the sisters are my family. I've been worried some about where I'd go and what I'd do. I'm thinkin' I wanna help, but can you give me a little time to ponder it?"

"I understand, Lottie."

"I won't make you wait long. I'll make up my mind by Christmas, so if things work out I can be ready to help when school starts."

That night while drifting to sleep, Ernest thanked God for His goodness. He'd been worried about how he would fulfill his promise to Lester. He couldn't live up the holler and watch out for Lottie in Big Creek. His original plan had been to recruit Doc and Rudy's assistance, but it would be even better to have Charlotte close by. He hoped her answer would be "yes."

"Okay, Red, you're tellin' me you wanna be a pig farmer?" Emie challenged her husband.

"I think it's an idea worth ponderin'."

"I ain't never seen myself as a hog wife."

"Emie, you are and will always be my wife. You won't ever be the wife of a hog," Rudy said, and then snorted like a pig. He placed his face close to Emie's neck and quoted the words his mother had shared with him repeatedly as a small boy, *Love you little, love you big, love you like a little pig.* He kept snorting and snorting softly just above her ear, until his darlin' broke into laughter.

"Red, stop now. This is serious business. I don't wanna turn into my mama!"

"Okay, I'll stop." He then snorted a couple more times for good measure. When Emie rolled her eyes, he couldn't help but repeat Ernest's story about the piglet that rolled her eyes. "The pig's eyes was blue and there was even blonde hairs comin' out her snout."

"Rudy, I've heard that story, and there ain't a lick of truth in it."

He went for her neck again but this time he didn't snort, instead he placed a series of gentle kisses on her smooth, creamy flesh. "Darlin', I love you, and your happiness means the world to me. If you don't want me to raise hogs, we'll find another way."

"Would we have to live next to the sows?"

"I don't think so. Lester started a house for him and Lottie. He put the foundation, walls in and tresses on top, but, with winter approachin', we won't get much further 'til spring."

"I saw it. Thankfully it ain't built on top the old house."

"Usin' what Lester started, what would you think about me buildin' a make-do place? I could sleep there when needed, but mostly be here with you and the baby. Then, in a couple years, we could build us a fine house in the meadow you love with them blue flags, cardinal flower and bluebells."

Emerald started to cry. Rudy reached for his wife and held her close. "Them happy or sad tears, darlin'?"

"Happy."

"I thought so. I'm puttin' lots of bedrooms in our nice house." He chuckled and asked, "Have you seen any dirty rats lately?"

Chapter Forty Eight

"If you eat snow before the third snowfall of the season
it will make you sick."
(Appalachian Folk Belief)

Emerald was enjoying the afternoon with Coral and Auntie. Rudy was in Big Creek visiting with his daddy about the game meat he'd been harvesting and the wares Ernest was procuring further up the holler. Emie was so relieved that Charlotte had made the decision to join Ernest in helping the learners. She had worried that her brother would be lonely. She had also worried that Lottie would somehow get lost in her in grief.

"I feel big as a whale." Emie said, looking down at her overgrown belly.

"I don't think you look like a whale, sister, more like a duck. You waddle when you walk." Coral added.

Aunt Ada laughed with her two girls. "From the back, Emie, you wouldn't know you're carryin' a baby, but then when you move it's definitely a waddle."

"I'm thinkin' it's time to have this baby," the expectant mother declared.

"That baby's gonna come when she or he is good and ready," Auntie said.

"Aunt Ada, I saw Granny Smith at the Christmas service at church. She said the oddest thing," Emie began. "She was at me and Rudy's weddin' and mentioned the special lily I was carryin'."

Coral pressed her hand to her heart, "I thought that the lily was beautiful, sister."

"Well, Granny Smith said she's been prayin' extra hard for me and the baby cause lilies that bloom out of time mean somethin' bad is gonna happen."

Auntie clicked her tongue on the roof of her mouth. "Granny is old. Some say close to a hundred. I asked her once and she don't even know her real age. She loves Jesus but still clings to some of them old wives' tales. I wouldn't worry none. God is takin' fine care of you and the baby."

"Thank you, Aunt Ada. I'm not really worried, but somehow Granny's words keep poppin' into my mind. When I told Rudy, he just laughed. He said it was nothin' but superstition, and that we don't believe in such nonsense."

"Sister, have you been thinkin' of any baby names?" Coral asked.

Emie knew that Coral in her own sweet way was changing the subject. It was just like her quiet and kind sister to be concerned about her older sibling's feelings. "Well, I have been thinkin' on it some. This will really get Granny Smith prayin', maybe even doin' some fastin'." Emie giggled. "If the baby's a girl, I want to name her 'Lily Jewel.' Lily like the special flower I carried and Jewel after all the sisters."

"What about boys' names?" Ada asked.

"I ain't rightly sure," Emie answered. "I was ponderin' about 'Lester,' but it still pains me to remember our loss. I know it won't always be like this, but it's a might soon."

The ladies shared a moment of silence. Emerald assumed that like her, the other two were thinking of Lester. *Other babies will come for me and Rudy*, she thought. *Maybe a namesake for my brother might be best down the road.*

Auntie broke the silence by offering more milk tea. The tea was like a soothing salve. *There's power enough in heaven to cure a sin-sick soul.*

Emie knew that Joseph's brothers had sold him to a caravan of men from Gilead carrying spices used to make healing balms. As she sipped her warm tea, she prayed in her heart. *Lord, let your healing balm comfort my family. We've lost so much. Protect me and this baby. Sooth my mind and erase the words that Granny Smith spoke.*

The newlyweds were enjoying a nice dinner of venison stew. The kitten was bathing herself in front of the fire, and the puppy was whining at the door. "Red, Rain has been actin' odd. He just piddled and is wantin' outside again," Emie shared with her husband.

"So I've noticed. I think he's lookin' for love. I talked with him a bit about dirty rats, but so far he ain't seen none."

"Rudy, quit playin'. I'm a might worried. 'Sides Rain's a bit young to have love on his mind."

The new husband smiled. "Darlin', he's almost seven in human years and that's about the time I laid eyes on you in first grade. I've had love on my mind ever since."

"Seriously, Red, do you ever think about love?"

"I think about love every day, Emie. I think about how much I love you and love our baby. I also think about God's great love in sending His Son."

"I'm scared, Red."

Rudy scooted his chair closer to his wife and laid his arm around her shoulders. "Darlin', there ain't no need for you to be scared."

"I'm havin' a baby, and I ain't ready."

"Emie, you're gonna be a great mommy."

"Thank you. I'm worried some about bein' a good mother, and I'm also worried about givin' birth. Granny Smith told me that she went blind from her labor pains when she brought her son into the world."

"Darlin', Granny's about 120 and full of mischief."

"Aunt Ada said that Granny Smith is maybe 100."

"It don't matter if she's 100 or 120. She is still speakin' out of turn and causin' you to worry."

"Well, it does give me some peace that her blindness wasn't permanent."

"Emie, women have been givin' birth since the beginnin' of time. I don't think blindness comes from givin' birth."

"Well, Red, there is that lady up the holler who is blind. I've seen her at church on a couple occasions. Maybe I could ask her about it."

"Darlin', she's blind due a childhood accident…"

"I'm a child, Red."

"Emie, you're not a child. You're a young woman, married, and getting' ready to have a baby. 'Sides, I don't think you should be askin' the infirm about their struggles. It could be off-puttin'."

"I think you're right. Maybe Coral could ask."

"Darlin', I think the best thing is to talk with Uncle Christian. He's delivered most of the babies in this holler. He's more of an expert than Granny Smith."

"Uncle is an expert at watchin' and helpin', not doin', Red."

"Let's go to bed, Emerald Ashby."

"That's not my name anymore, Red."

"Okay, let's go to bed, darlin'. I'm tired and needin' to comfort my wife."

"Rudy, thank you."

"Thank you for what?"

"Thinkin' of love every day, and also for letting Rain and Daffodil share our bed."

Rudy shook his head in mock frustration. "Once the baby gets here, there won't be any room for me in our bed. I'm thinkin' of asking Coral if I can move in with her and share the back porch bedroom."

As the time for the baby drew near, Emie experienced a burst of energy. She was always on the move – moving slowly but moving nonetheless. "Emie, you are wearin' me out," Rudy said late one evening. "Dark's long past and we're still puttin' things in order for the baby. Tomorrow is another day, darlin'."

"Red, I ain't tired. You go on to bed. Take Rain and Daffodil with you. They're gettin' in my way. Their fussin' is just plain aggravatin'."

"I ain't going to bed without you. How can I sleep knowin' that you're out here workin'? Although I'm not sure it's really workin' if you're just doin' the same things over and over. How many times have you folded that baby blanket? You're gonna wear holes in it before the baby even uses it."

Emie could tell that Rudy was getting exasperated. "I just want everything ready for the baby."

"I know you do, darlin', but everything is done ready. I'm worried you're tiring yourself out."

"Alright, I'll come to bed, but I want to show you somethin' first."

"Emerald, can't it wait 'til the mornin'?" Rudy yawned.

"I think you're gonna like this, Red. I drew you a picture." Emie went to the small table that rested between the two chairs next to the fireplace and gathered the drawing she'd prepared earlier in the day. The fire was dying down, and Rudy took the opportunity to stir the embers and add a couple logs. The bark on the wood immediately lit, and a fire sparked.

Her artwork was primitive, but Rudy easily recognized the picture of a long-tailed rat with a smile on his face. The caption read 'phew.' He burst out laughing. "Tonight, Emie? I'm tired, but we can make this happen."

She joined her husband in laughing. "I knew you'd say that. As soon as the baby comes and Doc says it's okay. I'm ready, Red. I want us to live like a real husband and wife."

"Darlin', we do live like a real husband and wife. There ain't nothin' fake about our life together, but this will make things ever more special." Rudy felt so loved by his beautiful wife. She was ready to give birth but still thinking of their marriage and future together.

Emie kept telling herself that Rudy would be home any minute. He'd spent the day with the hogs. She knew he'd come home smelling like the creatures; she had already drawn water for her husband and warmed it for a bath. Just to tease Red, she had added lavender and sweet smelling salts to the water. She wanted to wash Red's back, feed him dinner, and head to bed. Her tummy was twitching, her back was aching, and she felt tired. She had purposed in her heart to wait until Red had been taken care of to mention her ailments; she knew he would sacrifice his bath and dinner for her. Of course, was it really a sacrifice for her if Rudy smelled like a hog? The pig odor would linger in the air and make her stomach roll. She knew in her condition that it was normal to be sensitive to smells. She just didn't want her husband's scent to make her vomit. *It might hurt his feelings some,* she thought.

When Rain headed to the door, Emie figured Rudy was nearby. Of course, Rain did have a girlfriend. Rudy had spotted a female dog back by Amos and Andy's former coral. Rudy had said that the dog was mangy and skittish; he thought the pup was sleeping in the mule shelter. Emie, of course, wanted to bring the dog inside, but Red stayed steadfast with his opinion. "Darlin', we ain't needin' another critter livin' in our home. I'll put some scraps out back so she ain't goin' hungry."

Emerald understood her husband's feelings. They were both a little concerned about how Rain and Daffodil would react to the baby. She figured Rain would be curious but fine. Daffodil, however, was another story.

Granny Smith had also added her two cents about the kitten. "The cat will lay on top the babe and draw the breath right out of it." After Emie had told Granny that the baby was a he or she and not an it, she had immediately gone to visit with Uncle Christian. Doc had been headed out the cabin door on his way to see a patient, but had still taken a few minutes to address the expectant mother's concerns.

"Girlie, who told you such nonsense?" Uncle Christian asked.

"Granny Smith."

The good doctor slapped his thigh in frustration. "I should be thankful for her foolishness. It keeps me in business. Your kitten will be interested in the baby and you need to watch, but…," Uncle Christian stumbled for the right word, "the flower cat…"

"Daffodil," Emie interrupted.

"Daffodil," the doctor continued, "won't take the air from your baby."

Emie, knowing her uncle was in a hurry, swiftly offered her thanks and a quick embrace.

When the door to the little house opened, Rudy stepped in, and Rain headed out. Emie knew all would be well. Rudy was home, and his presence brought her peace.

"I stink," were the first words out of her husband's mouth. His next words were about the wellbeing of his wife. "Darlin', you're lookin' a might peaked. You doin' alright?"

"I'm fine. Let's get you in the washtub. I'm wantin' to wash your back."

Rudy quickly stripped and climbed into the tub. He didn't even attempt to be modest. Emie seemed curious about his body, and he was more than willing to accommodate her.

"I smelled like a hog. Now, I'm gonna smell like a field of flowers."

"Won't that be nice, Red?"

"If it's nice for you then it's nice for me, darlin'."

She slowly washed her husband's back. She enjoyed the view of his broad shoulders and muscled forearms. When she finished her ministrations and handed the soap back to Rudy, a sharp pain caused her to gasp. Both hands went immediately to her midsection. Red was out of the tub in matter of seconds. "I'm gonna help you to bed, Emie, and go get Doc."

"I think I'm okay, Rudy. Just let me rest a minute."

Her husband helped her to a chair and then stood naked in front of her. When the pain subsided, she started to giggle.

"What's so funny, darlin'? Are you okay?"

"I'm just laughin' 'cause you're standing here naked."

"Emie, I'm just gonna say one thing, and then we're gonna talk about your wellbein'. When naked, a man doesn't like to be laughed at by his girl."

"Sorry, Red."

"Now, tell me exactly how you're feelin' and don't leave nothin' out."

"I'm feelin' a might odd."

"How?"

"I feel funny, that's all," she added.

"Stay put, darlin', I'm goin' to get Doc." When Emie didn't respond he added, "Promise me you ain't gonna move."

"I promise," she answered. "Red are you thinkin' about puttin' some clothes on? I like you naked and all, but Aunt Ada and Coral could be a might surprised."

Rudy hurriedly reached for the clean clothes his wife had set out for him. "You don't think Doc might be surprised by my nakedness?"

"No, he sees naked people all the time," she smiled. "Red, don't worry. My pains are comin' and goin' and none too quick. If the baby's comin', it'll be awhile."

Rudy dressed in record time and was busy tying his shoes. "Just the same, we'll see what Doc has to say." He opened the door and called for Rain. When the dog bounded through the door, Rudy directed the pup to sit on the rug beside Emie's chair. He kissed his wife on her forehead. "Darlin', I love you. I'll be right back. Hopefully Doc's at home and can head over. If not, I'll bring Auntie back with me."

Emie closed her eyes and hummed. These days she mostly hummed lullabies. Every once in a while a hymn would pop into her mind, and she would sing it outright, but with Ernest gone hymn singing just didn't feel the same. As she hummed, she felt the baby move. Rain shifted from the rug and tried to crawl on her lap. He was much too big to be a lap dog, plus most of her lap was taken by the baby. Emie scratched the puppy's ears and kissed his head. Rain seemed to sense that she wasn't feeling well. Emie knew that he was doing his best to comfort her. He kept licking her arm and nudging up against her.

In mere minutes, Rudy and Uncle Christian barged through the door.

"So, my girl, I hear your baby is ready to make an appearance."

"I ain't sure, Uncle. I'm just feelin' out of sorts. I've some pains comin' and goin'. I think Rudy's more worried than me."

"It's generally that way with the daddies," Uncle Christian agreed.

Lily Jewel was born in the wee hours of the morning. With Uncle Christian's ministrations and Red's words of encouragement, Emie endured labor like an Appalachian coal miner working hard to obtain valued treasure. Through her pangs, Rudy never left her side. She loved her husband all the more for sitting, resting, standing, walking, and crying with her as she brought their baby into the world. With little Jewel's first cry, the new mommy cried herself. While Doc Bright severed the umbilical cord, Rudy held the baby, counting all her fingers and toes. Lily was then placed in Emie's arms.

"She's perfect," Emie softly spoke. Her voice filled with emotion. "Look, Rudy, she has little bits of red hair, and her eyes are blue."

The new papa responded with his own emotion, "You're right, darlin', she's perfect. Absolutely perfect, just like her mommy."

Chapter Forty Nine

"Dew on the grass means a dry day."
(Appalachian Folk Belief)

The new mother quickly regained her strength. The baby lost some weight at first, but then recouped what she had lost and gained even more. What little hair she had looked reddish in the light, and her eyes stayed blue − true blue, according to Aunt Ada. "I can see it in her eyes," the great aunt declared. "She's a beauty on the outside with a loyal and true heart on the inside."

The new parents lost sleep but gained the pleasure of Jewel becoming the center of their household. Both sides of the family doted on the baby. The holler people also doted and brought gifts: hand-carved wooden rattles to rag dolls, and hand-sewn quilts to clothing made from soft cotton cloth. Emie remembered her earlier concerns about the community accepting the baby. She chided herself for ever worrying. She had seen the holler people time and time again reveal their kind and generous hearts.

Spring was coming. The March calendar page hanging on the wall in the kitchen of the little house would soon be torn off and replaced by April dates. Emie couldn't believe Jewel was almost six weeks old. Uncle Christian had examined the baby earlier in the day and declared her fit and healthy. He had also briefly examined Emie. Mama and baby were both in glowing form. With Doc's approval, Emie decided to take Jewel for a stroll to see her daddy. She had kept her young one mostly confined to the house.

The weather had been unusually cold in February and March, but with spring coming and the air growing warmer, the new mommy thought it good for Jewel to enjoy some fresh air. "Let's visit the willows and blow the stink away," Emie told her little princess.

Rudy was at the old Ashby homestead. The sows had been bred the beginning of February, and the new pig farmer was worried that something might go wrong. On his last visit, Ernest had insisted that Rudy relax. "Brother, now is not the time for worryin'. When the birthin' comes that's when you worry, and pray to the Good Lord for help."

Sows were pregnant for three months, three weeks and three days. Ernest had told Emie once that the number three symbolized completeness. "Girlie, did you know that there are 27 books in the New Testament? Three times three times three is 27 – just like them books."

Emie always enjoyed Ernest and Charlotte's visits. She knew they were both grieving in their own ways, yet she prayed and hoped that the worst was over. Ernest never talked about Mercy, but if her name was mentioned the light in her brother's eyes seemed to dim a little. Lottie, on the other hand, freely talked about Lester. Her eyes would sometimes mist but, in the next moment, there would be the sound of her melodious laugher. Emerald loved hearing about the learners and the progress they were making in their studies. She also liked the stories Ernest and Lottie shared about the students' antics. During their visits, Ernest would tickle Jewel and sing her hymns; Lottie would whisper sweet nothings and kiss the baby's already chubby cheeks.

Emie missed Mercy. She wished her friend would contact her, yet she understood the reasons for her silence. At first, it pained Emie that Mercy couldn't see beyond the varying shades of skin color. She grew to realize, however, that it wasn't Mercy's prejudices but the prejudices of others that caused her heart sister to move away. She often thought fondly of Mercy's sweet voice. *When they've all had their quarrels and parted. We'll be the same as we started. Just travelin' along, singin' our song, side by side.* Emie prayed that one day she and her friend would once again travel along, singin' a song, side by side.

Emerald bundled the baby in a blanket and put a knitted hat on her tiny head. She also covered a portion of the baby's face with a soft cloth. Jewel was vibrant and healthy, but spring was just making an appearance and there was still a slight chill in the air. The new mommy wanted to protect her precious gift from the elements. She planned to show her little one the willows, cross the swinging bridge, and visit Red. She felt nervous; not only was this her first walk with the baby, but she was also ready to demonstrate her American Sign Language skills. Emie knew Rudy would grin and laugh when she showed him the "dirty rat" symbol. The young bride wasn't sure if she felt more nervous about her forwardness or what was sure to happen that evening as the couple went to bed.

"Sweet Jewel, Mommy will be right back," Emie spoke softly to the baby as she laid her in the cradle. Emerald walked quickly to the outdoor potty. She returned to the house speedily, washed her hands, and went to get the baby. Daffodil was lying in the cradle, and Jewel was gone.

Emie's heart began to race. *Where was the baby?* She frantically looked around the room. In her panic, the new mother didn't think about her baby not being old enough to move independently. At first nothing else seemed amiss in the room, but then she saw the facecloth lying to the side of the door. Next, she noticed large footprints that had left wet marks on the light colored rag rug by the threshold. The prints showed someone walking into the house and then exiting. Emie began to scream loudly. Thankfully, Coral arrived seconds later.

"Someone's taken the baby, sister," the panic-stricken mother cried. Without additional words, Emie showed Coral the footprints. "Head to get the sheriff, Coral, then get Rudy across the creek." Both of the sisters were sobbing, but trying to remain calm. There was no time to lose. "The baby's only been gone a few minutes. I'm takin' Rain and followin' the footprints." Emie hurriedly grabbed the fire poker and called for the pup.

The ground was wet with snow melt, so the footprints were easily tracked. She walked beside the prints and instructed Rain not only with her voice, but with hand signals, to stay by her side.

She was fear driven, yet knew it was important not cover the tracks of the abductor.

She hummed to calm herself and tried to stay focused. The tracks led, in a roundabout way, toward the creek. She'd neglected to grab her coat, and the breeze was cool. She wasn't mindful, however, of her own wellbeing, just the wellbeing of her baby. Each time she felt overwrought, she pushed down her emotions and prayed to God for help.

When she found Jewel's knitted cap lying by the trail, she felt relief that she was on the right path, but then she started to worry that her little girl would be cold. Tears rushed down her cheeks. She quickly wiped them with the back of her hand and willed herself to stay strong.

When she reached a small clearing by the creek, she thought she heard Jewel crying. She looked in the direction of the baby's cry but didn't see anything or anyone. Knowing she was close to whoever had taken the baby, she cautiously slowed her pace and moved from the creek banks into the willows. She gripped the poker until her knuckles turned white under the strain. Rain slowed his pace to match his mistress; his ears were alert. He was turning his head from side to side, listening to the baby whose cries were now growing in volume. When he started to move ahead of Emie, she held him back. She needed the element of surprise to overtake the large-footed man who had taken her precious Jewel. She motioned for Rain to stay and walked as quietly as possible through the trees.

As the baby's cries grew louder, she knew she was getting closer. When she heard a ruckus up ahead, she started to run toward the noise. Whatever was happening was drowning out Jewel's cry. She couldn't distinguish the noises she was hearing, and feared the baby's life was in immediate peril. When she spotted Charlie just ahead, she mentally scolded herself for not realizing earlier that he was the villain. The abductor was now abducted himself by a pair of feral hogs. The boars had him pinned against a tree and were biting at his legs. There was snow on the shaded ground under the willows and spots of blood could easily be seen. She knew Charlie would die if she didn't intervene. She had no concern for his life, but knew he held the key to Jewel's safety.

Emie yelled above the snarling hogs, "Charlie, where's the baby?"

"Get 'em off me. Get 'em off me, girlie."

"Where's Jewel? What did you do with the baby?"

One of the vicious hogs bit deeply into Charlie's calf. He yelped loudly in pain and fell to the ground. The wild beasts were frenzied. Rain startled Emie when he brushed against her leg, and she jumped with fright. She quickly remembered her puppy's instincts, grabbed him, and tried to hold him back. He escaped her grip and entered the fight. Without thought, Emie took the poker and began to beat the hogs. The iron stick was heavy in her hand, but she hit her targets time and time again. She prayed for strength and did her best to keep the assaults directed at the wild pigs. She wasn't concerned about hitting Charlie a time or two, but didn't want Rain injured. When the fight was finished, one hog lay wounded next to Charlie and the other had run off. Rain was whimpering. There were visible bites on her puppy's body. Charlie was barely conscious, and Emie had several deep wounds on her legs.

The mother gathered snow and rubbed it in Charlie's face. "You tell me where my baby is, or prepare to meet your Maker." Charlie moaned, but didn't open his eyes. Emie shoved him with her foot a couple times, collected more snow this time mingled with rocks and dirt, and threw it at his face. Charlie moved his head slightly and barely opened his eyes. "Where's Lily Jewel?" He didn't answer verbally, but pointed toward the direction she had come from at a cluster of willow trees.

Emie raced to the trees. She didn't see the baby. The grouping was large and wide in girth. She walked around the trees several times. She was beside herself. She didn't know what to do. "Jesus, help me. Help me," she prayed aloud over and over again.

"Emie, I'm here." Rudy yelled to his wife. "I can see her blanket. She's nestled in the branches of one of the trees."

Emerald looked up. "I can't see her, Red."

Rudy ran to the opposite side of the trees, placed his foot on a lower branch and climbed a few feet into the air. Emie breathed a sigh of relief. When she shifted positions, she could see the bundle he was reaching toward. When Rudy picked up the baby, she started mewing. "Darlin', I suspect she wore herself out cryin' for her mommy until she had no cries left."

Rudy gently handed the baby to Emie, and then jumped down from the tree. Together the parents looked her over from head to toe. All was well. The baby was safe.

"Darlin', she looks just fine. But I'm thinkin' we need to pay a visit to Doc."

"Take her, Rudy. I'll be right along, there's somethin' I need to finish."

"I ain't sure what you got in mind, Emerald, but I ain't leavin' you."

"This will only take a minute."

With Rudy by her side, Emie headed back to Charlie. When her husband snarled like a bear, Emie stopped in her tracks. "What is it, Red? The baby?"

"Darlin', Lily Jewel is just fine. I recognize those tracks and I'm grievin'. They're the same shoeprints the person left who killed Lester."

Emie was resolute about her actions. She walked past Charlie, who appeared to be awake, and knelt down next to Rain. The puppy's breath was gone. He'd been no match for a pair of wild boars. She picked up the poker that she'd dropped earlier. "Charlie, you raped me, you threatened Coral, you shot my brother, you took my baby, and you done killed my dog. Confess your sins and prepare to die." She raised the poker high in the air. As she started to swing, Rudy with one hand gripped the weapon.

"No, darlin', I want him gone too, but this ain't the way."

Chapter Fifty

"To break a spell, carry drinking water across a running stream."
(Appalachian Folk Belief)

Uncle Christian checked the baby over and deemed her just fine. He, however, expressed some concern over Emie's injuries. "It will take time for these wounds to heal, Emerald. I'm given you a powder to help you rest and a new medication called 'penicillin.' It should help with infection."

Rudy took his wife and baby home. He first washed the baby and dressed her in night clothes. Emie sat in a chair at the table and watched her husband's gentle hands at work. When finished, he laid the baby in her cradle and she almost instantly fell asleep. Next, he prepared a basin of water and bathed his wife. He followed Doc's instructions to the letter and gave his beloved her medicines. He helped her into a gown and put her to bed. "Darlin', Aunt Ada and Coral will keep watch over you and Jewel. I'll be back shortly."

He knew that the sheriff had collected Charlie. And, after Emie and Jewel's care, the raping, murdering, kidnapper had been examined by Doctor Bright. He also knew that Charlie had confessed to all his crimes. As soon as he was fit, he would go to prison. According to Sheriff Robbins, Charlie had no intention of harming the baby. He wanted Jewel as his own. When he saw the hogs, he knew that trouble would come, and placed the baby high among the willow branches for protection. When questioned about Lester's passing, Charlie admitted he was in cahoots with his cousin's business partners. When his own life had been threatened, he murdered to save himself.

Rudy headed toward the creek. He wanted to be sure the wounded boar was dead. He was confident it was one of the young pigs who had escaped during the fire. The other hog would need to be tracked and killed. They were vicious animals and, if given the opportunity, would tear other creatures and humans to shreds. He also wanted to bury Rain. He hoped he could find a piece of ground soft enough to dig a shallow grave. He planned to cover the grave with rocks to keep varmints away. When Emie felt better, he knew she would want to add something to mark the grave.

When he approached Big Creek, he saw Granny Smith poking at the hog with a stick. "He's dead, Rudy. Dead as can be. Mind if I take him home? He'll be good eatin'."

"Granny, feel free. I want nothin' to do with the beast."

"I done heard what happened; the Good Lord kept your wife and baby safe. I've been prayin'."

"I appreciate them prayers," Rudy said. He wanted to add "Stay away from my wife and quit filling her mind with foolishness," but he didn't have the energy to speak the right words in the manner needed to correct the old woman. "If you wait a bit, I'll help you get the pig home. I'm needin' to bury Emie's dog."

As suspected, the ground was still partially frozen. He dug a shallow grave and then laid Rain in his resting place. Rudy spoke a word of prayer. "Lord, thank you for a fine animal such as Rain. I appreciate the joy and comfort he brought to our lives."

Granny had brought her primitive butcher tools. The hog was cut into pieces. The boar was almost full grown and too big to carry in a single trip. Rudy was only willing to make one trek to the Smith house. "My wife and baby's needin' me. I'm sorry I can't be of more help."

"You go on now, son. I understand. There's plenty here for an old woman."

Rudy knew by morning the remainder of the carcass would be gone. It was the way of nature. It was also the way of the Appalachian people to not let anything go to waste. After what Emie and the baby had been through, Granny's taking of the hog meat seemed insensitive to Rudy. Yet, he didn't blame the old woman for wanting food for her and for others in the holler who often shared from her table.

Emie was awake and feeding the baby when Rudy arrived home. "We did fine today, Red. Just fine. We kept our baby safe."

"We did, darlin'."

"I'm thinkin' of Lester. I'm also grievin' for Rain, Rudy."

"I know, Emie."

"Red, how did you know where to find me?"

"The sheriff wasn't in his office, so Coral left him a note, and raced up the holler. She waited at the farm for the lawman, and I took off runnin', askin' God to help me care for you and Lily Jewel. There you were, Emie. I spotted you from the swingin' bridge."

"Rudy, I worried some that we were too young for marryin' and havin' a baby, but I'm thinkin' we'll be alright."

The young husband sat down on the bed next to his wife and baby. He kissed the back of the nursing baby's head and then kissed his wife's soft lips. "I love you, darlin'."

"Enough to share another baby with me?"

Rudy smiled. "More than enough…"

THE END.

Acknowledgments

The small town of Big Creek currently has a population of about 230 people — it doesn't appear that the town is home to anyone famous. The region surrounding Big Creek was the setting for the film, October Sky. Because my mother's family has its roots there, Big Creek also happens to be the historical setting for this novel.

In the Appalachian Mountain culture, stories are handed down from family members and friends in closely knit communities, each person adding or taking away something from the story. The same holds true for the novel, *The Whispering of the Willows.* Thank you to my publishing editor and formatter, Laura Bartnick, and to Charmayne Hafen, Lynn Byk and Marilyn Bay Wentz for adding and taking away at our monthly Writer's Group; including a special thank you to Linda Rae Collins, whose story on earth is finished. I would also like to thank Sue Lockwood Summers and Sue Carter for their superior editing abilities, and a small but mighty publishing group: Capture Books, for its support and invaluable assistance with getting into libraries, bookstores and reviews on the radio.

My beautiful and creative niece, Kara Elizabeth Hokes, is responsible for the photographs on the front and back book covers. I'm so proud of you. Special thanks are also expressed to Evelyn Engle. You're a lovely model, and your depiction of the book's heroine is amazing.

My heartfelt appreciation to my precious husband for his patience, encouragement, unconditional love and support, and to the ministry team that serves with us in South Africa for going above and beyond so I could enjoy quiet space for writing.

The Bible tells us to give honor to whom honor is due. I sincerely honor those who have aided me in the endeavor of writing.

Endnotes:

I obtained the folk beliefs at the beginning of each chapter from the following resources: www.hauntedcomputer.com/scottst41.htm www.appalachianlifestyles.blogspot.com/2009/08/gardening-folk-customs.html

Throughout the book, I cited typical community hymns and folksongs that were sung in the Big Creek region. The name of the song in each chapter is noted here with the author's name and date of publication.

Chapter One
Tell Me the Story of Jesus, Frances J. Crosby, Pub. 1880
Chapter Five
Leaning on the Everlasting Arms, Anthony J. Showalter and Elisha Hoffman, Pub. 1887
Chapter Six
Savior, Like a Shepherd Lead Us, Dorothy A. Thrupp and William B. Bradbury, Pub. 1901
Chapter Nine
Slumber My Darling, Stephen Collins Foster, Pub. 1862
A Mighty Fortress is Our God, Martin Luther, Circa 1529
Chapter Eleven
Slumber My Darling, Stephen Collins Foster, Pub. 1862
Chapter Twenty Two
There's a Fountain Filled with Blood, William Cowper, Pub 1772
Chapter Twenty Four
Someone to Watch Over Me, George Gershwin, Pub. 1926
Chapter Twenty Five
Peace, Perfect Peace, Edward Henry Bickersteth, Pub. 1875
Chapter Twenty Six
Black-Eyed Susan, John Gay, Circa 1723

Chapter Twenty Nine
  The Man I Love (original title The Girl I Love), George
  Gershwin and Ira Gershwin, Pub. 1924
Chapter Thirty Two
  Ain't Misbehavin', Fats Waller, Pub. 1929
  Tell Me the Story of Jesus, Fannie Crosby, Circa 1880
Chapter Thirty Three
  Jesus Promised Me a Home Over There, Traditional
  Unknown lullaby
Chapter Thirty Five
  Face to Face with Christ, My Savior, Carrie E. Breck and
  Grant C. Tullar, Pub. 1898
  In the Sweet By and By, S. Fillmore Bennett and Joseph P.
  Webster, Pub. 1868
Chapter Forty Two
  Great is Thy Faithfulness, Thomas Chisholm and William M.
  Runyan, Pub. 1923
Chapter Forty Three
  Side by Side, Gus Kahn and Harry M. Woods, Pub. 1928
Chapter Forty Five
  The Cradle Song, Johannes Brahm, Pub. 1869
Chapter Forty Six
  The Wayfaring Stranger, Traditional
Chapter Forty Nine
  Side by Side, Gus Kahn and Harry M. Woods, Pub. 1928

Go to: http://www.CaptureMeBooks.com
for other book selections

A Personal Note from Tonya:
Readers buy books based on other readers' endorsements.
I would appreciate yours!

Please rate my book if you enjoyed it.

Barnes & Noble

Here's direct link to reviews on Amazon:

 **I LOVE IT!**

https://www.amazon.com/review/create-review?ie=UTF8&asin=B01C6HMDUE&#

More about Tonya Jewel Blessing:

Growing up, Tonya spent numerous vacations and holidays in the Appalachian mountains of West Virginia. Most of her adult life has been spent in full time ministry with a focus on helping women. She has traveled nationally and internationally as a conference speaker. For a number of years, Tonya and her husband operated a retreat facility in Colorado for pastors and missionaries.

She and her husband currently live in South Africa. They are the directors of Strong Cross Ministries, a non-profit organization that assists local churches in providing spiritual reconciliation and humanitarian relief to the poorest in the world. Tonya has written a number of devotionals geared toward women in ministry. *The Whispering of the Willows* is her first novel. All of the proceeds from this book will be given to Strong Cross Ministries South Africa, www.strongcrossministries.org

Tonya Jewel Blessing is currently pursuing a degree in pastoral ministries. Follow Tonya on her author facebook page. Or check out her website: www.TonyaJewelBlessing.com.

Book Club Questions:

1. Do you think that hard work is good for children?

2. The names of the Ashby girls were precious names. How do you think Alma Ashby's character developed into the split qualities of light and dark that she exhibited?

3. What importance did church and music play in the working culture of Big Creek?

4. What can be done for families today who have a family member with a disability? How does modern assistance look different to the 1920s? – Or, look similar?

5. Do you think you would be capable of caring for a child at the end of your eighth grade year? What aid did Emie have?

6. Describe why it's important to help others?

7. How difficult would it be to share your home with a girl in need?

8. Does helping others create any benefit for the one who helps?

9. What part does poverty play in the morale of family members, such as choices they make involving their children?

10. Do you think that Charlie was destined for a life of crime? Why? Were there opportunities along the way for him to put his life on the right path?

11. How would it have made Charlie's life different had he experience a positive mentor?

CPSIA information can be obtained at www.ICGtesting.com
Printed in the USA
LVOW08s1811200616

493348LV00010B/1263/P